I0669322

Void of Course
Boulevard of Bad Spells and Broken Dreams, 1

CAROLE ANN MOLETI

CHAMPAGNE BOOK GROUP

Void of Course

Published by Champagne Book Group
712 SE Winchell Drive, Depoe Bay OR 97341 U.S.A.

~ ~ ~

First Edition 2022

pISBN: 978-1-957228-62-4

Cover Art by Melody Pond

www.champagnebooks.com

Version_1

This book is dedicated to the memory of the late, great Dr. Mary O'Gara who tutored many writers the science of astrology and the mysteries of The Tarot. Boulevard *would not be what it is today without her joyful enthusiasm, including an invitation to spend time with her in Albuquerque, New Mexico as this book was being developed. Mary pulled aside the curtain surrounding mystical practices and was always willing to welcome the uninitiated and bring them closer to deeper understanding and connectedness with their spiritual selves.*

Dear Reader,

Historical facts have informed this work. Real life events have been woven into a fictional story, which strives to give a voice to those whose stories have never been told.

Carole Ann

Chapter One
Void of Course

A metallic odor mixed with burning rubber turned Taina Aponte's stomach. Thuds and pings reverberated from underneath her car. "Please don't die here."

She scanned the avenue for a safe place to park, or a service station that looked like it really sold gas or had a mechanic who would fix the car rather than chop it up and sell it for a big profit. Nothing fit the description.

Window boxes filled with wilting flowers hung from fire escapes like tattered banners rallying anyone with any fight left in them to arms. A pigeon made eye contact, then swooped over the hood of the car. White and green turd splattered on her windshield.

Welcome to The Bronx. A spritz or two of fluid and a couple of wiper swipes later, the mess was gone, leaving a few residual stripes. A dude dressed in a black tee shirt and cargo shorts and wearing a do-rag watched her drive by. His rosary beads dangled a crucifix so large it resembled the one Christ died on. Did everyone and everything know the prodigal sister had returned after far too many years—and she'd be an easy mark?

That was Number Two of her ex-girlfriend Serena's many reasons to give up, to be content with what she had, to focus on the future. But the nightmares and restlessness were getting worse, and Taina had to find out who'd killed her family. So she was there, even in the face of Reason Number One: she'd be next if she got too close to the truth.

There was never a good time, astrologically or emotionally, to pay a visit to the place where your entire family had been murdered. Especially in this neighborhood where it wasn't a good time to go anywhere or do anything. Was it karma, the car breaking down as she was on the way there for the first time since that terrible night? Was it because she hadn't allowed enough time for the lingering effects of her void-of-course moon to wane? Or was it Reason Number Three: the South Bronx was no place to play amateur detective—or witch?

The car shimmied and thumped to a stop. The detached right front tire rolled free across the sidewalk and came to rest against a building. Horns blared as cabs and minivans swerved around her. Most people kept walking, but a few kids ran over and waved through the closed window at Taina like she was a monkey at the Bronx Zoo.

"Damn!" She pounded the steering wheel, then fumbled in her pocket. That lipstick-wand-athame multi-tool Serena had given Taina wouldn't do much good in this situation. The lead pipe under her seat was useless for spell work, but the time for subtlety had run out.

She stepped out into blinding sunlight and surveyed the axel resting on asphalt. Might as well start with the jack. She dug it out of the trunk, but the wrench slipped every time she turned the bolts holding the spare in place.

"Looks like you need some help, *chica*." The tall light-skinned guy had somehow gotten behind her. His designer jeans hung so low off his ass it looked like he'd just finished taking a piss up against a wall.

Only friends were allowed to call her little girl. "No, I'm fine." Serena had warned Taina naïve girls from Puerto Rico were targets, and she'd better act bold, bitchy, Bronx.

The boxers underneath were adorned with skulls. His teeth too big, too white, and his hair too neat in the late July heat and humidity amplified a red aura. In broad daylight.

Dhampir crossbreeds, who'd evolved to be more human than vampire, were particularly suited to warm, sunny climates.

"There's probably damage to the rim. Let me call a tow." He whipped out a cellphone.

"I don't have enough cash," she bluffed.

"No need to pay me back." His aura flickered like a candle flame with odd silver highlights.

Sure, just a quick bite, then I'll be yours forever. But she couldn't hit him over the head with the lug wrench for trying to "help."

He dialed anyway. *"Ven aqui."* His voice, as deep and murky as the ocean, seemed like one of an older, more sophisticated man than his style of dress implied. "My friends will be here in a minute."

The dude with the crucifix and do-rag was walking toward her much too fast to be using only his legs. The head covering disguised a pale green tint along the outline of his scraggly hair. No one would notice unless they knew what to look for. Serena had drilled her on auras—green was the only sure way to identify a witch.

A tight-lipped smile cracked the dude's face. He was no kid. His arms were covered with runic tattoos—and he liked gold jewelry. "I'll change it. For free." He stared at *el guapo* with piano-keyboard teeth like he meant business.

"A tow is on the way." The dhamp wasn't giving up.

The dude swaggered closer. "Cancel it."

Neither backed down or averted their gazes.

The dhamp's sick smile turned to a snarl. "Don't try that shit with me, Arnaldo."

"Out early, Raul? Leave the lady alone." The witch snickered.

Raul snapped his fingers. Several men marched out of alleyways and down the block toward them. Demon's haloes, a red aura with a hint of yellow at the crown, pulsed over their heads like a beacon. The Bronx dhampirs had evolved into a super-species far beyond the threats posed by the more solitary nocturnal Puerto Rican dhamps.

Sparks of fear tingled along her spine. Instead of being relieved by the presence of a good Samaritan, worry bubbled up from her gut, realizing this Arnaldo was the guy Serena had entrusted her to.

Taina fingered her wand. Would the distraction spell she'd been practicing work against this gang, or should she fight the mundane way and swing the lug wrench like a baseball bat?

The sun dipped behind a massive gray cloud. The sky darkened, and a fork of lightning hit a huge rock formation in the park across the street. Thunder cracked like the stone had been split in two. People screamed and scattered.

If Arnaldo was nervous he didn't show it. He breathed in and out, slow and deep, and with each exhalation came another round of forked lightning and a teeth-rattling crash. Electricity crackled along Tania's scalp. Her stupid spell wasn't worth shit compared to this magickal maelstrom.

Passersby ran for shelter. The dhampir gang stood behind Raul in the now-deserted street.

Arnaldo took a deep breath, held it, and jerked his hands together, then rapidly apart as he exhaled. Another spear of lightning split a huge tree in the park across the street in half. It took down a power line in a shower of sparks. The leaves ignited like a bundle of dry straw as it flailed like a snake. Flames shot into the air.

Ozone vapor from the rain clutched Taina's throat like skeletal hands. She struggled to breathe through it.

Plumes of smoke, the acrid odor of burning leaves, flecks of soot, the whine of a distant fire engine... Then screams, vomit in her mouth that smelled like gasoline, flying through the air, bodies being carried away...

Powerless, unable to move, let alone perform magick, her fingers and toes numb... Ghostly wails and shrieks echoed in her ears.

Rain and pea-sized hail pinged on metal. A police car screeched around the left corner toward them, and two officers leaped out. "Get back!"

A fire engine screamed down 149th Street from the opposite-side direction. A firefighter jumped out, hauling an extinguisher and covered the smoking, flailing wire with what looked like melted marshmallow.

The rest of the crew quenched the flames devouring the dead grass with a torrent of water.

Flashing strobe kicked behind her eyeballs with each rotation. She had to get out of there before she passed out.

Arnaldo took Taina's arm and guided her back onto the sidewalk, behind her car.

The dhamps slithered away and blended into the rest of the crowd now fleeing the park.

Raul was the last to leave, fangs protruding onto his lower lip in a snarl.

Arnaldo pursed his lips and shook his head. "Didn't take very long for you to get into trouble, Taina."

"Couldn't you have done something less dramatic? I mean, look at all the people who could have gotten hurt!"

His cocky grin faded. "I can't let them get away with anything—neither can you."

"How did you find me?" She raked wet hair off her face and tacked it up into a knot.

He chortled. "Your aura is bright enough to attract every fucking deviant in The Bronx. Better learn how to turn that down, *chica*."

She didn't trust the witch sporting a Catholic icon any more than the dhamp. Reason Number Four: Arnaldo was a player. Unfortunately, her only means of transport out of there was about as reliable as a broom missing most of its bristles.

"Can you fix it?"

"Pffft." He examined the wheel. It wiggled like an exotic dancer as he rolled it over. "Where did you buy this car?" He dug out the spare tire and jack.

"Off Bruckner Boulevard. That creep told me it was in tip-top shape. What the hell did I expect for a grand?" Could she trust anyone in this place, where things were never certain, never reliable, never what they seemed?

"The prick left the lugs just loose enough that they'd jiggle off by the time you got to here, to Ritual Rock, ground zero of the magickal holy wars. Did you tell him where you were from, or going?" Arnaldo huffed as he positioned the jack and pumped, raising the car off the ground.

"No, but he knows where I live since he registered the car."

"You got deadbolts? Grates over the windows?" He dragged the spare over. Grease and dirt stained his hands. It didn't seem to trouble him in the least.

"On the third floor?"

"You got a fire escape, right? Raul will be dogging you, now he got a look at the goods." He winked and gave her the once-over.

She needed a whole host of protective spells, but in the meantime wrenches and lead pipes would have to suffice.

Arnaldo tried to position the spare onto the lugs, but one was bent sideways. One wave of his hand, and the tire moved into place. "All better." He tightened the nuts and stowed the damaged tire, jack, and tools in the trunk.

Only an accomplished witch could manipulate weather and move matter. The crucifix was just a diversion for the mundanes.

He brushed his hands together. "I'll take you to a repair shop to see if they can salvage that tire. After you, princess." He opened the driver's door, then eyed her thighs as the shorts moved north.

Taina started the car. His silly grin and the dangling cross earring in his ear were seriously getting on her nerves.

Arnaldo put on the radio, turned up the volume, and pounded out a rousing bongo beat on the dashboard.

She turned off the blaring music. "Look, thanks for helping me with the tire. Where can I drop you off?"

"Serena told me I better watch out for you, and I'm not going to piss off that witch." Despite the sarcasm in his voice, a flash of tenderness lit his eyes. "Turn right at the next light. My buddy owns a garage off 149th, and he'll treat you like a lady."

Ticked, disoriented, frazzled, Taina took the turn too fast and ran up onto the curb. A bum on the corner rummaged through the contents of a wire trashcan. A shopping cart attached to a bicycle frame stood by his side, draped with six bulging black garbage bags, all covered by a canopy fashioned from wood and blue plastic.

She jammed her foot onto the brake pedal. *"Pare."* Taina struggled to intone the spell calmly, to focus, to stop the goddamn car.

A weak shudder ran through her. They fishtailed and sideswiped the guy, tossing him about five feet in the air. He landed in the middle of the street. Bottles smashed. Cans clanked. The car screeched to a halt just before it hit a light pole.

"Omigod!" She put the car in park before leaping out. Crushed metal scattered. Glass scrunched as she ran to the crumpled figure. "Please don't be dead!"

"Good try, but you have to infuse more energy to work that spell in an emergency." Arnaldo walked over to the motionless bum. "Get up, Jesús. You're scaring the poor kid."

The guy pushed himself up, a toothless, bemused grin on his face. There was no blood, though his lower leg stuck out at a right angle from the knee. An odor of stale urine, with just a whiff of rot, hung around him along with a pale yellow zombie aura.

He popped his leg back into place. "Can't kill me, cutie. I've been dead for years. But why don't you let Arnaldo drive from now on?"

Chapter Two
Burned Out

Taina knelt beside the zombie. "Let me help you up." How could Arnaldo have kicked him like a piece of trash and just stand there and let the poor man—well zombie—fend for himself.

She took Jesús's bony hand and hauled him to his feet. Long dead, he weighed far less than a life-size doll. Insects wriggled in his stringy hair. A few crawled across her arm.

His green eyes struggled to focus, blank, unblinking, like he was looking straight through her. His smile, though marred by the few remaining rotten teeth, projected the remnants of a gentle, good nature.

"C'mon, Jesús. You have to pay attention to what's going on around you." Arnaldo stood on the curb, his arms crossed over his chest.

She instinctively brushed the bugs off, expecting Jesús to show some reaction; anger, maybe embarrassment, but he was more concerned about retrieving his cans and any intact bottles. She scurried around to help.

Damn, if it wasn't for Arnaldo's distractions, none of this would have happened. She hadn't been off the plane more than a week, and already Serena's dire prophecies were coming to pass. "We've got to get him out of here."

"He's got nothing else to do, and we need to get your car inside a garage before dark." Arnaldo swaggered over.

Taina almost threw a sticky Corona bottle filled with bees at him. "I can take care of myself." Even she didn't believe that, hadn't shown him any evidence it was remotely true.

A balding man, wearing a filthy mechanic's jumpsuit, hurried out of an open garage bay. "*¿Que pasó? Ay,* Arnaldo, Jesús. Who is this young lady?" He winked at Arnaldo.

No way did she want to be taken for that shithead's girlfriend. "Taina Aponte. I'm visiting from Puerto Rico."

"Mucho gusto, mi amor." He shook her hand and bowed. No aura, no supernatural vibe, only the gallantry and respect so common among Puerto Rican elders, *Los Boricuas.*

Arnaldo gestured to the car, two wheels still up on the curb. "She bought this piece of crap off Bruckner, and the damn wheel fell off. I put the spare on, but can you see if there's any damage? And you better check to be sure there is nothing else wrong."

"Of course." Miguel whistled through his teeth so loud she expected a pack of dogs to come running.

Four laborers rushed out of the garage and swarmed around Jesús, goosing his butt as he stooped to pick up his treasures.

"Stop, please. Leave him alone." Taina got in between them and the zombie.

"¡Bastante, ya!" Miguel boomed. "Bring that car in and go over every inch of it."

One hopped into the driver's seat and pulled her white Ford sedan in with the door still open. The others walked back, still grinning, pushing each other, goofing like silly schoolboys.

Miguel wagged his head and smoothed silver strands of what hair he had left across his pate. *"Ah, La Isla.* Someday I'm going back to *Culebra.* But we're in The Bronx now, *nena.* This is no place for a nice girl like you to go wandering around."

Her father would have been this age, if he weren't dead, along with every single one of her family members. So much for trying to forget she was an orphan in a big city where she didn't know anyone, and no one knew her. Maybe she should just go back to the apartment, explain to her landlady she made a big mistake, get into a taxi, and head back to Kennedy Airport. *"Gracias,* Miguel."

"I'll be looking after her." Arnaldo's tone had softened. He almost looked like he felt sorry for her.

"I need my bag." How stupid could she be, leaving her wallet, money, keys, and phone in the car?

"I'll get it for you." Miguel headed back.

Taina watched Jesús fill a black bag with his treasures. "Is he going to be all right?"

"He'll be fine. *Las Tombas* won't let anything happen to their workers, unless they become too sentient." Arnaldo took her arm and led her toward the garage.

"¿Las Tombas? Are they gang members?" Taina glanced over her shoulder, but the zombie didn't even appear to recall there had been

an accident. The overstuffed bags on his cart swayed like giant balloons as he shambled away.

"Bingo! Lupo Lopez's thugs. This is their territory. Long story, not now."

Miguel brought her purse, wrapped in plastic so he didn't soil the white leather.

Taina fished through it and found everything was still there. She tore a page out of her notebook and scrawled the address.

Miguel and Arnaldo looked at each other with raised eyebrows and grinned like dirty old men.

So, hot pink gel pens were not bold, bitchy, Bronx. "I live on Prospect Avenue."

Miguel wagged a finger. "I'll bring the car to you. Don't come over this way alone." He bowed his head, doffed his Yankees cap, then returned to work.

She and Arnaldo walked out of the side street, past rows of warehouses and alleged auto body repair shops. They passed a fish market, a Chinese restaurant, a drug store, a bakery.

It looked like a normal neighborhood, and it would be very nice if the trucks rattling by on the elevated Bruckner Expressway weren't spewing plumes of diesel exhaust.

A caravan of eighteen wheelers rattled the loose metal roadbed, threatening the poor women below as they dodged traffic, pushing strollers covered with plastic rain shields to keep soot off the babies.

"Is there a place we can get coffee and chat?" she asked.

"Chat? We don't chat here, *chica*. We rap.

"There's a new witch in The Bronx.

She wants to dish in The Bronx.

She wants to dish in The Bronx.

This new bitch in The Bronx." Arnaldo wiggled his butt and guffawed, very amused by his own antics.

Asshole. "I wouldn't quit your day job."

"No chance. I run *Sonrisa* Community Center to give folks a place to hang out besides the streets. *Bueno*, coffee. There ain't no Starbucks within miles of this place. The closest we can get is the McCafe." He patted his belly. "Love those apple pies!"

~ * ~

Taina sipped hazelnut iced coffee with skim milk.

Arnaldo swigged his hot, black, three sugars, to wash down an apple pie. "Want the other one?"

She did, but her booty was already bigger than she cared it to be. "No thanks. Too many calories, too much fat."

"Live a little, mama." He wiped his mouth with the back of a hand. "Now I need a cigar."

"You're going to kill yourself like that, Arnaldo."

He held his breath and exhaled pure venom. "You know the trouble with people who didn't grow up here? They don't have a fuckin' clue."

"I'm sorry." As much as she disliked this man, there was no one else to get her street-ready.

He shook his head. "You'll learn. Like we all did. So, why are you here?" He sneered and took a long swallow.

"The detective who investigated the fire that killed my family is about to retire. I need to pick his brain, try and find the motherfuckers responsible, and send them to jail."

He choked on his coffee. A fist pounded his chest like a penitent. "It's mo fo's. Less vulgar. Do you really think just wiggling your cute ass on the way into a police precinct is going to get them to solve a crime from, what, twenty-five years ago?"

Clearing her throat was a technique she'd learned in the law office to remind her to keep her voice down. "Actually, it was thirty-five years ago. And unlike you, my brains are in my head. I'm a paralegal and worked for an attorney in Puerto Rico who prosecuted criminal cases."

The insult rolled off his back like water off a windshield. "You ain't gonna find anyone responsible for those fires."

He then attacked. "Let me fill you in on what happened while you were hiding out in the *La Isla Encantada*. The police and fire department brass wasted time fighting over who had jurisdiction, while firefighters sprayed enough water on this borough to empty the East River."

She didn't bother to clear her throat this time. "Don't you think I already know that?"

Everyone in the restaurant tuned into the live novella.

Arnaldo didn't seem to mind the studio audience. "*Las Tombas* took over from the inside out when that undead Abe Beame was in charge. The Bronx almost burned to the ground. The whiteys figured it would be a good way to get rid of us spics and niggers, anyway."

"Yeah, yeah, you tell her, bro." A kid too young to have pimples brandished one Black Power fist high while holding up droopy gangsta pants with the other.

Arnaldo lowered his voice to a serpentine whisper. "Then came crack and AIDS. Those mutated vamps and weres got hold and wouldn't let go until they drained the lifeblood out of the people.

And now the good witch returns from paradise to the rescue?"

Taina's cheeks burned. She pushed back her chair, and it clattered to the floor. Everyone went silent, staring and smirking. Resisting the temptation to give Arnaldo an iced hazelnut coffee shampoo, she walked out the door.

Groups of teenagers applauded, hooted, and whistled as she passed.

"Whoa, man, she's pissed at you."

"Not gonna get any tonight, bro."

Putrid, humid air closed around her. She ran all the way to her apartment. Arnaldo didn't bother to follow. How dare he lecture? Her entire family had been wiped out. She had nothing left, nothing.

Taina fumbled with the lock on the black wrought-iron security gate. The landlady watched out her window. Taina waved like nothing was wrong and ducked inside, climbed to the third floor, then secured the deadbolt and three locks behind her.

Sirens blared. A fire engine raced down Southern Boulevard. Enough of a well-timed reminder. She gagged, recalling the smoke, the soot. The smell of gasoline wafted through the room like a ghostly mist. Wails faded into the distance.

A suitcase lay open on the floor. She fell to her knees and clutched a family portrait to her chest.

Her mother, with caramel-colored hair, mocha skin, and dark-brown eyes that looked just like Taina's, cradled the child she tossed to safety before the smoke and flames overcame her. Her father, who everyone said resembled a young Desi Arnaz, held her older sister. Ana screamed, "Papa, help me!" but burned to death in his arms before he could crawl out.

A warm breeze came through the tiny kitchen window and blew away the nightmare. This apartment might be empty, sweltering and lonesome, but she'd make it her own and accomplish what she set out to do.

For them. Without anyone's help. Or die trying.

Chapter Three
Fae Magick

Dusk painted the sky gunmetal gray. Skeletal fingers of purple clouds grasped ghostly orange digits of sunlight. Someone, somewhere, was reaching out. Taina sorely needed a confidante to tear through the dark curtain that had come down in front of her.

Once she got a job she'd make friends, but for now she was trapped in an inner city limbo so hot it bordered on hell. Taina craved the tropical comfort of a piña colada, with a shot of the best rum she could get to take the edge off the heat—and her nerves.

But there wasn't much time to get to the store and back inside before dark.

A crowd of men, with gray mundane auras, stood outside the liquor store on 149th. They undressed her with their eyes.

Regretting wearing shorts and a tank top, Taina pushed past, ignoring the lewd comments.

One guy pulled her ponytail, then grabbed her ass. She whipped around and whacked him across the face with her forearm. The crack of his nose reverberated up to her elbow.

He dropped to his knees, both hands trying in vain to stem the bloody torrent.

She hoped it was broken.

The men rallied around their fallen comrade, which attracted the attention of the shop's owner. He plowed through the crowd encircling the victim.

"Ay, señorita, I'm sorry. *Entra."* He escorted her into the shop and ran back outside, gesticulating wildly. *"¡Vete, ya!* Don't hang around here *molestando* my paying customers."

The group wandered toward Prospect Avenue. Taina selected a bottle of Puerto Rican rum. "Where can I buy a blender?"

The proprietor had reinstalled himself behind the counter to watch the ball game. "The Yankees are having a bad night. Here you go." He plunked a tiny mixer on the counter, just enough to make piña coladas for two—and she was thirsty enough to drink both.

He rang her up. "Anything else?"

"Do you have *crema de coco*?" She collected her bundle.

The crack of a bat hitting a ball drew his focus back to the baseball game. "Gotta go to C-Town."

The shop bell tinkled when the door slammed and locked behind her. The closest grocery was on the other side of the already deserted park.

Taina hustled through and took all the *crema de coco* they had on the shelf. The bottle of rum clinked against the cans as she grabbed the shopping bag from the checkout counter and headed home.

Mountains of black plastic bags sat in front of the stores and apartments. Rusty elevated train tracks shed lead-laden paint chips like poison manna. She picked up her pace and detoured through the only green space within miles to avoid the dog shit smeared on the sidewalks.

Her chest tightened in the hazy air as she carried the heavy packages up a grassy knoll toward 149th Street. She had no inhaler, and struggled to breathe as her lungs, long ago damaged by smoke-inhalation, couldn't expand.

A pigeon flew so close Taina expected the poop to plop on her back. It flapped its wings to challenge a squirrel scavenging through an overflowing pail filled with remnants of fried chicken, egg rolls, and pizza crusts.

The rodent was faster, though, and it scaled a tree with a crescent-shaped remainder of something in its mouth.

As she passed Ritual Rock, a gray bird, its wing tips and breast streaked with blue and green bright enough to adorn a peacock's tail, landed in front of her. It blocked the way like it had set up a force field.

"What the fuck?" She tried to push past but couldn't.

"Humans really like that word." A creature, waist high to Taina, with a Cheshire-Cat grin, a British accent, two iridescent blue wings, and a squat, leaf-green body materialized. His choice bits were barely concealed by a brown rag.

"What the fuck! A fairy in this human wasteland?"

Like a true New Yorker, he ignored the duplicate expletive. "Allow me to introduce myself. Bridge Rat, minion to Hawk Claw, Fairy King of New Yorke at your service, Lady Taina. I am in charge of this sector of The Bronx. My liege lord shall arrive in a moment."

Bridge Rat bowed, and his arm gestured like he was sweeping the sidewalk. "I daresay the foul language you've acquired in such a short time bodes well for your ability to rise to your duties."

Tonight couldn't get weirder. First, she'd broken some punk's nose. Now she'd dropped the F-bomb on a fairy. Twice. She didn't give a shit about either transgression.

"Knock it off. The only court around here is on 161st Street and the Grand Concourse. This isn't Camelot, and I'm not a lady. I'm a woman and don't rise to do anyone's duty."

The fairy rustled his wings. Magick tingled along Taina's spine and soothed the angst roiling in her gut since she'd gotten off the plane and into that fetid yellow cab at Kennedy airport two weeks ago.

"Ah, I beg to differ, my lady." Bridge Rat turned his eyes skyward.

A majestic ruddy hawk glided to a landing on top of Ritual Rock. Another fae-induced shiver crawled down Taina's back like a spider.

The haughty fairy king coalesced out of a rusty dust spiral. Red hair hung in wavy tendrils over his shoulders, obscuring much of a bare chest. Pointed ears, adorned with cuffs, spikes, and jeweled earrings, wiggled. A lime-green cape swept the gum-stained asphalt as he flitted toward her, bare, six-toed feet hovering only inches above the ground, maroon and ochre wings beating like a translucent heart.

Bridge Rat announced him. "Hawk Claw, King of The Fairydom of New Yorke."

Hawk Claw alighted, swept the cape over one shoulder, and bowed. "Hail and welcome, White Witch. Long have we awaited your return."

Yes, this night could get even weirder. "I think you must be confusing me with someone else. I'm brown and barely a witch at all."

"On the contrary, Lady Taina. You are just beginning to realize your powers. We trust that Sir Arnaldo will be at your side during the impending battle."

She suppressed a giggle at that image. "I'm just trying to get to the bottom of a mystery, then get my bottom out of the Fairydom of New Yorke."

The fairies in PR were more like fireflies, quiet, silly, tricky. Of course, everything in The Bronx mutated to the most extreme degree possible.

"Fear not, it has been foreseen and will occur." Hawk Claw pronounced, expressionless, like one who hasn't had good news in a long time. "Bridge Rat will summon me and the others when the time comes." He fluttered his wings, rose into the air, and transformed back into a majestic bird as he flew west over Ritual Rock toward the Manhattan skyline.

Taina shivered despite the hot, humid night. Streetlights blinked on.

"I don't mean to be rude, Bridge Rat, but I need to get this royal ass inside. My powers aren't strong enough to fight off the dhamps and weres. I doubt I'd be much use in a real battle."

The fairy crinkled his mouth and scratched a fuzzy chin. "Need an amplifier then, do you, Lady Taina?" He flapped his wings rapid-fire and transformed back into a common pigeon, flying east.

A trace of fae glitter, perhaps some of their glamour, sparkled on Taina's arms and hands, and she couldn't wipe it off. As she walked, dark shadows surrounded by red auras crept out behind Ritual Rock and the other smaller boulders scattered about the park. The temperature dropped. *Los Sangueros* were coming out to play, and she'd missed the sunset curfew.

More shrouded figures rustled through deserted streets and alleyways. Taina made it to the corner of her block before Hawk Claw swooped overhead, a white fur ball dangling from his talons. Bridge Rat alighted on the wrought iron fence surrounding her apartment.

A pack of pit bulls wearing red collars and nasty snarls padded out of the garbage and rubble strewn lot that had once been a gas station. Hawk Claw did not transform but deposited his prey at Taina's feet.

She gasped at the sight of the tiny dog, bloodied and limp. "What did you do to him?"

Hawk Claw departed without an answer. Bridge Rat hopped from rung to rung on the rusty metal fence. He couldn't very well shed his glamour and let the mundanes outside the bar across the street see him shape-shift.

His voice was far louder than such a tiny body could muster without great magick. "His Lordship rescued this poor pup from that roving band. His name is Zeus, and he will serve you well." The pigeon fluttered to the eaves just above her apartment window and disappeared into a duct.

The pit bulls seemed to sense the drop in magickal energy and crept closer, teeth bared, prepared to fight Taina for their precious morsel. Glass and metal clanked as she tossed away the shopping bag and gathered the injured animal into her arms. The dog looked into her eyes with his own wide in fear, desperate. She fumbled, almost losing her tenuous grip on the pooch.

The pack circled, moving closer, closer. One nipped at Taina's heel. Just like when the man pulled her ponytail, the breach of boundary sent a surge from the point on her foot that his fangs had scratched to the top of her head.

She thrust her right arm out, palm outstretched, and traced a circle around her while moving clockwise. A protective spell spewed out from somewhere deep inside, and she intoned it, visualizing energy pulsing toward the pack.

"White light, shine bright.
Banish the night.
Bring back the light.
White light, shine bright.
Banish the night.
Bring back the light.
White light, shine bright.
Banish the night.
Bring back the light."

The dogs moved back.

She clutched the pup close to her chest, stamped her foot, and waved away the pit bulls. "Shoo!"

One lunged at her in defiance.

"¡*Vete para carajo!*" The words spilled from her mouth, guttural as a canine's growl, surprising her as much as the dog pack.

She slipped out the wand and re-traced the circle. *"Ahora!"* Sparkling dust scattered.

The mongrels yelped, clawed, and bit themselves as magickal motes alighted on their coats. The smell of burning sulfur filled the air.

A large alpha took off at a gallop. The pack followed, all stopping to lick their wounds. Men outside the bar applauded. The mundane bastards probably thought the sparks were flame from a cigarette lighter.

Taina retrieved her shopping bag, unlocked the outside gate, and hurried inside. She laid the tiny white dog on a towel and cleaned his bloody, tattered ears, the bite marks on his back, and the claw marks on his neck.

Bundled into her arms like a baby, she rocked him. Her tears fell on his matted coat. The animal's gasps of fear slowed.

Would he make it until the vet's office down the street opened the next morning?

"Please don't die."

He sighed and raised his head. A ribbon of pink tongue tickled her chin. The spindly tail wagged.

"Tomorrow I'll take you get checked out. No time for piña coladas tonight, my friend. You need food and water, and a good rest. Me too."

She laid him down and put away her things. The dog struggled to his feet, lapped the water and ate the pieces of leftover meat she'd cut and placed on the floor.

The glass wasn't broken, the cans weren't dented, the dog was alive, her magick was stronger. Was that fairy influence or the familiar? He was so cute it didn't matter.

Taina opened the window and called to the pigeon in the eaves of the dormer. "Thank you, Bridge Rat."

Chapter Four
Bitter Fruit

Taina wiped the daily accumulation of gritty dust off the windowsill. She watered the palm tree on the black metal fire escape. There wasn't an air conditioner left in any hardware store in New York City, and the oscillating fan circulated the heat around like a convection oven.

In PR, there would be ocean breezes blowing through the rooms, the sound of songbirds, the smell of bougainvillea, sand between her toes. But her plan for the day was picking up her car and having furniture delivered.

"Be right back, Zeus." She tousled the dog's ears, avoiding the healing wound on the back of his neck.

He gazed at her for a moment, then tucked his head between his front paws and closed his eyes. She hated to leave him, but the vet had told her to not take him out until he'd recovered.

Taina stuffed the $300 deep into her pocket and hurried down the stairs. She crossed 149th Street at the juncture with *Las Tombas* territory.

Males and females exuding a yellow-zombie aura clustered in groups, wearing dark glasses, scanning for rival gang members or likely targets. Weakened by the mid-day sun, they hung back in the shadows under awnings or in alleys.

She put on her best bold, bitchy, Bronx strut. But as she got closer to the industrial park and the rows of auto-body shops, the elevated roadway obscured a good deal of the light. The temperature dropped, but she was sweating—the nervous kind that smelled like a men's locker room.

The zombies' hard glares bored into her. They growled.

"Arnaldo's new *puta*," one bitch antagonized.

She'd spent less than two hours with the man, in broad daylight and public places, and had already been labeled. Taina didn't take the bait and ducked through the open garage bay.

The startled mechanic's wrench clattered on the concrete floor. "Go back outside and come in the front. It's dangerous to walk through this area."

What an understatement. "I'm here to pick up my car." She walked toward the office, right under the cars up on lifts.

Miguel hurried to meet her. "¡Hola, nena! Didn't you get my message to call me to arrange delivery?" His smile was as warm as the day.

"I've been busy setting up my apartment." She didn't want to get into all the adventures she had since the car accident.

His eyes narrowed. "Isn't Arnaldo here with you?"

She hadn't seen the bastard since their altercation. "No, he...he's working."

"Ay, sí. The man gives his life to that center. The car is out back." He held the door and let her pass first.

"I brought cash." She dug the wad of bills out of her pocket and counted it out.

He didn't verify there were enough twenties and took her keys off a pegboard. "I'll let you out directly onto Timpson Place. It's safer, but keep your doors—"

"Locked and my windows closed."

He smiled. "Arnaldo knows of what he speaks, nena. Don't come over here alone again, please."

Miguel escorted her into an alleyway. Her car faced a solid metal door. He opened the driver's side and stood next to her while she slipped in.

"You're James Aponte's daughter, right?" He cringed, likely anticipating a shower of emotion.

Instead, joy swept over her. "You knew my father?"

Miguel lowered his eyes. "I'll never forget that picture of a soot-covered child on the cover of the Daily News and New York Post the day after the fire. James was very dedicated to the community."

She blinked back tears, but a hope had her heart pounding. "I'm trying to find out who started it, Miguel. Do you know?"

"Everyone, and no one. Throw gasoline and light matches. It's only bricks and cement. Just a game. The landlords and the gangs didn't think about the people left homeless, and the ones who died. They still don't. Only the weapons are different."

She exhaled in frustration. "I won't rest until I find out."

Miguel stroked the graying stubble on his chin. "Go away, before something happens. It won't change anything, and if you get hurt they'll have won again."

Everyone had just given up. "Why do you stay here in the middle of gang territory?"

"Because I'm a stubborn old man with a wife, a daughter, and grandchild back in PR to support. I keep my nose out of their business, and they leave me alone. But if you go looking, trouble will find you."

Taina glanced at her watch. Furniture delivery in an hour—but she had to follow this lead. "Can we talk about my family sometime? Abuelita took me to PR and never wanted to discuss even happy memories."

He took her hand. "My friend owns a place near Jackson Avenue, and they make *lo mejor pollo guisado en El Bronx*. Call me when you have time for dinner."

"I'd like that." This was the first glimmer of hope that she might be able to find out important details about the arson.

The metal gate rattled as he unlocked the gate and pulled it up. As soon as it clanked shut behind her, a crowd of *Las Tombas* rushed the car and blocked her way. The weres wore dark glasses and sported yellow halos, too aware, too intent and focused to be zombies.

She eased forward, but they didn't move. Taina leaned on the horn, but the sound didn't trouble them. Her hand found the lead pipe. The crowd leaped onto the hood and pounded on the windshield.

The car lunged forward as the accelerator met the floor and fishtailed. Two weres tumbled onto the asphalt; two others smashed against her windshield. One's head cracked the passenger-side glass.

A female, bushy mane blowing, held on to the windshield wiper. Taina took a right turn up over the curb, and the werewolf flew off, taking the blade arm along as a souvenir. The remaining soldier, unsettled as the car veered left, and it jumped off before he fell.

No one paid any attention to the blaring horn, the squealing tires. She gunned through a yellow light to get off the side street, back onto 149th Street where gray-haloed mundanes stopped to stare at the crazy bitch behind the wheel.

Still shaking, adrenaline surging, Taina's heart pounded. Her head ached from staring through the hazy auras and the effort of even minimal magic. She watched in the rearview mirror at *Las Tombas* in pursuit, ducking from awning to awning to avoid the sunlight. With a few quick turns, one the wrong direction up a one-way street, she lost them. Tailed, tagged, and targeted, she feared someone would follow her home.

~ * ~

Taina propped her laptop on the windowsill to pirate a neighbor's wi-fi connection. She could have two million dollars, a date with a sexy Asian single, a female cougar, or a hot, hunky jock. But she couldn't get her ex-girlfriend to answer an email.

Their breakup had seemed amicable, but Serena was obviously taking it hard. Or perhaps Arnaldo had filled her in and the two of them were having their own private chuckle. Click, spam deleted, shutdown. Miguel, the perfect stranger who just happened to be a gentleman, had done more for her than the jerk-off Serena had entrusted her to. But he was a mundane who knew nothing about magickal matters.

Taina knelt by her altar and lit rosemary incense. She needed a smudge stick to purify her new home. The mismatched, colored candles from the dollar store looked ridiculous, but the goddesses would have to understand. Zeus raised his head, and his ears pricked. He struggled to his feet, limped over, then settled at Taina's feet.

She patted the dog's head. "Interested in magick, are you?"

He watched as she sprinkled salted water from a black vessel into the bristles of her broom and swept widdershins to banish the negative energy. She flicked salt water on the windows, the doors and chanted, walking clockwise.

"Salt and sea, of ill stay free.

Fire and air, draw all that is fair.

Around and around, the circle is bound."

The perimeter gave way as she ran for the buzzer. No wonder her magick was so erratic—she was too distracted, too scattered, too unfocused.

The deliverymen clomped up the narrow staircase. Zeus hobbled away and hid behind some books stacked on the floor.

Taina got in front of them lest they trample through her ritual space. "Can you put it over there?"

They maneuvered the unwieldy load around her and plunked the sofa down. "Be right back with the rest."

The men brought the mattress, and then the box spring. Their sidewise glances betrayed their annoyance at her blocking the fastest route through the room. Arnaldo followed, carrying the bed frame under one arm and the headboard under the other. He flashed a close-lipped smile.

"The guys needed some help." He paused at the door until the deliverymen hauled the bedding into her room. "May I enter?"

So, he had some decorum. She invited him in.

"The circle is open, but unbroken

May the peace of the Goddess go in our hearts.
Merry meet, merry part, and merry meet again.
Blessed be."

He closed his eyes for a moment, whispered something to himself, then bowed as he carried the furniture across the living room. Acting like a proper witch.

Taina's cheeks burned like they'd been slapped. Had Serena shamed him into coming back, or did he feel guilty?

"All done, miss." The deliveryman reappeared, looking askance as he handed her a clipboard. "Sign here."

Taina shook off the distraction. "Let me check to make sure everything is all right." She pulled the sofa a bit further from the perimeter of her circle, checked for damage, and bounced on the bed to be sure it was steady.

The three men waited near the door until she came out of the bedroom.

"Thanks. Everything seems to be fine." She gave them each a five-dollar tip.

They beat it, leaving Arnaldo standing alone and empty-handed. Zeus peered out from his hiding place.

Arnaldo jumped. "What the hell is that?"

"My familiar," she said.

He screwed up the left side of his face. "Looks like a dirty mop."

Zeus growled, and Taina stroked him. "He's a Westie."

Arnaldo tittered. "A Whattie?"

"A West Highland Terrier. He needs a good grooming. But I can't take him until his wounds are healed. He's my familiar."

Arnaldo hung on the doorframe, laughing so hard tears ran down his cheeks. "Where did you get this killer?"

Zeus growled.

"It's a long story." She wasn't ready to get into another altercation about where she couldn't and shouldn't go.

Arnaldo changed the subject. "Your circle is a kind of weak, and I'm concerned about that protective spell holding up, particularly with the windows open."

No use denying it. "Yeah, I sensed that too. Any idea where I can find a sage smudge stick around here?"

"There's a magick shop on Webster Avenue, but your weakness is internal. You lack confidence and focus, therefore power. That's what Serena told me about you, and I agree." He wandered about, nose lifted like he was sniffing out the weak spots.

Just as I thought. "So, she made you come?"

"Tee, hee, hee. She told me to get my hairy ass over here to train you in urban magick. Hasn't seen my ass for twenty-nine years, but some things never change. It's too hot to go all the way over to Webster Avenue. Why don't we go for a walk in St. Mary's Park? I'll show you Ritual Rock and take you to a *botánica.*"

They'd been together long before Serena swore off The Bronx and off men. He must know she and Serena had been a couple until recently, but she let that go for now.

"I don't practice *Santería.*" Abuelita's fervor had been placed on Catholic rites, daily masses, recitations of the rosary, lighting candles to St. Anthony, St. Jude, cleaning the church, ironing altar linens—and trying to persuade Taina to become a nun.

"Serena never put much faith in it either, so I'm not surprised she taught you traditional magick."

"A lot happens in twenty-nine years." Taina couldn't picture her bejeweled, classy ex-girlfriend with Arnaldo.

For sure." His chin drooped as much as his voice. "Wanna go?"

Traveling with him as an escort was too good an opportunity to miss—particularly after this morning's episode. *"Sí.* But only to the park. I don't want too many new experiences on the same day." She tucked Zeus into his bed and locked the door behind them.

Hot air hit her in the face like a blowtorch. Sunlight beat down on the asphalt, raising a smoldering gray aura over the streets and the few people out at what would have been siesta in other places where it was this hot. Taina blinked to clear them, her vision, her head.

She better warn him. "A bunch of *Las Tombas* just cornered me when I went to pick up my car."

No sense of surprise or worry touched his face.

"Why do you think Raul was on your tail the minute you arrived? The dark magicks sense fresh blood, and they don't abide by any code of ethics. "What did you do?"

They stopped at the corner to wait for the light to change. "I gunned the accelerator and sent them flying."

He gave a thumbs up. "Good, next time run them down. Let Lupo come and scrape them off the street with a shovel and remake them into zombies. You can't let them ever get the upper hand."

"How come they don't bother you?"

Arnaldo fidgeted, put his hands into his pockets. "Well, let's just say we have an uneasy truce. Sort of like the Arabs and the Israelis. We fire a few rockets back and forth, take out a few soldiers, sometimes some civilians as collateral damage, and move on."

Her blood chilled. "Innocent bystanders?"

"Let's cross before we get hit by a bus, then I'll explain." He led the way into the park.

The few patches of grass were crisped by the heat. Tree branches drooped. Dried leaves already scattered the ground. A few moms pushed babies in swings. Older kids skateboarded on a makeshift ramp fashioned from a plank and a chunk of wood.

Arnaldo chose a bench in the shade. "Raul Rivera is the half-breed vamp who was trying to 'help you out.' *El jefe de Los Sangueros.* More sophisticated, but just as dangerous as *Las Tombas.* The police think they're rival gangs, but they only fight with each other when there is nothing else to do.

"Both are always looking for new meat, though Raul focuses on his stable of girls and boys. Lupo will take anyone who follows instructions, even the likes of Jesús."

"What happened to him?" she asked.

"He shot heroin, then crack, then got AIDS. Desperate for a cure, he accepted Lupo's offer to join *Las Tombas.* But his brain was so fried he couldn't be relied upon in a fight.

"So he panhandles on a fixed schedule: Bottles-and-cans Monday, candy-in-the-subway Tuesday, windshield-washing Wednesday, thrifty-picky-pocket Thursday, dumpster-diving Friday, cash it all in and turn it over to the boss on Saturday, and on the seventh day he rests."

Not even a trace of sadness afflicted his voice.

"I can't believe he chose to exist like that," she said.

Arnaldo couldn't disguise his resignation. "Yep. Die a nobody or live forever making mayhem without getting caught. That's why I took over an abandoned building and rebuilt it from the ground up, inside out, when Jesús was still alive and knew how to do electrical and plumbing without flooding the basement or blowing the fucking place up. It's a place the kids can go to learn about hope. *La esperanza es todo que tenemos.*"

"*Sí,* hope is all we have." Taina didn't have any left, but she wasn't going to admit that to him.

Barefoot children waded in a filthy puddle under an open fire hydrant. One sat on top of the plug, while the others dodged traffic to run under the high-pressure stream of water strong enough to shove their bodies under the cars whizzing down St. Ann's Avenue.

Arnaldo's gaze fixed on the same sight. "*Benditos.* They think a seventy-percent average is doing great in school. But they get one hundred in sex and drugs, courtesy of Raul Rivera."

The plume of water, the spray alighting on her face conjured a memory of the fire. She suppressed it. "There are lots of saint's names in this neighborhood. Aren't there any angels to fight back?"

He humpfed. "Never saw any, but I don't hang out with the heavenly sort. A few fairies here and there."

The image brought a smile to her face, and she played dumb. "Fairies in The Bronx?"

Arnaldo stared past her at the huge rock formation that rose to the eighth floor of the housing project hulking behind it. A few pigeons waddled across the top, creating a green-and-white collage of droppings.

"Yeah. They spent too much time at the Whitestone Drive-In back in the 1970s—before it became a ten-plex annex to Rikers Island. While I was getting it on in the back seat with Serena, they watched *Star Wars* and got the idea someone would come along and stop the destruction before the ley lines were corrupted. They were wrong, and most of them have gone to Westchester and beyond."

"How can all this be stopped?"

"A revolution, and a revelation of the extent of dhamp and were involvement. But the mundanes won't believe any of it. There are just too few white magicians with the *cohones* to stand together against the dark magicks."

Fingernails of foreboding scraped down Taina's back, and she shivered in the light mist. "Which side are you on, given the collateral damage you've caused?"

Arnaldo finally looked her in the eye. "Listen, *chica*. Forget about pure black or pure white. Turn on the auras. Anything but green or washed-out gray is an enemy. Any hesitation, you're dead, or forever undead like Jesús.

"The mundanes who happen to be around when shit goes down, well, they'd be dead even if you weren't there." Great pain, and deep regret, seeped under his ornery façade.

"Why do you stay here, Arnaldo?"

"I don't want these kids to wind up like me. My mother was a Hunts Point whore and goddess only knows who my father was. My grandmother took me in. I rewarded her by being sent to prison for drug dealing and grand larceny. She turned me in just as I was about to join *Las Tombas*. If I wasn't in the joint getting detoxed, I'd have been sharing needles with Jesús, have AIDS, and be as cracked out and undead as him."

He got up and walked a circle in the shadow of Ritual Rock. Taina opened her mind and sensed the energy surge. This was a magickal battlefield with great significance, great power, great moments of triumph, yet monumental loss.

He paused, lips moving in silent meditation, then traveled widdershins before stroking a white vein in the dark-gray stone and resting his forehead on the surface.

She turned away, giving him privacy with his grief. She knew only too well of waking nightmares filled with guilt, regret, remorse, fury, helplessness, hopelessness.

"¡Piraguas!" A woman under a green umbrella near the edge of the park, hawked shaved ice drizzled with syrup.

Taina read her aura, a soft gray, like Abuelita's hair. Comforting, mundane, safe.

"One lemon and one coconut, please." Taina regarded the woman's grubby dress and threadbare sandals and handed her five bucks for three dollars' worth of ices. *"Ya. Enough."*

A toothless grin cracked her face. *"Que Díos se bendiga."*

Arnaldo came up behind her. "What's He gonna bless you for, *chica?"*

"I'm going to need all the blessings I can get." Taina handed him the coconut ice instead of the lemon.

He'd already shared enough bitter fruit.

Chapter Five
Angels and Zombies

The ices were dripping down their arms by the time they got back to Taina's apartment.

She unlocked the outside security gate. "Would you like to come up?"

"No. If I'm not there for the pick-up basketball game, the kids wander off and get into trouble."

Unease wriggled like worms in her belly. After his confession, his swagger was gone, and he regarded her with narrowed eyes. New respect? Perhaps. Or maybe recollections of younger days with Serena?

Bile rose into Taina's throat. He was after her tail, trying to recapture the relationship he'd had with Serena by taking up with the woman who'd been her apprentice—and her lover. Too creepy.

Arnaldo seemed in no hurry to leave. "Tomorrow, we should get working on spell casting and self-defense."

"I have a job interview." That wasn't untrue, but too convenient to not seem contrived.

"Where?" His eyebrows rose.

"The Bronx County Courthouse. For a position as a victim's advocate."

"You're in The Bronx, not Puerto Rico. You'll need to harden your shell, perfect that magick. The next morning then." His sarcasm, the deriding sneer, the insistence was more than annoying.

"What if I get the job?"

He almost spat with frustration. "Come by *Sonrisa*, when you're ready. Southern Boulevard and Longwood Avenue. Where *Las Tombas and Los Sangueros* territories form a trine with mine."

An invitation—or a dare?

"Okay, sure." Taina fled into the apartment.

Zeus met her at the door, his stub of a tail wagging. She knelt to pet him, and the dog settled back onto his bed.

A cool shower freshened her enough to make resting on the new sofa almost a pleasure. She imagined Serena looking at the caller ID, making the decision whether to answer, then focused on establishing a mental connection.

Taina fingered an aquamarine crystal from her former mentor and partner for the final magickal push.

"Travel a while, over the miles,
I sense you are home,
So answer the phone."

It worked. Anxiety tightened Serena's voice like an overstretched rubber band. "Taina, *que pasa, hija?*"

Her heart hurt that the only person still alive who really knew her was so far way, so unavailable. "I was with Arnaldo today. We're going to meet this week to do some training."

"Bueno." Serena must have already known as the inflection in her voice didn't change.

"What has he been telling you about me?"

Serena's voice quavered. "That you must focus, have confidence."

"Then why are you crying?" Unease, a sense they'd been plotting something, tickled Taina's mind. She took deep breaths to stay in control.

"Because I remember what it was like to learn the hard way." Serena sobbed like they were breaking up all over again.

Tears streamed down Taina's cheeks. "I think Arnaldo sees me as your replacement."

Zeus pattered over and settled at her feet, gazing up. She picked him up and puppy kisses eased her discomfort.

"That was a lifetime ago—for both of us." Composure returned to the older woman's voice, but it was still tinged with regret. "You were called back to the place of your birth, and only he can help you now."

"Serena…"

"Calm yourself, *mi amor.*

"This circle is cast
Between worlds,
Between night and day
To build a bridge
Between the present and past,
Between all creatures

That herein dwell."

"Use that chant during your next ritual with Arnaldo." Serena disconnected.

Why such mystery? Taina stared at the phone like it was going to answer. With Zeus tucked under one arm, she knelt by her altar and lit the white candle.

Shadows flickered across the glass, giving an illusion that her mother, father, and sister were shaking their heads.

~ * ~

Taina paused atop the twenty-three steps outside the majestic courthouse, which overlooked what had once been the showplace of The Bronx. A few steps from Yankee Stadium, the posh hotels and residences of lawyers, judges, and movie stars were now subsidized housing or welfare hotels.

The building towered behind her like a temple over what had been the seat of great power and wealth, before it crumbled away to dust, memories, shattered dreams, and broken glass. The lives of those remaining were held together by old chewing gum, spat like bullets from the mouths of angry gods.

In the quadrangle that resembled the Roman Forum, crimes were prosecuted, victims compensated, births, deaths, marriages, and divorces certified. The life of The Bronx was filed in heavy metal cabinets with giant wheel-shaped-locks, which, such as those on a bank vault, sealed them tight—like coffins.

Immersion in the order and formality of the court environment distracted her for a while. As a bilingual Latina with legal experience who hungered for justice, Taina had made a good impression. After the background check was complete, she'd be summoned to report for duty, a magickal blending into mundania.

Her heels clacked the marble surface, steady despite the slippery sheen from a light rain shower. Sun peeked out from behind clouds, bathing Joyce Kilmer Park in golden light. She wandered through high tufts of ornamental grasses before going downhill to the subway.

Funky, underground energy distorted even mundane machinery. The Metrocard read only after three swipes. A pair of rats scurried along the tracks and stopped to regard Taina like they knew her, whiskers twitching, tails undulating. Good will radiated from them, and she leaned over to get a better look.

"Stand back, girlie. Those disgusting creatures bite, if the train doesn't run you over first." The graying black man didn't take his gaze off her until she backed away.

A woman, clad in the garb of a West-African priestess, spoke in an accent somewhere between French and exotic. "They mean you no harm."

Her smile twinkled as bright as her eyes. The green aura blended so well into the lime glyphs on her robes it was nearly imperceptible.

Taina opened her mouth to respond to the magickal spirit, but the woman turned away. New Yorkers didn't speak to strangers on the subways, unless it was a matter of life and death, lest it become a matter of life and death.

Clammy heat trapped underground joined the smell of mold, stale piss, and grease. She stripped off her suit jacket. The underarms of her blouse already drenched with sweat. The ground trembled like an earthquake as the train rumbled in on the uptown tracks. Metal wheels screamed like a tortured cat. Before the din and tremors disappeared the arrival of the downtown Number 4 joined its counterpart in a deafening crescendo.

She ducked into the nearly deserted car, the temperature a good thirty degrees colder, its windows frosted over like it was midwinter. She put her jacket back on, wiped away the fog, and counted off the stops from 161st Street to 125th Street.

New York was a city of extremes, nothing stable, nothing predictable, but at this moment she was in synch with that rhythm—aware, alert, ready.

Almost on cue, Jesús shuffled in from a neighboring car, swaying as if on a Maypole as the train slowed. He gripped the rail with his left hand while clutching a tattered box in his right. "Greetings, ladies and gentlemen. I'm trying to stay out of trouble. Please buy some of my candy so I can eat some dinner."

Taina giggled. There were only two people in the car—she and the man who'd warned her away from the tracks. "Hello, Jesús. It's Taina, Arnaldo's friend."

The old man glowered at her. He had no way of knowing the bum, who looked like a wolf had chewed him up and spit him out—because it had—and smelled like the subway tracks, wasn't a complete stranger.

Jesús didn't remember her or the unfortunate circumstances of their meeting. "Arnaldo? Where's Arnaldo?"

"Working, Jesús." She wanted to take his hand, buy his crappy candy, show him some concern, but the money would go to Lupo, to no good.

"Skittles?" He proffered the filthy display.

"Not today." Sadness welled. She could do nothing to help him.

Jesús shambled into the next car.

"You better learn how to act on the subway, girlie." The old man wagged his finger.

"Thanks for the tips." She ascended into the shadows of hulking housing projects, upstairs crusted with wads of spit, cigarette butts, and scraps of paper.

Sweaty, grimy, muddy, back where she belonged, but where she wanted least to be.

Chapter Six
The Dhampir's Challenge

"I talked to Serena the other day." Taina's hands gripped the steering wheel as tandem tractor-trailers blasted by on either side.

Arnaldo adjusted the seat belt over his shoulder—again. He fidgeted and looked in the visor mirror. "What a handsome devil you are, Arnaldo Reyes. Keep right here, Taina."

"Okay." She signaled and changed lanes. "Serena mentioned you'd spoken."

"Watch that guy!" He gave the man who cut them off the finger.

"Why are you ignoring me?" She stopped short as another driver cut in front of her then braked, setting off a chain reaction.

Wheels screeched behind them. She gritted her teeth, but there was no impact, no sound of glass shattering, only angry horns.

"Because you are a bad enough driver and don't need any more distractions. You go too slow and let everyone squeeze in. See what that bastard did?"

"That's my fault? Isn't there a *botánica* closer to where I live?"

"Not one where you can go in and buy something without having to hear how your stars are crossed, what trouble will befall you for lighting the candles in the wrong order, or don't follow exact instructions for doing your *brujería.*"

The light turned red. She took a deep breath, grateful for the respite. Teenage girls who thought they were invincible, with their skirts up to *here* and blouses down to *there*, shook ass and bopped along, singing off-key karaoke. Men with nothing else to do enjoyed the view.

Adolescent boys dodged in between cars, buses, and double-parked Coca Cola delivery trucks with no regard for traffic signals and flashing 'Don't Walk' signs. Mothers walked their children home from the park, on alert for drive-by shooters out for some target practice.

Two kids rode skateboards down the middle of the street. Taina accelerated—very slowly.

Arnaldo shook his head. "They see the immortals doing that shit and try it themselves. First step to being lured into the gangs."

A young man rushed out between two buildings and charged the car.

"Hit him!" Arnaldo didn't hesitate to pronounce the sentence.

She jammed on the brake pedal. The guy tiptoed over the hood of the car, paused for an instant to kick the windshield, then disappeared into an alleyway on the other side. The crack left from the previous werewolf attack crawled up and across. A car behind her jumped the curb and hit a light pole.

"I told you to hit him." Arnaldo got out and slammed the door so hard the windshield disintegrated. Baubles of glass tinkled onto her lap and the empty seat.

Taina ran after him to the other car. The driver, an elderly man, sat stunned, covered in airbag dust, but conscious. A passerby called 911.

Arnaldo put his hand on the man's shoulder. "You're okay, Guillermo. I'll go with you to the hospital." He turned to her. "If you'd listened, this accident would never have happened." His words could have punched holes in metal.

"Am I supposed to run over pedestrians just because you say so?"

He bent to whisper in her ear, "You hit Jose, and nothing happened. My friend could have been killed. Turn on your auras, sweetheart. Raul is just letting us know he's watching every move you make. Now that he's won this round, he'll be back for more."

She tried to keep the conversation private. "It's too distracting to drive with auras enabled. All those mixed colors give me a headache."

"Take a fucking aspirin. This is not a game. You can't hurt *Una Tomba* or *Un Sanguero*."

"What if I make a mistake and kill someone who's innocent?"

"That's going to happen, Taina. Just like in any other war. Those are the playground rules. If you don't want to join the game, take your toys and go home." He turned his back on her.

The shock of Arnaldo's heartlessness never ceased to horrify her.

"No! It doesn't have to be that way."

An ambulance and police car arrived and took over. The tension dropped five notches when the ambulance door closed on Arnaldo's glare.

A cop touched her shoulder. "Miss, are you injured in any way?"

"No."

"Can you tell me what happened?" His demeanor was polite, but the way he stared her down implied she'd been at fault.

She took another step down the slippery slope, trying to be bold, bitchy, Bronx. "A stupid kid ran into the street. I stopped short. The other driver swerved to avoid hitting me."

The officer put his hands on his hips. "Can I see your license, registration, and insurance card?"

Taina retrieved them from the glove compartment, knocked the rest of the dangling glass into the car, and brushed off the seats so she could drive home.

Arnaldo was right. No matter what choices she made, someone was going to get hurt. And if she'd told the cop a dhampir had challenged her, he'd take her to the psych ward.

"Okay, miss. Be sure to call the insurance company right away."

She stuffed her papers back into the glove box, drove home, and duct-taped cardboard over the windshield. With any luck, someone would steal the car.

At least two beings wanted her out of the way, and they were not likely to give up.

Zeus danced at her feet. She picked him up, and the softness of his fur, and gentle kisses soothed and calmed her nerves.

Safe inside her apartment, she locked the door, all the windows, and reinforced her circle.

~ * ~

"Tell me that wasn't the best *pollo guisado* you've ever had." Miguel patted his belly. He took Taina's arm as they crossed Westchester Avenue.

"*Deliciosa.*" She waited until the train above them clattered past the Jackson Avenue station and they could hear each other again. "After you fix my car, sell it, Miguel. I've had two accidents already, and the parking is a pain in the ass. Keep whatever you can get and whatever the insurance company gives you. Take a nice vacation in PR this winter."

"I'll get rid of it for you, Taina, but I won't take your money. I'll be retired by fall, sunning on the beach, playing with my granddaughter.

Culebra is the most beautiful place in the world." He put his hand on her shoulder.

"I've never been there." She'd love to be anywhere near *La Isla* right now.

He took her hand. "Then you'll visit us."

"When I finish what I came to do." Every time she repeated that mantra, the cold dark shroud of reality closed around her again.

His grip tightened. *"Nena,* no one should have to live through what you did. But let it go. Find a nice man, settle down. No one moves into this neighborhood unless they have no choices."

"I need to find out who killed my family." She squeezed his hand.

"Your father made a lot of enemies with his community organizing." He looked side-to-side and loosened his grip. "And I've said too much already. Where's Arnaldo?"

Ahh! A clue. She took a step back. "Working, and soon I will be too. At the courthouse."

They'd reached the corner of Prospect Avenue and 149th Street. "You'll be safe in there. I'll walk you to your door."

"I'll be fine." It was much harder to argue with Miguel, a simple, caring man, than with Arnaldo, who was a jerk.

Miguel glanced around. "Walk in the street so no one can grab you. I'll watch until you get in. And call when I sell the car so you can cancel the insurance and pick up the money."

"Okay, Miguel." She handed him the registration.

He clasped her hand, raised it to his lips, and kissed it. *"Te veo."*

"Yes, see you soon." Taina saw tears in his eyes.

She walked down the center yellow line, auras enabled, turned and waved to Miguel when she got to her house. He ducked around the corner. Could Lupo be putting the squeeze on him—because of her?

I'm buying your ticket back to Culebra, Miguel. I owe you for all the trouble I've stirred up.

Chapter Seven
Sonrisa

Taina walked down Southern Boulevard to *Sonrisa* Community Center. She'd put off seeing Arnaldo since the car accident, but precious time was passing.

The row house, missing the ones on either side, stood up like a middle finger, dissing everything around it. A golden sun and moon etched on the glass transom over the door projected a protective spell out a few feet onto the sidewalk.

She chuckled as clueless mundanes stopped in front of the building, pivoted like they were lost, or crossed the street as they went by. Taina stepped over the pulsing energy field and rang the bell outside the chain link gate. She pushed through at the buzzer and right in the front door.

A group of senior citizens sat in gray metal chairs around rickety tables covered with red-and-black-plaid vinyl cloths. Laughter and the aroma of coffee wafted through the room. Two couples valiantly attempted a salsa to Tito Puente on a tinny boom box. The others applauded.

Good will pervaded the space. Zeus poked his way out of the blanket she'd wrapped him in. Taina rubbed behind his ears, and he rewarded her hand with a few grateful licks.

Arnaldo came down the stairs, waved, then paused to chat with the seniors.

He took his time coming over. "You should have called first. I won't have time for training until later this afternoon."

Zeus retreated under the blanket.

"Just paying a visit. I've had a lot to do the last couple of weeks." A twinge of guilt pricked her conscience. Taina had ignored his invitation, and now she was here only to extract information.

Arnaldo extended his arms like a priest giving a benediction. "The senior citizens stay until after lunch. Kids start to arrive at three. I supervise sports in the backyard, and they can play games, watch movies, hang out."

He patted the crucifix on his chest and pointed to an even larger one on the wall.

"Catholic Charities gives me a lot of help. Some funding from the Police Athletic League and the city and state. A few private foundations. Meals on Wheels. Come see my apartment." Joy lit up his face, and he ascended the stairs.

She braced for a slovenly bachelor's studio, but freshly washed dishes sat on a counter in the tiny kitchen. The toaster oven, coffee pot, and microwave barely fit on a dinette with two chairs.

The windows along the back of the room looked out on the brick wall of the building behind. The sofa bed was open, unmade, sheets trailing onto the floor, pillows dented as if he'd just picked his head up off them.

"I didn't have time to make my bed. I had to let Jenna from the NYC Office of the Aging in to set up." Arnaldo swept the linens into a ball and stuffed them into an already overflowing laundry basket. He folded the mattress and pushed down the mechanism with one foot while retrieving cushions from the floor.

The finish on the bare wood was worn thin, but there were no dust bunnies in the corner. His altar sat next to a television.

He saw her staring. "My bag of tricks is over there." He pointed to a collection of *Santería* candles, none ever lit, a peg rack dangling rosaries and colored bead necklaces, and a collage of statuary representing the most popular deities, with *Changó* front and center.

"You're a *santero?*" From the looks of the dust coating the icons, they weren't in regular use.

He grinned, winked, and wagged his head. "Sometimes one or another of them helps me mix up some *brujería.*"

It was a place to sleep alone, eat alone, but nothing to soften the hard edges. No rugs, no curtains, sun to banish the gloom, no pictures to offer companionship and memories, not a thing out of place, probably because there was not much here to begin with.

"Want some coffee?" He pointed to the sofa.

"Thanks. I didn't have time for breakfast." Taina sank onto the couch and put Zeus on the floor by her feet.

Arnaldo ignored the dog's tail-wag greeting. "Be right back." He clumped down the stairs and was up in less than three minutes balancing two plates on top of paper cups stenciled with the Acropolis.

"*Café, y un bagel con* cream cheese." He put the load down on a chipped wood coffee table and nestled into the couch cushions, cup in hand.

Spanglish always made her laugh, especially when rendered in his particularly rough Bronx accent.

"What's so funny?" He clearly didn't realize he'd spit a ball bearing into the musical rhythm of the Spanish language.

"I'm just happy today."

Zeus sidled closer.

Arnaldo *humpf*ed. "So, where did you get your Westie?"

She'd hoped for a way to bring the fairy issue up. "When I went to the grocery store about a week ago, I met two fairies in the park. They gave him to me." She took a bite of her bagel.

Arnaldo's smile disappeared, and he moved to the edge of the sofa. "St. Mary's Park? At night?"

"I would have been home before sundown if Bridge Rat and Hawk Claw hadn't stopped me. In fact, I didn't have any problem until I got almost to my front door. That's when they brought me Zeus." She deliberately left out the mob details.

"That fluffy puff thing is named after the greatest and most powerful of all gods?" Arnaldo was trying to joke but looked like someone was twisting his balls.

Taina sipped coffee, but it was far too strong. And too hot. "It fits." Her tongue burned.

He swallowed some bagel and took a swig. "Like a man and a goat."

She put her cup down. "Oh, stop. Let me tell you about the fairies."

Arnaldo gestured like he was swatting flies. "I'll tell you. One shifts into a red-tailed hawk that lives on the Dakota apartment building in Manhattan. How much assistance and protection did the great and noble king provide John Lennon the night he was shot?"

She'd learned to ignore him by now. "They called me Lady Taina."

He cleared his throat as he tossed the rest of his bagel onto the plate. "Get a grip, Guinevere. They're frisky when there's a new witch in town. Especially a female one."

"Arnaldo, they told me I was the White Witch, and that you and I would be joining them in battle."

"They said that?" He rubbed his chest like he had a bad case of indigestion.

She forced a laugh. "Yeah, me."

"The fairies are determined to reclaim their territories, but I don't think that's ever gonna be possible. In the meantime, stay out of the fuckin' park until you're better at self-defense. The lessons for which, by the way, haven't happened."

Zeus growled his disapproval.

What was this man's problem? "I saw a few *Los Sangueros* on my way back, but they didn't come near me. After the fairies brought me Zeus, I sent a pack of pit bulls away whimpering. My magic is stronger because of this familiar."

He ignored the dog's warning and leaned closer. "Taina, you're in the middle of a supernatural ground zero. Fairy magick is so disrupted by iron and steel and carved up ley lines they're recruiting anyone and anything they can."

She'd tired of him perpetually ruining her optimism and good spirits. "They mentioned you were my ally. If that's true, how come the gangs aren't targeting you and this center? I've asked you that before, and you never really answered me."

He sat back and folded his arms across his chest. "Because I've been around a long time and know things about them that could cause, let's say, some inconvenience. You don't want to know the details."

The dog whimpered. Arnaldo reached over to pat his head. Zeus snapped.

He pulled his hand back just in time. "Stupid shit. The two of you are like cute baby lambs waiting for slaughter."

She really did want to know the details, but this wasn't the time. Taina gathered her things. "Why does every conversation we have end with you insulting me? I've survived without you until the age of thirty-five, including being thrown out of a burning building."

He winced, then got in her face. "Zeus got lucky—this time. And so did you. Better take your little doggy back to PR now, before something happens."

Uh, huh. Reasons Number Five and Six on the 'don't fly' list: He had involved Serena in his screw-ups and now Taina had to leave for her safety. He might be jealous, angry over the breakup, uncomfortable being part of a pansexual love triangle. Or unwilling to drag someone else into his messy affairs. Maybe all of the above.

"I'm not leaving before I find out who set that fire, Arnaldo." Taina tucked Zeus under the blanket, hurried down the stairs, then headed home.

~ * ~

Taina gave up on sleep about an hour before sunrise. Arnaldo's parting tirades were getting more and more troubling, and she hadn't slept well since the last salvo. Her body ached while her eyes fought to close. Not a good way to start a new job.

Could someone in the courthouse help her contact the detective? Calls to the precinct had been met with "hold on" that went on forever.

In-person appeals netted blank stares, furrowed eyebrows, and "Michael Kelly, arson task force? Never heard of him."

Linked-In said he was a detective with the New York City Police Department but didn't list a phone number or address. She'd messaged him, but he hadn't returned the email. No social media—what detective would want to be that recognizable?

Zeus whimpered to go out. She put him in the litter box. "We'll go for a walk before I leave." She didn't dare go out until daylight.

He scratched at the dust, sneezed, but relented and peed. She was a prisoner in this apartment with the windows closed, curtains drawn, doors triple locked, protection spell reinforced daily, and a lead pipe under her pillow just in case something got past it all.

The coffee and oatmeal tasted like glue washed down with battery acid and burned her stomach accordingly. She popped some chewable antacid and showered.

The gray suit restricted her movement, making her even more vulnerable. Her feet ached as she forced them into matching pumps. The blouse clung to her like a damp rag.

She opened the window to let in the cool morning air and perched on the windowsill. Zeus crawled into her lap and peered out, head cocked right, then left like he knew what he was looking for.

When the caravan of Coca Cola trucks double-parked in front of the bakery, she got the leash. "Safe to go for a walk now."

The mundanes in green uniforms, jovial despite the fact it was before seven in the morning, sipped coffee, ate buttered rolls, and smiled.

"Morning, ma'am. Cute pooch." One patted the dog.

"Good morning." There were normal, civilized people there and, dressed in business attire, she was one of them.

A garbage truck squealed, backed into the curb. The men hauled bags off a mound and tossed them in one-by-one. Drivers stuck behind them leaned on horns. Mundane bums rolled makeshift carts loaded with scrap metal to the junkyard. All perfectly routine, un-magickal.

Zeus sniffed every lamppost, every hydrant, and lifted his leg until nothing was left in his bladder. She scooped him up and hurried back.

The window remained open. No sense of menace or threat drifted in on the humid breeze. Taina jammed a wooden spoon between the upper sash and top window frame so no one could push it open and climb in. How they would do that so remote from the fire escape, in the front of the house, in full view of a busy avenue remained to be seen, but Arnaldo's prophesies of doom buzzed like bees around her.

If she didn't act like a witch, they wouldn't bother her more than other mundanes, who seemed to get on just fine unless they happened to be in the wrong place at the wrong time.

Being around judges, lawyers, plaintiffs, defendants, and legalese was what she was used to, and she was good at it. Forget dhamps. Forget weres and zombies. Forget fairies. Forget witchcraft.

She'd gotten by just fine all these years as a paralegal and would keep away from the park, *Las Tombas, Los Sangueros*, magickal creatures, and from Arnaldo Reyes.

Chapter Eight
The Temple of Justice

Taina was far from fresh when she got to 125th Street. The subway platform disguised as a sauna was packed with commuters wilting in the stifling, stagnant, stinking underground. Everyone that streamed off the Downtown Number 6 raced for the already packed uptown Number 4 when it pulled in.

She allowed herself to be shoehorned in by those behind her, pressed between men in suits, women in sundresses and sandals, and an assortment of folk on the way to Yankee Stadium very early for the 1:00 PM game—sporting banners, backward caps, and T-shirts proclaiming, "I Hate the Fucking Boston Red Sox."

She wallowed in mundane shit, not worried about auras and spells and dark and light magick. Vengeance crossed her mind as her toes, already pinched in the pumps, got stomped by some idiot with an air horn and an open can of beer. And it was only 8:15 AM.

Outside air was actually refreshing. She hobbled up the twenty-three imposing marble steps, then another six, along with the stream of humanity outside the massive brass and glass doors, waiting in the already blazing sun for the stroke of nine.

Clutching the letter of introduction to obtain her identification card, Taina ducked in behind another worker before the staff entry door snapped shut. The guards looked like someone had elbowed them in the ribs or had an underwire digging into a boob. And it was only 8:30 AM.

One called her out, "ID should be out and on your person, ma'am."

She put on her best, professional smile and forced herself not to limp. "It's my first day, and I'm supposed to report to the Victim's Advocate office. My photo has already been taken."

The woman perused the letter, checked something out on a clipboard, then rummaged through the unlocked drawer of a battered desk. "Do you have a picture ID?"

Taina handed over her Puerto Rican driver's license, the image oddly unfamiliar, taken during another life, another time.

The guard studied Taina's face before handing them back. She fished a laminated ID out of an alphabetized box. "Must be worn, picture out, at all times when on court premises. Employees normally do not need to go through the metal detectors but, since it's your first day, pass through and take the elevator to the sixth floor. The office is the second on your left."

She got into the queue and studied the basket-weave detail around brass pillars in the doors, white marble floors with brownish-gray, block-style tiles adorned with glimmering gold mosaics. An odd color combination, but it worked.

"Empty your pockets. Remove your belts. All electronics in the bins," called out the vinyl-gloved officer.

She obliged, put her purse on the conveyer, and it went through the scanner. The examiner frowned at the screen and rummaged through and picked out the wand/athame multi-tool. He couldn't unmask and unscrew the lipstick case baffle.

He twirled up until 'Peach Melba' stained his fingers, closed and set it aside, and sent the bag through again. Satisfied that what he'd seen on X-ray had been some artifact, pushed both toward her.

Everyone in the elevator knew one another, and no one paid any attention to her. They chatted about boyfriends, kids, their plans for next weekend. She had none of that to occupy her mind, no friends, no family.

No one.

Taina's sweaty palm slipped as she tried to turn the knob on the office door. She dried it on her skirt and gave a firm twist. A faint tingle ran through her, and the lock clunked.

The door creaked open on a dark, empty office. Those daily rituals she'd been performing, plus the familiar, had boosted her powers enough she didn't have to do more than try to perform simple magick.

She flipped on the light and surveyed the regiment of wooden chairs, the finish worn off the seats by countless bottoms sliding on and off, nicked by keys and God only knew what else.

An oak desk that looked like a relic from the day the courthouse had opened sat in a corner of the room that would soon hold grieving, frightened people in need of a soft shoulder and a firm hand.

"Good mooring, Taina. I see you had no trouble getting your ID." The African American woman who'd hired her swept in, heels clicking, keys jingling.

"Hello, Simone."

"Sandy will be here any minute. Sit down. Relax. I'll make some coffee. Clients usually don't start arriving until about 10:00." Simone fiddled with the coffee maker.

The pot hissed and dripped, the aroma as enticing as the yummiest dessert. Taina's mouth watered.

Her boss settled behind the desk, locked her bag in a drawer, and folded her hands on the blotter. "We usually alternate picking up cases as they come in, unless one of us is in court or in session. Sandy keeps things organized."

Either anxiety or excitement, perhaps a bit of both, welled up inside. "In PR, the dockets are so full it takes far too much time to move forward. I can only imagine here."

Simone frowned. "Taina, being a paralegal is very different than being an advocate. Our job is to help a client through this day, this problem, not to resolve or fix it for them. We take the punches from the defendants, the defense attorneys, the press, the police, and the detectives, so the clients don't get hurt any worse than they have already.

"The odds are so stacked against these women—let's face it, most of them are women—we're the only ones who stand between them and a system that gives them less rights than the perps."

"No legal advice, just support, information, and reassurance." Taina had once researched the law, prepared briefs, counseled clients. A new role, plus figuring out what went on in each building this temple towered over, would be a big change.

"Correct. The assistant DAs and court officers are very kindly disposed to us. But not the attorneys, not the cops, and certainly not the perps. We have to have big mouths and balls as big as the rest of the guys, even if they aren't a natural part of our anatomy." Simone poured two cups. "How do you like it?"

"Milk, no sugar." Taina accepted the cup.

"I take mine black." Simone sipped. "Ah, nectar of the gods. Milk's in that mini fridge over there." She took a breath, another swig. "Your office key is in the desk drawer. We'll work together for the first couple days, until you get your phone list updated.

"Won't take long to have every city agency dreading your number on the caller ID." Simone plunked into her seat and dialed into voicemail.

The litany of troubles emanating from the messages wasn't soothing Taina's pounding head. She went out for more caffeine. A few clients were already taking seats in the waiting room.

A harried woman, gray hair in neat cornrows, was handing out clipboards. "Hi, Taina. I'll be right in to properly introduce myself."

The clients raised vacant eyes, pupils pinpoint from fear, to meet Taina's, then resumed scrawling with trembling hands.

She pushed open her door, turned on the air conditioner to banish the musty heat, slugged her coffee. There was a job to do. Better get ready.

~ * ~

Taina, the only one in the office who spoke Spanish, spent the morning interpreting for clients too distraught to try and translate their troubles. The grateful look in their eyes soothed her first day jitters. By lunch she already had a good feeling for the job and a list of community agencies for client referrals.

"Break time." Sandy locked the door. "How ya doin'?"

"She's doing fantastic." Simone rapped her on the back. "I hope you're not too tender for this."

Taina had worked in a high-powered law firm in Puerto Rico with plenty of badass clients. But she didn't grow up in a neighborhood where the women had bigger *cohones* than the men. And there was still work to do to qualify as bold, bitchy, Bronx. "Well, it's different than in PR, but the work is the same."

"Got lunch?" Simone went to the fridge, took out a sandwich, and started munching.

"No, I'll go to the cafeteria." Taina fished money out of her desk drawer.

"Hell, no. There's only vending machines with junk food and mystery meat sandwiches." Simone washed the last bite down with her morning coffee. "It's a public area filled with jurors, attorneys, anyone and everyone. Someone will remember you from somewhere and chew your ear off with the latest chapter in their bad romance. I've got to run to the bank." She dashed.

Sandy headed toward the door. "I'm going out. "Pizza? Chinese?" She collected her purse.

"A slice. And a bottle of water." Taina handed her a five dollar bill. "This enough?"

"Plenty." She stuffed it into her pocket. "You answer the phone. I'll relieve you when I get back."

Taina passed the time neatly re-writing phone numbers onto a list. Her stomach growled, and she regretted not having gone to the machine for a day-old bologna sandwich wrapped in stiff, crinkly plastic.

The phone startled her. "Victim's Advocate Office. Ms. Aponte speaking."

"Uh…is Simone there?" The woman on the other end sounded…troubled.

"She's at lunch. Can I help with something?" *Where the hell was Sandy?*

"Not unless you're an advocate who speaks Spanish."

"As a matter of fact, I am. Taina Aponte." She didn't mention it was her first day.

The woman exhaled. "Can you come to Borough Command? I've got a real tough case here."

"Sure. Where?"

"198 East 161st Street." She hung up.

Taina put the receiver in the cradle. *Don't know where that is or what to do when I find it.* She scrawled a note to Simone. 'Got called to Borough Command.'

There were no directories to keep miscreants from easily finding places they shouldn't be able to access unless escorted in handcuffs.

Security directed Taina two blocks away and across the street to another court building. After passing through the metal detectors again, she asked the guard how to find Borough Command.

He pointed to an elevator. "Fourth floor, Part B."

After wandering the entire perimeter she saw a faded Part A stenciled above a doorway with a nearly invisible arrow pointing down a tiny hallway to Part B.

Taina knocked. Before her knuckles were off the door a harried blonde in a blue suit with matching pumps nearly dragged her inside. Her cheeks were the color of her hot-pink blouse, and she looked like she was about to hit someone.

"Katherine Sullivan, assistant district attorney with the Special Victims Division. Let me brief you quickly. We've got a teenager who was date raped yesterday. The detectives and the SANES nurse saw her in the emergency room and collected all the evidence. The police picked up the guy.

"We're ready to do a line up, and she won't go in the room, even though we've assured her no one can see her. If the DNA evidence is as compelling as her statement in the ER, he'll be going away for a long time. Can you figure out what the issue is? If she walks out, so does he. To do it again."

"I'll give it my best." Taina pushed open the door to find a petite

Latina, mascara so smeared under her eyes they looked blackened.

Taina introduced herself in Spanish. Hello, my name is Taina from the Court Advocate's Office. Can I speak with you for a few minutes?"

"Si, señora."

The ADA closed the door behind them, leaving Taina alone with a desperate, frightened victim. Time to take the punches.

She explained that all the girl had to do was identify the man, and that she wouldn't have to face him until the trial, which might never happen if the evidence was good and he plea-bargained.

The kid clutched Taina's hand as they went behind the one-way mirror with the ADA.

With the other, the girl pointed to a man, smack in the middle, his aura like yellow fuzz, his eyes outlined in deep red. *"El!* He did it."

Shit. Did flagging both yellow and red colors mean he was both *Un Sanguero* and *Una Tomba*, or a go-between? "Are you afraid of him?"

The poor girl didn't answer and looked down.

Taina tried in Spanish *"¿Tú tienes miedo de el?"* How could she assure this kid nothing was going to happen to her?

"Sí." The girl started to cry. *"Hizo un error.* A big mistake."

Taina wanted to ask why the girl had gotten involved with the gangs. And if she was being pressured into prostitution. And tell the lawyer about the kind of operation Raul Rivera and Lupo Lopez were running. But she wasn't here to deliver punches.

She turned to the ADA. "Did she nail him?"

"Yep," Sullivan said.

Just translate, don't explain. No relating that the DNA evidence would be worth nothing because he wasn't human and the whole case would fall apart. "She's scared. She made a mistake."

Sullivan nodded. "We've seen a disturbing pattern of young girls lured into prostitution. Does she want to press charges? Will she accept relocation, for both herself and her relations?"

Taina asked.

The girl shook her head. *"No. Si el me molesta otra vez. Por ahora, no."*

"She said only if he bothers her again."

Sullivan's head wagged like a bobble-head doll. "Tell her if she changes her mind, we have the evidence preserved and will go forward with the case. She has my card."

Taina complied and gave the client a business card for the advocacy office.

"I'll take you home." The detective, dark circles under his eyes, his shoulders slumped with exhaustion, shrugged and ushered the girl out.

Simone was waiting when they stepped outside.

Sullivan strode over to her. "You finally got a Latina advocate. The kid won't press charges—they never do—but Taina did her best."

"You owe her lunch. Her pizza is as cold as a block of ice." Simone patted Taina on the arm.

"What do you want? I'll have it delivered." Sullivan smiled.

Taina wasn't hungry anymore. Not only did she have more reason to hate Lupo Lopez and Raul Rivera, she needed something more than a sandwich from the ADA.

"I like cold pizza. But I could use your help with something else. It's...well...my family died in a fire when I was five. I'd like to talk to someone from the joint homicide and arson task force who investigated, but no one knows where he is."

Simone's eyebrows knitted into a straight line.

Sullivan crinkled her nose. "Do you have any more details?"

"It was August 25, 1985. Detective Michael Kelly. Pent-up emotion leaked out. Taina's voice quavered. "He was originally in the 41st Precinct, but no one wants to give me his current location."

The ADA scrolled through numbers and placed a call. "Sullivan from Special Victims here. Listen, find out where Detective Michael Kelly is. He was once on the arson task force at the 41st."

During the pregnant pause, Simone hugged Taina in the shabby, darkened room. "Oh, this sounds like a terrible story."

"I need answers." Taina wanted a lot more, but no one in the police department could work magick.

"Thanks." Sullivan scribbled on the back of her card. "He's at the 49th Precinct now. If you run into trouble making contact, call me. Good luck."

"Thanks." Taina's knees shook as she walked up the hill with Simone holding onto her hand like a child.

Once back in the office, Simone hovered while Taina ate the cold pizza and drank warm water. Sandy deflected calls. Then Taina registered two clients. Then she called the 49th and found out Kelly would be on duty until 5:00 PM.

"Go," Simone said.

"But it's my first day!"

Simone wagged a finger. "All of us who work here have our own stories to tell or we'd be somewhere else. You've got to take care of yourself, or you'll never be able to stay centered enough to help clients. You had no lunch. It's already four, and I am used to handling things by myself. Get yourself over to the 49th and tell us what happened tomorrow morning."

Taina downed the rest of the water in one gulp. Even after all these years, the thought of one more day was intolerable. She grabbed her bag and ran to hail a cab.

No matter how much it cost, she had to get there before Michael Kelly left.

Chapter Nine
Cold Case

Every street came to a dead end or wound through a park. Taina could have walked faster than the traffic was moving. The cabbie swerved around slower vehicles and buses, cut in front of a truck, and took a curve on what felt like two wheels past the Bronx Zoo and the Botanical Garden.

"49th Precinct, miss."

Taina pushed the agreed-upon $15.00 through the bulletproof shield. "What subway line is near here?"

"None. Over there is the Metro North Commuter Station. You could take it to Fordham Road and get the D train."

No line she knew began with letters. "How can I get back to Prospect Avenue?"

"I'll wait. I have to drive back anyway. Might as well have a fare." A fuzzy gray aura, with a smudge of purple laced through, glinted in his eyes.

Taina read it as kindness. "Thank you, sir." She slipped out the passenger side.

"My name is Sambir, miss. Might I know your name?"

"Taina." Enough courtesies. It was 4:50 PM.

The building looked like it had been plucked out of Disney World and plopped in the middle of a block of apartment buildings. The windows were fitted with restored leaded glass and delft-blue-and-white-patterned tiles set into the brick face beneath them. It's a small world, after all. There was even a goddamn clock tower on one end.

A black, wrought-iron fence, with sword-like tips that looked like replicas of Excalibur, topped the surrounding brick wall. Curled metal projections that had once held lamps would have been useful to string up a body.

"Excuse me." She cut between a few cops outside smoking, probably off duty but still in full uniform, with so much gear strung around their waists they looked like they'd wobble when trying to walk, let alone run.

"How can I help you, ma'am?" Officer Grogan stood behind a high desk. His hair was buzzed marine style, and he wore a NYPD blue mock turtle and a holstered gun on his hip.

"Detective Sullivan called ahead. I'm here to see Detective Kelly. My name is Taina Aponte."

He frowned and called to a chubby Asian female officer seated in front of a computer. "Kelly still here?"

She didn't take her sights off the screen. "Don't know. Never says hello, never says goodbye." The phone rang. "49th Precinct, Officer Shu."

Grogan didn't move.

"Can you please find out? It took forever to get here from the courthouse." Taina tapped her foot to discharge the nervous energy.

He hit speaker on his phone and dialed. It rang through the receiver. Once. Twice. Three times. Four. Five. "Guess he's gone. Sorry."

Taina put her face in her hands and wiped the anguish off with her palms. "Can I leave him a message?"

"Sure." He handed her a piece of paper and a pen.

She stood on tiptoe and started to write exactly what she'd intended to say when her scalp tingled, and a shiver crawled down her back. Before she turned Taina knew that the man behind her, in a white button-down, khaki slacks, and yellow tie, was Michael Kelly.

Resignation, boredom, frustration, or some combination of all was etched around a mouth turned down like a backward smile. His eyes, like the yellow-gray hair, showed no spark of life, enthusiasm, or interest.

His hands were jammed into side pockets, a gun on the right hip. "You the person Sullivan from Special Victims called about?"

Disgust oozed out of the man like slime. She'd wasted her time—and he wouldn't be nice about it, either.

"Thank you for waiting, Detective Kelly. I'm Taina Aponte and want to ask you a few questions about an old case that involved me—and my family." Her voice quavered, and she took deep breaths to stay in control.

One side of his mouth quirked. He looked inside a room labeled 'Detectives,' full of plainclothes officers taking reports. "Let's go upstairs."

The cops behind the desk raised their eyebrows at each other. She jogged up, pushed through the double doors on the second floor, and waited.

"I'm getting too old to keep up with you. First door on the left. It's open." He stayed a few steps behind, probably some police procedure.

The office was no bigger than a closet, with a view of the busy street below. A fan oscillated, blowing hot air, dust, and disinterest back and forth.

If there were such thing as a black aura, this room would have it. There were no pictures on the desk, no personal items. Just piles of papers, chewed-off pencils, yellow sticky notes on the computer screen, and a map of The Bronx dotted with purple and green thumbtacks on the wall.

"Sit down, Ms. Aponte." He gestured to a blue plastic seat on a pitted silver frame and sank into his, on wheels, the tattered fabric stained with dribbles of what looked like some conglomeration of salsa and black coffee.

Taina had rehearsed this so many times, the words spilled out like she was reading a script. "You probably don't recall investigating the fire that killed my parents and sister. 4452 Eagle Avenue. In 1985. I just wanted to…"

"I've often wondered what became of that poor kid with a bad case of smoke inhalation. I feel very old right now, Ms. Aponte. Real old, real tired." The detective's demeanor softened, just a tinge. His head nodded while his lips pursed.

Tears filled her eyes. "You remember?"

Kelly knitted his fingers together then turned his hands palm out and stretched. "I could never forget that scene. Someone knew who'd started that fire, or paid to have it started, but wouldn't talk, no matter what."

She wiped tears of her cheeks them with her palms. "I'm looking for anything that would give me some insight into what happened—and who did it."

He plucked a tissue out of dusty box and handed it to her. "James Aponte's efforts to stop the drug traffic were not, let's say, well received. Gasoline was poured directly on the ground underneath what was your apartment. When they tossed a match, flames shot up, caught the draperies just inside the open window, and the place went up like a bundle of hay."

"That's it? No names, no leads?" How hard could he have tried?

"Taina, I hope you don't mind me calling you by your first name, but I'll always remember you staring at the window, calling for your mother." His voice turned husky as he said, "We scoured the neighborhood to find the guy who caught you, figuring he might know something. But that soot-dusted crack head was so high off the ground, it's a miracle he had the presence of mind to hand you to a firefighter and not just toss you into a dumpster.

"Claimed he was walking by and looked up to see a woman screaming. His friends were like those monkeys—hear no evil, see no evil, speak no evil."

Taina pounded the desk. "That's all a matter of public record, Detective Kelly."

He raised his voice in defense. "I investigated every lead for links to what amounted to a serial killer. The statute of limitations on arson murder never runs out, but I won't see any justice until I arrive at the pearly gates and look down at the perps in Hell."

"Do you at least know the name of the man who caught me? I'd like to look him up and thank him." She wanted to grill him over hot coals but would never admit it.

"There were dozens like him, strung out and so desperate they mainlined anything—with dirty needles. AIDS was their death penalty."

A wave of nausea washed over her. Her vision blurred. Somewhere, deep in the recesses of her memory, she recalled a younger Kelly, not wrinkled, with teeth stained yellow from too much coffee and too many cigarettes. Then the smell of gasoline, sirens, screams, police radios blaring…

"Are you all right?" The detective leaned forward in his chair.

Taina shook it off. Serena's Reason Number Seven echoed in her head: *Let it go, Taina. Get over it.*

"Thank you, Detective Kelly." She got to her feet.

Kelly stood, looked her in the eye. "So, where have you been all these years?"

"My grandmother raised me in Puerto Rico. But I needed to come back and face this."

"Let me walk you down." He took her by the arm and led her to the exit, to where Sambir's black car idled by the medieval gate.

Kelly opened the door for her and handed her his card. "Call me anytime, even after I'm retired. Taina, if they find out who you are, those men won't hesitate to come after you."

The door thudded. "Where to, Miss Taina?" Sambir asked.

"Prospect Avenue and 149th." She slumped back in the seat.

The cabbie made a U-turn and passed by Kelly, still with hands in his pockets, watching.

Let it go. Let it go. Fucking easy for all of them to say. Her lungs reminded her every time she ran too fast. Whenever she got sick, Taina hacked like an old man.

No, she wouldn't let go and give up like everyone else.

Chapter Ten
No Escape

"Did you make it?" Simone stood in the doorway of Taina's office.

"Yeah, but he wasn't much help." She closed the folder on her desk. "I came in early this morning to finish the reports from yesterday."

"I'm sorry. Want to talk about it?"

"No thanks, Simone. I was hoping for a miracle, but Detective Kelly was fresh out." She brought the pile out to be filed.

Simone patted her back as she passed. "Take a break."

Sandy stroked Taina's arm as she took the bundle, and then ushered the first client into her office.

Taina plunked down at her desk, stared out the window at the bustling street below.

Her intercom buzzed. "They need an advocate in the Borough Command Center."

Taina took her purse. "I'll get lunch. My treat."

"Sounds good." Sandy got back to the paperwork.

What would it be this time?

Once she got there, the detective, tie loose and askew, perspiration beading on his face, dribbling down a pudgy neck, leaped up.

"Are you the advocate?" He didn't wait for an answer. "Rosa Nuñez. A prostitute allegedly assaulted by a john. She won't cooperate, and she has a young child that we have to ascertain the safety of."

"So why is she in Borough Command?" Taina stopped before adding, "right next to Central Booking? Why was she even arrested?"

He put his hands on his hips. "We're investigating gang-related prostitution and need her testimony. That's all I can say."

She didn't want to talk to him, either. She pulled the door closed behind her. "Hello, I'm Taina Aponte from the Victim's Advocate Office."

The sullen Latina sat at a table, alone, her right leg jumping up and down like a puppet on a string. A faded-out red aura pulsed over her head. She stared straight ahead and didn't acknowledge the greeting.

"Yo hablo español." Taina sat down, made eye contact.

Rosa got to her feet, paced, stared at the wall. "I don't care what you speak. I don't need any help."

"Ms. Nuñez, whatever you tell me is confidential. I can't give you legal advice, but I can make sure you have support services, including a lawyer if you need one. You're right not to answer any questions you're uncomfortable with. But if I don't know what's going on, I can't help."

Rosa's face softened, and she sat down. "They want information about my…situation. They're not even trying to find the guy who roughed me up then ran out without paying."

A spider of trepidation crawled up Taina's spine as the faint red aura glowered around Rosa's head.

Raul was this woman's protector.

"No one can force you to press charges against the man who attacked you. Did they arrest you or read your rights?"

"When I refused to go to the hospital because I have to pick up my son from school, they brought me here. They told me if I don't say who I work for they'll turn him over to children's services."

Rosa pounded the table. "My kid is happy. He's safe. We have an apartment, food." She looked down. "And I need drugs to stay healthy."

What Raul put in HIV cocktails to keep the newly changed dhamps addicted and enslaved Taina could only imagine. "We can help you get away and any kind of treatment you need. There are safe havens, and you can bring your son."

"You don't understand, miss. I made a deal there is no going back on."

Should Taina tell Rosa she knew about Raul? Was any shelter going to be secure enough to prevent intrusion by *Los Sangueros*? Was that kid really safe?

"Let me talk to the detective." Taina exited, then stepped into the anteroom.

He came at her, thuggish, like *Un Sanguero,* but his aura was thick, steel gray. "Well?"

"You know, I never got your name." Taina struck the bold, bitchy, Bronx pose: One hip jutted out, hand on it, head cocked, chin up, lips puckered, eyes daring him to try any shit.

"Detective Kidman." He crossed his arms over his chest.

"Nice to meet you. Why is she here if she doesn't want to press charges?"

He got in Taina's face. "Because she lives at 4855 Cauldwell Avenue, a drug den known for prostitution. I have a responsibility to be sure that kid is safe. I've already called the Administration for Children's Services. If she tells me who the pimp is, the ADA says we can make a deal."

Time to take the beating. "Detective Kidman, your concern for the child has been addressed and ACS will follow through. Ms. Nuñez has not expressed any fear about her living or working situation. She wants to go home."

He pounded the wall just to the right of Tania's head. "Goddamnit. Every time we get a lead, these women refuse to cooperate. Don't they want to get away from this life, make something better for themselves? How else can we put these punks behind bars?"

Taina stared him down. "She is not the perpetrator. I'll follow up with her about safe havens and other services. Perhaps Special Victims and the Integrated Domestic Violence Unit might be able to enlist her cooperation. They are ideally suited to this type of situation."

Kidman backed away, his lip curled in a lopsided sneer. "Thank you for your opinion, Ms. Aponte. I'm taking her to pick up the kid then home to meet with ACS. If there is evidence of prostitution when ACS investigates, she will be arrested and be right back here."

"In which case, I will see you in court." Taina went back into Rosa. "Detective Kidman will bring you home to meet with a child welfare worker. That's mandated by law at this point."

Tears slid down Rosa's cheeks. "No clients ever come into our apartments. But they're never going to believe that. Thanks—for nothing." She rolled her eyes, and her leg started to bounce again.

Taina handed her a card. "If it was a sexual assault, even an attempted one, we might be able to get the case reassigned to a detective and judge that would be more sympathetic. Please call me tomorrow and let me know what's happening." She had the woman's name and address—should she go over there while the cops and ACS were there? Of course she should, but…

Raul, all dressed up in black leather, stood outside, leaning against the wall, tapping his foot. A fiery red aura blazed around his dark hair.

Taina pivoted and hurried down the back stairs but was sure he had seen her.

There was no getting away from magick.

Arnaldo had been right—again.

Chapter Eleven
The Dhampir's Kiss

Simone paused in between bites of a sloppy, overstuffed Italian hero. "We used to do home visits, but now it's just too damn dangerous. You already told Ms. Nuñez to contact you if she needs help."

Taina picked at the other half. "I think I should go over to Rosa's apartment while ACS is there. That detective is pressuring her to give him information to crack a prostitution ring. And she hasn't even been arrested or spoken to a lawyer. Simone, I don't think she's going to be able to stand up to that."

"Do what you think is best but get the hell out of there when the cops leave. Better still, let them take you home. Two more waiting. We'll each take one, then you better get going if you're going to pay Ms. Nuñez a visit." Simone took a giant swig from her water bottle.

"Thanks." Taina nibbled bread crust before tossing it into the trash.

Sandy was playing with a child in the waiting area. She handed Taina the file. "This is Ms. Precious Bonsu. Do you speak any French?"

"Some." She'd taken it in school, but her accent sounded like Puerto Rican with a bad cold. "*Madame*, I'm Taina Aponte from the Victim's Advocate Office. *Parlez anglais?*" She hoped the answer was yes. Conducting this interview in French would take three times longer.

"Yes." Precious's accent was heavy, but she seemed to understand. More importantly, the only thing colored around her was the clothing.

"*Bon, mais si vous.* If you don't understand, tell me." Would that be called Franglish? Fringlish? "Come into my office. Your son will be fine out here with Sandy."

Precious carried herself like royalty; her orange-green-and-gold garments and head wrap made her seem taller, more regal. The curve of the woman's neck, as graceful as a swan's, seemed too delicate to support the huge bundle of fabric.

How could anyone have hit her hard enough to cause that bruise across the whole right side of her face?

Taina ignored the indigestion—and the injury. "Please sit down. May I call you Precious?"

"Yes, please do, Miss Taina." She blinked back tears. "I don't want my son to ever have to see his father again. In Ghana, he killed a man who looked at me."

She gave the woman a chance to compose herself.

Precious sniffed, sat up. "The detective said they will send a police car to watch my house until I change the locks. I have this paper, but what will it do to keep him away from me?"

Orders of protection weren't enough to mop up the bloodshed they failed to prevent. "Do you want to be relocated? With your son, of course. The police will take you home to pack your things, and you will be escorted directly there."

"Oh, God bless you. Yes, I need to get away from him. Far away."

Dealing with mundanes was far easier than immortals with supernatural powers. Locks. Bullets. Relocations. None of them would stop a dhamp or werewolf intent on finding tracking down one of their captives.

"It will take me a while to make the phone calls and get a police escort. Have you been seen by a doctor? Are you in pain?"

"I am fine. The police took us to Lincoln Hospital last night. They brought us here this morning."

"You both must be exhausted." How could this woman still be so pleasant, so composed?

"Yes, it will be nice to sleep safely tonight. God will bless you, Miss Taina." Precious smiled, the bruised cheek so swollen the right side of her face didn't move.

Taina led her outside where Sandy was building block towers with the boy, about six, with eyes so big and bright they could have lit up the room if it weren't for the fear and exhaustion lingering behind them.

He ran to his mother, and she picked him up. It wasn't until he wrapped his legs around her and hitched up the skirt that Taina noticed the bulging belly. Few shelters could accommodate pregnant women.

"How far along are you, Precious?" Taina had to know.

She smoothed her dress over the baby bump, as if that would wipe it all away. "I was afraid to tell, Miss Taina. Six months."

"No need to apologize." Taina checked her watch—2:00 PM. Chances she would make it to Rosa Nuñez's apartment before the child welfare worker left faded fast. Maybe the gods were trying to tell her something.

~ * ~

Just when Taina was about to give up, the Hands Clasped, Hearts Linked Shelter, somewhere in the grand borough of Brooklyn called back with a spot for Precious and her son. The Special Victims Unit was so frenzied it was steaming like a teakettle, so they diverted a patrol car from the 41st Precinct to take them to the safe house.

Once they had buckled them into the back of the cruiser, Taina bolted for the subway.

The rush hour crush, the heat, the smell of sweat, her aching feet, her sore back, her throbbing skull, none of it mattered. She'd be home soon, free, comfortable, able to come and go. but Rosa couldn't. She would get a look at the building before deciding if it was safe to go in.

A couple of stops later, she descended the stairs to Jackson Avenue. Red auras glimmered as she walked into *Los Sangueros* territory and paused for a moment on the opposite side of the street from Rosa's building.

The butter-colored brick structure, much smaller than a housing project, but still eight stories, had interesting architectural detail, including a mock medieval tower on one corner. A storefront on one side sported a sign for Romeo's Lounge with most of the light bulbs broken or missing. The corrugated security grate pulled down over it was decorated with two champagne glasses clinking, spewing dirty gray bubbles across the entire expanse of steel.

She imagined the inside to be a dilapidated bar where dhampirs and werewolves dropped in to let their hair down while, blowing smoke all over the place, imbibing far too much since it didn't matter what they did to their bodies or anyone else, laying on crushed velvet sofas stained with semen, blood, and spilled drinks. Whatever went on in there—and she had no desire to find out what it was—didn't involve anyone with zest for life. The reason dhamps were concentrated in this area was the general lack of light and sunshine due to the tall buildings-and the preexisting underworld that attracted people with no choices to succumb to the promise of an easier life.

Negative energy and sadness pulsed around the structure, pulling Taina closer though she wanted nothing more than to run. She opened the courtyard gate then peered into the deserted lobby at what should have been the busiest time of a summer day.

A child's cry emanated from a third floor window barricaded with window guards. She searched for the button for apartment 4C.

"Taina, my dear." Raul's saccharine smile telegraphed his malevolent intent. He'd been waiting under the stairs.

Her heart almost thudded. "I have a client expecting me."

"There is already a cop and a social worker up there. I'm sure they can manage without you while we chat." He slithered closer.

Be bold, bitchy, Bronx. "No, I need to get up there right away. Official business." She pushed past him.

Raul caught her arm, held it with enough strength he'd dislocate her elbow if she tried to get away. "Taina, let me explain the way I do business. You see, *mi amor, Los Sangueros* are much more civilized than *Los Tombas*—and Arnaldo. Lupo strong-arms the thugs, the imbeciles, the riffraff. We prefer those who want to preserve their humanity, yet live life full of pleasure."

She wanted to throw up. "They have other options."

Raul sniggered. "Sure. They can get out of The Bronx by enlisting in the army, get shot and die—or worse get maimed and live. Or they can pass Lupo's admittance test: selling flowers and water under the Bruckner Expressway or hawking newspapers in rush hour traffic on the service roads. They can go it alone and turn tricks for a pimp, get AIDS, and die. I give them an apartment, food, and immunity from disease."

"They can also finish school, get a job, stay clean, and live a normal life."

He chortled. "What's normal? Have several children—all with different men who do nothing except beat and steal from them? I take those kids in, even though they're mundanes, and let them go to school.

"You want information about what happened to your family? I have what you're looking for." Raul backed her against the wall of mailboxes. "Think of our offspring—dhampirs with the powers of a witch." He was as turned on by the promise of eternal dictatorship as he was by rubbing his crotch against Taina's thigh.

Had the cop and ACS worker already left? How could she get away? "I don't think so, Raul. Now, let me get to work. They're expecting me."

Raul didn't fall for the lie. "Taina, you have three choices. Align with Arnaldo, who is one step above *Las Tombas*—crude, rude, far beneath what a lovely witch like you deserves." He reached out to stroke her hair, her cheek, her neck.

"Or with Lupo, who would see your lovely, smooth skin covered with coarse, dark hair. Banish you to dark shadows and underground orgies at every full moon."

A manicured fingernail traced down her cheek. "Make your choice now, before it's made for you." His smile didn't lose its gleam, or his fangs their seductive menace.

The scent, musky, not unpleasant, a hint of spice, licorice, relaxed the tension in her neck and shoulders. His voice, barely a whisper, made love with words. "Come be my queen, Taina. Together we will create immortal witches with unsurpassed magickal powers. For all eternity you shall be known as the mother of a new race."

The bulge in his pants throbbed against her, his fangs fully extended, his breath fruity, sweet.

She slumped forward, her muscles too flaccid to resist. He enfolded her in his arms, moved his hands up to her breast, unbuttoned her blouse, circled his fingers over the lacy bra cups. Her nipples, erect, firm, tingling, met them.

"Yes, Taina. Say yes." His fang scraped her neck.

A baby wailed. The spell dissipated.

She pulled out of his grasp, clutched her blouse closed. "No." She ran toward the door.

"I hope Lupo doesn't get to you first. That would be a terrible waste."

Prepared to kick her way through the glass if need be, she wiped a sweaty palm on her skirt and gripped the knob enough to turn and release the lock.

Hot, putrid air assaulted her, far less enchanting that Raul's olfactory preview of paradise. Taina sprinted down the narrow, crowded sidewalk, turning to see if anyone was following, expecting one of his henchmen to grab her.

Like a madwoman, she bumped into people and knocked over a convenience store display of tropical-colored mini fans that sprayed cooling mist.

She'd dropped the bag containing her wallet, work ID, her keys, and her driver's license. But she still had her life and her freedom.

He could have bitten her, restrained her, changed her—but hadn't. Why not?

By the time she limped up to the gate around her apartment, her white leather handbag was hooked over a gatepost.

Raul might be many things, but he wasn't a thief.

Chapter Twelve
Banishing, Cleansing, Sacrifice

Taina emerged from the subway into the blazing sun on 149th Street.

"How's the job going?" Arnaldo appeared so suddenly she wondered if he'd done that cool few-inches-off-the-ground roll like on the day they'd first met.

"Not bad." After trying to convince herself that things would get better once she'd adjusted, why invite the eternally cantankerous Arnaldo to aggravate her even more?

"Been threatened yet?" His smirk invited a slap.

"As a matter of fact, yes." She walked faster.

He was in better shape than he looked, barely breaking a sweat as he jogged to catch her arm. "No wonder. Half of the cases are domestic abuse and sexual assault, and Raul and Lupo are behind most of them."

He raised his nose like he smelled fear and fixed his gaze on her neck where Raul's fang had brushed.

He spared her a response. "Lupo sent his toughs to mark you the day you went to pick up your car, but you got away. Raul got to you yesterday, it seems. He plays human, but that damp is as much a fuckin' animal as the werewolf."

"How do you know what happened?" She couldn't get the slimy feel off her body, even though the clothes had been washed and she'd scrubbed herself, inside and out, until everything itched.

He settled into a stride next to her. "I smell vamp musk. Too sweet to be real, stale, but not quite rancid. Raul keeps himself nice."

Taina wasn't about to tell him she'd been fondled and how close she'd come to being seduced. "He tried, then let me leave."

Arnaldo nodded. "Damps start slow to wear the victim down.

Make them vulnerable, insecure. He marked you, so no male will dare touch you."

How could he know Raul had made her feel dirty and complicit? "I'll never get that close to him again."

"That's what you say now. But when human men get a whiff, they'll just back away, stay away, sense you're trouble without knowing why. Life gets awful lonely."

That posed no threat, but maybe he didn't know her and Serena had been more than just girlfriends. "You're human, how come you're not running?"

His eyes went blank, unblinking. "I've been around and in places I wish I'd never gone. Places I don't want to think about you even visiting."

His attention snapped back to her. "You think he can't get at you because you prefer girls?"

"I prefer to be alone." Her entire family had been taken away without warning.

Once the bottom had dropped out of her world, there was no one she wanted to be with, nothing she aspired to, nothing she looked forward to besides facing the murderers in a court of law.

Arnaldo took her by the arms, his grip too tight for comfort. "What were you doing near him?"

This guy always found the vulnerable spot. "I was on my way home from work and needed to see a client."

"Don't you get it? Lupo and Raul both want claim to a fertile witch to produce some sort of hybrid offspring with incredible powers."

She pulled her arm away. "I'm not a flower waiting to be pollinated."

"If you continue to work in the courts, you'll never be far from someone they've changed and you can't help, no matter how hard you try. Once they've broken your spirit, they'll claim the prize. And will likely share you. Lupo doesn't care about damp scat."

"I'm always so uplifted after a conversation with you, Arnaldo."

"I've never been known as Mr. Sunshine. You've gotten into nothing but trouble since you came here because you're looking through a periscope and don't see the torpedo until it's ready to hit. That measly dog isn't going to even the balance of power, ever.

"I close up at *Sonrisa* every night at nine. Come over, we'll have dinner, we'll train." His swagger and the normally condescending pursed lip and left-eye squint on his face had vanished. He looked ten years younger. He was trying.

"'That dog' was a fairy gift, and I treasure him more than anything or anyone else." But it was now clear that she needed Arnaldo's help to survive another confrontation. "Tomorrow night. By the way, you never took me to find sage." She needed cleansing, clarification, and centering right now.

It took a while for him to respond. "There's a *botánica* a few blocks down." He walked like he'd rather be going in the other direction.

Botánicas offered a different option than acquiescence to fate: A bit of mystery and magic, if even just the illusion of control.

A statue of the Virgin Mary, big enough to adorn a church altar, stood in the window flanked by smaller icons of *Santería* saints. The Blessed Mother had years of dirt caked in the folds of her robes and had lost a few of the metal rods protruding from her fingers, signifying her Grace flowing out into the neighborhood.

The door wouldn't open until Arnaldo threw his full weight behind it. A bell tinkled. A conglomeration of odd scents escaped. Taina tapped to be sure the asthma inhaler was in her pocket.

He shoved the door closed behind them. "Josefa?"

"¿Quien es?" A woman pushed aside a threadbare velvet curtain and hobbled out. A smile cracked her wrinkled face. "Arnaldo! I thought you'd given it up after Abuela died."

He shoved his hands into the pocket of his cargo shorts and lowered his head like a chagrined schoolboy. "I do things my own way. Works for me."

Josefa pursed her lips, nodded so slowly the sadness seemed to project around the room. *"Ay, sí.* What's your name, *hija?"*

She extended her hand. "Taina Aponte. I wonder if you have sage to bundle for me? I…"

"You're a witch." Josefa said it without question, without judgment, without malice.

Taina looked at Arnaldo.

"It's okay." He'd lingered near the door instead of following her to the counter.

"Do you need anything, Arnaldo?" Josefa settled herself on a stool.

"Nope."

"Bueno, leave us. We need privacy." The *santera's* voice was so dry and raspy Taina wanted to clear her own throat.

"Josefa is an old friend. Ask her for anything you need." When he pulled hard on the door it swung in so fast he almost fell on his ass. The chuckle was cut off as it latched shut.

Josefa wagged her head like a patient grandmother. "Don't be afraid, *mi amor*. I keep secrets. Witches and *santeras* are like sisters. So you have need of cleansing?"

"I need to banish bad karma. Burning sage will help."

"It won't hurt." She rose and sighed. "But these old knees and hips do. Don't get old, *hija*." Josefa cackled.

Taina perused a display of necklaces and bracelets made from shells, wood, and colored beads. Dolls hung on hooks, some made of felt with heart-shaped patches on the chest, some fashioned from sticks and yarn, others with wings or capes made of corn husks. She chose one that looked like a straw fairy.

"For your harvest ritual you will also need a rooster, fresh killed, seasoned with oil, *azafrán*, and red pepper." Josefa closed her eyes, frowned. *"Yemayá* can give you the most help right now. Put some of the bird's blood on these stones." The blue and white translucent beads clinked as the *santera* placed them into an abalone shell.

She settled on her stool. Arthritic fingers pieced together a bundle of sage that smelled like a cross between a weed-strewn lot and a pot party.

Josefa possessed an odd aura, pale green with a hint of gold, which emanated psychic energy and a deep abiding wisdom. "Come."

Taina followed her behind the velvet curtain, into a room filled with small black cauldrons, a riot of statuary, and flickering, jarred candles immersed in glass bowls of cloudy water.

Her lungs wheezed at the combination of floral and medicinal essences seasoned with just the right amount of mold. She took two puffs on her inhaler.

Josefa gestured to a seat. "Following in your mother's footprints. I suppose *tu abuela* never took you to a *botánica* in Puerto Rico, so you don't understand *Santería."*

Taina stopped midway between standing and sitting. "You knew my mother—and my grandmother?"

"Si, both of them. But Antonella had to find her own way, just like her daughter. Do you want *un registro?"*

"I'll try the sage first, thanks." Taina didn't need more bad news.

Josefa brushed the back of Taina's right hand and turned it to examine the palm. "There is much I would like to tell you, but not while Arnaldo is waiting out in the heat getting into mischief." She dropped Taina's hand and hobbled back out to the counter. "I'm glad he found someone of like mind."

"We're just friends." She just wanted the damn sage and to be rid of both of them.

"Ah, so no love potions needed." Josefa's gnarled fingers struggled to tie thin filaments of blue and white thread around the sage fronds.

"Let me help." Taina tried to keep the annoyance out of her voice.

Josefa raised her eyes, grinned. "Antonella was the same, not content to wait for *los santos* to act. She had to do her own magick." Scorn dripped from her mouth like venom. Her fingers ceased their work.

Taina reconsidered. "Can you tell me about my mother? I know almost nothing about her."

"In time. You should know your mama sent you here."

"Perhaps."

Was it too much to hope she'd ever learn more about her mother and her practices?

Josefa went back to wrapping the green cone in a blue and white web. "Looks like a penis." She smiled, accentuating with the wrinkles around her eyes and mouth.

The mischief in the old woman's voice unearthed a laugh from somewhere underneath Taina's frustration. "How much do I owe you?"

"*Un regalo,* a gift." Josefa's smile faded. "May I give you some advice?"

Taina took the bait and switch. *"Sí."* Whatever it took to get more information.

The *santera* added what looked like a giant red firecracker to the pile of sage and beads. "Burn incense this Friday and Saturday. Always walk from the highest point and leave it to finish outside."

She took a blue and a white candle off the shelf. "Burn *Yemayá's candela* next to your guardian angel's." She packed the lot into a box.

Tania had to curry the *santera's* favor. "I must pay you for all this."

"Thirty dollars." Josefa waved a crooked finger. "And be careful with Arnaldo. He's a good man, but inside lives a very bad boy."

"What else do you recall about my mother?" Any details of her magickal practice—things her grandmother had refused to discuss—would create precious memories.

"Return after you complete these tasks. I'll read your chart and tell you what I can."

"Pues, gracias." Taina took the phallic stub in a brown paper lunch bag and stuffed it into her pocket. She put two twenties on the counter and took the box.

Josefa opened the door with no difficulty.

The floral conglomeration and the mystique had started a throbbing behind Taina's eyes. Only a matter of time before the migraine set in, and she'd need two puffs on her inhaler.

"So she gave you the introductory special?" Arnaldo was leaning against the door of an adjacent shop talking to a couple of older men.

"Got the sage." Taina ignored their smirks.

Arnaldo gave a thumbs up to his amigos, took the bulky box from her, and started walking.

Relieved of the burden, and breathing fresher air, her wheezing eased.

"And what did she say?" He grinned and questioned Taina like a three-year-old intent on getting his mother to let him eat cookies for breakfast.

She played dumb. "That she knew my mother."

His saccharine demeanor turned sour, too fast to be good. "Really?"

So that must be significant. "Yes, and we're going to talk more, another day."

"She's a matchmaker, you know."

By now, he was a few steps in front, and the heat was too intense for Taina to consider catching up. "Josefa said you were a good man but that there is a bad boy lives that lives inside. And for me to come back alone another day so you didn't get into any mischief while waiting."

He stopped, whirled to face her. "Fuck you! Fuck all you women. You sit and chatter about girlie nonsense and blame men for all your troubles."

It always came to this. "Arnaldo, what's bothering you?"

"Abuela followed Josefa as if she were a goddess. If she had the courage to use more powerful magick instead of praying in front of statues, wearing beads, and doing silly spells with lemons and razor blades, maybe things would have turned out different. And then she blamed Serena for corrupting me, and for blaspheming her *santos*."

The guy wasn't over all the women in his life.

"Everyone has different ways of doing things. Did you deserve the karma you inherited? Did I deserve to even be born to that whore?" He blinked back tears.

"I'm sorry, this has brought up so many bad memories." Why had he taken her to a place charged with such bad memories? There were other *botánicas.*

She took the box before he dropped it—or threw it at her. "I'm going home now? Where can I get a fresh-killed chicken?"

"Josefa told you to sacrifice one?" He snapped out of the melancholy.

"No, she said I should cook a fresh killed rooster and put some of the blood on the stones."

"There's plenty of human blood flowing around here—more than enough sacrifice to appease whatever goddamn saint, god, goddess, angel, elf, dwarf, fairy, orc, troll, or gremlin is around. Did I miss anything?" He blew out his frustration and kept walking.

She heaved the box to her opposite hip.

Arnaldo's arm waving kept pace with his feet. "The old women's ways of doing things don't work around here. *Santería* takes time, and we don't have it."

He stopped to let her catch up. "A fucking chicken? Are you serious?" He snatched the box back.

Between the heat and aggravation being relieved of the physical burden did nothing to ease the tightening in her chest. "Josefa knew my mother, and that means a lot to me. I learned long ago to follow my intuition. It's never led me down the wrong path."

"Fine. Whatever. This way to the slaughterhouse." He took her free hand, his grip as angry as his grimace.

~ * ~

The makeshift entry smelled of sawdust cut with the metallic edge of blood, seasoned with the stench of chicken shit.

A man flapped through the slit rubber doorway. "How can I help you, *mi amor?*"

Taina eyed rows of white chickens in stacked cages. "I need *un gallo*, a rooster."

The butcher gestured to some cages against the wall. "Want to pick him out?"

"No, I trust you." She had no idea how they killed them and no desire to find out.

The butcher winked at Arnaldo. "*Gallos* are tough old birds. How about a nice young hen?"

Taina ignored the innuendo. "No, I need a rooster. And can you remove the feathers and cut it up for me?"

"You should just go to C-Town." He disappeared behind the slats.

"You're really going to eat it?" Arnaldo looked at her with a crinkled left eye.

"It's for First Harvest." She didn't know if she could bring herself to eat the bird, but the most important thing was the intent.

"Bring it to our block party this weekend. We'll have mundane New York City-style hot dogs and hamburgers, corn on the cob, and watermelon from the Jamaican guys who park their truck under the elevated Bruckner Expressway."

"Is it part of a harvest ritual?" The idea of a routine mundane celebration was very attractive.

That distracted, dreamy look returned to his face. "I haven't celebrated with anyone since Serena left. This is a neighborhood tradition that started with the Take Back the Night Movement."

"Maybe. I've got a lot to do Friday and Saturday." Taina needed to be mindful of her intent through all the steps of the prescribed process, especially when propitiating a deity.

As the butcher came through the door, two of the rubber strips on the end hung over his shoulder like reins. "Here you go. Three pounds, six dollars." He handed her the bag and wiped his hands on a bloody apron.

As she rummaged for money, somewhere deep in her memory, she remembered being here with Abuelita and a man just like this chasing a chicken through a cackling horde, grabbing and wringing its neck while the others shrieked in horror.

He'd carried it by the feet to a block, hacked, and the severed head fell into the sawdust. Blood congealed, and he'd kicked it out of the way before plunging the bird into a boiling vat to steam off the feathers.

But that time, Abuelita had pointed out the bird she wanted, watched closely to be sure everything was done to her approval, and took home the bird to chop it up herself.

Maybe Puerto Rican chickens were noisier. Maybe Puerto Rican grandmothers were tougher. How come Taina could remember every stinking detail of a *vivera* when she was a kid and yet couldn't remember anything about the night her family died except smells, screams, and sirens?

The butcher turned to Arnaldo. Another wink. "Women nowadays want someone else to do the dirty work for them."

He seemed to know better than to respond. "*Gracias.* This is a short cut to Prospect Avenue."

Taina followed him out a side entrance, past the open back door of the *vivera*. Birds fluttered around in a cage the length of an entire block. Black and brown goats in pens lowed. The butcher strode in, and the flock scattered, squawked. One screeched in terror. She turned away, wheezing from the fetid cloud and the smell of chicken fear.

Thwack. The butcher's feet scraped the sawdust.

Arnaldo heaved the box at her and didn't break stride toward Southern Boulevard. "My kids will be climbing the fence if I'm not there. See you tomorrow night."

"Sí, mañana." Taina hurried home and dumped the plastic bag of chicken parts into the sink.

The dog could barely wait until they got outside, and while he watered every hydrant along Prospect Avenue, she steeled herself for the unpalatable task ahead.

Zeus watched with great interest as she drained the blood into a cup and ran cold water over the hacked up bird until it looked the same as a package from C-Town—at double the price.

She washed her hands with salt and water three times then put the beads and the doll on the altar. Following the written instructions, she sprinkled blood over the stones, lit the candles, and rested the smudge stick next to them.

Taina itched to light the sage, get on with it, get it over with. But haste diluted her energy, destroyed her focus, caused the goddess to turn her back.

Only three more days. Three long days.

Chapter Thirteen
Let the Games Begin

Arnaldo was on his own turf in the basement of *Sonrisa* and in a much happier mood then he'd been in three days ago. "Surprise is your best friend. I'll show you a couple of moves, then you can use a spell work to enhance your speed, agility, power. But *Las Tombas* and *Los Sangueros* have some tricks too. And sometimes, like when the weres cornered you outside Miguel's, you don't have time to get your magick up."

The floor mats were sticky, even with the air conditioning on. Perspiration dripped down Tania's forehead and between her breasts.

Zeus sat to the side, watching Arnaldo's every move.

"Fighting stance." He took her waist and shifted the left side of her body forward. "Dominant side back, so you can punch or kick with more power. Be sure you can see all around you. Hop to the right, then back to the left, so no one can sneak up."

He demonstrated. She followed.

Zeus's ears pricked.

"Good. Let me see how hard you can kick." Arnaldo picked up a padded vest and held it against his chest.

She had taken a self-defense course and knew how to spin from dance classes—even executed a double *fouetté* when she was younger. But surprise was her best friend.

She raised a bent knee parallel to the floor and thrust her right heel hard into his chest.

He grabbed her foot. Old trick, but she found her balance, focused on her spot, and whirled, using her arms like a windmill to augment the turn.

Her head snapped back to face him. He never saw her freed leg coming.

"How...come...you didn't...tell me you...knew this already?" He rubbed the spot where her blow had connected with his unprotected flank.

"Surprise is my best friend."

Zeus growled and nipped at Arnaldo's feet. "Whoa, killer! I'm just trying to help." He pranced like he was running through a tire-strewn obstacle course to get away from the dog's needle-like teeth.

She suppressed a giggle. "Down, Zeus."

He halted mid-snap and walked to the side, still not taking his gaze off Arnaldo.

The worry lines on his face relaxed. "You've got more ability than I expected. And more power than you realize. Now you just need to learn to use it, no matter what the cost."

Butterflies of worry fluttered in her stomach. She'd broken that guy's nose, but Raul had rendered her powerless. And if she smelled gasoline, saw flames, heard sirens she could barely remain conscious.

"Let's get to the magick, okay?" Drills had always helped her find focus in the heat of necessity.

"Just a couple more evasive maneuvers." Arnaldo grabbed Taina's arm and drew her closer. "Where's that animal?" He stayed in fighting stance and scanned around.

The dog crouched, ready to leap.

Taina held up a palm. "Stay, Zeus. We're playing."

Arnaldo drew her closer until her head was next to his chest. "Two choices. Pull back hard so all my effort goes into holding on to you. Then move toward me, fast, preferably when you've got a magickal boost ready to go. Or execute some of that fancy footwork and bring your head up, hard, under my chin."

He smelled like Ivory soap and baby shampoo. Taina let him lead her through the steps.

Arnaldo's hands lingered on her back and traced down her arms. "Don't get too cocky, Taina. There will be more than one. Muddling and confounding spells throw them off balance, things that make them trip or cause something to fall on top of them give you some time to figure out your next move. Do you know those?"

"Sure, but I don't have time to practice."

"So why don't you commit them to memory and rehearse the ones that work for you." He backed away.

She alternated being relieved at her choice of concealing workout clothes and disappointment that the session was over.

He wiped his forehead with the back of his hand, still breathing heavy. "You coming Sunday?"

"I'd planned to go to Ritual Rock for a short ceremony."

"Haven't done a real sabbat for a while. How about I join you? We'll go to the party afterward?"

"Umm…"

Arnaldo stayed too close, for too long. His eyes had that look of admiration, one step before male lust.

Magickal energy had gotten her into trouble before, and it would be buzzing with them inside a traditional circle, after a *Santería* appetizer and main course, and possibly sly fairy magic for dessert.

"Sure, why not? It's getting late, and I have to work tomorrow. Thanks, Arnaldo." She collected her purse and her pooch.

"I'll walk you home." He sat on the floor, put on his sneakers.

"I'll be fine."

"Once I'm sure you can fight back, okay?"

Zeus growled.

"What's with that mutt?"

The tingle told her Zeus was reading her thoughts, feelings. "He doesn't like it when anything or anyone gets too close." She stroked the dog's head and he snuggled into his favorite spot over her heart as she ascended the narrow staircase. Arnaldo's breath tickled the back of her neck.

Rats scampered around the trashcans as they went out the front door and down the front walkway. A pigeon fluttered to rest on the roof.

"Damn fairies." The magickal fence around *Sonrisa* gave way as he cut it with his hand.

Positive energy shimmered off the glamour the shifters had left behind. Zeus stopped squirming. If only she could get all that good will concentrated and stored. They walked into the night, and no one or nothing dared come near.

~ * ~

Taina locked her desk drawer and retrieved her bag. "Friday at last. I'm going to a barbecue on Sunday.

"And I can see from the way your eyes lit up that it's with someone special." Simone did her finger-pointing, hip-swinging jig. "Oh yeah, oh yeah, Taina's got a date."

"It's just a gathering with a few friends." The dual bombshells of her bisexuality and paganism were best kept buried at least until she was off probation. It didn't seem like Simone or Sandy would have a problem with either, but why take chances?

Simone stopped her happy dance. "I didn't mean to pry. Hope you have a good time." Her heels clacked out. "Night, Sandy."

"I'm leaving too, Taina. Have a good one. Be sure and lock the door."

"Night, all." Taina needed to finish this report and stay focused and on task for the ritual.

But even those simple goodbyes had derailed the effort. Arnaldo wasn't picking on her nearly as much. She was enjoying his company. Her powers were getting stronger. It was nothing more than friendship, nothing more.

The door creaked open. Why hadn't Sandy locked it? She walked into the outer office ready to be cold and ruthless. "How can I help you?"

"Ms. Aponte. I was in court for a case and hoped I wasn't too late to catch you." The dark business suit, tie, and white shirt made Detective Kelly seem more competent.

Her heart fluttered. "Please come in." This time she motioned him into *her* office. He perched on the edge of the same seat her clients used.

Was he unable to relax because he could sense the restless energy in there, because he had some news for her, or because she was imagining all this?

"Your case was one of the most troubling I handled. Seeing you, talking to you brought that all back. So I pulled the files and reviewed my notes. There isn't much that you don't already know. Except one thing."

She almost leaped across the desk. "What did you find?"

"The guy who caught you was named Jesús Rivera. Last known address 5514 St. Ann's Avenue. The building no longer exists. Good luck searching the phone directory to try and find him. If he's still alive."

Taina's stomach flopped so hard she nearly puked. Jesús? The zombie? She recalled the eyes, now vacant, lifeless, trolling the same haunts, the same territory—all he had ever known.

She smelled gasoline, heard screams, sirens. Red lights flashed, her vision blurred. Police radios chattered.

She bobbled in his arms—obviously he'd never held a child. Green eyes darted side-to-side, as he shoved her toward a figure in an oversized black coat, red hat, his face streaked with soot.

Taina screamed, reached for the window three stories above, where she and Mama had been just a moment ago. Orange flames licked the bricks. Thick black smoke spiraled out, clutching her lungs in its death grasp. Pungent odors bit at her like a rabid dog.

Her chest ached as she struggled to breathe fresh air. The monstrous man ran, holding her so tight she couldn't cry or scream. Others dressed like him surrounded her. One pressed a plastic cap over her nose and mouth. She wriggled. They held her still.

"Breathe, baby, breathe."

"Ya, nena. Respira."

"Mama!" Her words were swallowed by the mask over her face, her cries drowned out by yelling, more sirens.

Air, she needed air. Taina stood, clutched the desk, and swayed.

The detective's feet tangled in the chair legs as he leaped to grab her. It toppled backward with a sickening crash. She slumped into his arms.

"Ms. Aponte, are you okay?" Kelly's voice was muffled, tinny, distant.

The cacophony died away, and it was just Taina and a detective, locked in an embrace. If anyone walked in now...

"I'm sorry, Detective Kelly. I get these flashbacks whenever some recollection is triggered." Her tongue was still thick. She forced herself to stand upright.

"Post-traumatic stress. I see it all the time." He eased her into the chair, then righted his own. "Did you remember Jesús? Is there something I should know about?"

"No, nothing." *Just a coincidence, that's all. The guy was so cracked out he'd never remember anything.*

Kelly patted her shoulders. "I apologize for upsetting you. How about a ride home?"

"No, thanks." As tempting as it was to avoid a summer Friday rush hour, Taina couldn't face more time alone with him. Or anyone in the neighborhood questioning why a cop was bringing her home. They couldn't see crimes happening while hanging out the windows but sniffed out a good scandal with no trouble.

"Are you sure you're okay? Can I call you Taina?"

"Sure."

"I'd like to die knowing I solved at least one cold case. The thread that will lead to a lot of others is knotted up in this one. The precinct can always find me."

"Thank you, Detective Kelly. I will." The bubble of hope burst, and her heart ached even worse now that the one person she'd believed could give her some answers had nothing to offer.

"And Taina, no sniffing this out yourself. Those creeps have woven a tight web of protection and will trap and eat you alive. Good night." He closed the door behind him.

She locked it. *Bastante* for one day, one week. Every clue, every thought about what happened, just resurrected the pain again.

Taina grabbed her things and bolted. The cleansing would help clear her thoughts.

Chapter Fourteen
Mishmash Magick

She should have gotten in the damn car with the detective. She should have let *Señora* Duarte wonder why she was being escorted home in an unmarked police car. She should have treated Michael Kelly to dinner at Paloma and picked his brain.

Instead, she'd just missed the Downtown Number 4 and stood alone on the platform in mid-summer watching what she first thought was a heat crazed mundane juiced up on something push a very pregnant woman onto the tracks. But the devil's halo left a streak as he jostled past, and ran up the steps, pausing to flash a sick grin.

Taina burrowed for her phone. *Please, let this call go through.* "Help! Call the police, stop the trains, someone fell on the tracks!" She screamed, hoping the clerk in the booth safely outside the turnstile could hear her, but the uptown clattered by on the opposite side.

Dialing 911 yielded nothing but a 'no service' error. The woman lay motionless in the gravel, her legs draped over the rails.

Having been in NYC long enough, Taina knew that when the train went by in one direction, another would come barreling along a few minutes later in the opposite direction. Could LED display that the next downtown train was in five minutes be trusted? Now four. No time to center or remember any spells.

She took three deep breaths, wiped the sweat off her face with the sleeve of her blouse, and eased her way down.

"Hey, some crazy bitch just jumped onto the tracks." A few people straggled onto the platform. A couple whipped out phone cameras, but at least one person was yelling for help.

The woman stirred and moaned.

"Please, wake up." Taina patted her scratched face, the swollen belly. The baby kicked. "Don't worry, I'll get you and mama out of here."

Several spectators gathered near the edge of the platform.

"Pull her over here, and we'll drag her up."

"For God's sake, lady, get moving or get the hell out of there."

Seconds ticked off like a bomb in her head. The rumble of a distant train shook the ground. She slid beneath the woman, took a deep breath, visualized an ebony-skinned goddess, dressed in flowing blue and white robes. *"Yemayá, please, give me strength."*

Arnaldo's warning tingled in her ears, *Santería takes time, and we don't have it.*

Two men lay face down on the platform. Their hands reached into the pit. "Please, miss, just drag her over here. You'll never be able to lift someone twice your weight."

The rumble grew closer. She'd die right here before she left this woman and the unborn baby. Taina heaved the woman up and off the tracks, toward the wall. A sickly chill prickled her stomach. She trembled with fear, and sweat poured off her body.

Goddess, protector of women, make my burden light.
Goddess, protector of women, make my arms do right.
Goddess, protector of women, make my burden light.

Taina huddled next to the wall, clutching the woman against her, catching her breath. Another uptown train squealed by. Relief flooded over her, but a low level tremor rattled her teeth.

Goddess, protector of women, make my burden light.
Goddess, protector of women, make my arms do right.
Goddess, protector of women, make my burden light."

A rat darted out from a hole in the concrete and scampered under Taina's skirt. Only a sparkle of fairy dust glimmering on its back kept her from panicking.

But not the onlookers. "Omigod. A rat just ran up her legs." More screams.

"Don't make me come down there to get both of you. Shit, woman, c'mon."

Goddess, protector of women, make my burden light.
Goddess, protector of women, make my arms do right,
Goddess, protector of women, make my burden light.

With her last burst of energy, Taina slipped her hands under the woman's knees and behind her head then lifted her toward them. The men pulled her up the rest of the way. Another braced himself and hauled Taina out. Both shoes fell back onto the tracks. Her skirt hitched up so high they were all treated to a coochie flash.

The commuters gathered around the still unconscious woman, leaving Taina alone on the platform, which was fine with her.

Cops and EMT's flooded the station.

Static crackled through the public address system. "Ladies and gentlemen, due to police and EMS activity at 161st Street, all service on the Number 4 has been suspended."

One cop with lots of authority and a bullhorn took over. "Please leave the station now." He moved the crowd back with high-decibel squeals while the EMTs attended to the victim.

"That lady jumped down and dragged her out." One of the men who'd helped pointed the police her way.

A phalanx of reporters and cameras headed toward her. She'd make another excuse for a dhampir attack, lest she be labeled a nut. Then ask for a ride home.

~ * ~

"Thank you, officer." The cop opened the door and helped her out like a barefoot actress who'd just completed shooting a stunt scene. Only this wasn't the finale.

The dark magicks were following her, watching her every move, tracking her a like an animal. Just as Arnaldo had predicted.

"No problem, miss. You're crazy, but very brave."

"Yeah, well I just did what I had to do."

He waited until she was inside the perimeter gate and opened her front door before toggling the siren in salute and driving away. A pigeon fluttered from the eaves to the awning, then peered over the edge.

"Hi, Bridge Rat."

"Greetings, Lady Taina. Moving along nicely on your quest, I see."

Every time that British voice projected out of a bird's beak, Taina had to suppress a laugh. "One of your comrades flicked a ratty tail in support. I'll open the window of my apartment so you can come in and chat. After I take Zeus for a walk."

"Very good." He fluttered back to the eaves.

Zeus scurried about her feet. He picked up his leash and waited by the door. Seeming to sense the need to hurry, he piddled as soon as they got to the gutter and scampered back upstairs trailing the lead.

Taina unlocked the window, removed the brace, and pushed it up far enough for the pigeon to squeeze through.

"I don't have a lot of time. Tonight I have a ritual to perform and a festival to prepare for."

Bridge Rat cocked his head like a real bird. "Indeed, *Lammas* approaches. You are celebrating?"

"Yes, Arnaldo and I."

The bird's feathers shimmered and sparkled. With a flash of light, a wizened fairy form appeared with a huge smile on his face. "Ah, very good. So the two of you are consorting…"

"No! We're just friends." Why was everyone trying to match make between her and Arnaldo?

He clapped. "You have much to teach each other and much to learn about each other before you will be able to fulfill your destinies."

Enough of that. "Want to watch me on the seven o'clock news?" Taina turned on the television. "I'm the star of 'Hot as Hell Heroics in the Subway.'"

The fairy wiggled with delight, and perched on the edge of her sofa, one stick figure leg crossed over the other, bobbing up and down. "I do so love mundane movies."

Right on schedule: her—bedraggled, greasy, sweaty, answering questions in such a way as not to arouse any suspicion of magickal activity, postulating that the stricken woman was overcome by the heat and jostled by a distracted commuter. At least they'd edited out the footage of her ladyship's royal ass as the Rasta guy hauled her off the tracks.

Bridge Rat rubbed his chin with a gnarled brown finger, the green nail pointed toward her like a weapon. "Very good, my lady. Soon all will recognize and hail the White Witch."

The question burned her tongue. "Why me?"

His hand lowered, his silly grin cracking a wrinkled face. "Because only you can conjure the powerful magick necessary to accomplish this, but if only you have faith, Lady Taina. Tonight was testimony to that, is it not?"

"I think it was just luck." A momentary blaze of glory, which would soon be over as the mundane world went back to its sensationalistic stupor.

But plenty of attention to fuel Raul and Lupo's desire to bring her under their control.

"Soon, soon you will believe." Bridge Rat spoke with authority, his jaw lifted. He swept his cloak. As it lapped the air, he shimmered and reconstituted as the pigeon. "I shall return with a gift that Hawk Claw has been awaiting the proper moment to bestow."

Weakness and despair had seeped into her muscles and bones. Everything ached. "Tomorrow, Bridge Rat, okay? I'm tired. I need a bath. I need to sleep."

"I shall not disturb you further, Lady Taina. Simply check the sill before you retire." He ducked through the open window and disappeared into the darkening sky.

The sick feeling in her stomach, the blurry vision, the weakness. She'd performed a difficult magical task tonight and would pay for it for the rest of the weekend.

Mishmash magick might work for Arnaldo, but she wasn't an accomplished witch. If she ever needed cleansing it was now.

Taina looked at her family's picture on the altar, next to the shell filled with blood-spattered blue and white beads, with the sage on the other side. Tomorrow she'd do the rest.

The ache in her back could have been from the exertion tracks, but she barely made it to the toilet before she threw up. Then cramps and bleeding were two weeks earlier than expected.

It took some scrubbing to get the grease off. At long last, warm water suffused with lavender cradled her in its comforting embrace. Taina leaned back and closed her eyes. Zeus awakened her by kissing her toes.

The water had cooled during the snooze, extinguishing the perpetual heat in her core. She got out and wandered into the living room wrapped in a towel and ignored the four messages on her phone. The last thing she wanted to do while in a post-magickal exertion stupor was listen to Arnaldo's bullshit.

Taina turned out the light and glanced out onto the hazy, yellow glow bathing everything. *Las Tombas* were about. A light rain had fallen. The street steamed. Cloudy, with no stars, no moon, it seemed especially ominous.

She checked the locks on all her windows and reluctantly closed the open one. Just before the sash slipped into the grove, she saw a reddish-gold feather resting along the entire length of the outside sill. From Hawk Claw's mighty wing, it would spread sage smoke as it was intended to be done. She touched the sharp quill, stroked the soft yet strong fronds extending from the central base. Traces of glamour and fairy dust sparkled on her fingers.

But her head still throbbed, cramps ripped at her insides, and she could barely push the window closed and get to bed. Her damp towel crumpled to the floor. She slid under the covers. Zeus nestled by her feet. The cushy mattress cradled her overwrought body. Taina turned to her side, cuddled her pillow, and braced the small of her back with another to soothe the ache.

Zeus circled three times and lay at the head of her bed.

The room spun, her stomach lurched. Tomorrow, she'd go see Josefa for more advice. Tomorrow. She'd be better tomorrow.

She'd better be.

Chapter Fifteen
Cleansing

Desperate for his walk and scraps of roll and butter from the Coca Cola deliverymen, Zeus kissed her awake. Early morning sunshine poked through the blinds, preheating the second floor apartment to oven temperature.

Taina slipped out of bed, loathing the need to ruin her glorious naked romp. Serena's Reason Number Eight not to come to The Bronx: Being sky clad in in New York City got you arrested and being in a bathing suit got you a reputation. She chose a halter-top, shorts, and sandals as a compromise.

Zeus nearly pulled her down the stairs and explored the spoils of the Friday night before—a few beer bottles, fried chicken wrappers, a smattering of cigarette butts, other random contents of the corner garbage pail that had been overturned. He peed on every upright object that wasn't moving.

Shadows caught his attention. He snarled.

"You're silly, Zeus. Those are yours and mine."

The dog continued to growl. Then she saw the bigger, third shadow off to the side. She looked behind. Nothing. No one.

The dog stopped yapping and resumed sniffing at the ghostly image of a small dog and a grey figure whose hand waved when hers did.

How had those specters cloaked their presence? Had it been one of Lupo's zombies tailing her again? Could they get inside her apartment by attaching themselves to her in some way? No, Zeus would have noticed, just like he had this time.

The soda deliverymen—one of the few bastions of normalcy—were either off or long gone. The bakery was empty save for two women, one older the other younger, working a different kind of spell—dispensing comfort in the form of sweet, smooth black coffee and delectable confections.

Her back crackled. Thanks to Josefa's potion, her uterus was still struggling to expel whatever foul curse might have been sent her way. Taina already needed another bath.

"Let's go back, puppy dog. I have a lot of things to do." She followed Zeus up the stairs, sipping coffee, centering.

She opened the windows as wide as possible and intoned a purifying spell.

"Sacred smoke,
Carry away all that is evil
Make room for bright blessings
Fellowship and merriment."

Taina pulled out the smoke detector battery, then sneaked down to the first floor and lit the smudge stick, dropping ash as she walked up, waving Hawk Claw's feather to disseminate the smoke. She directed the cloud toward the windows to banish evil, around the doorways, and finally, her altar.

The sight of congealed blood worsened the nausea. She lit the candles and read the prayer on the back of her pillar and extinguished the sage stub in a dish of salt water before resting it in the shell.

"For the honor and glory of *Olorun*, owner of heaven, *Yemayá*, goddess of the sea, protector of women, give me the strength, the courage, to do what I must. Give me the gift of sight to know what you wish, to proceed without reservation." She added her own plea, "Teach me, guide me, as you have done for daughters Josefa, Antonella, and Serena who have walked this path before me."

Her lungs twitched from the lingering haze. Taina took two pumps of her inhaler and sank to her knees in front of the sacred space, spiritually cleansed but sweaty and bleeding like the slaughtered chicken.

She'd only been up for an hour and was ready for a nap.

Arnaldo's voice ascended the stairs on the remnants of sage smudge.

"Taina, you done with that *Santería* crap yet? Smells like a pot party in here." The front door closed then his footsteps thudded on the stairs.

How could she maintain her focus with him around? "Yes, I'm here but not feeling well enough for company."

He must have magicked his way through the gate and the front door. "You okay after last night? Girl, you did good." He grinned. "Now tell me exactly what you did."

"I don't know."

"Hee hee, I told you to have confidence, use your instincts. I'm proud of you, baby." He punched her shoulder and almost knocked her over.

"I am not your baby. And I told you I'm sick."

"Whoa." He steadied her and lost the grin, the swagger. "You look terrible, which means it was magick. It can wipe you out for a few days to concentrate that kind of energy under circumstances like that." He almost looked like he was worried.

"More likely a long week at work, the antics in the subway, and to top it off, female troubles. I'm going back to bed."

"Did you eat?"

"I'm not hungry." Her head pounded so hard she couldn't stand to be upright. Even the muted light diffusing through the blinds scalded her eyes.

He bit his lips and stroked her cheek. "Let me bring you something. Get into bed."

"Raul and Lupo are watching me. They'll take anyone standing around with them." She wobbled and leaned against him.

Arnaldo took her chin in his fingers. "I told you to be prepared, and you were. It will get easier." He gestured with his chin toward the bloody beads. "Do you think that worked?"

"All I know is I have a terrible migraine and awful cramps." If he didn't get going she'd have no chance of getting to Josefa's today. And she really needed to be in the company of a woman.

He put up his hands in resignation. "Okay."

She curled up on top of the bedspread. Zeus leaped up and snuggled next to her butt.

Before she realized any time passed, Arnaldo placed a brown bag on her nightstand. He stood with his legs apart, arms folded in front. "Got you some food. Hope you can make it tomorrow."

"You take care of her, Zeus." Arnaldo patted the dog's head. For once, he didn't growl.

Taina fought to keep her eyes open. She ripped the bag, took a bite of the roll and butter and a sip of sweet tea. "I'll be there. My spare key is on the kitchen counter. Take it, and lock up on the way out."

She didn't remember him leaving.

~ * ~

Her knees shook as she got out of bed, and she sat for a minute sipping the now cold tea. The sugar quelled her nausea so by the time she got to the bathroom, all she needed to do was pee and wash up.

Zeus danced around her feet, and she picked him up, found his leash, and hurried downstairs—4:45. Would Josefa still be there? Taina shot up her hand.

A gypsy cab stopped.

"Prospect and Leggett," she said.

The driver, done up in black and gold African garb, said something unintelligible. The smell of aftershave on top of stale body odor did nothing for the queasies.

The dog leaned his front paws on the door and watched the world go by. Taina breathed deeply to keep from throwing up.

"Five dollars, miss."

She gave him six, put the leashed dog down, and escaped to fresh air.

Taina rang the bell. A buzzer sounded. She pushed the sticky door hard, and it creaked open.

"*Hola, nena. Ay Díos,* I saw you on the news last night. No wonder you look so tired. Cute doggy. Let me get some water for him and tea for you. Sit." Josefa moved faster than Taina remembered, but in this situation she was traveling in reverse.

Taina eased onto the stool and leaned on the counter. Her head threatened to sink onto it. Josefa returned and put a steaming cup down and bent to slide a ceramic bowl underneath for Zeus. He lapped. Taina sipped. He curled up and lay down.

"This will help." Josefa handed her a cup.

"I have my period. I have a migraine. I'm ready to throw up. Every muscle in my body aches from pushing that woman up onto the subway platform."

The *santera* took Taina's hand and traced the palm. "It's all related. Drink. I mixed it especially for you."

It tasted like dead grass and smelled like mud.

She ushered Taina through the velvet curtain, past dusty racks of herbs in old mayonnaise jars, names scrawled on them in black marker. "Normally, I do a reading before *un sacurate,* but I know your story—and your situation—all too well."

Cardboard boxes lined the shelves, along with beads in glass vases, candles labeled 'seven day' and 'reversible' in a spectrum of colors. Josefa directed her to a card table covered by a silken black cloth.

Zeus had followed and plunked under the chair.

Taina peeked over her shoulder.

The *santera* stood behind her, donned a multicolored silken shawl, and prayed to a statue draped with green and yellow beads. She set out a bottle the size of liquor they serve on airplanes. The scent of

Agua Florida, faintly musty, like the old lady's bath powder Abuelita had sprinkled on Taina when she had heat rash, relaxed her immediately.

Josefa invoked *los santos* under her breath, *San Cristobal* being the only one spoken clearly. She massaged the fluid over Taina's arms, shoulders, back, legs, temples, face, and neck. Dampened fabric soothed and cooled her skin.

"Put both hands over the glass and tap them rapidly. No, not like that." She took Taina's hands and demonstrated a rapid up and downbeat on the rim of the glass.

After she got it right, Josefa snapped a bright orange and brown cloth around Taina like a silken whip.

She opened her mind to receive *la cura*. Her womb cramped, but the pounding in her head eased.

"You will be better after the purge and some rest. Wait outside while I prepare things." Josefa took two steps, swayed, then sank into an empty chair. "I have the gift, or the curse, of sight."

"What is it you see?"

The *santera* stared into the half-empty glass. "There are those who are jealous or fearful of your abilities." She gazed into a crystal triangle filled with golden icons and tiny stars. "Antonella died before she could finish."

Taina's guts contracted even more. She groped for her inhaler, took two quick puffs." Finish what?"

"Your grandmother never allowed Antonella to stray from Catholic teaching. And I doubt your father knew anything about your mother's visits to me. Even as a baby, you wore a gold crucifix. Perhaps she now wants her daughter to study *los santos*."

Her heart fluttered from the medication—and fear. "I still have that crucifix."

"It is among other blessings your mother dispensed. And that, *nena*, is more than enough about the past for today. It is healing you need." The subtle nature of Josefa's divination did not mask its naked power. The crucifix at the end of a string of rosary beads around the *santera's* neck rested on the table. The statue of San Francisco appeared to blink. Taina's vision blurred.

The *santera* paid no mind to her distress. "Did you recite the prayer and burn candles to *Yemayá*, and to your *angel guardia?* "

"Yes, after I put the blood on the stones and burned sage."

"Evil has attached itself to you by the hand of another. Wash with the green, then throw out the mop. Then rinse with the pink—and a new mop. Burn this incense, from the highest point down to outside. Then banish and cleanse your body. The brown liquid first, then the white."

Muddled, quaking, Taina grasped the table edge. "I can't remember all that."

"I'll write it down and prepare a potion. Take two droppers each day, morning and night."

Taina coughed. Couldn't the woman hear her wheezing? "I'm allergic…"

"*Ta, ta, ta, ta, ta.*" Josefa's tongue clicked like the beads around her neck. "Do you not trust me?"

"Yes, I do," Taina lied. Sweat drenched her clothes, dripped between her breasts. Blood oozed between her legs.

"May I use your bathroom?" She clutched for her purse.

"Through the curtain, on the right. That's the cohosh working." Josefa's lips curled into a mischievous grin. "I'll pack everything up for you."

Taina tripped over the threshold as she entered the bathroom.

The lone window, covered with contact plastic that looked like stained glass, let in no light. She shoved her fingers through the grating and opened it a crack for air. Blood soaked her inner thighs. Miraculously, the dark denim masked the stain on her shorts.

Taina cleaned up as best she could with some grainy paper towels. That would have to do until she got home.

Her head buzzed as flashes of things Josefa had prophesized collided in her brain, coalescing into globs that Taina couldn't categorize or understand.

Why me? How did I get caught up in all this? The racks of oils, essences, and herbs she passed on the way only confused her more.

Josefa, recovered from her weakness, gestured to a large box with a thick red candle swimming in a fragrant oil, a prayer card of *San Miguel* tucked behind it. Next to it she'd put, two-liter soda bottles filled with the baths, and two smaller ones filled with green and pink turbid liquid.

Taina gulped the now cool tea. Her vision cleared. The trembling stopped. The wheezing abated.

"Place this candle on the floor near your doorway and ask San Miguel to keep intruders from your home. Speak to him of who threatens you by name."

Josefa shoved a sheet of parchment paper and a pencil toward Taina.

She considered writing 'From all those who mean me harm,' but San Miguel likely needed more specifics. 'Raul Rivera and Lupo Lopez, plus all their soldiers and followers.' Taina pushed it across the counter.

"¿Ya?" Josefa didn't read it. She tipped the red candle out of the bottle and dropped the paper into the oil before replacing it.

"How much?" Taina's voice croaked.

"Thirty dollars. Remember, sometimes it is best to walk the path and not know what waits around the bend." Josefa winked.

Zeus stood and stretched, his ears pricked to attention as he came back to Taina's side.

She paid but could barely hold onto the box of potions. The sticky door gave. The bell tinkled. She raised her hand. A silver gypsy cab pulled to the curb.

The driver turned to her as Zeus leaped in and she slid into the back seat, his white teeth garish in the dark face, his Franglish providing a bit more intrigue to this already mysterious weekend.

"Where to, *madame?*"

"149th Street and Prospect."

She thudded against the back seat as he accelerated from zero to forty. She fastened her seatbelt and cradled the dog on her lap.

~ * ~

She stopped and leaned against a lamppost while Zeus did his business.

One of the fried chicken place's servers was out for her cigarette break. "Are you okay, miss?"

"Yeah." Taina picked up the pooch. Bending over accentuated the dizziness, but she managed to get back upstairs.

The menstrual flow had slowed to almost nothing, and despite the most profound exhaustion she could ever imagine, the migraine, nausea, and breathing problems had abated.

Somehow she found the strength to mop the floors with the green solution, then the pink.

Pleasant at first, the fragrance became progressively more cloying and objectionable. The incense wasn't as smoky as the sage, but it smelled like burning rubber.

Taina stripped off her stinky clothes and sat in the tub. She poured the pungent solution that looked like cola and smelled like tobacco and cloves over her. Far from offering comfort, nausea gripped her again.

Only a chill rewarded her as the pink floral concoction flowed over her head, down her face, her neck, her back. No way could she leave this odiferous mix on her body one minute longer.

Warm water and lavender soap offered relief, and probably guaranteed *los santos* would turn their backs since they couldn't smell her.

Iron—she needed something to recharge her depleted blood supply. Craisins would have to do, along with the stale sandwich on her nightstand and a fresh cup of tea.

She lit the candles, fingered the bloody beads, sprinkled salted water over the altar. "*Yemayá,* why?"

And cried. For her mother, Arnaldo's grandmother—both defeated. For Serena, who'd fled. And for all the women she tried to help every day at work, even though it was like shoveling shit against the pigpen fence. Too many things to ponder, and the need for sleep overrode it all.

Taina closed the windows and left all the candles burning in the bathtub.

She crawled into her bed to sweat it out and awoke when the clock read 7:00.

Was it morning or night? The headache, the cramps, the bleeding, the malaise had vanished in the candle smoke.

Her stomach growled from hunger. Zeus's cold nose lifted her hand as if taking it to lead her on a walk.

"Okay, puppy dog. Hang on." A quick shower. A swipe with the toothbrush. Another pair of shorts and tank top.

She peered out the window. A few bums collected cans and bottles from overflowing trash cans. People lined up outside the bakery. Morning.

She took enough money for a big breakfast, if the fried chicken place was open and served anything she could stomach. She had to be ready for tonight—and there was much to prepare.

Chapter Sixteen
First Harvest

Ritual Rock, set in the only green space in the area, was bordered on one side by a big building, which helped contain energy.

Zeus, his tail and ears pricked, seated himself on the south side.

Taina's scalp tingled as she walked counterclockwise around the eastern side of the boulder. Haphazard vestiges of magickal jamborees reverberated. She focused on only those in the green spectrum and imagined the others burrowing deep underground where they could do no harm.

This secluded dark side exuded a forbidding mishmash of auras as well as a subtle odor of evil that drove away all but the most unaware, desperate, or stupid mundanes.

A few of them clustered behind smaller boulders doing mundane things like smoking weed, dissing, and cursing anyone who walked by. Including her.

But the foolish *prosaicos* couldn't get closer. The myriad of circles cast around Ritual Rock over the years created shields that repelled all who had no business there.

Even in midsummer, leaves in shades of fire crackled under her feet. Absent sunlight, she still broke a sweat. *Los Sangueros* had claimed this place.

The northern side, which faced the street, provided momentary respite. Only when the turf wars spilled over did mundanes realize the power and danger here. She continued widdershins to claim her circle.

A musty, musky odor emanated from a crag near *Las Tombas* turf, to the west. Veins in the black granite glowed yellow. She hurried past the werewolf portal back to the southern aspect, deeply shaded by a stand of trees.

Zeus hadn't moved, but his eyes followed her progress.

Arnaldo, Serena, and quite possibly Taina's mother had consecrated this area for sabbats in the mossy green area witches preferred. She reclaimed the space for tonight and had hopefully resurrected the link.

She traced the white vein of quartz that ran through the granite like a root anchoring it beneath the earth. Lingering bits of witchy presence rose around her. She and Arnaldo would celebrate there tonight under the influence of the new moon, a good time for building positive energy.

She turned and walked deasil. Once she returned into the shadow of the housing project, a shock of negative energy rose through her feet, tingled along her spine, and raised hairs on the back of her neck.

She made the final turn to the south. A dark-skinned woman, dressed in a green and gold wrap dress with a matching headscarf and beads on her neck, wrists, and ankles stood just outside the perimeter. Green mist swirled about her bare feet.

Taina smiled and bowed her head. "Blessed be."

The woman nodded in response and picked her way around until she'd found a clear space for her own circle. There was enough room for everyone there as long as boundaries were respected.

Taina emerged into the sunlight once again, the fully exposed public area filled with mundanes sitting on bed sheets and folding chairs in the shade, kids chasing each other, skateboarding, squealing in delight.

It was easy, too easy, to deny the magickal world existed and she was a part of it—being drawn deeper and deeper into its mysteries and dark secrets. Zeus bounded toward her, his tail wagging, yapping in delight. Or was it relief?

Straying off the path and carving out new trails had never been her thing, and this was territory with no map, no guide, and no clear destination.

~ * ~

Arnaldo's voice drifted up the stairs. "You ready, Taina?" Footsteps followed, then the rest of him ducked into the doorway. *"Ay, señor.* Must be feeling better." He surveyed her head-to-toe in white shorts, a peach shirt, gold sandals—far more tropically flavored than usual.

She'd tried on several things before deciding what to wear. "Much better since I slept all day yesterday." No mention of the foul potions that had cured whatever magickal hangover she had.

"Are we taking this?" He lifted the Styrofoam cooler.

"Yes, that's the chicken. It's all ready for the grill. And corn. And some piña coladas."

"The party is already going strong. I don't drink alcohol any more, though." He started down the stairs.

"We don't need the rum. I don't need to wake up for work tomorrow feeling like I did this morning." Taina clipped on Zeus's leash, and he danced around her ankles.

"You're bringing the dog?" He closed the perimeter gate and shook to be sure it was latched.

"Of course. He'll just sit quietly in the circle."

Zeus seemed to have become more tolerant but still tangled the leash around Taina's legs to stay closer to her than to Arnaldo. She freed herself and carried the dog to the park.

She easily located her spot and re-claimed it by retracing her steps. Zeus ignored Arnaldo, chased his tail for four rotations at the southern point, and lay down, his back to the center.

Here the candle, red for Fire, would ignite the passion to do what was right, call out the dead, and allow new vital energy to spring from the ground.

Continuing East, Taina laid the green candle for Earth, its musty sweet odor, subtle, like mowed grass left to dry in the sun.

To the North, a blue candle represented Water, life, the realm of *Yemayá,* fittingly at the juncture between her circle and the mundane world.

She placed a golden candle to the west, along with Hawk Claw's feather in homage to Air and her fae friends.

Arnaldo waited, head bowed, until she completed her rounds, then looked up and smiled.

"You've prepared this well, Taina. The perimeter is strong." He struck a match, lit a stubby cigar, and walked the same path, igniting the candles, pausing to whisper something at each point. When he reached South, he knelt and invoked *Changó.*

She waited until he rose and crushed the cigar beneath a foot— his offering to *el santo del fuego*: fire, thunder, lightning.

Taina saw the African woman alone, cross-legged in the grass and touched Arnaldo's shoulder. "Should we ask her to join us?"

He looked at her with an expression somewhere between surprise and hurt—like she'd violated some sacred trust. "Invite a stranger into our circle?"

"I can feel her energy around me. Can't you?"

"She's gone." He didn't seem upset.

Just as fast as she'd appeared, the woman had vanished.

He closed his eyes and bowed. He rested his hand on Taina's shoulder. The spot he touched warmed, then tingled. A shudder of electricity moved down her arm, across her shoulders, diffused to her toes.

She started to walk deosil once again, chanting.
"This circle is cast
Between worlds,
Between night and day
To build a bridge
Between the present and past,
Between all creatures
that herein dwell."

He followed, right foot for right foot, left for left. Taina lapsed into a trance.

She and Arnaldo came together in a burst of bright light, their feet barely on the ground. They danced. His hands moved from her shoulders to her neck, ran through her hair, down her back. What was he doing to her, with her? No wonder he hadn't wanted anyone else in the circle.

Energy tingled along her spine. Her heart pulsed. Her hands trembled. She could do anything, achieve anything. The candles flickered. Arnaldo, his hand still on the same shoulder, steered her deosil until they completed three circuits. Taina's chest ached like a lead weight was sitting on it.

Not until a crow alighted on Ritual Rock and cocked its head to look at both of them, did her breathing ease. *Los Santos*, and the gods and goddesses, were either pleased or confused by the mishmash of spiritual practices.

She walked widdershins to unbind the circle, blew out, and collected the candles. Her tiny athame, too confounding to be noticed as a concealed weapon, nevertheless sufficed to open the energy field and allow them passage.

He let her go out first, then offered his arm. She took it, grateful for the grounding his solid presence provided after the energy peak. The tension between them had evaporated, and all that was left was a man and woman strolling in the park on a hot summer night. Arnaldo picked up the heavy cooler. She picked up Zeus.

Arnaldo looked younger, happier than she had ever seen him. "Time for a block party. The neighbors can feel the magick even if they don't know what it is or where it's coming from."

Los Sangueros were notably absent. *Las Tombas*, far from full moon, were elsewhere. Arnaldo guided her down a side street that was once a city block. Instead of housing units, chain link fences, cut and bent akimbo, provided the perimeter for a picnic area.

A charcoal grill fashioned out of a half a metal drum mounted on sawhorses belched smoke and flames tinged with the chemical tang of lighter fluid. Folding picnic tables held rows of chicken and sausages, hot dogs and hamburgers, salads, plates, cups, utensils, soda, beer.

A fire hydrant gushed a plume of water and kids ducked in an out of the spray while their parents sat on beach chairs and towels spread out over glistening recycled glass mixed into the asphalt sipping *coquito* out of clear plastic tumblers with seashells etched on them.

Zeus, petted almost bald by the children, licked their sticky fingers clean.

A few couples did what looked like tango to *"Bailamos"* until it shuffled into a Tito Puente riff that had even Arnaldo tapping his feet. "Let me put that chicken on the grill. Then we can dance."

Taina held the plastic bag while Arnaldo used the community fork to place the sacrificial bird over the coals. She tossed on the ears of corn, husks still on, and dropped the poppet doll in between, only to watch it flare and burn. The traditional offering, as well as those to *Yemayá*, the goddess of women and of the sea, and *Changó, the god of fire*, were now complete.

Arnaldo led her to the corner, and a dry, free space on the dance floor in the past had likely sported dirty needles, smashed bottles, crack vials, and cigarette butts.

They did *merengue* and s*alsa*, with a couple of breaks to turn the chicken, until her feet hurt and her back ached, and she was breathless, and she needed a drink. They ate, drank, then they danced some more with neighbors Taina had never met.

A man took his seat behind a stand of drums. The rhythm picked up as his hands moved faster and faster, blurred. The beat pounded in her head; her feet barely touched the ground.

They spun, twirled, hips gyrating. Arnaldo moved with a grace Taina had never seen and led her with gallantry. His hands held hers, his fingers touched her neck, her bare shoulders, traced her back. Their eyes, their feet, their bodies moved as if they were one.

The sweet smell of coconut and pineapple swirled around them. Invisible spirals of energy trapped them in a vortex.

It was nearly midnight before the drumbeat stopped and the magick dissipated.

Couples collected their coolers, their kids, their blankets, chairs and, finally, the boom box. They departed, some in cars, some walking home down the middle of the street from habit, though the ever-present threat seemed less ominous tonight.

Arnaldo doused the coals and helped the other men put the cap back on the sprinkler. The flow slowed to a trickle, dribbled and tinkled through the sewer grates, wiping the street clean, providing hope that it could always be like this.

Tipsy from the ritual and joyous energy, they laughed all the way home about the kids' antics, the crazy dance moves, anything, everything.

Taina paused at the gate in front of her house, not wanting the night to end, not wanting to be alone, wanting Arnaldo to kiss her, wanting him to come upstairs, hating herself for not asking, afraid to ask.

He hesitated, then kissed her on the forehead, his breath still tinged with tropical fruit. "Good night, Taina. Thanks for helping me conjure some magick. This neighborhood really needs more nights like this. We all really need more nights like this."

"It was wonderful, Arnaldo." She was about to ask him up when the African woman passed by on the other side of the street, her gaze riveted to them. A coincidence, a sign—or a warning?

Taina unlocked the gate. He stood as forlorn as a jilted teenager. Zeus jumped around her feet, but by the time she'd untangled the leash and released him, Arnaldo had closed it behind him and shook to be sure it was locked.

"Goodnight." No kiss, not even a handshake.

After the physical closeness, his evasion seemed forced. He pulled a Yankees cap out of his back pocket and twisted it as he walked way. In a few breaths, he was a lone stick figure, wandering down the middle of the street, toward Southern Boulevard, toward *Sonrisa*, toward his empty apartment.

She retrieved Zeus, who'd been watering the garbage cans.

A shot pierced the calm. Tires screeched. A woman screamed. Arnaldo kept going—in the opposite direction. Police sirens wailed.

The afterglow contracted, dissipated. Red eyes glinted out of the alleyways as *Los Sangueros* emerged. Something howled, and it wasn't a dog. Whatever healing energy was raised during new moon, or peace spell they'd cast was gone now, and the bad boyz and girlz could come out to play.

Taina hurried inside, locked the three deadbolts, tightened her circle, snuggled up to the dog and her pillow. Was her wish that Arnaldo was holding her in his arms, that the spell was still intact, the magick extant.

Chapter Seventeen
Order in the Court

Taina crept into the office.

Simone nearly dropped the coffee carafe. "Girl, I tried calling after I saw you on the news. Shit, I don't know if I would have jumped onto the tracks."

"I didn't have much time to think but leaving her there wasn't an option."

"How was the weekend? Pretty good, I bet, since you never called me back." Simone's raised eyebrow and pursed lip smile belied her lascivious imaginings.

"I was really sick Saturday. I think it was the combination of the end of the workweek, the subway incident, and the heat. But Sunday was really nice."

Sandy had come in and was changing from sneakers to pumps. "Really nice?"

"I went to a block party. We ate, danced salsa." It had been quite a bit more, but how could Taina even begin to explain a pagan ritual?

"And?" both coworkers asked at the same time.

"We? Did you go *with* someone?" Simone pumped her hand like a traffic cop trying to move things along.

"With my friend. Arnaldo." Arnaldo's attentiveness when Taina was sick, and the magick of the weekend had elicited feelings that it really could be more.

Sandy rubbed her bare right foot like she'd forgotten to put on the second shoe. "Is he nice to you? Good in bed? You don't need anything more."

"I'm still not over my ex. Let me double check the time and place of those proceedings for today." Taina fled to her office and waited for the computer to boot up.

She didn't know what the hell she wanted, except to do it all over again tonight. More than six weeks until fall equinox—the next excuse for a sabbat. Maybe by then she'd have her head screwed on straight.

The court docket opened. Precious Bonsu and Rosa Nuñez both had court dates today.

"Shit."

Who needed her more? The mundane, battered woman in a safe house, whose husband was out on bail pending the outcome of his plea deal? Or Rosa, charged with prostitution, who'd lost custody of her son, and either named the pimp and walked or the case would go to trial?

Precious's case was scheduled in the Major Crimes Unit, a half-hour after Rosa's, which was in the regular criminal part. Precious needed and wanted Taina's help. But she needed to stand up to Raul or his fangs would grow another inch just anticipating wearing her down and sinking them into her neck.

"Two clients waiting, Taina." Sandy was back to business.

Her boss's door was closed, the 'In Session' sign up. Sandy was arguing with someone on the phone about a similar scheduling situation for Simone.

"I apologize for the wait," Taina said to the man and woman in the waiting room. "I'll be with you shortly."

The shell-shocked survivors were in no position to complain. And they were sitting so far apart that they were likely two separate matters. Two cases to be opened, and she had an hour and a half to do the intakes, reach the assistant district attorneys, find out who the public defenders assigned to Precious and Rosa were, and strike Taina's own deal. This job was like juggling eggs.

She rifled through her numbers and visualized the Criminal Court Building.

"Haste makes waste, so time waste negate.

Haste makes waste, so time waste negate.

Haste makes waste, so time waste negate."

Then she imagined Rosa Nuñez and Raul outside the courtroom.

"Haste makes waste, so time waste negate.

Haste makes waste, so time waste negate.

Haste makes waste, so time waste negate."

Next she thought of Precious and her son.

"Haste makes waste, so time waste negate.

Haste makes waste, so time waste negate.

Haste makes waste, so time waste negate."

Taina dialed the DA's office, tapping her foot to keep the energy flow ticking forward. "Good morning, Taina Aponte, victim's advocate. Who's handling the Bonsu case today? I have some scheduling issues. Yes, I'll hold."

~ * ~

Taina had spent years as a paralegal at the firm of Montalvo and Mercado, wearing this same light gray suit, matching pumps, and white blouse. In PR, and today in The Bronx, all she could hear as she negotiated through the crowd in front of the courtroom was Spanish.

"Can I help you, counselor?" The gun toting, radio-equipped court officer wasn't a familiar face.

"No, I'm the advocate assigned to the Nuñez case."

He studied her ID. "They're just waiting for the defendant. Lemminsky is the assistant district attorney. Blackstein is the public defender."

"Thank you." For good measure, she recited the spell under her breath three more times as she walked down the central aisle.

The assistant DA had agreed to hold the *Bonsu vs Bonsu* matter until she got there, but Precious would be forced to wait with her violent husband eyeing every move far longer than necessary.

The ADA and the judge were conversing about the Yankees. The public defender wore a trough in the floor. Detective Kidman was immersed in his cellphone. They all turned as Taina passed the railing that divided the seating area from the lawyers' tables.

"Good morning." She introduced herself like a scratched CD.

If Kidman recognized her, he didn't let on.

"Have you spoken with Ms. Nuñez recently?" Blackstein looked like he was worrying far more about the outcome than Rosa herself.

"Not since the day Detective Kidman called me in on the case." A backdraft of energy pushed her into the attorney. "Sorry, I twisted my ankle."

Taina didn't need to turn around. Raul was behind her. Right on the stroke of eleven. Right on time. Right on cue.

He took a seat in the courtroom, along with a striking young woman in a blouse with a plunging neckline and a red aura.

The child welfare caseworker, a mundane woman in a blue suit, sat next to them.

Rosa was dressed to impress. Her breasts bulged out of a leopard push up that showed through the pale yellow top. Her pants were the skinny type, and she wasn't thin. Her heels were so high Taina's feet hurt just looking at Rosa strut down the aisle.

The harried public defender intercepted her before she could join Raul. "Good morning, Ms. Nuñez. Ms. Aponte and I would like to speak with you for a few moments before we begin."

The ADA took a seat at a table and organized his legal pads. Taina would be far more comfortable in that role than in the one she was acting right now.

The court officer and stenographer debated why the Yankees were having such a bad series run against the Devil Rays. Raul smirked as Taina walked out, his gaze focused on her breasts until she passed, then kissed her ass with a magickal stare.

The public defender and Rosa plunked on a bench near the back of the room. "Ms. Nuñez, I've been trying to contact you for several days about the plea deal the District Attorney's office is offering. We don't have much time to discuss this as the case is about to be called."

The red aura throbbed around Rosa's head. "An old boyfriend beat me up, and they arrested me and charged me with prostitution. That detective has it out for me. My babysitter and the ACS worker are here to testify on my behalf. And my landlord too. What's she here for?"

Taina picked up her cue. "Ms. Nuñez, I have also been trying to reach you, and even came to your building, but the landlord wouldn't let me up to your apartment. I'm here today for support." *I'm out of here at 11:30 to go to someone who wants my help.*

Rosa's eyes shot daggers. "I don't need either of you."

A vein in Blackstein's temple throbbed. "Ms. Nuñez, you need an attorney. If the main concern is custody of your son, then perhaps you should consider the deal. If this goes to trial..."

"You're my fuckin' lawyer. You're supposed to get me an ACD." Rosa had obviously been in trouble before.

Now Blackstein's neck veins pulsed in time. "There is no medical or crime scene evidence. You admitted participating in an intimate encounter with the man before he struck you. You will not give his name so he can be subpoenaed. I can put in a motion for dismissal. If it's denied, a jury might acquit you, but they might not. You'll have to wait longer to regain custody of your son."

Taina tried to advocate. "Look, someone else called the police. They didn't take her to the hospital. They took her in. That was wrong."

"Counselor, if you need more time with your client, well go on to the next case and adjourn this matter for today." The court officer stood a respectful distance away but had still likely heard everything.

"No deals." Rosa folded both arms under her breasts, which made them pop out even more.

"No, we're ready to proceed." Blackstein walked directly to his table.

The surly Detective Kidman sat in the spectator's area behind ADA Lemminsky, who was tapping his fingers on the desk.

This mess was everybody's fault and nobody's fault. Rosa should have returned the phone calls. The lawyer should have investigated further. The detective shouldn't have arrested this woman. Taina shouldn't have done the time spell, should have let things run late, made her excuses, and left.

But she and Rosa were alone, and it was time for the last push. "I know all about Raul and the deal you have with him," Taina whispered. "Take the plea bargain. I'll get you and your son out of New York City."

Rosa bit the hand Taina offered. "My man is gonna take care of everything. He'll steal my son back if he has to."

"I see. Let's have a seat until the judge calls you." 11:33. Taina was trapped here, wasting time, missing the opportunity to help a person who needed and wanted it.

"Judge William Kravitz, presiding in the matter of *The People vs. Rosa Nuñez*. All rise please." The court officer's heels clicked across the courtroom.

The gray-haired, stubble-faced man flapped his arms, so the black robe fanned out like bat's wings, then sat down. The court reporter settled into place. Chairs scraped, feet clomped. Raul took his time slipping into the row but remained standing.

"Please be seated, everyone. Ms. Nuñez, come forward." Judge Kravitz perched on the end of his seat, his back so bent into a C position, it appeared he was leaning forward.

Rosa walked to the bench without any fanfare. Blackstein stood next to her.

The court officer gestured her toward the witness stand. "Raise your right hand and repeat after me. 'I promise to tell the truth, the whole truth, and nothing but the truth'."

Rosa repeated the sentence, with her affect as flat as cardboard. She was already trapped in Hell and one more lie wouldn't matter.

The judge spoke slowly, his demeanor as hopeless as everything else in this stinking courthouse. "Mr. Blackstein has submitted a request to dismiss all charges. It seems you have three witnesses who have come forward to testify on your behalf. As I understand, you were assaulted. By whom?"

Rosa's gaze darted side-to-side, but she didn't look at Raul. "An old friend came to visit. I asked him to leave. He wouldn't. One thing led to another."

"Ms. Nuñez, you let him in to your apartment. The complaint further alleges that you have a six-year-old son, who was not home at the time, but that the Administration for Children's Services removed to foster care pending the outcome of this case. You have been charged with prostitution and obstruction of justice and were offered a chance to have the charges dismissed if you provide the name of the man—or men—putting you into this situation."

Rosa raised her chin and put her hands on her hips. "The detective wanted his collar. I want to let this whole thing die."

"Might I remind you, Ms. Nuñez, that you are under oath."

"Yeah, so?"

Blackstein exhaled his frustration. "Your honor, Ms. Nuñez's witnesses did not come forward in enough time for me to have proper statements prepared. I believe you already have a copy of Ms. Chalmer's full report on the status of the ACS investigation." He handed the court officer a paper to bring to the bench.

Maybe the judge would adjourn this matter until witness statements could be properly collected, but Taina didn't dare try any more spells.

He glanced at the courtroom clock, then put on reading glasses and studied the document. "The 12:00 case was adjudicated while we were waiting for Ms. Nuñez. In the matter of expediency, let's just dispense with this before lunch.

"Ms. Nuñez, you may step down. Ms. Ermilenda Sepulveda, Mr. Raul Rivera, and Ms. Karen Chalmers, please approach the bench. Officer Brandeis, please swear these individuals simultaneously."

Sweat trickled between Taina's breasts. *That's what I get for magickal schedule keeping.*

The trio walked with such regimentation, it appeared they had done this before. The court officer stepped forward. The ACS worker's well-practiced hand shot up immediately, while Raul and Ermilenda's palms turned toward their faces, wrists as limp as a dead fish.

Human law and ethics were not operational in their world, but even if the judge and attorneys noticed it, there was nothing they could do anyway.

Judge Kravitz removed his glasses and stared Raul in the eye, as if to warn him he'd better tell the truth. "Mr. Rivera, what do you want to tell the court about Ms. Rosa Nuñez?"

Taina's admiration for the judge went up one hundred percent. At least he'd noticed the schism between word and action.

Raul was also on one hundred percent—black suit, pants belted at the waistline, white shirt, tasteful tie, perfect English, serious countenance, fangs under cover of lip. "Ms. Nuñez has been a tenant in my building for the last five years. Her rent is always paid on time, and I've never had issues prior to this with any questionable or illegal activity in her apartment or in the public areas of the property. She does volunteer work at the *Boricua* Shelter for Women in Crisis, which is the reason she has not needed the court advocate's kind offer of advice." He bared his teeth at Taina.

The judge's narrowed eyes widened, and a smirk tickled his lips. "Thank you, Mr. Rivera. In what capacity are you familiar with the *Boricua* Shelter?"

"I started it as a place for those having difficulties with obtaining housing, child support, domestic violence, necessary health care services, and so on to avoid becoming homeless with no resources. Women helping women, right in their own neighborhood."

Taina almost gagged.

"Might I assume that you, Ms. Sepulveda, are one of the members of Mr. Rivera's organization?"

Ermilenda blinked like a light had been shone in her eyes. *"No hablo ingles."*

Crap. Now we have to wait for a translator. Hopefully, he'll read the ACS statement while we're waiting.

The judge looked at Taina like a homing beacon was rotating on the top of her head.

"Ms. Aponte, as an employee of the court, might I impose upon you for translation to save some time?"

That's the second kickback. One more to go before this bad dream is over. "Of course, your honor." Now, she was just a sewer pipeline. Did this center even exist? Vetting that out would have been one of her jobs as a paralegal.

She walked down the central aisle, introducing herself on the way to save time. *"Muy buenas, Señorita Sepulveda. Me llamo Taina Aponte. Yo trabajo con la Oficina de Los Defensores en El Bronx. El corte tiene la necesitidad de saber que quiere decir sobre Rosa Nuñez."*

"Soy cangura del Ariel, el hijo." She looked at Raul.

"Ms. Sepulveda is Ariel's babysitter. *Continua, Senora.*" Taina stayed in charge.

"Ella es lo mejor madre que alguien pudiera sepa. Nunca le hicieria algo mal al su hijo. El se ama la madre muchisimo. El apartamento es limpia, y el siempre tiene a el todo que necesita—la ropa, las comidas, las juguetes." Ermilenda counted off on her fingers, looked at Raul, then the judge before she tucked a peeking bra strap back under the shoulder of her blouse.

Taina turned to the judge. "Rosa Nunez is the best mother anyone could know. At no time has she done anything bad to her son. He loves his mother more than anything. The apartment is clean, and he always has everything he needs: clothing, meals, and toys."

The judge frowned. "What is Ms. Nuñez doing that requires her to hire a babysitter?"

Ermilenda obviously spoke more English than she let on because her eyes teared up, and she trembled.

Raul remained impassive.

Taina glanced at Rosa, sitting next to Blackstein doing her leg-shake comfort ritual. The tapping twanged Taina's nerves like a finger-pick did a banjo, but it appeared Raul's prep work had failed to consider a judge who could see the mud at the bottom of the swamp. Rosa spoke in Spanish, her gaze fixed on Raul.

You're just here to translate. Don't ask questions. "When Ariel is with Ms. Sepulveda, Rosa goes places with women who need assistance and cleans houses in the neighborhood."

The only regret Taina had was that Ermelinda was sweating more than Raul—and that both women might end up in jail for perjury. But only if the judge ordered more investigation of *Boricua.*

The judge chewed a corner of his pen. "I see. Thank you very much, Mr. Rivera and Ms. Sepulveda. You may both be seated."

They shuffled their feet.

"Ms. Chalmers, I've read the report and see that you've recommended closing the ACS case. There appears to be no evidence of child abuse, maltreatment, or neglect. Why hasn't the son been returned to his mother's custody?"

The well-practiced ACS caseworker delivered her statement. "Given the nature of the accusations, my supervisor felt it would be best to await the court's decision whether or not to proceed to trial. In addition, continuance of foster care would be indicated if Ms. Nuñez were to be incarcerated."

Judge Kravitz nodded. "Understood, but we don't remand single mothers before they are convicted. Please, be seated. Ms. Aponte, many thanks for translating."

Taina walked back to her seat next to Mr. Blackstein, who also had a full day of bullshit like this ahead of him.

"Mr. Blackstein and Mr. Lemminsky, could you please approach the bench?"

Let's make a deal time. Rosa is going to get her ACD. Taina contemplated one more magickal push but resisted.

Raul stared her down. She tried to not blink. As uncomfortable as this was, she wouldn't acquiesce to his veiled threats and pompous arrogance.

Rosa's leg thumped. Ermelinda picked her cuticles. Neither looked up at their pimp/ ringleader/master or at each other.

The judge and two attorneys nodded in unison after what seemed like an hour but was really only seven minutes. The ADA rifled papers.

Blackstein sat next to Taina and whispered, "All charges dismissed."

The judge put on his glasses. "Thanks to all of you. We all agree the best course of action given the testimony today is to dismiss all charges in one month, provided that Ms. Nuñez has no further arrests. That will enable Ms. Chalmers to take the necessary steps to close the ACS case and return the child to his mother immediately. Ms. Aponte, I suggest you have a look at Mr. Rivera's shelter and set up a referral system. It might be a good resource for the women your office serves."

"I certainly will, your honor. And I'll send you a report as well." Seeing Raul beatified had to be the final kickback.

As usual, the ADA, the public defender, the judge, and the officer didn't bother with any goodbyes before they got busy with their next case. And they never got to see Ermelinda and Rosa outside, running their hands up and down Raul's back, staring at him as if he was their god.

He had his arms around both his girls but dropped them and was at Taina's side in a heartbeat. "I'd love to take you on a personal tour of *Boricua* Center, my lovely young witch. Anytime. Remember, I've offered you the opportunity to be in charge of it all." He winked, moved too close then brought his face near hers and bared his teeth.

"Get out of my way, or I will press charges for harassment." She tried to push past, but he clutched her arm and twisted just enough to let her know he'd hurt her if necessary.

"I'll win in the end, Taina, because I have plenty of time. This system is a joke, a total failure, along with everyone in it. You belong with the winners. Don't cross me. I don't make deals like they do around here."

Taina pulled back, then fell forward, unbalancing Raul enough to break free of his hold. A well-timed elevator going up provided and exit. She could escape his physical presence, but not his infiltration of every stinking place in The Bronx his fangs had penetrated.

When would her luck run out?

Chapter Eighteen
Court Date

A few sips of rotgut coffee from the canteen machine on the sixth floor eased the irritation. But caffeine mixed with what tasted like sludge did nothing to ease the beginnings of Taina's post-magickal migraine.

Even Josefa's potion, which Taina had taken faithfully twice a day, hadn't eliminated that side effect. Would she ever be as nonchalant as Arnaldo, who conjured thunder and lightning without missing a breath? Or Serena, who could knock a determined stalker into an enchanted bougainvillea lock-up and never lose stride?

More irritating stops on each floor, from six to three, with elbow poking, toe smashing, and butt bumping as people excused themselves to exit and others crammed in.

She limped toward the courtroom.

"Hi, Ms. Aponte." The court officer spoke into his radio. "The advocate for the Bonsu case just arrived."

Among friends, if they could be called that, the tension in her neck, the throbbing in her head eased.

The officer frowned at the static in his ear. "Hang on. They're almost done adjudicating this case. We shifted the morning schedule around so you could be here."

"I'm sorry I held things up." An hour and a half longer than necessary.

"Ah, no biggie. Things are running strangely well today. All the defendants have been on time, the lawyers, the DA's too." He peeked inside the courtroom. "The plaintiff is being escorted in, and the defendant is coming down." The officer held the door for her.

As customary, she took a seat in the observer's area, right behind the assistant district attorney's table. No magickal auras in here.

Only the specter of sad, plodding justice for incidents that should never have happened lingered like ghosts in the aisles or cobwebs in the corners.

A black man in a brown-and-gold kembe tunic and pant set walked in a side door with the public defender. His face, adorned with a few war-stripe scars, showed no expression, no tension. His breathing was slow and even, his body still. The public defender gestured for him to sit. She settled into place and read her notes.

Precious entered, her arms clasped around her chest, making the pregnant belly seem even bigger, eyes darting, teeth biting her lower lip. When she saw Taina, she smiled, wiped a tear, then slid into the seat next to the ADA.

The court officer called the cast's names and beckoned the two lawyers to the bench. The trio traded paperwork.

Precious turned and clasped Taina's hand over the railing. "Thank you for coming."

"Has he found you?" Taina whispered.

"No, but I live in fear for me, for my son."

The assistant DA, named Kennedy, smiled at them both as she returned.

The judge, his New Yawk accent so thick you could slice and serve it on a bagel, banged his gavel. "Let's come to order in the matter of *The People vs Kwaku Bonsu*. Mr. Bonsu, you're here to answer to the charges of assaulting your wife with a chair leg in front of your five-year-old son. The district attorney has offered you the option of pleading guilty to avoid a trial, limiting your jail time to that already served. While on probation, you must attend regular meetings with a parole officer, anger management classes, and agree to abide by the order of protection your wife, Precious Bonsu, has obtained. That order prohibits you from having any contact, physical, verbal, written or electronic with her, your son, and the baby due to be born on or about September 25.

"I will warn you, Mr. Bonsu, that any transgression, no matter how slight, will land you back in jail, and this case will be re-opened. And of course, if you are arrested for any other reason, your past record will not be viewed favorably by the court. Do you have any questions or objections to this proposal?"

"No, your honor." Kwaku continued staring straight ahead.

The judge looked at Precious and smiled. "Mrs. Bonsu, have you any objections to this proposal? I must also ascertain that your husband has made no attempt to contact you or your son in any physical, verbal, electronic, or written way since the date the order of protection was obtained."

"No, your honor. But he has not paid any money to me to buy things for myself, the baby coming, or my son."

"I see." The judge pursed his lips and stared at Kwaku. "Mr. Bonsu, are you working?"

"No. I drive a taxi, but they fired me when I got arrested."

"Yes, Mr. Bonsu, another unpleasant fact of life when one breaks the law. Where are you living now?"

"In a shelter."

He was too well groomed, too nicely dressed, too full of shit. Taina considered a hex. An itchy asshole, maybe some cramps in the toes, but it would likely backdraft on her in some equally awful fashion.

"I see. Counselors, has the issue of finances been addressed with your clients?"

"Yes, your honor." They'd answered in unison.

"And both parties are receiving housing and public assistance?"

"Yes, your honor."

"Do you need time to discuss any further terms with your clients?"

Taina gave the ADA a time-out sign.

The ADA stood. "Five minutes, please, your honor."

"Very well." The judge's robes fluttered as he hopped down from the bench and retreated into his chambers.

Precious eased her chair around.

The ADA leaned over the rail and whispered, "We could have child support entered into the agreement, but it will hold up divorce proceedings."

"And he probably will never pay you anyway, Precious. But it's up to you." Taina hated the kind of deal that let the guy off so easy, but severing ties was usually the best course of action.

"I'd rather starve than have to be in contact with him or come back to court." She spoke with certainty.

"Understood." The lawyer turned forward as the judge returned.

"I can help you find childcare for when the baby is born." That was the best Taina could do now.

"Yes." A blue-and-white beaded bracelet tinkled on Precious's wrist. She fingered each bead, then moved her chair to face front.

More subtle magick, but at least it was someone else's doing.

The judge sat down. "Counselors, please approach the bench."

They did. Comments were murmured.

"Mrs. Bonsu, be sure to inform the police, the district attorney, and your advocate if there are any violations of this order. We'll adjourn for a one-hour lunch and return at 2:15 PM. Officer." He grabbed his glasses then retreated.

"I will be in touch, Precious. Taina, thanks for coming." The ADA hustled out.

They followed and paused outside for a hug. Precious's belly was surprisingly hard, and Taina bounced off it. "Good luck."

"May *Yemayá* bless and keep you safe. You are a wonderful person in a terrible world." Precious slipped the bracelet off and gave it to Taina.

"No, you keep it. I know it's spiritual protection." She couldn't accept a *Ileke* charged with such intensity—and her client's only real means of defense.

"I want to do something to thank you." Precious slipped the beads back on.

"This is my job and my pleasure." No coincidence that they shared the same deity, of that Taina was sure.

Their hands clasped.

"Say a prayer to your *orisha* on my behalf." Precious waddled to the stern matron near the elevator and departed. All the good feelings from the weekend vanished with her.

The hallways and elevators were full of the lunch going masses. Simone and Sandy were gone, and the only office greeting was a ringing phone.

"Ms. Aponte, Detective Browning from Special Victims here. I've got someone who needs a lot of help. She's...I don't know, mentally challenged, and she was beaten and gang-raped last night. Is there any way you can get her on your schedule today?"

"Yes, bring her right up."

That spell was not finished kicking Taina's ass.

~ * ~

If she practiced some community service spells on the way home to build resistance, maybe her head wouldn't feel like it had been hammered on from the inside every time she did magick.

The guy bopping along to music so loud she could hear it through the ear buds was way too close to the edge of the platform. She blew gently, visualized the flow of energy toward his chest and whispered,

"Don't play, stay away.
Don't play, stay away.

Don't play, stay away."
He moved back like someone was pulling him. Even looked around to see who it was.

When she got to Arnaldo's she'd have some good news. Then she'd hit him with the fact she'd pissed off Raul and opened a new case this afternoon involving Lupo and a sickening initiation rite of a girl so limited she didn't even understand that six hairy men having sex with her under a train trestle was a bad thing. How would he suggest Taina magick her way out of this?

She stopped a block away from *Sonrisa* and watched soldiers from each gang line up in front. No time to warn him.

Arnaldo came outside. "Get the hell away from my property." The protective spell around the perimeter pulsed with each rise and fall of his chest.

The two lines of soldiers shot warning glances like bullets at each him, then filed away, one group toward *Las Tombas* territory, the other toward *Los Sangueros* turf. Lupo and Raul lingered.

She hid behind a car. Could this have anything to do with her? So soon?

"We have a deal, Arnaldo. Don't let her fuck it up." Lupo, his recruit being the most recent case Taina was involved with, was clearly the aggrieved here.

But Raul didn't suffer in silence. "She had a full docket in court today. But I won. I always do."

Arnaldo's aura flickered like green tongues of fire. "Stop luring my kids."

Coño. If the DNA netted anything, the zombie teenager case would dispatch a whole new bunch of Lupo's recruits to jail. No plea deals for a gang who'd raped a child, particularly a disabled one.

Taina waited, unwilling to disrupt the wobbly, pheromone-laced triangle or give them an excuse to start throwing more than words at each other.

When the dhamp and were walked away, she ran to the gate. *"Que pasó?"*

Arnaldo's face registered the usual disgust. "The kids see them cross in front of buses, ride the tops of subway trains into the tunnels and survive. They suck them into the ultimate video game, promise them money, sex, drugs. But when kids shoot guns at each other, they don't just re-materialize and go back for more."

"This is my fault." her stomach ached. Her head throbbed anew. "Raul put in quite a performance in court. He reiterated his previous offer and got very nasty when I refused. I used some of those maneuvers to get out of his grasp."

"He got that close?" Arnaldo's laugh lines deepened far too much to indicate humor.

"Yep." A suspicion that there was some underhanded agreement between Raul and Arnaldo rose to her lips, but she suppressed it. Now was not the time to tell him about Raul's groping incident.

"You have to do what you have to do." Sarcasm dripped from Arnaldo's mouth. "Raul Rivera is able to manipulate everyone and make everything go his way. The cops and the detectives have a bead on him, but he manages to worm himself out of trouble all the time."

"I do my best but have the beginnings of another migraine from a time-management ditty."

He rubbed her temples with his thumbs. "You draw everyone's magick into your sphere. Plus you've got all these conflicts about what's white or black or good or bad. Let them have it full-force because they're not going to spare you."

Taina's heart pounded so fast her chest hurt. "The police found one of Lupo's initiates wandering the streets naked and took her to the hospital. She's only sixteen. The detective is salivating until the DNA evidence is ready so they can pick up the perps. If there is anything usable there."

Arnaldo knotted his fingers together. "Now that you've crossed both bosses, every gang member in the hood has his or her sights on you. They'll get a nice reward if they deliver the prize. Taina, this is your last chance to get out of here."

"Even if I wasn't here, those cases would still be investigated." She was now at the point, like Serena had been, of deciding if threats would drive her out The Bronx forever. And Serena was a much more confident, powerful witch than her headache plagued initiate.

"When the war starts, nothing, no one—no courthouse, no cop, no district attorney—is going to save you. You're gonna have to save yourself." A strange expression, something between pain and anguish, registered on his face. "Lemme walk you home."

Taina didn't argue.

Chapter Nineteen
Werewolf Infiltration

"Girl, you're having one week from Hell." Simone put her coffee cup down and scrunched her nose.

Taina thumbed through the report. "I've seen this before in kids from the tiny *campos* in PR with a history of educational neglect. I think the best strategy is to get her placed in a group for intense vocational rehab."

Likely the offspring of some drug-addicted werewolf pairing, Zoraida had been banished to the zombie sect because of her low functional status. Of course, she couldn't tell Simone that.

"Egads. What a terrible story. What time are the proceedings?"

"Ten AM in Family Court. There are no arrests imminent and no testimony or evidence to implicate anyone in a criminal case."

Taina flipped to the end of the story. "Zoraida has no parents who could be found and is assumed to be a runaway, though no missing person reports have been filed for anyone meeting her description. The psychiatrist believes she is schizophrenic, unable to answer questions or cooperate with testing."

"Good luck. At least it's Friday. Got any dates to look forward to this weekend?" Simone's eyebrows rose.

"No plans." Taina went back to her office. She wanted to hit the repeat button from last week and see Arnaldo, with no agenda and no conflicts. But having him as an annoying bodyguard was worse than being alone.

As expected, the DNA evidence from the sixteen-year old well on her way to initiation as a zombie soldier in *Las Tombas*, was inconclusive, muddled, or otherwise unintelligible.

The lure of the streets, of the clan, of the gang that had given the poor kid a sense of person and place, of family, and made her feel wanted, would win—even if it involved sex with werewolves.

Taina checked the day's planetary hours. No wonder this had been a crazy week; her moon was just emerging from being void, of course. She'd need to be better about checking her charts, though the real world didn't surrender to, or even believe in, the validity of an astrological forecast. No matter what, the outcome of this case wouldn't be good.

Taina made it a point to arrive just in time so that Zoraida would focus her anger on the caseworkers who'd brought her there.

The teenager sat next to the law-guardian appointed to represent her interests. She stared at the elaborate woodcarvings, the architecture of the ceiling, the pattern on the floor.

Judge Winslet, a youngish black woman with a luscious Caribbean accent, tried to get her attention. "Miss Maisonet?"

The kid's gaze focused on the judge's braided hairstyle piled in a complex beehive.

"Zoraida, do you speak English or Spanish?"

No answer.

Judge Winslet tried again. "*¿Habla ingles o español?*"

Zoraida blinked. "*Ingles y español.*"

The judge exhaled. "Then please answer me. We want to figure out the best way to help you."

"Let me go back to *mi tio*. He came to rescue me last night." Zoraida had such a dreamy voice, she had to be living in some netherworld.

The lawyer and the ACS worker looked at each other.

The judge frowned. "Where did you see your uncle?"

"He came to my window and told me to come with him. I couldn't get out."

The judge looked toward ACS. "Ms. McIntyre, is this true?"

The worker pursed her lips and shook her head. "She lives on the eighth floor of a locked ward."

No sweat for a magickal being with an army at his command.

The law-guardian walked over to Zoraida and touched her arm. "What is your uncle's name? Tell us where he lives so we can call him."

Zoraida's eyes brimmed bright with tears. "I know how to walk there. Please let me go."

Taina had to do something or her heart would beat out of her chest. "Your honor, if I might interject here. I'm Taina Aponte, from the Victim's Advocate Office. I met Zoraida when the assistant district attorney brought her in from the hospital."

"Please come up and tell us what you know, Ms. Aponte." The judge beckoned to the stand next to her.

Taina gave a gentle magickal push under her breath while on the way to the bench. Risky, under a waxing crescent moon and just past void of course, but this situation dictated an all-out effort.

"Hide, shelter, protect.
Remove her from this sect.
Hide, shelter, protect.
Remove her from this sect.
Hide, shelter, protect.
Remove her from this sect."

Taina settled into the seat. "Zoraida said she had sexual relations with some boys she met while walking down 138th Street near the entrance to the Robert F. Kennedy Bridge. Zoraida didn't seem to think there was a problem and that the boys were her friends. There is an educational deficit I believe, which makes this a particularly challenging—"

"Your honor, if I might interrupt." The law-guardian stood like she was going to grill her.

"Go ahead, Ms. Williamson."

"Ms. Aponte, without any evidence the criminal aspects of this are moot. We must investigate placing her with any known next of kin."

The ACS worker and judge bobbed their heads in unison. Zoraida alternated studying the ceiling and the floor. Taina's heart sagged.

Judge Winslet looked at Taina with a resigned kindness. "In the interest of expediency, I propose that Zoraida take either or both of you to her uncle's home, under police supervision, to ascertain the veracity of the relationship. Once we have a full report, I can decide. I want every effort made to vet this fully. Step down, please."

Could the kickback be that fast? *I have to walk into Lupo's lair?*

The judge waited until Taina was back in her seat to speak. "The date for a follow-up report is August 19 at 9 AM. That should give everyone time to gather the information. Zoraida, you must answer questions, and you must take us to your uncle. For now, you'll stay in the shelter."

She tapped the gavel.

They all filed out. Taina handed her card to both the ACS worker and the law-guardian. Hopefully, they wouldn't bother to call her.

"*Tio* is calling me." Zoraida looked around, out the window, into the crowd of miserable people waiting behind bullet proof glass while distraught, screaming families stumbled out of courtrooms.

The ACS worker guided the teenager to the back elevator where a cop joined as escort.

"*¡Tio, por favor, ayudame!* Save me!" They pulled Zoraida in. The closing door silenced her, though there was more than enough anguish lingering in her wake.

The tendrils of alarm that curled down Taina's neck signaled danger. She bumped into Lupo Lopez.

His musk, a cross between a wet dog and stale tobacco, assaulted her like a punch in the kisser. He was even more hairy close up, with a coarse curly weave of beard that continued down his neck, to below the collar of his yellowed *guayabera* shirt.

Wiry strands pushed through the delicate cotton fabric. His eyebrows ran together in the middle of his forehead, giving him the countenance of a permanent frown, but with the scowl on his lips, it was likely a common enough expression.

Taina focused on the court officer with a gun right at the entrance to the bulletproof playpen. But everyone was huddled close, trying to keep very personal discussions private in a very public place. How could one officer pick out anything unusual in this horde?

Family Court cases had the potential for as much violence as criminal ones. Why the hell weren't more officers here, scanning the crowd, walking about like goddamn lifeguards at the beach to make sure no one was drowning?

Lupo twisted her arm behind her back. "Move." He pushed Taina toward a corner window overlooking Sherman Avenue.

Traffic crawled by. People came and went. Life went on as usual. Shots could ring out anywhere around there, anytime and even in the short interval she'd been here, Taina was always looking for an exit. But there was none.

"What did you tell them?" he snarled.

"My conversations with clients are confidential." Taina prepared one of the tricks she'd practiced with Arnaldo to give her time to run toward the officer.

Lupo was too chunky, his legs too short, and his body too muscle bound to move as fast as she could. His weapon of choice was not a gun, so she wouldn't get it in the back. Anything was better than being bitten.

Lupo jerked her arm and pain shot through the elbow. "Don't give me your official crap. I want to know what you told them."

She fell against him. What spell could augment a head butt under the chin? A good swift kick in the nuts or stomp on his foot would likely be as effective, especially given the luck she was having this week.

He twisted her elbow until it threatened to dislocate. She couldn't get near enough to do anything.

"That she should be given some education, some job training." No lie, just omissions. "It's not my decision anyway."

"It isn't your business either."

She leaned closer to relieve the pressure on her elbow. Would he dare try and bite her in public? Did it matter? Even if he was arrested, she'd be changed.

"I don't play nice like Raul. If you come anywhere near me, or my people, I'll have to invite you to join us." He gave one final jerk on her arm, then disappeared into the crowd, leaving her slumped into an orange molded plastic seat, crying in pain.

No one noticed. She looked like the rest of *les miserables* in this pit of despair. Taina stood up to Raul and twice he'd backed away. Was Lupo bluffing? She'd find out in two weeks.

~ * ~

"Here you go." Simone handed her a cup of high-test coffee—black.

Taina swallowed two aspirin and gagged from the combination of bitter dust and bitter brew. Her head sagged like a lead weight.

"You never recovered from last week's adventures and this week started out with a short fuse that just burned down." Sandy pressed a cold cloth to the back of Taina's neck.

She needed to immerse her elbow in a cup of ice, but how could she explain not reporting an assault and threat after a hearing?

But if she'd called for help and fingered Lupo, *Las Tombas* would be all over her as soon as she took one step out of the courthouse. They might even come in here after her, and that wasn't fair to any of the court employees, especially her co-workers.

If she went on that home visit, the entire team would be in danger. Arnaldo, having held off the pair of gang leaders for years, would know what to do.

Waves of nausea swept over her. She was sick. The situation was sick. What the were and the dhampir were doing was sick. The world was sick. Could any of it could be cured?

"Let me try and get something done while the medicine kicks in." Taina went to her office and worked using the dim light from her computer.

Five more hours to go, seven before the moon got out of this crazy cycle and things would settle down. Plenty of time for something else to go wrong. She should have just stayed home for all the good being in court had done.

After re-writing the same paragraph three times she gave up and buried her face in her hands.

She'd only been working here three weeks, and if it weren't for the fact her co-workers were seriously kind women, she'd have been fired. If this trend continued, it would do more harm than just letting her mother, father, and sister rest in peace.

"Taina, how are you doing?" Sandy brought her some files.

"Better, thanks." No way would she let them pick up for her again.

Simone carried in a plastic bag. "How you feelin'? I got you some salad and soup."

Their kindness and sisterhood brought tears to her eyes. "Good. Ready to work. Monday, I treat for lunch."

Simone unpacked the food. "Staffing this courthouse office is always a problem because most people can't take the pressure, the politics, or the intensity of clients right out of the ER or jail cell. They like being over there." She pointed to the home office of the Victim Advocacy Center, to have 'distance' from the clients.

"There aren't too many with your knowledge and skill, Taina. And your dedication. In the couple of weeks you've been here, I swear there has been more strange shit than I've ever seen. But you caught that nasty 'ole cat by the tail and swung it. Slow down, take it easy, or you'll burn out."

"Simone, I…"

"It's Friday afternoon in mid-summer. The lawyers and judges want to get to the Hamptons or the Jersey Shore. Next disaster is mine. Tidy up your paperwork."

How could she let Simone pretend she wasn't working extra to make up for the slack? "I've caused nothing but problems since the day I started."

"Girl, this place is nothing but trouble." Simone massaged Taina's neck, then went back to the pile on her own desk.

You should only know. She ate, drank, and distracted herself, trying not to think about dilemmas and decisions.

"See you Monday." Simone hung on the doorframe. "Better leave early. Last week you wound up meeting with that detective and got into that subway mayhem."

"I'm almost done with this report."

"I hope you'll reconsider and see your man this weekend." She winked and shimmied.

"Maybe we'll get together." Let them think this was a romantic fling. By Monday Taina needed to figure out a way to tell them the gangs were tailing her. Arnaldo might have some idea of how to let it be known without blowing the whole thing apart.

She switched the message machine to the emergency weekend call line. She filed her papers, threw out the rest of the food and cold coffee, turned out the lights, dialed down the air conditioning. Checked the hallways. Locked the door. The fact this office was down a dead end corridor hadn't bothered her before, but all the offices were empty now. Silence sent prickles of fear down her back.

Tania paced in front of the elevator with her phone in one hand, and her keys, two poking between the middle and ring finger, in the other. She'd never take the stairs again, even just one floor.

The car ran express to the first floor, courtesy of the cleaning man's override key. He acknowledged her stare with a nod.

She checked for auras or any color flags—some of *Las Tombas* were decrepit like this fellow: hunch-backed, balding with what hair he had left greasy and yellow. Blue uniform, black boots, belt, no chains.

Her gaze lingered over his scalp. Artifact from the gray-blond hair caused some interference, but it was not contiguous over the pate or the back of his neck. A grizzled, gray mundane.

"Goodnight." She bolted through the lobby, empty save a couple of court officers on high alert, chatting about the goddamn Yankees. Shit, the place could be overrun, and they'd let the wolf man escort her right out.

Out the doors, down the marble stairs. The August blast furnace hit her. The ever-present smell of garbage from overflowing trashcans irritated her still tender stomach. No subway tonight.

Her hand shot up. The gypsy cab stopped.

"How much to Prospect and 149th?" She didn't care, but it allowed time for an aura scan before she got in. Taina checked him out like a thief sizing up a victim.

"Ten dollars." The green kufi cap with brown lightning bolts embroidered in was a bit of a baffle over his head, but this guy was covered by a tunic and pants she couldn't find any skin save his sandal clad feet.

Gray swirled around the gas pedal. "Miss? Yes or no?"

As he faced her, she examined his neck and chest—so much gray it filled the front seat.

"Yes. Sorry. I'm tired."

He chuckled. "Long week?" His teeth were like ivory chips, and though crooked, the smile was genuine, beautifully mundane.

"For sure." She settled into the back seat.

The cab made a U-turn across rush hour traffic. Her seat belt locked when he stopped short and tires squealed.

For a short while, all she had to worry about were other cars and utility poles.

Chapter Twenty
Call to Duty

Taina's head threatened to burst. She knocked everything off the cluttered nightstand until her hands found the rubber stopper, unscrewed the cap, and downed the whole bottle of potion. It might kill her, but that would end the misery.

A firebrand burned its way from gullet to belly, but within minutes the smoggy haze dispersed like smoke leaving everything sharp, clear, the spaces in between, no matter how narrow, open, and bursting with fine detail.

Handy. She'd be able to detect Lupo's tobacco laced musky odor or Raul's seductive licorice scat emanating from musty alleyway. It was a relief to finally open the blinds and let light into the room. Flashes of fairy glamour sparkled on the ground around the garbage pails. Instead of a mingling sense of rot, each smell emanating from the containers remained distinct. Though foul, the odors of banana peels, fish, and sour milk were easier to take by themselves.

Vibrant colors popped off yellow awnings on the strip of stores across the street from her apartment. Red stoplights flashed danger, green ones blinked reassurance, jewel-toned Afro-Caribbean apparel sauntered along, stretched over butts and breasts of women of every shape, size, and age.

Whatever she'd overdosed on was miraculous or psychotropic, maybe both. Everyone here was alive and out and about in the bright sunshine, and she could be one of them again.

Zeus scrambled around Taina's feet, his nails clicking as he ran in circles anticipating a kiss and hug, a walk, and curling up on the couch—in that order.

"Let's walk to Arnaldo's before it gets too late."

His tongue kissed her cheek like a sloppy lover. As long as he was with her, Zeus was content.

She changed out of proper court attire into shorts, a tee, and sandals, normal, free—though she'd still have to walk a gauntlet to Paloma for some dinner. If she was going to ruin Arnaldo's night, she might as well feed the guy first.

"Where's Miguel?" the counter guy asked as he packed her order

"Working, I guess." Taina waited for him to make change and put a tip in the jar.

"This is more than enough for two." Could he actually think she and Miguel were an item? She didn't offer any explanation because whey should she?

In front of his place with *pollo guisado* in hand, Taina tried to get through Arnaldo's shield. The gate didn't budge, the latch appeared rusted and frozen shut. Some of that enhancement on her windows, already sticky from humidity, wouldn't hurt.

He always seemed to know when someone was trying to enter. His head peeked out the door. "Come in. Wassup?"

The latch clicked. The gate swung wide.

"I brought dinner. From Paloma." She let Zeus off the leash, and he ran in circles around them, yapping.

Arnaldo took the bag. "What happened?"

"Who said anything happened?"

"I can tell by the look on your face."

Was he psychic, or was she just a lousy liar? "Let's eat first. No use ruining our appetites."

Zeus padded next to her as they walked out to the back where a few kids were playing basketball despite the heat.

"Night, Arnaldo." As the boys passed by, each one pounded his shoulder or met his high five.

He brushed dust off the top of a white plastic table tucked under a rusted awning. She unpacked the food, paper plates, plastic knives and forks, cold soda, and napkins.

Eyes narrowed, he watched. "Lupo causing trouble today?"

She blew dirt off a chair and sat. "Here are some hand wipes. You must be connected to his information flow."

He tore open the square packet with his teeth and cleaned his mitts. "No, but after you told me about that kid, I figured something was going down."

"The hearing was today, in Family Court. It's bad enough when it's an older person, but she's only sixteen—with the intellect of five-year old."

"You can't help a zombie." Arnaldo took a bite of chicken, spit the bones into a napkin.

"Is that how you justify everything?" Taina picked at her rice.

He stared at her for what seemed like five minutes before responding. "Am I wrong?"

"She's sixteen and has no capacity to make that kind of decision. They're going to track down her 'uncle' and want me to go along."

He dropped his fork. "Take yourself off that case, right away. Lupo can breach any security."

"He already did. After the hearing. Just like Raul did the last time I was out on official business." Taina braced for his tirade.

Arnaldo stroked his chin. "Normally, he'd just let this kid go to stay out of trouble. She's the bait."

"Everyone is in danger here. Me, the kid, all the court employees."

He eyed her so intently she turned away. "They both want you bad enough to risk blowing their cover. You know how many detectives are looking for a reason to arrest them?"

Taina dared not bring up Michael Kelly. "Is this what convinced Serena to leave?"

He winced. "Serena was just another witch they'd kill in a New York minute. Now you're at the top of the ladder. That job will constantly put you in contact with some stinking thing they're masterminding.

"Quit. Come live here. Do legal advocacy work at *Sonrisa.* Together we'll have a chance."

"So you can be the one to claim victory?" She'd never admit it, but the thought of his protection was the only comfort she'd felt all day.

He laughed without mirth, only resignation that sputtered out like a candle in the breeze. "I'm not looking to breed a master race. I just want to die in peace—of natural causes."

Was it all part of the game? "I should have expected trouble today. My moon was void this morning."

The elusive moment of détente passed. The old arm-waving Arnaldo roared back. "You can try astrology. You can try The Tarot. You can try crystals. You can try *Santería,* voodoo, *brujería.* They're not going to wait until the moon phase is correct for spell casting, or your planets are in the right house, or the right card comes up in your spread."

She couldn't hold back on this any longer. Taina stood to leave. "Yet you defy Lupe and Raul over and over. What's your secret?"

He looked up, then down, to the side, and bit his lower lip, until he couldn't avoid her stare anymore. "I'm stronger than you are physically and magically. And we have a mutual pact not to disclose certain…past transgressions. You're packing some major power inside behind that pretty, petite body of yours—and they know you're afraid to use it.

Arnaldo took her hand with an expression on his face one might see at a deathbed scene. "You must agree to join an alliance with me. If you're taken against your will, those powers will weaken."

A novel pick-up line. "I have Zeus."

"That stinking mutt and your wimpy spells are like mosquito bites. They'll hit you as hard as they can, until you break, then fight each other to the finish."

Taina got a whiff of Arnaldo's spicy bullshit buried in disingenuous advice. Whose side was he really on? What was he hiding?

"Come, Zeus." The dog leaped to his feet and ran to her.

Arnaldo mopped the back of his neck with a towel. "I'll take you home."

"No. I can take care of myself."

He walked her to the gate the kids had left open. It slammed shut. He gestured, and a circle of pulsing energy re-sealed behind her. "So you like being a damsel locked in an ivory tower?"

"Fuck you, Arnaldo." Bold, bitchy, Bronx was getting easier every day.

Taina blended into the streets teeming with people trying to get some relief from the heat oozing from the surrounding brick and mortar. Music blared from open windows. Fireflies, ever resilient even in this urban wasteland, clustered over any patch of weeds they could find.

Zeus sniffed in a patch of brown grass and cocked his head as specks of glamour skittered about. Fairies shifted into bugs. She'd have to adapt, just like everything else around here.

Bridge Rat fluttered to the perimeter gate around her apartment as she unlocked it. "Good evening, Lady Taina."

No matter how bad her mood, the talking pigeon never failed to crack her up. "Meet me upstairs."

"I'd be positively delighted." He fluttered to the eaves.

By the time she got up, he was pecking at the window. She disengaged the lock, removed the broomstick chock, sliced open her own protective ring. Bridge Rat fluttered in, transformed mid-air and tumbled gracefully head over heels as he materialized.

A sumptuous breeze tousled the curtains. Zeus leaped onto the chair she kept there for him to look out, propped his paws on the sill, and scanned the street below.

"So, my dear, what can I tell you?" Bridge Rat collected himself, shook out his cape, and exercised his wings.

"Raul Rivera, Lupo Lopez, and Arnaldo Arroyo are all vying for me. Why? I'm a magickal nobody."

Bridge Rat fluttered to the window and perched on the sill, legs crossed, cape folded under him like a cushion. "Look around at the streets, schools, and housing projects named after those who dared to battle evildoers. They were far less powerful than the White Witch. Fear not, my lady, the fae will assist you as much as our laws allow."

A very dramatic speech, obviously rehearsed. Fairies loved theatrics.

"So I must choose the lesser of three evils? Become something I'm not. Do things I feel are wrong?"

Bridge Rat leaped onto the floor with a surprisingly heavy thud. "I exist in your world as a common pigeon. My kin choose the forms of insects, rodents, whatever set of wings or legs will enable them to fight, to win back at least a portion of what was once our realm."

He tossed his cape so that it draped evenly, raised his chin to peer up at her in defiance. "Canadian geese are the stupidest, dirtiest birds around. Who do you think helped effect the Miracle on the Hudson when two of the daft creatures were sucked into the plane engine? The Fae. How were they rewarded? Barely escaped being rounded up and gassed, my brethren did. Do we worry about being something we're not? No! All for the common good. Whatever it takes."

She squatted on the floor so she could see eye-to-eye with the fairy. Her heart hurt. "I didn't mean to offend you, Bridge Rat. I'm confused and scared. I never expected to be a heroine." She sat back on her bum with a thump and crossed her legs to relieve the ache in her muscles.

Bridge Rat half-fluttered, half-walked over and perched on her left knee. Zeus scampered down and rested his head on her right. Taina tousled the dog's soft fur and gently traced the delicate yet firm, muscular line of the fairy's back and wing sockets.

Zeus licked her hand.

Bridge Rat stroked her arm, took her hand in his palm, and encircled it with his long, gnarled fingers. "Your mother empowered you to unite the good folk to fight the dark forces which plundered this fine forest world and defile it still."

"How do you know all this?"

Bridge Rat's firm squeeze stopped her hand from shaking. "The Fae have been around long enough." He chuckled. "Others who practice The Crafts—in whatever form—no doubt have divined it."

Zeus leaned up on one paw to kiss the tears off her face. A dose of comfort, but neither her familiar nor fairy honor guard could wipe away the reality. "So what do I do now?"

"Ask for guidance. Answers will come."

Taina got to her knees. "I need a shower—and an air conditioner."

"I can provide none of that. But I can stand guard with Zeus to ensure a restful night and cool zephyr for clarity of dreams." Bridge Rat flapped to the window and sat, tailor-style, on the sill, his legs curled up inside the sash.

Zeus hopped onto his chair, then crawled next to him.

Taina showered and put on her nightgown, not wanting to be naked in front of a male fairy. She brewed chamomile tea with honey and sipped, in front of the candles burning to *Yemayá* and *San Miguel*. She smelled, for the first time, Zeus's warm, smoky magick on a whiff of dog.

A glorious breeze scattered flecks of glamour from Bridge Rat's cape.

"Good night." She let sleep take her.

She left her body and walked about the apartment, past the sentinels in the window. Her mother in corporeal form, sat cross-legged on the floor inside Tania's sacred circle.

For the first time since she died, Antonella looked at Taina, anguish painted on a ghostly pale face, back-lit like a tragic mask. Could this be the moment she'd been waiting for?

"Mama, help me!" She reached out, desperate to make contact or glean some insight, or to receive some instruction from her mother, but Antonella turned and walked away, chanting

"White light, shine bright.
Banish the night.
Bring back the light.
White light, shine bright.
Banish the night.
Bring back the light.
White light, shine bright.
Banish the night.
Bring back the light."

Chapter Twenty-One
The Ivory Tower

Morning light sealed the veil, leaving Taina on the side of the living, her mother once again a memory, or a dream, which had offered no advice or solace. Now, she knew the chant, which had come to her the night she'd banished the dog pack had been imparted by her mother before she died. Had recalling it been a blessing or a curse? A command or a wish? A charge or a warning?

Bridge Rat yawned and stretched. "Fare thee well, Lady Taina. Rested and rejuvenated, I trust."

"No. Bridge Rat." She walked to the windowsill and rubbed Zeus's ears. "I've been installed in a position for which I'm not qualified."

The dog flopped on his back and let her scratch his belly before jumping down. He waited by the door for his walk. Just like any other day.

"Of course, you're qualified. Ever vigilant, we remain at your service." Bridge Rat swirled his cloak and disintegrated. Fairy dust rematerialized in his avian form. He fluttered between the window guards and to his eave for a well-earned respite.

A void opened inside her, a yawning loneliness, a yearning for a real person to talk to when fear surrounded her.

Taina dressed quickly, hurried down to the reality of an early Saturday morning of bottles, an odd shoe, overflowing garbage. The shopkeepers swept and hosed off the sidewalks to take back some control, though their agency was tenuous.

The fish-store proprietor smiled and nodded as she and Zeus passed. The bakery patrons and counter girls waved. Taina was already recognized, accepted. If they only knew what her presence here might bring to bear.

Hot sun scorched her eyes. There was enough shade in the park for mundane relief. Zeus, thrilled, sniffed everything he could reach and strained against the leash at every opportunity, barking at every shadow.

She sat on her usual bench to study Ritual Rock and tried to divine any spiritual presence. A fuzzy aura, golden, warm, lay just beyond her reach. Instead of comfort, the smell of spring rain reinforced her loneliness, her despair, her confusion.

Josefa could help her connect with her mother's spirit. "Let's go, Zeus."

They walked on the shady side of the street, past the early morning shoppers with their two-wheeled carts, the leather-clad guy on his duded-up motorcycle, and women laden with huge bundles headed to Laundromats.

She was not the first patron at the *botánica.* A group of women prayed while Josefa lit yellow and orange candles in tribute to the river goddess *Oshun*, Our Lady of Charity.

"Desculpe." Taina turned to leave.

"No te vayas, nena," a wizened old woman croaked.

"Entra, Taina. We have completed our daily prayers. How can I help you today?" Josefa took her hand and led her in. "Hello, little doggy." She patted Zeus and went to her counter.

"I need advice."

"Sit." Josefa pointed to the chair and got some water for Zeus. A marmalade tabby, bigger than the dog, poked out from under the black-velvet curtain, tail curling in disgust at the invading canine. *"Vete, Canela."*

The cat disappeared.

One by one the women embraced and departed, rosaries and beads draped around their necks, packages of herbs and bottles of oil in their hands.

Finally, she and Josefa were alone. "Trouble with Arnaldo?"

"Just trouble."

Josefa stroked Tania's hands and closed her eyes. "You're in pain. Confused. Perhaps the charts will show us something."

Josefa reached under the counter and pulled out a laptop. "Birthdate?"

The contrast of the decrepit shop and a brand new computer seemed surreal.

"October 31, 1980."

Music played as the computer booted. Josefa tapped the keys. "Time?"

"Ten PM."

A few more taps. "Hmm, very interesting."

"What?"

"Scorpio is a water sign." She copied something onto a scratch pad and tallied. "But your signature is Sagittarius. Water and fire."

"I've tried to douse those memories all my life." This was hardly a revelation.

Josefa printed the chart and pointed with the tip of her pencil. "Taurus inconjunct with Mercury—in retrograde so it feels like you'll never get there. You're moon squares Uranus, so there are lots of battles in your life."

Taina couldn't make any sense out of the tangle of red, blue, green geometric figures. "Sounds pretty hopeless."

"That Mercury is retrograde, always making adaptability a struggle." Josefa's eyes narrowed as she read, scrawled, and did more math. "Eleventh house, friends, hopes, dreams—empty. Eighth, rebirth, regeneration, sexual identity." She paused, looked at Taina. "Empty."

"Great, on the decline, no friends, no sex, no chance." How many people had committed suicide from astrology this frank?

"Josefa, yesterday my moon was void, of course. Many things happened, but three, now I have three…men threatening me. I want nothing to do with them, but we keep getting thrown together. Arnaldo offers me some protection and accepts my practices, but I don't know if I can trust him."

"*Bueno*. Your north node is in the same house as your moon. That means a calamity or crisis surrounds things affected by it."

"Is there anything good in this chart?" She sat at the counter and placed her palms against the *santera's* upturned ones.

Josefa squeezed both hands. "The influence of Jupiter and Venus compels you to find stability, closure. Also truth. You seek truth."

Her anger boiled over. "Josefa, you've told me what I already know."

She dropped Taina's hands. "I can't do this for you, *nena*."

This was useless, a stock reading. "I'm seeing my mother, hearing her. I smell her and see glimmers behind the veil."

Josefa picked up Taina's hands again, closed her eyes. "You are at a crossroads, and your mother is reaching out to help you. Are you taking your potion? Have you done what I asked to honor *Yemayá?*"

"Yes."

"Bathe in the sea. Let the sand run through your fingers. Place some in the bottom of a shell, filled with salt water. Ask *Yemayá* for guidance." Josefa stood, ending the session.

Taina gave her a $20.00 bill.

"Gracias, amor. Bring me Arnaldo's date and time of birth. His chart may provide the answers you seek about his suitability as a friend—or a lover. I'm tired from so much work this morning." She yawned and rubbed her right hip.

"Let's go, Zeus." Taina hadn't disconnected his leash, and it trailed as he stretched and walked to the door. It was still stuck shut.

~ * ~

Taina waited until Simone had her coffee and finished her bacon, egg, and cheese on a roll before she knocked.

She pointed to a chair. "You look like you're carrying a big weight."

"When I got out of Family Court on Friday, the man impersonating Zoraida's uncle cornered me."

Simone's eyes widened, and her chest heaved. "In the waiting room? Where were the court officers?"

"By the time I figured out what was happening, the man was gone." She hated to lie.

"You should've reported it right away so they could detain him. If he goes into court next time and says he's the uncle, it's your word against his. Plus, he could come after you."

Simone picked up her phone. "I need Grayson up here to take a report. Someone roughed up an advocate in Family Court waiting last week. Yes, that's right and you guys gotta keep a watch on things over there. Uh, huh. Uh, huh. They're all criminals."

Hiding behind the protection of the court wouldn't work in the magickal world. But Taina would have to play this game.

She went back into her office, did more paperwork. Simone took the first case. Taina paced. Drank coffee. Drank more coffee.

The uniformed officer came in while Sandy was on the phone. Taina waved him inside.

"You the one who had the problem?" He could barely get his hands into his pockets what with all that crap on the belt: gun, holster, bullets, flashlight, summons book, cellphone, belly.

"Yes, Taina Aponte. Friday morning, about ten-thirty. After a hearing involving a teenage runaway, a man accosted me from behind, and told me to back off and leave her alone. Then he left."

"You didn't see what he looked like?" Disgust registered on his face. "Why did you wait until now? Where was the court officer?"

"He was seated at the entrance to the fishbowl. I was in the far corner courtroom. He was stocky, taller than me, gruff voice." Keep it vague, no untruths but not the full truth.

"We'll review surveillance video and put out a bulletin to all the staff warning them to report incidents of intimidation immediately. Next time, don't be a hero."

She walked him outside. Sandy was registering a client. Simone's door was still closed.

Sandy handed Taina the clipboard with the client's name.

"Ms. Alvarez, I'm Taina Aponte. Please come in." She gestured to the chair in front of her desk and read the aura as the woman passed. Gray. Thank whatever god, *orisha, santo,* or savior was in charge for the day.

Would they keep the werewolves at bay tonight, when they came out to play under the light of the full moon?

Chapter Twenty-Two
First Alarm

Troubled dreams, always the same, of smoke and flames, screams, sirens, the smell of gasoline. Taina awoke gasping, but it wasn't asthma or the heat. Her back hurt, her legs stung with pins and needles from being curled in an odd position on the sofa. An old movie was playing, but she couldn't recall its name or the actors. Zeus yapped and jumped on top of her. Flickers of light danced in the windows, yellow, then orange. Spirals of smoke coalesced into black clouds. She touched the glass and pulled away as her fingertips burned. Flames licked the façade. *I will not be trapped like last time.*

She grabbed Zeus then ran to the window that she'd propped slightly ajar and knocked the broomstick chock away. Then came the cough, insistent, like she'd inhaled dust and couldn't clear it.

She covered her mouth and nose with the crook of her elbow and charged to the door, felt it from top to bottom before opening. Dark mist already filled the stairway. Smoke detectors screeched.

Señora Duarte came out of her apartment, banging the doors and walls. *"¡Fuego! Despierte!* Get out!"

Hugging the dog against her chest, Taina lurched down. Sirens wailed. Horns blared. She hacked, her throat closed, and she fell backward onto the stairs in a free-fall flashback.

Thick smoke, her hair singed, screams, her mother's arms, fresh air as Mama kicked out the window, her mother's last kiss, flying, thudding into the man's arms.

He caught her as if she'd been tossed like Daddy used to play with her, not for her life. "Shit, what do I do with it?" He smelled like sweat, reefer, tobacco. His green eyes darted.

"Give it to a fireman! We've got to get the hell out of here."

More screams, sirens. The fireman held her against his chest, elbows poked, water sprayed, droplets fell like rain, steam hissed off burning wood, metal clanked.

"She threw the kid from that window. Someone get her into an ambulance. We're going into the apartment."

Another pair of arms, a stiff, hard coat, heat, soot stained face, funny hat. Clanking. "You're okay."

"You're okay, miss. Just breathe."

Vomit filled her mouth. She flung the oxygen mask to the side and spit into the street like a bum. How had she gotten out of the stairwell?

Terror snaked through her gut. *"Señora Duarte?"*

The bunker-coated firefighter led her to the perimeter gate.

"She's fine. Bring the dog over here. There are less fumes and smoke."

Taina shook like a tree branch in the wind. "He's after me."

"Who?"

"I'm not sure." She swayed, dizzy from the smoke, fear. Muddled, confused, tired of telling outright lies.

"I'll get the fire marshal. Tell him what you know." The man was old enough that he could very well have been the same fireman who'd been at the scene a few blocks from here—way back then. "You knew how to get out, crawling with one hand over your mouth and one over the dog's."

Heavy boots clunked as he dragged a hose out of the way.

Had she really done that?

"Wait outside. They're inspecting the interior of the building for damage now. Good thing those upstairs windows were closed. The fire was confined to the trashcan in the alleyway, but the smoke headed right up into your apartment."

"I need to talk to detective Michael Kelly from the 49th Precinct. He knows me very well and said he should be called anytime."

"This is not his jurisdiction. If the marshal thinks it's necessary, he'll call a detective from the 41st." The firefighter removed his hat. His hair stood up like spikes on his head. "Ask the fire marshal to call your detective friend, okay?"

"Yeah, sure." Taina hugged the quivering dog to her chest.

"That's my friend. Let me through, goddamnit!" Arnaldo tussled with a group of firemen and police officers. "Taina! Taina, are you okay?"

He was submerged in the sea of gawkers who'd poured out their apartments in the dead of night like crazed spectators at a prizefight. Did any of them realize it was full moon and the weres were snarfing around just waiting to leap?

She raised her hand in acknowledgement and went to the cop standing just inside perimeter gate. "Can you let my friend in?"

"Is that the guy who's after you?"

News traveled fast. "No, he'd never do anything like that."

"He can come in after the marshal is done with his investigation." The cop gestured for people to move back.

No one budged.

Arnaldo pushed to the front of the crowd. Cupped hands formed a bullhorn around his mouth. "You okay?"

"Just wheezing a bit." And yelling wasn't helping. "Come upstairs when they let you in."

"Sir, please, we've got an active crime scene here and need to talk to the witnesses first. Everyone is safe."

The crowd of black and blue coalesced, and Arnaldo disappeared.

All she cared about now was finding out who was the other voice, the one telling Jesús to get rid of "it," meaning her, the five-year-old whose mother, father, and sister were already dead.

"This blaze was started to alarm, not to kill." The marshal, very official with his title emblazoned across the back of his jacket, pointed to a pitted steel drum—the type the homeless set fires in to keep themselves warm on street corners or in abandoned buildings.

Situated in between Taina's windows on the side of the house, it was out of view and far from the rat/fairy outpost in the front yard.

Charred rags, still stinking of gasoline, hung over the sides, spent after they'd sent a warning flare directly from Lupo to Taina, leaving shingles singed and sooty. The foam the firemen had sprayed looked like blackened scum, and the whole area smelled like wet charcoal. Sand scrunched under her feet.

Señora Duarte sat on the front steps, hugging her knees and crying. "This was our dream house. My husband and I spent every penny we had to buy it. He only lived a year after we moved in. *Bendito,* he got killed in a car accident."

Taina squeezed in next to her.

Señora sobbed into sleeve of her sooty bathrobe.

"Let's go inside." Taina helped her up, and they huddled together in the downstairs apartment for a miserable pajama party.

"Who would do this to me? I don't bother anyone." The landlady cried softy on Taina's shoulder.

Guilt stung her like an uncovered nest of ants.

"I have no idea." She patted the woman on the back.

"I have nowhere else to go."

"You don't need to go anywhere *Señora* Duarte." *I'm the one who needs to leave.*

The fire marshal rapped on the molding of the open door. "Miss, you indicated to a firefighter that…"

She leaped to her feet and steered him out into the hall, away from her landlady's vulnerable ears. "She's very upset. Can we talk outside?"

"So, you think someone set this fire to get you?"

Taina had uttered those words in a post-flashback stupor and now had to deal with the consequences. "I work in the courthouse as a victim's advocate. There are a lot of people who'd like to get me. Which is why I asked that Detective Kelly be called. He knows how unique my situation is."

"Yeah, right. Well, you can ask the police officers to notify him." He poked his head inside her landlady's door. "Ladies, leave the windows open so any smoke inside dissipates. There is no structural damage, just some cosmetic repairs needed to the exterior. Call the insurance company about filing a claim. The police will have a patrol car here while the investigation is going on."

Señora Duarte shot a long, disapproving glance at Taina. The woman spoke more English than she let on and had heard enough to suspect.

Taina paused in the doorway of the building to watch boots shuffling, hoses grating as they were rewound. Ladders clanked. Radios chirped. Strobes flashed. Firefighters closed off the fire hydrant. Cops wrapped yellow crime scene tape around the entrance to the alleyway.

She dialed the 49th Precinct from the privacy of her apartment. "I need to speak to Detective Michael Kelly. My name is Taina Aponte. Someone set a fire outside my house tonight. He told me to call him, anytime, if I had any information about another arson he was investigating."

"What is your address, ma'am?"

"2330 Prospect Avenue."

"That's the 41st, not the 49th. Didn't the officers on duty explain jurisdiction?"

"I work for the court and know all about jurisdiction. This is related to a case Detective Kelly has investigated for years. He'd want to know. Can you please call and say Taina needs to see him right away."

"It's three-thirty in the morning, ma'am." Her dismissive voice was reminiscent of the fire marshal's.

"I'm fully aware of that, but Detective Kelly made a point of saying I could contact him anytime."

The phone clicked in her ear. She'd have to go over there tomorrow and find him.

"Taina! Taina, you upstairs?" Arnaldo's footsteps thudded in the foyer.

"Shhh! Come up. *Señora* Duarte is going to throw me out of here right now."

He was upstairs with his hand was on her arm before she finished the sentence.

"How the hell do you do that?"

"Do what?"

"That gliding thing."

"I'm just fucking fast."

"You're fucking full of shit."

Arnaldo looked hurt. "I hear all the sirens and the commotion and know you're involved—because I have some telepathy with you. Then I run over to help, and you insult me."

To continue this would be descending to Arnaldo-like behavior. "Okay, I'm sorry—and very upset. What do you think of Lupo's full-moon mischief?"

He concealed himself behind a curtain so no one could see his silhouette from outside. "You saw Lupo?"

"Why are you hiding over there? The whole fucking neighborhood saw—and heard—you trying to get past the cops. And no, I didn't see Lupo, but there is that case and there was that incident at *Sonrisa* last week."

He wrinkled his nose and shimmied his hips. "Did the whole fucking neighborhood come to see if you were trapped?"

The female impersonation was as bad as his jokes. "No, why should they risk their lives? Like I'm risking *Señora* Duarte's."

He walked over, brushed the soot off her nose and smoothed her hair. "Come stay with me Taina. You're not safe here." His voice rasped like gravel. His touch was gentle, seductive.

A chill ran through her. "If I run, they'll chase me, overtake me, change me. If I face them and fight back, maybe they'll realize I'm serious."

He returned to his window post. "Heart attacks are serious. And if they don't kill you, you're changed after having one. You can't do this alone, Taina."

Could this be part of a plan? Some pact he had with Lupo and

Raul to "not let her fuck things up?" Lupo and Raul act out, then Arnaldo to the rescue?

"I'm not alone. I have Zeus and the fairies." She paced.

"Oh yeah, like you, a Westie, and a bunch of three-feet-tall, winged crusaders have a chance against guns, knives, dark magick, and two legions of loyal followers who will do anything their leaders tell them to. Anything. C'mon, Taina, you've got to get serious."

"If I back down it would mean quitting my job."

"Lupo doesn't play it smooth like Raul. Especially at the full moon. By next month, if this case doesn't work out his way, he'll go even further."

"How can I get off the case, knowing the danger someone else covering it will be in?"

"You can't help that kid. No one can." Arnaldo moved way too close, especially since she was in her nightgown. Just like a Raul Rivera move, at 4:00 AM, in the dark, after an attempt on her life.

Taina pulled away. "I have lots of options to consider." Like trying to negotiate a truce with each leg of the magickal triangle separately, but Arnaldo would ridicule her for even suggesting it.

The knock at the door was opportune. "NYPD."

She ran downstairs before *Señora* Duarte answered. "Detective Sparagna, 41st Precinct. Are you Taina Aponte?"

"Yes, please come upstairs." She turned midway. "I don't suppose anyone told you I'd asked to speak to Detective Michael Kelly."

"Sure did, and he just ran right into my back."

Kelly waved. "Kinda crowded here. Can we keep moving?"

Of all the men now standing in her apartment while she was soot-stained and wearing a nightgown with no underwear, Kelly's face was the most comforting, probably because he remembered her as a soot-stained five-year-old wearing pajamas.

"Thank you for coming, Detective Kelly. I'm sorry they had to wake you up."

Arnaldo stood behind the cops performing a jiggling, pantomime mimicry.

She resisted the temptation to give him the finger.

The other cop looked at her with a what-am-I-a-piece-of-gum-on-the-bottom-of-your-shoe expression and flashed his shield. "I called Detective Kelly because of information indicating you knew who did this and it was related to a case in his precinct many years ago."

"This is my friend, Arnaldo Reyes. Please sit down." She stood in the middle of her circle, so they didn't tramp through it, but Arnaldo deliberately goosed by her in retaliation.

She flashed him the prettiest, most disingenuous smile possible. "Would any of you like a drink?"

After the chorus of "No thanks" she headed for the bedroom. "Excuse me one minute. I ran out without a bathrobe." Surely arson detectives were used to interviewing people in even greater states of undress, but three men staring at her tits was getting too creepy.

Once under cover, now sweating bullets, she struggled to open the windows. Each man joined her, and soon they were all sitting around like a group of friends getting ready to watch a movie.

She kept to the mundane facts. "I'm officially involved, as an advocate, in an assault case that involves Lupo Lopez. He's not happy about it. Then this happened."

Arnaldo winced.

Taina sensed a bomb detonate. He had his own plans for world domination and it depended upon placating Raul and Lupo.

Kelly, clearly the senior detective, nodded. "This has all the hallmarks of *Las Tombas* and their brand of witness intimidation. Are you snooping around doing detective work on your own?"

"No, but the clients I deal with aren't the wholesome, let's-talk-out-our-differences type." Now that was totally the truth.

"Taina, it's an odd coincidence that this is happening to you. I mean, it's like a repeat." He didn't seem to believe her.

Arnaldo cleared his throat and shifted in his seat.

"What?" she asked.

"The smoky odor is getting to me." He got up, paced, looked out the window.

Sparagna took back his jurisdiction. "Taina. Detective Kelly briefed me, and I'll read all his files. I suggest you recuse yourself from the case in question to avoid more trouble. We could consider a sting to try and catch Lupo, but that will take some time to initiate and only if you're willing."

"I'll speak to my boss tomorrow about taking me off the case." A sting meant surveillance, with her as a decoy, and this duck wasn't interested swimming with the alligators.

"Yes, but undercover we may finally nab him." Sparagna rubbed his hands together. "Think about it."

The two men stood. Taina took Sparagna's card.

"Mr. Reyes." Kelly held out his hand.

Arnaldo's reflexes had slowed to those of a stroke victim. Tension crackled in the room until his hand took the detective's. Silence threatened to explode her eardrums as the empathic link to

Arnaldo's fury connected.

Kelly and Sparagna sensed the energy surge. Like most mundanes, their brains weren't open or sufficiently developed to understand and just assumed Arnaldo was acting crazy. They'd likely ride away asking, "What was up his ass?"

The car had just disappeared around the corner of 149th Street and the Bruckner Expressway before Arnaldo exploded. "You've been talking to the cops trying to dig up dead bones, haven't you?"

She returned fire. "I told you I intended to find the motherfuckers responsible for killing my family and get them arrested. Now it appears that might just happen."

He shot back. "And, if you remember, I told you that wiggling your pretty behind wasn't enough to solve a cold case. But you did it anyway, going to get a bathrobe, after you stood there in a negligee just to pique their interest, then putting on that 'I'm so police-savvy' amateur detective act."

"A negligee? It's an old lady nightie." She ripped open her robe. Buttons scattered all over the floor. "I'm not a sex kitten. I'm a pissed-off motherfucker and am not going to run away and leave my co-workers, or my clients, to the wolves—or dhampirs."

He held up his hand. "Go ahead. Trust the cops more than me to solve a magickal problem I've dealt with very effectively for the same last thirty years you were living in paradise. With Serena, who also bailed when the situation got to be more than she could control. You go in with the cops and see what happens. Can you spell Witness Protection Program?"

"Arnaldo, I have to figure out a way to work in both magickal and mundane circles."

His breaths came shallow. His fists clenched. "So I guess you want me to go." The jilted-schoolboy look came back.

Spiders of fear crawled down her back. "No, it's 5:00 AM, and it's too dangerous with *Las Tombas* running with the moon. Stay here. We'll figure out what do tomorrow. I need your help, but I have to do things my way."

Zeus, who'd licked most of the soot off his paws and legs, hadn't moved from the windowsill. He jumped down and sat at Arnaldo's feet, tail wagging.

He bent and patted the dog's head. "The boss approves. Okay? I've got the couch. Reinforce your circle, and let's get some sleep."

While he was in the bathroom, she tried to concentrate as hard as she could despite the ideas, emotions, fears, and hope—yes hope, bubbling in her brain. A traditional binding ritual hardly seemed appropriate, given the *Santería* beads and candles next to her implements, the complex web of magickal forces she was confronting, and the unpleasant choices with which she was faced.

Still, she spun a thread of magickal energy with the tiny athame clutched in her right fist.

"Around and around,
So the circle is bound
Protect those within
From harm and from sin."

Taina got Arnaldo a pillow and sheet and traded places, allowing him private time to do whatever he wanted to augment her efforts. By the time she'd washed up, he was snoring on the couch.

She fell into an exhausted sleep but awoke tingling. Zeus slept, heavy and still, in his place near her feet. Arnaldo stood in the doorway watching her.

How dare he come into her room while she lay on top of the covers, her nightgown hitched up over her ass, a specimen to be examined, probed, and used? He might not hurt her physically, but did his deed by emotionally wearing her down, undermining her confidence, pretending to help while enforcing her dependency.

Taina didn't move. Didn't call him out. Didn't even bother to pull the sheet up or the nightgown down

What was the currency this trio used to determine who'd offered the highest bid?

Chapter Twenty-Three
Bronx Beaches and Island Dreams

Taina flipped pancakes, an odd choice at 3:00 PM, but they'd slept the day away. "Don't wait for me. They taste better hot."

"So, you're going to cooperate with the cops on an undercover stakeout?" Arnaldo had calmed down. He poured warmed maple syrup over his stack but didn't dig in.

"Maybe." One of the malevolent bands would spill to the others, and she needed to keep her mouth shut and not offer too many clues until things reached the tipping point. How she'd know when remained to be seen.

She turned the last of the pancakes onto a serving plate and sat at the table with him. "Was the couch comfortable?"

"I can sleep anywhere, anytime. Learned that trick in jail—along with how to do just about anything with an audience." He sliced a triangle into the pile and jabbed it with a fork. "You really want cops crawling up your ass?"

Taina bit her lip to avoid a wisecrack about how he'd been up hers last night. "If it means keeping *Señora* Duarte, my clients, and my co-workers safe, yes. Don't you work with the Police Athletic League and the community affairs officers?"

He paused while lifting the dripping forkful to his mouth. "The Police Athletic League is not a detective agency, but I don't want them seeing things that would raise questions I wouldn't want to answer."

This opportunity couldn't be passed up. "You've got something to hide?"

"We all do, Taina. Even you." He put down his fork, sipped coffee.

"For example?"

"I don't want them watching me walk circles, do rituals, and asking about my candles and my altar. Some of my protective spells involve disrupting radio waves and energy fields. That would fuck with their surveillance equipment. How would your boss feel about you being a witch?"

"I don't think she'd care." Taina stayed cool as a clam on ice.

She fingered the beads on her altar and rearranged her accouterments.

He was back at the window. "Let's go to Baretto Point Park today since it's so hot."

"Swim in the Bronx River? Yuk." Not even close to enticing.

"They've got a pool barge."

"That's like jumping into a public toilet."

Arnaldo sighed. "Well, I have to admit the view of Rikers Island unsettles me. You're going to stay at *Sonrisa* until the full moon wanes and this court case is resolved, right?"

"No. I can't leave *Señora* Duarte alone here, even if I have to sit up all night with a lantern shining on the alleyways." She started on the pancakes. Her coffee was already cold.

As soon as dusk came, Taina would be holed up there, alone, so she could enlist Bridge Rat and the other shifters to keep watch. And find out where the hell they'd been last night.

"The cops are going to be here a couple more days—at least until something happens somewhere else. If you're gone, Lupo's thugs won't hassle your landlady." Arnaldo washed not only his own place setting, but also the batter bowl, the spatula, the griddle—then wiped off the stove and countertop. He could be downright useful to have around and endearing—when he wanted to be.

"Mind if I take a shower? Then we'll go get my bathing suit—just in case we decide to go swimming—and grab a cab over the park, okay?" He wasn't giving up on the beach.

If she spent the afternoon locked up here, by the time night closed in she'd be one tick of the clock from crazy. "Sure, I guess. I mean go take a shower, and we can check it out."

The door closed, locked. How come being with him felt so natural and pleasant sometimes? Taina washed her dish, pulled out a towel, and her bathing suit.

Arnaldo came out in his shorts, bare-chested, toweling dripping curls. Middle-age paunch notwithstanding, his biceps bulged and his pecs twitched.

No man had ever sent shivers of desire through her like that. No woman either, for that matter. Arnaldo pushed all her buttons, sometimes one at a time, sometimes all at the same time, but it appeared he was trying to win her over for more than one type of unholy alliance.

Was it a love spell, a distracting charm, or just an act to convince her that he was the best choice to hook up with?

Was he cooking up one of his own surprises? Was he succeeding?

~ * ~

The fourth gypsy cab blew past them. Arnaldo lowered his hand and shook it. "I've got pins and needles from holding my arm up so long. When are you getting that car back?"

"Never. Miguel is selling it for me."

"Can't we just go take it out for the day? You still got insurance, right?"

"I don't want Miguel to think I'm just using his shop as a free garage."

Arnaldo looked at her sideways. "The guy takes you out to dinner and treats you like a princess. Why would he think that?"

Something in the tone of his voice, more than the actual words, made it sound sleazy. "What are you suggesting?"

He put up his hand again. *"Dios mío,* all I meant is that he cares about you like a family member," Arnaldo paused to execute an exaggerated bow, "and that he'd do anything for you. I think you remind him of his daughter in PR. She's your age."

Was she reading conspiracy into everything? "Okay, but I still feel funny just showing up without calling ahead. Maybe next time."

"Then you try and get a cab."

Taina crept closer to the corner and waved. One look at Arnaldo, and the black car went by.

His throaty laugh irritated her as much as the heat. *"¿Que tú haces?* You do that, and they'll think you're a Hunts Point *puta* who wandered off course. If you're hanging with me, you gotta be bold."

"And bitchy and Bronx." She raised her arm higher, stepped off the curb into the street, wiped the smile off her face. It probably wouldn't hurt to jut one hip.

A gypsy cab stopped, and the driver rolled down the window. The salsa beat nearly drowned out his words. *"¿Adonde vas, mi amor?"*

Arnaldo took over. "How much to Baretto Point Park?"

The guy's smile turned back to business. *"Quince,* fifteen."

"Bueno." Taina opened the door and got into the back seat.

"You got cash?" Arnaldo loaded the cooler into the car first, then got in.

Meaning he probably didn't. "Yeah, my treat. You bought the drinks and food."

She buckled her belt and stared at him until he was shamed into doing the same.

She'd almost forgotten how her ex-fiancé Jaime used to insist on doing everything for her. Far from Arnaldo's style, he never pampered or sweet-talked her. Both were equally annoying.

The cabbie had a thing for horns, leaning on it every time someone ahead of him slowed down, even for a red light or stop sign. Taina pressed her head against the back seat to avoid whiplash. Only a left, a couple blocks, and a right before they reached the shoreline.

"Seven dollars now. The rest when you come back in two hours." Arnaldo didn't give the guy a chance to argue, picked up his cooler then slammed the door.

"You think he'll really come back?"

"Hopefully. Hard to get a taxi to come over here. Well, maybe not for you."

Taina ignored the quip. She didn't need to defend her reputation to another aggressive, possessive man.

The park was as sad as the degraded industrial area along a maze of train tracks. Weeds threatened to cover freight cars laced with gang-related graffiti scrawled in the dust. A few apartment buildings survived, scattered amongst decrepit warehouses.

Light diffused through the roadbed of the elevated Bruckner Expressway and stained everything in shades of black and gray. Defiant trees remaining after the rape of the landscape grew crooked, starved for light.

The weedy green tangle of grass beckoned sunbathers like a desert oasis. A cool breeze blew off the East River. Muddied waters lapped the shoreline where a few children shoveled blackened sand into pails. A faint whiff of sulfur tickled Taina's nose.

"Low tide." Arnaldo scrunched his face and walked to the water's edge. "But it's coming in. Want to go to the pool barge?"

Taina looked at the chlorinated pit filled with so many bodies twitching, jumping over each other, screaming, laughing, and pushing it looked like a nest of roaches after an exterminator had blasted them.

"Nope." She spread her towel on a patch of sand without too many rocks or pieces of gravel and asphalt mixed in.

This poor excuse for a beach was all these people had, and she was now one of those poor people, who'd almost been burned out of her apartment—again. And so desperate for company she was with a guy who was no better for her than the lawyer from San Juan she'd ditched, with a hell of a lot less money and even less class.

She'd thought Serena was the answer—and Taina's dissatisfaction with men a sign her life partner should be a woman. And now this.

Arnaldo peeled off his shirt and sat next to her on the sand.

"No towel?" She moved over so he could share hers.

"I want to keep it clean to dry off." He accepted her offer and perched on the opposite side of the terry cloth. "I bet this is nothing like Puerto Rico."

"You've never been there?"

"No. Abuela was saving money so we could go see her brother, her nieces and nephews, and introduce me to my aunts and uncles. But she spent it all when I got arrested on the drug rap to get me out of Rikers Island on bail and for a real lawyer." He swallowed and pointed at the nondescript complex. "I still went to prison. Right there. She finally went to PR—in a coffin. They didn't even let me go to her wake."

The sadness in his voice was as palpable as the stones under the beach towel—and as uncomfortable. "I'm so sorry, Arnaldo. Why don't you go now?"

"My aunts and uncles never met me, never wanted to. '*Como la madre*', 'like the mother.' That's how they referred to me." He blew out a defeated *pfft*.

She put her hand on his shoulder. "You should go, even for a few days."

"Who knows what condition *Sonrisa* would be in when I get back? Always wanted to see Serena again. I've often wondered, if I hadn't screwed up, if we'd still be together. I think, because of me, she had it with men all together."

"Some people know their sexual orientation from childhood. Others pretend to be what we think we should be, or what others want us to be, and deny what we really are. I was engaged. I didn't break up with him because of Serena. But shit just happened."

He nodded. "It's over between you and Serena?"

"We started out as teacher and student and should have just kept things that way. You know how it is during rituals with all that energy. One thing led to another, but we were so different, so star-crossed."

He stroked her arm. "Opposites attract, don't they?"

A tingle ran down her arms and diffused through the rest of her body, concentrating in her core, her nipples, her groin. "I still can't figure out what I really am."

"You are what you are, in any given moment." Arnaldo stared at her intently.

She tried to break the contact, sever the bond, deny the attraction, her arousal. "At this point, I think it's better for me to be alone." Done, conversation complete.

He drew circles in the sand with an index finger.

Taina put her hand on his shoulder. "Close your eyes. Good. It's hot like this in PR, only the breeze smells like this." She opened her purse and spritzed floral perfume into the air. "And the trees are tall palms that wave in the breeze like the grasses we passed on the way here. Imagine a white sandy beach, water so warm and so clear you can see the bottom no matter how deep. And the fish are colorful, and everyone is laughing and chattering in Spanish.

"They drive crazy there too. Just like our cabbie. And whistle at the girls. The men wear *guayabera* shirts and big straw hats. And the women wear bathing suits that look like torn napkins and rub scented oil all over themselves, so they glisten in the sun like bronze goddesses."

He titled his head up eyes still closed, smiling. "Thanks. I'll hold on to those images until I get there to see it myself and to apologize to Abuela in person instead of during one of Josefa's rituals."

Arnaldo shook his head and opened his eyes. The vision she'd conjured had softened the features of his face. "The tide came up. Let's go for a swim."

Taina slipped off her shorts, her tee, and ran after him, past the teenyboppers in string bikinis. No one ogled her in a sensible one-piece, coral and cream, which covered a little-too-ample posterior.

Her feet sank in the mud. Shells pricked her soles. A rock stubbed her toe as she waded into the water. A barge stenciled with the name 'Traprock' motored by, kicking up waves that lapped along the shore.

Arnaldo dove into the water, a dingy gray green like everything else. Seaweed on the rocks smelled of fish and hard-boiled eggs. "Come on out into the deep water. It's refreshing."

Josefa had directed they bathe in the sea, and this was as good as it was going to get. Environmental justice was yet another issue, but there were only so many things Taina could handle at the same time.

Terrified she'd step on broken glass or some other disgusting trash, she dog-paddled, holding her head above water so as not to ingest carcinogens or toxins. One foot brushed through sticky mud.

Keep moving, she had to keep moving so she didn't get sucked in, trapped. A faint whiff of her floral perfume lingered.

"Pretend you're in PR!" Arnaldo bellowed.

Several bystanders chuckled and gave a thumbs up.

"Yeah, imagine. Imagine this is PR." The water welcomed her, warm yet surprisingly refreshing, salty, not greasy or polluted.

They dried off in the sun, listening to the sound of waves breaking over the sand and kids squealing with delight as they ran barefoot under the ever watchful eyes of parents and caregivers.

Her phone tingled. The cabbie was outside the entrance to the beach, as promised.

"I guess we have to go." Arnaldo got up and hauled Taina to her feet.

"Yeah."

They rode back in silence, hands clasped as if to acknowledge somewhat of a détente in their rocky relationship.

Taina gave the cabbie a five-buck tip.

Arnaldo paused at the perimeter gate around her apartment. "Are you sure you want to stay here by yourself?"

"I'm not alone. Zeus is upstairs." Wet hair clung to her back, soaking her T-shirt. Dusk furled across the sky like a purple flag. She shivered.

"Okay." He lingered for a minute, saluted, then walked on.

The sun dipped behind the housing projects, casting its final golden light like a blanket of fairy glamour over the neighborhood. Her eyes, sharper than ever, spotted them everywhere. Pigeons that flew when the genuine articles were roosting for the night. Rats bold enough to poke their heads out before the cover of darkness. A hawk circling over an area that had no prey for miles.

Being out amongst mundanes was good for her and for Arnaldo as well. But getting too close to him would ruin her plan, distract her from her goal.

There was no way to strike the testimony that had already hog-tied her to Zoraida's case. If Taina didn't show up, Lupo would win a round. This might be the only opportunity to negotiate with some measure of protection.

She locked the gate behind her.

Chapter Twenty-Four
Showdown

Taina slipped into the back of the courtroom to distance herself during the proceedings. The ACS worker read a report of the home visit. Taina needn't have worried about missing the heavily staged act, which included an 'aunt' who lived in the two-bedroom apartment but only had enough clothes in a dresser drawer for one day. And no toothbrushes in the bathroom. Almost funny.

The description of the woman sounded an awful lot like the one who had been recruited to serve as Rosa Nunez's nanny, but Lupo could never, ever, muster enough smarts or sophistication, like Raul, to charm everyone in the courtroom. Even stuffed into a white shirt and dress slacks, he was too hairy and too grungy and too creepy to trust with a disabled minor.

Judge Winslet agreed. "After careful consideration of the facts in this case, as well as the psychiatrist's opinion, I feel this young lady would do far better in a placement where occupational and vocational therapy could be administered along with the proper medications to control her psychosis."

Zoraida's tantrum exceeded Taina's expectations with a rambling, sniveling, whining monologue accusing the foster home of beating, chaining, and starving her. She raved about uncle's kindness.

She pointed directly at Taina and spoke in the first focused, complete sentences the court reporter was able to type. "You did this. You. You told them to take me away."

Everyone in the courtroom swiveled in their seats to see the object of such animosity. Lupo's gaze penetrated her like daggers.

The judge banged her gavel. "Clear the courtroom."

Court officers escorted Taina, the ACS worker, and the lawyer out of the fishbowl as quickly as they could, but Lupo did some magick trick to get next to her as soon as the officers went back to help restrain the hysterical Zoraida.

Good thing Taina's first attempt to propose the terms of how they'd 'work together,' would be in here and not on the street with *Las Tombas* backup.

He stood, inches away, on the other side of the security tape, and nodded in the direction of the screams. "Are you happy now?"

This was as close as Taina was willing to get. "I recused myself from the case, Lupo. You sank the boat by setting that fire outside my apartment. If you keep calling attention to yourself, the cops will be all over you and your enterprises like flies on dung. Take my advice and stay away from kids. There are laws, very strict ones, and you will get caught. It's bad enough you recruit adults."

His lip curled, baring teeth. "I'm not bargaining with you, witch. You're interfering with my business." He stuffed his hands into his pockets.

The gap accentuated his short legs and sagging middle. Walking on all fours, he'd be more proportional.

She made her offer. "Stay out of my way, and I'll stay out of yours. If you continue to target me, I report you're targeting a court employee. And that investigation might very well lead to what you did to my family."

A snarl tinged with a smile tickled his lips. A bulbous pink tongue licked tobacco-stained jowls. Lupo wandered away.

It was over for now. It wouldn't be long before he made the next move.

Wails emanated from the courtroom. Four court officers dragged Zoraida toward the elevator, keening as shrill as five mourning women. She bit one's hand, stomped another's foot. "Uncle, Uncle, please don't leave me. Rescue me! You," she shrieked, pointing at Taina, "the devil will take you. You will burn in hell."

The elevator door closed. Howls faded, like Zoraida had dropped off a cliff. Lupo watched from the same corner he'd accosted Taina the last time.

A pyrrhic victory. Zoraida was now headed to a locked ward of a different type, which would protect her physically, but she was too limited to understand why.

Taina returned to her office, watching over her shoulder all the way across the Grand Concourse. She saw new clients, made follow up phone calls. Did paperwork. Stared at the same words, read the sentences over and over.

At the stroke of five, she gave up. Still distracted, her eyes aching from reading a spectrum of auras, she missed her subway stop and had to walk even further through gang territory without her familiar's protection.

She unlocked the perimeter gate and heard Zeus whimpering. "I'm coming puppy dog. Sorry I'm late." She pushed it open and recoiled.

A sticky substance coated her palm. The smell of shit, fresh and ripe, brought bile to her throat. She dragged a plastic garbage bag from the pail and tried to get it off her hands, but couldn't touch anything, do anything without spreading it around. Banging on the door brought no answer.

Zeus howled. Had he been hurt? Had they roughed up *Señora Duarte*?

Giving up on staying clean, Taina turned the knob and rushed in. Her landlady's door was secure, no paint chips or scratches around the frame. Lupo wasn't after her yet.

Taina took the stairs two by two. Opened her door. Only fear kept her from gagging as she surveyed werewolf scat smeared on the floor, the walls. Zeus hopped around her feet, unharmed. Where had he hidden?

Despite her broom handle chock, pressure lock and protection spell, the window she'd left open had been breached. How had they scaled a brick wall and come in through the window on the front of the building in broad daylight? Someone, or something, in *Las Tombas* had shifting abilities or spectral energy.

She washed her hands, took Zeus for a quick walk, along with rubber gloves, a roll of paper towels and a spray bottle of disinfectant. Taina gulped fresh air and retraced her route on the way back upstairs, scrubbing as she went.

How naïve to try and negotiate with a murderer. But backing down now would mean going back to Puerto Rico, hiding and regretting it for the rest of her life.

Each time Lupo had retaliated the fairies had been nowhere in sight, even where there was enough space and free flow of energy for their powers to function. Were they letting her do the dirty work in the hopes she'd succeed against all odds, freeing them to flutter and scamper about singing Long live The White Witch?"

Even after hours of scrubbing, ten rolls of paper towels and a bottle of disinfectant the smell lingered, killing her appetite, dousing her spirit.

She finally called Arnaldo. "They did what?" His voice was loud enough to hear without putting the phone on speaker.

"Marked me." Taina tried to maintain her composure, but the tears broke through.

"Pack up and get over here right now. Take a cab."

"I can't leave *Señora* Duarte. What if they come back and she chases them with her broom like she does to the vandals and homeless people scavenging in the garbage?"

"What the hell happened to the cops keeping an eye on things?"

"I still haven't decided about setting up surveillance, so I guess they just gave up and moved on to the next problem."

"Cast another protective spell before you leave. *Las Tombas* will know that you're gone. And they'll know where you're going." There was a sharp edge in Arnaldo's voice Taina had never heard before.

Talons of fear pricked her skin. "I'll call the detective back and let them do what they need to do." She couldn't tell him she'd told them no, flat out. Lupo, Raul, and Arnaldo had to think the option was still open.

"Why did you call me if you didn't want my advice—or my help?" He hung up.

Playing one off against the other was a risky strategy. Raul and Arnaldo couldn't be trusted, and Lupo was desperate.

Taking the clear path—the easy way out—and running into Arnaldo's arms was too easy, too good to be wise. Likely her destination lay outside the lines the rogue witch, the dhampir, and the werewolf had drawn in the sacred soil around Ritual Rock, in new territory she had to carve and claim for herself.

Should she call in sick tomorrow? No, then she'd be in trouble again for not reporting what happened after the hearing and Lupo's threats, particularly after the fire. She had to keep going to work.

Taina used throwing out the trash as an excuse to walk the perimeter of the building, visualizing white light pulsing like barbed wire around the yard. Not a rat or a pigeon in sight, though dark shadows appeared and disappeared next to her. Zeus growled down on the scene from his windowsill perch, something he never did when the fae were about.

She wandered around the apartment, gathering her most precious belongings: the picture of her family, Hawk Claw's feather, the abalone shell and beads Josefa had given her, and the vial of all-purpose soothing *Agua Florida*. Some clothes, underwear. Just in case she had to leave in a hurry.

~ * ~

Taina awakened before daylight touched the sky, before the moon gave up its waning glow. "A good time for banishing spells, Zeus."

Nothing came to her as she stared into the bowl of cloudy water in which the protective candle of San Miguel burned. Was he on duty? Were the cops on duty? Were the fairies off at some late summer jamboree?

Zeus's wet nose nuzzled her hand, and his paws rested on her arm as if to say, "I'm here, doing the best I can." His pink tongue caressed her cheek.

What spell could be useful? "Moonlight, give up the fight...No, that sucks. Moonlight, so bright. Shit, sounds like a sappy love song from the 70s."

Taina took three deep breaths, visualizing *Las Tombas* in wolf form stopping, one leg raised facing in her direction like Pointers who'd caught a whiff of a doe's scent, waiting for the cornered animals next move. "I will not sit here and wait for you to come for me again."

She turned to the moon, which looked like a bite had been taken out of it, retreating far too slowly.

"Good night, moonlight.
You've lit up the night.
Now take flight,
and with it the fight."

Zeus's tail wagged in approval. Taina smiled, opened the window, and spoke with renewed energy.

"Good night, moonlight.
You've lit up the night.
Now take flight,
and with it the fight.
Good night, moonlight.
You've lit up the night.
Now take flight,
and with it the fight."

Sunshine pricked the horizon with needles of light. The moon remained high in the sky, its luminosity dimmed, still struggling with all it had to remain in control.

Red lights flashed on the wall. San Miguel's candle flared. The wick sputtered.

Black smoke rose out of the jar, disappearing like wisps of smoke into the air.

The flame in *Yemayá's* blue candle on the altar dimmed, and a carbon residue scorched the rim of the holder.

Taina sprinkled *Agua Florida* around the apartment and ran dampened fingers through her hair. "Give me strength, guidance, protection."

The floral aroma lingered as she went back to the window and watched the sky turn into a giant Creamsicle, reducing the moon to an ivory marble in the west. Zeus languished in her arms, transfixed at the sight.

In her mind's ear Taina heard *Las Tombas* whimper. Within the bowl of San Miguel's water, doglike figures backed away from the red pillar, then turned tail and disappeared.

She picked up the jar and read the prayer. 'Defend me in the fight, give me protection against the perversity and snares of the demon. Grant that God demonstrates his power through the strength that He has bestowed upon you, keep away all who malign and threaten my soul with damnation. Amen.'

"It seems to have worked very well, didn't it, Zeus?"

"Bravo, Lady Taina. Most impressive." Bridge Rat poked through the window and clapped his pigeon's wings.

She whirled. "You have one hell of a nerve to show up now. What happened to all the help you were going to give me?"

Bridge Rat's neck retreated like a chicken escaping a chopping block. Beady, birdlike eyes blinked in indignation. "Really. The rat patrol dragged you down the stairs and couldn't have done much short of shifting and riding in on the firefighter's backs. They were writhing in pain when their wings contacted the iron oxygen tanks. If there is one thing mortals do well in New York City, it's put out fires. Got a jolly good amount of practice at it, after all. I mean, they were here in the flutter of a wing."

"Couldn't you have swooped down and pecked those filthy lupine eyes out?"

"With all the iron about there isn't much magick could we have performed, particularly covered with glamour." His voice softened. "Now, if we were in the parklands…"

Taina tired of the excuses, no matter how amusing his performance. "Next time, just be sure Lupo and Raul know to come after me in the park, so they set me up to win."

"What have you lost, Lady Taina? You've not retreated."

"Lupo and his thugs threatened to burn me out of my apartment. And he's not wasting time in making sure I know he can get to me. No matter where I go or what I do, I can't rest or let my guard down."

"Well, you could stay with Master Arnaldo. He's quite good in a pinch."

What fae benefit there was to a good witch/bad witch duo eluded her understanding. "I'm not sure I can trust him either, Bridge Rat. My knowledge and my powers are so limited."

"On the contrary, Lady Taina. It is the magickal beings that are limited. You are fully human, able to walk between both worlds unencumbered. We are held prisoner by our weaknesses. The fae to the disruption of iron and steel, werewolves to the cycles of the moon, and the dhampirs to bright light. Even our adaptations, our evolutions, do not allow us to easily traverse the veil between the magickal and mundane."

"Is that why Arnaldo can hold them off? Is that why you want me to ally with him?"

"There are many advantages to your union. But if you choose to soldier on without him, I daresay that given the aplomb with which you just handled the battle between the moon and sun on your own, with Zeus's help of course, there shan't be a problem." His beak actually bent into a grin. Bridge Rat tucked his head under one wing and bowed before flitting through the window.

Taina slammed it closed, locked it, braced it. "Enough magickal bullshit. Back to work."

Chapter Twenty-Five
Seismic Shift

"Say what?" Simone almost dropped the coffee cup in her lap. "Do you have any proof he set the fire?"

Taina's newfound bravado faded in the bright sunlight. Tears built up behind her eyes, clogged her nose and throat. "No, none. But the detectives believe it was a *Las Tombas* attack, and Lupo Lopez is their leader."

"We've got to keep you away from any clients that have gang connections, so this doesn't ignite The Bronx like a match thrown into a hay bale. Anytime you get even a whiff of it, you're off the case. I'm going to contact the head of the gang task force the DA convened, so they're aware. Maybe you need police protection..."

What Simone was proposing made perfect sense in the mundane world. But not in Taina's. "They've already offered me the opportunity to be under surveillance. I said no. Simone, there are things in my life I'd like to keep private—nothing criminal, but..."

"You don't have to explain that to me. No one wants every move monitored. But the gangs will find another target if they know the cops are on you. Think about it. In the meantime, let me give the DA a call." Simone clacked into her office..

Taina opened the blinds and peered out onto the teeming streets below. *Walk with ease between the worlds? I feel like I don't belong in either. How can I do the best for my clients if I'm always on edge, and my co-workers have to keep catching the hot potatoes? Maybe I should consider working for Arnaldo.*

As crazy as it seems, maybe Raul can mediate. He does have some control over Lupo. Time to see what this Boricua *Shelter is all about. If his organization is real maybe I can set up an alliance with the Victim's Advocacy Program for 'selected' clients like Rosa and*

Zoraida.

Taina's stomach knotted, remembering the last official visit that left a cancer of fear growing inside her. Anticipation hung in the air like stray energy, prickling her scalp, humming like a mosquito in her ears.

This week would tick away like a clock with a dying battery. A late summer funk hung over the city like a bank of smog. The weekend backlog cleared and the Friday scramble to get done and get away seemed a long way off.

In between was Thursday—August 25—the anniversary of the fire that killed her family. Yeah, that had to be what was buzzing inside her like a beehive.

Simone plowed through a drawer, dumping old files into the shredder box. Sandy tapped away at a spreadsheet—some report she'd been asked to do for the home office.

Taina didn't bother to knock on Simone's door. "Ever heard of *Boricua* Women's Shelter?"

"Nope. Where are they located?"

"Cauldwell Avenue and 149th. I met this guy in the courthouse a couple of weeks ago, and he invited me to take a tour. Do either of you mind if I take a long lunch? I'd like to check it out."

"Nope." Sandy's fingers didn't break their rhythm.

"Sure, go ahead." Simone tossed a manila folder into the box and missed. Sheets of paper flew like a pack of pigeons scared by an oncoming train.

Taina helped her pick up the mess. "It's very near where I live, actually. "Supposedly it's women helping women."

"What does *Boricua* mean? I hear it all the time." Sandy finally took a break.

"People linked by their indigenous Puerto Rican heritage." It meant so much more as a cultural community that transcended distance and national boundaries.

"Like Black persons calling each other brother, sister?" Simone tore some pages in half, paused, and did it again.

"Yes." Raul had big balls to have appropriated a revered ancient moniker for a brothel.

"Don't come back if it's so close to your apartment. Write up a report to justify the time away, and I'll send it to the office."

"Thanks." Taina took her time getting ready, hoping the phone would ring or the door would open, and some clients would walk in. But it didn't, and they didn't.

"See ya!"

Simone and Sandy were so distracted by monotony they just waved as Taina left.

The streets teemed like an anthill. She passed the falafel and hot dog vendors, scruffy men with sandwich board signs offering legal help for bail bonds, pretty girls enticing passersby into pawn shops promising needed cash for gold, and brazen sidewalk displays of *Santería* beads and bracelets, knock-off designer bags, and stolen or counterfeit electronics.

The train wasn't crowded, allowing Taina to squirm in the hard plastic seat wondering why the hell she was going to Romeo's Lounge, or what was left of it.

The corrugated steel security door, stenciled with a champagne glass dripping dirt-stained bubbles, was never pulled up. With one tail of the R missing as well as the O dangling off the cracked white background, the club was to mundane eyes an abandoned storefront.

A sickly smell emanated from under the door, distinctly different than the odor of greasy exhaust from the Chinese/Cuban/Mexican take-out place next door. Sweet, like licorice and overripe fruit, with an underlying acidic bite.

A red cloud of dust slithered out from underneath and rose like smoke into the sky. A blast of warm air tousled her hair, though there wasn't a breeze rustling the leaves on a stunted tree near the corner. A cloud of evil energy scraped over her bare arms and wound down her body, spiraled around her toes.

Mundanes at the laundromat, the *bodega,* and the ninety-nine-cents store, whose display Taina had trashed the last time she ran away from Raul, smoked cigarettes, ate chips, guzzled energy drinks, laughed, rough-housed—oblivious to it all.

How could they not notice? She wandered around the corner to the apartment building entrance. A man and a woman stood outside. She hung on him like a vine from a tree.

"I'm looking for Raul Rivera."

The woman unwound. *"No esta."* The response was too slow, too deliberate. A challenge.

"He's out, and no one is allowed in unless Raul says so." A male sentry swaggered over, his toothy grin too perfect to be true.

"Tell Raul that Taina is sorry to have missed him." She wasn't and resisted the temptation to run.

Taina walked back to the subway. A colossal waste of time.

The ground trembled as a monster truck rumbled by. Burnt orange paint with black skeletons in bas-relief adorned the entire vehicle. Bony arms reached out to grab whatever they could, their faces locked in sinister smiles. The body was jacked up so high the entire undercarriage was visible.

It motored by way too slow, on tires so impossibly big the treads could have sheltered any mouse that got in the way. Lingering to make the biggest impression worked. Kids and teenagers, plus a few older men, ran out.

"Cool. Look at that."

"C'mon, maybe he'll give us a ride."

"Yo, dude, wait."

One boy hung off the tailgate, feet dragging along the asphalt, a hair's breadth away from the steaming exhaust pipe. The others followed, like lemmings charging toward a cliff about to meet their doom. Another truck, its yellow paint muted by whispers of black bones strewn across the body like a pilfered graveyard, attracted the stragglers.

Taina hurried up the hill. There was no doubt who they were— and where they were headed.

The street curved, as most of them did around here, and led back to Prospect Avenue. Despite the fragile control she had on her breathing, she ran all the way.

Two lines of gang soldiers flanked *Sonrisa, Las Tombas* on the right, *Los Sangueros* on the left. In the middle of the street, kids sat in the trucks, blew the horns, and pretended to steer.

The cool factor negated the macabre, and parents stood alongside, smiling, chatting, snapping pictures and recording videos of their children in vehicles flaunting death and destruction.

Raul and Lupo came down the street from opposite directions; each went to stand with their soldiers.

Arnaldo's laugh lines deepened, his upper lip curled over his teeth. Anger smoldered like embers in rage-narrowed eyes.

His breathing, so slow, so deep, pulled the air from her lungs, choked her. Taina had seen him do this weather manipulation before but had no idea how.

He gazed solidly ahead, paying no attention to the puffed chest, hip thrust forward aggressive stance of *Los Sangueros* and the hunched, about-to-pounce crouch of *Las Tombas.*

The sky remained crystal blue, but they'd timed the action for the exact moment the sun moved far enough west to cast deep shadows of hi-rise buildings over the street.

She waited for thunder, lightning, hail. The ground trembled like a train going by underground, except there was no subway nearby. The shaking intensified, jostling the soldiers into each other.

Taina hung onto the fence. Traffic signals swayed. Loose metal, stones, and scraps of concrete fell from the elevated Bruckner onto the pedestrians below, sending them screaming and running for cover.

The fucker had conjured an earthquake!

The kids bouncing in the trucks, and their parents, oblivious, paid no heed until people flooded out of the high-rises and milled in the street. Sirens wailed. Police cars whooped. Cars snaked through the crowded avenue and side streets.

Chatter in Spanish, English, Jamaican *patois*, and a conglomeration of African dialects spoke of the Mayan calendar, the wrath of God, the second coming of Jesus, and global warming, among other things.

The mood turned festive, like they'd just survived the big one, even though it had been a blip, a momentary tremble, albeit an ominous portent of what was to come.

Anyone that didn't perceive the magickal realm hadn't realized that a supernatural gang fight had been brewing right then, right there. Anyone who didn't know wouldn't suspect that the tension building between three rivals would soon spill mundane blood, much of it that of the very children being lured to a *Las Tombas's and Los Sangueros's* open house.

Lupo led his soldiers away. The remainder followed Raul into the mundanes' post earthquake melee.

Arnaldo staggered toward her.

She held onto an arm to steady him. "How did you do that?"

"It helps to be way pissed. Professional witch on a closed course. Don't try it." He tweaked her chin and finally smiled. He might brush it off, but the guy was shot from that effort.

"Let me get you something to eat and drink." She cut through the gate spell and held it open for him.

He paused, winded, still holding onto her. "They'll be back, Taina. A pile of sticks has been thrown up in the air and everyone is scrambling to grab what they can. All because of you."

"Pretty flowery talk for someone who isn't a politician or minister." She helped him up the stairs and inside.

"I finished my BA in political science and sociology behind bars."

"So, what do you propose we do that we're not doing already—me at the courthouse and you at *Sonrisa?*"

He sank into a chair vacated by the seniors who'd just gone home in time. All ten fingers drummed the plaid, plastic tablecloth. "I can't hold them off unless you ally with me and make it clear you're gonna fight."

She mixed two teaspoons of sugar into tea and brought it to him with a plate of leftover sandwiches. "There are times we go with the mundane flow. But far too many times we're like gasoline and a match. How long will it be before we blow one another up?"

He had no comeback, no snide remark. "Thanks." Nibbles and sips were so un-Arnaldo like. "Well, waddah you say?"

"I need something more concrete than lofty goals, Arnaldo."

He finished half a cheese sandwich, drained his cup, then threw it into the trashcan across the room. It missed. "Concrete? Chunks of it are going to fall on you, *chica.*"

He leaned close, took her hand, stared into her eyes. "I know you think I'm in league with them. I've made my mistakes but have more than made up for them. I'm only looking out for your best interests. But they'll try and turn you against me."

She wanted to believe him, but there were too many questions he couldn't or wouldn't answer, and too much sadness and ambivalence on his face.

Chapter Twenty-Six
Hurricane Watch

Death day was always difficult but being so close to where it had happened weighed Taina down with boulder-sized melancholy. Grief hovered over her like restless spirits. The only reason she dragged herself out of bed was Zeus, who desperately needed his morning walk.

He did his business right away, though he looked longingly toward the bakery where someone always gave him a treat. She started to cross the street, to buy a coffee and buttered roll, but the sight of life going on as usual: the delivery men, the garbage collectors, kids being dragged to the camp bus stop by sleepy parents on their way to work, froze her in a moment she'd long forgotten—or suppressed.

Twenty-six years ago today her mother and father had gotten up, went to work, did the laundry and shopping, ate breakfast, lunch, and dinner, having no inkling it would be the last day of their lives.

What had she and Ana done that summer afternoon? Had they gone across the street to St. Mary's Park and played in the shadow of Ritual Rock? Shopped for school supplies?

Taina would have started kindergarten that September and had dreamed of a new book bag, pencils, crayons, glue. She'd loved pasting strips of construction paper together to make cards and gifts.

The smell of school glue still made her smile, the feel of it drying on her hands, the cracking of it like a second skin oddly comforting. It had been the one constant, the one thing she was able to do in Puerto Rico, just like she had in New York, as the days, weeks, months, and finally years ticked away until she got too old to do it anymore.

Then she buried herself in math and social studies and wrote script neat enough to make the nuns happy, which was as impossible as forgetting and moving on.

Everyone stopped asking why she lived with her grandmother. They forgot that Taina Aponte was an orphan, but she never did. Neither did Abuelita, who never smiled, never hugged, never kissed. She just did her duty because there was no one left to do it, wishing out loud from time to time that she could go places with her friends, or take vacations, or enjoy her old age instead of taking care of a sullen, confused, grieving child who grew up to be a sullen, confused, grieving, bisexual who couldn't stay in a relationship because she wouldn't let anyone take care of her.

She was haunted by a memory as elusive as a whisper in the wind. Tortured by the memory of flames biting her like an angry dog. The only people who had truly loved her were gone, and she was the only one who'd survived. How could she go to work today and take care of people in need when she was as fragile and empty as a hollowed out eggshell?

The dog, tired of waiting through Taina's daydream, strained at the leash.

"Let's take a walk before it gets too hot."

Zeus whimpered as they passed the bakery on the opposite side of the street.

Leaving a message on Simone's voicemail was a lot easier than having to call out sick in person. "Today is the anniversary of my family's… Of the fire that killed my family. I woke up with a terrible headache and just can't come in today. I'm sorry, Simone. See you tomorrow."

This hadn't been the best job choice, but there were a lot of decisions Taina would have made differently if only she hadn't ignored her charts and forecasts that warned of unsettled times around retrogrades and void moons—more ominous than Serena's reasons—which had all come to pass.

Today's vibe warned of nothing in particular, but something rippled along the magickal energy pathway. It twanged like a tuning fork, beckoning Taina like an enchanted piper to join a dance with the dead.

Eagle Avenue, where she'd soared like a bird into a stranger's arms, was just past Cauldwell Avenue, the cauldron across the street from Ritual Rock. Smack in the middle of magick central. And bordered by Trinity Avenue, the aptly named juncture of *Las Tombas*'s and *Los Sangueros*'s turf, with Arnaldo holding his own near the perimeter.

No fairies, as usual when she wanted to ask Bridge Rat a question or feel that there was someone on her side. The only pigeons around were the real deal, pecking at a discarded bag of potato chips. And the rats were doing a mating dance inside plastic garbage bags piled curbside.

Zeus growled. Taina pulled him along.

Humidity hung in the air despite a hot breeze that tousled awnings and rustled papers overflowing from trashcans. The *bodega* owner had taken in all the displays in front of the shop.

"¿No hay frutas?" A peach or plum would taste very good about now.

"Ay, señorita, the storm stopped all deliveries."

She hadn't listened to the news, seen a paper, or turned on her computer. "A storm?"

"Hurricane Irene is gonna pass right over the city. They're evacuating Coney Island." He mimicked a bird in flight to make the point. "King Mayor Bloomberg says we have to take everything inside or else. That mayor, he'll fine you for taking a piss in your own toilet."

"Good luck." So that's what had her head buzzing. But when hurricanes hit PR it never felt like this. Then again, this was The Bronx.

Taina put one foot in front of the other. All she had was the address and a five-year old's memory of a blackened, shattered window overlooking a courtyard. It couldn't be that far from the corner of 149th Street, since there was also a recollection of seeing the park from the kitchen while eating breakfast.

The plaque above the archway read 854. She pushed through the open wrought iron gate and ducked under the brick semicircle arch. Her gaze instinctively moved left as she ascended three steps and entered the circular remains of a garden, now a weedy area with some ramshackle playground equipment and a few benches in desperate need of paint. Apartments on that side overlooked both this area and the street. She counted three stories.

Her stomach flip-flopped. Bright yellow curtains adorned it now. A window box full of trailing vines with purple flowers hung off the sill, sporting a Puerto Rican flag on a stick crisscrossed with the blue and white NY Yankees banner.

No memorial for a tragedy long forgotten, a legacy erased, an injustice never brought to judgment, a wrong never made right, remembered only by a lone woman and a tired, retired detective.

Zeus sat at Taina's feet, still, silent, his eyes fixed on his mistress's focal point.

"I never should have come here, puppy dog."

Tears stung her eyes. Her lungs wheezed, as if the smoke she'd inhaled that night was spiraling through them once again. She fumbled in her pocket, but she hadn't taken the inhaler, just a change purse and her phone for what was to have been a quick walk.

She sank to the ground, forced herself to take deep breaths and not panic, to not waste whatever air was flowing at the moment. Zeus stretched himself over her lap. His tiny heart beat against her chest, reminding her that she wasn't all alone.

"I'm sorry, Taina." Raul's unmistakable honey-sweetened voice, with a bitter-saccharine aftertaste, intruded on an already terrible moment. He put out his hand.

She dragged herself to her feet without taking it. "Because you set the fire?" She would not allow him to intrude on her private grief with such platitudes.

"I can assure you I did not strike a single match during the burning times." His hand remained extended.

Zeus wiggled a warning against her shins, but she couldn't hold back. "You just paid off those who did."

Raul lowered his arm and bowed his head. "The landlords commissioned the jobs."

She barely restrained herself from slapping him in the face. "Blame everything on Lupo, why don't you?"

"My business is not real estate. And Lupo has been behaving badly for years." He took her elbow. "Walk with me. There is a lot about my past you should know."

She shook his hand off. "I know all I need to about you from *el bochinche.*" The gossip on the street, even among mundanes, had always linked Raul to providing the rewards, in gratitude for Lupo providing space for his seedy enterprises.

Raul smirked like he could see right through her clothes, right into her soul. "But you came looking for me."

"Yesterday. And you weren't there. Today my mind is elsewhere, and I'd like to be alone with my memories."

"As you wish. I hope that someday soon you'll allow me to share mine. We have much in common, Taina. More than you know." He slithered down the stairs.

Chapter Twenty-Seven
The Tower, The Fool, and The Wheel of Fortune

Taina sat like a homeless person on the low stone wall surrounding the grassy oval. People came and went without a passing glance at the strange woman and the white dog. There was nothing left here for her, not even the faintest trace of her mother, father, and sister.

She picked up Zeus. "Let's go get ready for the storm."

Taina emerged from the shady courtyard. Concentric rings of hazy sunlight glowed through the clouds. Her breath caught in her throat.

Raul sat atop Ritual Rock, his image distorted by the motes of humidity dancing in the air, stripping away whatever magickal glamour he possessed.

To her eyes, he appeared nothing more than a mass of black with a fiery halo, arms wrapped around pulled-up knees. Despair hung in the air, sodden with moisture.

A hot wind blew from the north to the east, which should have pushed her away. But instead, Taina walked into it, into the park.

This was not the right time to approach the dhampir, but there would never be one.

He'd sought her out today. That would put her on higher ground, prove that she could maintain control.

Zeus growled his displeasure.

A few birds roosted atop streetlamp. Real or fae? She glanced around, then called up to them. "Tell Bridge Rat the White Witch needs him."

The birds didn't move, didn't respond. Common pigeons and a few sparrows. A few black squirrels and a couple of gray ones scampered through the trees, their nails scratching the bark, sending a shower of chips to the ground. Cute, but not fae.

Raul slid down. His feet sank into the blackened dust in the dhampir area. "Taina."

She put the dog down, and Zeus immediately put himself in between them. She visualized roots growing from her feet into the soft brown soil consecrated to the goddess and God by countless witchy circles.

Grounded, connected to that energy, she prepared to hear what he had to say, prayed silently for guidance to say and do the right thing, since she had no idea what to do or who to believe at this moment. "Why did you follow me today, of all days, Raul?"

"I've long anticipated the opportunity to spend some time getting to know you, White Witch. And I believe your reluctance to join forces with me will fade. We have the same goals, you see." Here in the shadows, stripped of all glamour, Raul's sinister countenance, his pallor, his lips darkened by the promise of new blood could not be disguised.

His smile disappeared. "Enough game playing. You are no ordinary court official and know very well that I am no ordinary community organizer. All of the men and women in my organization are recruited, and they pass a very stringent initiation. By their own choice.

"When our paths cross with the legal system, even if we lose we win. Mortals can't keep us locked up forever. I'm trying to avoid unfortunate complications—as I did with Rosa. If you'd been able to recommend Lupo's latest Lolita to me, she would have been better served. And Lupo wouldn't be so out of control."

"I certainly agree the outcome of that case disturbed me." Taina was violating a lot of rules right now. Making deals with dhampirs and werewolves wasn't in the Court Advocate's Policy and Procedure Manual.

He settled back, quite comfy on his own turf. "Rivalries born in one era die off long before we do. I don't relish Lupo's brand of initiation and operations, but right now it's expedient for us to ally on certain...projects. Taina, you can't defeat us or outsmart us."

"I told him to let the kid go, but he kept at it. He set that fire. And smeared scat all over my apartment."

Raul exhaled. "I said from the beginning that *Las Tombas* are uncouth, ignorant, crass, and brainless. Now Lupo is in a frenzy. My soldiers will contain him. A lot better than your fairy friends—and Arnaldo Arroyo. If Lupo knows you've allied with me, he wouldn't dare go near you again."

Supposedly, Raul had marked her the last time, but it hadn't interfered with either Lupo or Arnaldo's pursuit. "I'm not forming an alliance with anyone. Whatever deal the three of you have doesn't interest me."

He slid forward. "Oh, but it should, *mi amor.* Arnaldo is not a poor innocent witch. He was nearly initiated into *Las Tombas* but reconsidered. He doesn't have long enough left on Earth to put his past behind him. Believe me, Lupo and I protect him too."

She suppressed a shiver. Was Raul exaggerating for effect? The visit wasn't about Arnaldo or Lupo. It was about *Boricua* Center, and the role she could play as a court insider to cover up Los Sangueros's misdeeds.

"Agreed. Let me take you on the tour you requested." He extended his hand.

She didn't take it. "Not today."

He smirked. "My touch isn't venomous."

Taina pulled herself up to her full height and pretended she was looking into the eyes of a murderer—because she was. Except murderers were usually behind bars or a glass partition, and armed guards stood nearby—just in case. "The last time, you got way too close."

He lowered his arm. "Last time we met, you declined all the options. You know my fondest wish is to have you as my equal, my queen, my partner.

"Dhampirs don't rut like animals at every full moon. We maintain our human character. Our principles are based on free choice to join the clan. To resist the ravages of disease and to share our life essences through our intact bodies—with consent. Thus over the last few decades we're no longer creatures of the night, better able blend into mundnania. Having you join would raise that to a new level of class and respectability.

"So, my lady," he bowed, with a lot less charm than Bridge Rat and Hawk Claw, "I shall offer you a three-card spread to consider."

Did he really think she was that naïve? "I didn't know dhampirs read The Tarot." This would be interesting.

His shoulders wriggled. "I dabble." He took a deck out of his pocket, shuffled, cut, handed them to her.

She chose three cards from the top, middle, bottom, laid them on a stone and turned them over so she could see them first. The Tower, The Fool, The Wheel of Fortune.

Raul didn't even know the rule that the reader faced the cards. Full of shit—as usual.

She pushed them toward him, the portent of The Tower under

attack, The Fool, blissfully walking while a cat scratched his ass, and the Wheel of Fortune being turned by three rodent caricatures—abundantly clear.

"Hmmm. See my lovely. The knight has fallen from The Tower ramparts, and the savior is emerging. The Fool, well certainly not you, but perhaps those giving your counsel and advice? Where will your Wheel stop, Taina? Who will put an end to the endless games?"

"I'm not sure I concur with your reading, Raul. Who is the fallen knight, who is the fool, and who will be victorious?"

Taina gathered strength from the energies swirling beneath her. She stepped back into the morass of witchy circles—the baffles many generations had set up to cause those with impure intent to stumble over the invisible roots of a fairy and sage dusted maze. "What might those shared goals be? You invited me to *Boricua* Center. I wanted to see if it could be a legitimate referral source for selected clients."

"Let's go. Right now. Unannounced. Perhaps then you'll believe the community I've fostered for my women really does exist." He gestured toward the street, bustling with mundanes taping windows and carrying bags of groceries and cases of bottled water.

"I shall not lay a hand on you. Nor will any of my soldiers." As Raul walked toward her, a sliver of light pierced through the leafy trees, and his image reverted to the human side.

"I lost my mother. Right here. In her zeal to save me from being changed, she fell victim to my master." He stared into the woods. "We both believe that everyone has the freedom to decide their own destiny, but then they bear the burden of that choice.

"I, like the others who are now in my service, chose to enter *Los Sangueros*, to share my blood and my body with my brothers and sisters rather than struggle to survive on my own in this neighborhood. My mother preferred death, but if she had not followed me the night I was to be initiated perhaps…"

"Yet you convict them to a life of imprisonment, prostitution, and servitude?"

"Taina, there is no one in my clan who did not willingly accept my invitation. They have ample opportunity for them to change their minds before they make the final commitment. I can't say the same for the wolf man—or the mundane gangs for that matter."

"What about those death trucks, luring children into thinking gang life is a brother or sisterhood, a hedonistic romp?"

Raul sneered. "Arnaldo is tampering with a system that fosters stability, camaraderie…"

Who did he think he was talking to? "Thuggery. Slavery, sexual and otherwise."

He shook his head, began walking toward her. "Come see before you judge."

Zeus snapped at Raul's heels as he stepped over him.

The dog's snarl toggled a switch in her brain. Snippets of unrecognizable voices raised a warning.

Taina backed off. "Today I will honor my family's memory. And there are preparations I must make for the storm." She picked her way through the minefield of competing energies clutching at her feet. She gestured, palms down, and intoned under her breath.

"Goddesses and mothers,
Sisters and brothers.
Saints and sinners alike,
Show me the path to the light."

"Wait, Taina." Raul reached to grab her and promptly stumbled as wisps of brown dust engulfed his feet like shackles.

Above their heads, disguised in the wind-rustled leaves, two pigeons with iridescent wing markings nestled together, beady eyes following his every move.

Zeus scampered effortlessly through the labyrinth. The point was made. Raul knew she had the power, the allies, and the means to repel him.

She now knew it too.

Would he stand by his vow? Palms up, she reversed her spell.

"Goddesses and mothers,
Sisters and brothers.
Saints and sinners alike,
End this strife.
Show me the path to the light."

Siempre suave, always cool, as expected for someone with only a smidgen of human blood flowing through his veins, Raul stepped defiantly into the witches' territory and was immediately bound in place by its magick.

He gripped her elbow, and so failed the test. "I'm disappointed you can't accept my invitation."

"Another day."

Zeus crouched, ready to pounce. The pigeons above and behind him rose from roosting position onto their feet. Their tail feathers wiggled, and their wings twitched.

Raul released her, and his too-perfect smile returned. "Anytime. No pets allowed." His gaze flicked toward the trees. "And bring no one else with you."

Taina made her way through the circles with ease. The dhampir's gaze dripped like a melting ice pack down her back. Safe on the busy avenue, she turned to watch as Raul moved back onto dhampir turf and ascended to the top of Ritual Rock.

She picked up Zeus and hailed a cab, hoping a New York City taxi driver could outrun *Un Sanguero*.

Chapter Twenty-Eight
Dead Man's Curve

"Pull into the garage, please."

The cabbie looked back at Taina.

"*Ay, sí, mi amor.* The only girls who walk over here aren't nice ones." He maneuvered onto the sidewalk.

Shea handed him the money and kept her head low, sunglasses on, as she ducked inside. *Las Tombas* or *Los Sangueros* would recognize her no matter what, but they'd have to catch up first.

Clanging of metal on concrete, the swish of an automatic drill, the *pfft, pfft, pfft* of an air hose, all to a *salsa* beat, drifted through the split rubber curtain dividing the garage from the empty office. She tucked the dog under her arm and leaned over the counter to look for Miguel.

"What do you need, *nena?*"

Taina bumped an elbow on the wooden ledge so hard it screamed in pain. She didn't.

"Miguel. I didn't hear you come in." So her enhanced perception was not functional away from Ritual Rock. Her powers weren't, either.

He smiled and patted Zeus on the head. "What's wrong?"

"Nothing," she lied. "Have you sold my car yet?"

"I've got a few dealers interested but first the earthquake, now the hurricane."

"Would it be too much trouble to take it out? I want to go to the cemetery and can't trust the subways today." She struggled to keep her voice from quivering as much as her insides.

"The trains are going to be shut down completely in advance of the storm. The buses...well, never mind. Traffic will be terrible with everyone headed for higher ground."

"I'm going to St. Raymond's Cemetery, then coming right home."

He raised his arms, palms up, in frustration. "Why today?"

"I want to bring my family some flowers for the anniversary." Tears dripped down her face.

He hugged her, the big bear type. "*Ay, sí.* I forgot the date. I'll go with you. You should not be out alone on a day like this."

Funny how mundanes sensed things, even though they had no idea what was amiss. He couldn't know a dhampir and a werewolf were chasing her tail. He just figured some mundane creep was.

"No, you're busy, and the weather is turning bad." No way would she allow Miguel to be swept up in this.

"You know the way?" He fished in a drawer for a map. "Can't Arnaldo go with you?"

"He's busy too. I'll find it." She looked at the route he traced with his finger.

"Take the Bruckner north. Be careful going over the Westchester Creek drawbridge. They call it Dead Man's Curve."

"Nice." *How fitting.*

"Hutchinson Parkway to the Local Streets exit. It takes you right to the old section."

Could the fact that Dead Man's Curve led straight to them be an omen? "That's exactly where they're buried."

"Getting back take Tremont to Bruckner Boulevard. Make a right and stay left over that drawbridge or you'll be stuck on the Cross Bronx Expressway."

Taina scribbled the instructions on the back of the shop's business card. But her family would lead her to them. "Don't wait for me."

"*Nena,* I live on the fifth floor. What preparations do I need to make besides buying milk, bread, and water?"

"Yeah, they make such a big deal about weather around here."

He chuckled. "I'll wait for you—and drive you home." He fished the keys off a pegboard and led her through the garage into the fenced-in lot. "Keep an eye on her, killer." He scratched Zeus's ears.

He should only know. She put the dog on the passenger seat, slid behind the wheel, fastened her seatbelt. As soon as the door opened, she peeled out, not giving anyone or anything hanging out a chance to get anywhere near the vehicle. But this time she'd run them over. The time for being nice and civilized had long since passed.

The lights were green from the first to the last, surely a good sign. And with everyone scared off the roads, she had plenty of time to find her way to the cemetery. Zeus perched on the front seat, staring out the windshield like he knew where they were going.

She consulted a map outside the deserted gatehouse and made her way amongst the monoliths, struggling to read the moss-covered numbers. Even after so many years, a jagged knife of anguish stabbed her heart when she saw the inscription:

Aponte
James, beloved Son and Father
Antonella, beloved Daughter-in-Law and Mother
Ana, beloved Daughter and Granddaughter
Eternal Rest Grant Unto Them O Lord
And Let Perpetual Light Shine Upon Them
August 25, 1985

Taina recalled Abuelita's whispered prayers, the clanking of the devout Catholic's rosary beads as she knelt in front of their picture in their safe haven in Puerto Rico. Did her grandmother know about her daughter's magickal gift? Were the years of warnings about the sacrilege of *Santería*, prayers recited by rote, daily Masses, white Communion dresses, and red Confirmation gowns a backlash?

Taina slipped off her shoes while standing on top of their remains. Her feet connected with the Earth, her toes tangled in the damp grass.

She waited for their spirits to wind around her waist like Papa's arm, stroke her hair like Mama, tickle her ribs like Ana trying to steal a candy.

But their bones lay silent beneath the earth. Not a glimmer of her family's presence manifested itself. Nor had they met her in the courtyard of the building they'd died in. Would they be among the spirits with her at Ritual Rock?

Taina sank to her knees, raked her fingers through the dirt, and watered the grass with tears.

"Salt and water,
Inner and outer, Soul and body,
Be cleansed!
Cast out all that is harmful!
Take in all that is good and healing!
By the powers of life, death, and rebirth.
So mote it be."

She wiped the mud off her feet and hands with grass and dead leaves. She looked toward the heavens. "When will I feel your presence again, Mama, Papa, Ana?"

She kissed the granite. Only cold, dead stone met her lips.

Zeus sat immobile, facing away from his mistress, nose raised to sniff out trouble, eyes scanning for any sign of intrusion.

The humidity-soaked wind picked up, blowing her hair into a tangled mess. She trembled as the first raindrops, driven sideways, touched her bare shoulders.

Taina laid the bouquets against the headstone and pushed the floral stakes deep into the ground, but the tender blossoms would never survive the fierce winds.

She hugged Zeus to her chest and ran for the car as the rain fell like giant teardrops.

Miguel insisted on driving her home and waited until she'd closed the perimeter gate and hurried to the front door through the torrential rain. Jittery, Taina expected something to leap out and grab her. But nothing besides garbage, branches, and leaves skittered along. A turbid river of water streamed toward lower ground, churning like a whirlpool above the already overburdened sewer grates.

Zeus was sopping wet and led the dash upstairs. *Las Tombas* were in their cave, *Los Sangueros* in their den. The fairies were who knew where? And all the good people and good witches belonged inside their homes, candles at the ready, to weather the storm.

A warm bath, dry clothes, and a hot cup of tea later, Taina finally got to the messages.

Simone's idiomatic voice came up first. "Hope you're okay. Jeez, an earthquake, a bad anniversary, and a hurricane in the same week. What's next? Anyway, the courts will be closed tomorrow. Stay home. Stay dry."

Damn if Taina knew what was next, except that it made a wimpy earthquake and hurricane seem insignificant.

Next up, Arnaldo. "Taina, where the hell are you? They said you didn't come in to work. You got food and bottled water? Come stay with me here at *Sonrisa.*"

The time on that one was 3:30—about when she was at the cemetery.

His second message at 5:00 was less jolly. "Now I'm getting worried. Call me before the power goes out. Please."

Talking to Arnaldo rarely made things better, but not calling him was mean. Wind shook the windowpanes, and rain clattered through the gutters. The phone still worked.

He picked up, breathless, shouting over the message in progress, "Taina, hold on until this thing stops." *Beeeeeep.* "Pain in the ass. The message, not you. Where the hell you been?"

"I had a terrible headache and slept late. Then went to run some errands." She hadn't lied, just omitted a lot of facts. "Anyway, Zeus and I are home in our PJ's and just fine. Is this storm your doing?"

"Let's just say the rumbles I caused the other day might have stirred up the winds over the Atlantic. This damn city needs a good cleansing."

"You do realize people could lose their homes or die because of your 'acts of nature.'"

"The gods and goddesses control the fates of others, not me. Where the storm blows itself isn't my doing. You sure you don't want to come here?" Disappointment had replaced the relieved lilt in his voice.

"No. *Señora* Duarte might need help. Things are far worse in PR during hurricanes than on the third floor of a city apartment building. New Yorkers are real wimps." Good thing he couldn't see her hands shaking.

"Sure you're okay? No one should be alone in a storm."

"No thanks. Bye." Taina hung up before he heard her crying. Why did he always tie her up in knots like this? Why was the thought of his imposing presence and his strong arms around her so comforting?

A gust of wind howled around the building. Rain fell like angry gods tossing giant buckets of water from the heavens. The lights blinked on and off, then the power went out. She sat cross-legged on the floor next to her altar, Zeus in her lap. San Miguel's and *Yemayá's* flickering candles provided illumination, but no answers.

The one who could give her the information she needed to mete out justice would demand allegiance for immortal life. Would she rather die with her quest incomplete or outlive everyone, with no chance of ever meeting her family in some other place, in some other life? Who could be trusted to deliver what they promised, the witch with his own self-serving megalomania, or the dhampir with the intoxicating kiss?

No one should be alone in a storm. But she was always on her own.

Always had been. Always would be.

Chapter Twenty-Nine
The Eye of the Storm

Hurricanes in Puerto Rico made this one look like a spring breeze, but this was New York and they awfulized everything except the things they should.

Taina cleaned up the water that leaked around the window frames and puddled on the floor. She coaxed information from her cellphone news before the battery died. Spending the night in the dark, alone, was far from appealing, but the howling winds dissipated with daylight and the rain let up.

Sick of the litter box and a grumpy, restless mistress, Zeus danced on his back legs, front paws pumping up and down to stay upright.

She snapped on his leash. "Let's go."

Now, cramping and bleeding despite whatever the hell Josefa had concocted for Taina, or perhaps because of it, a trip to the *botánica* seemed essential enough to brave the eye of the storm.

Shop owners swept up debris, clearing piles of trash from the sewer grates so the flooded streets would drain water tinged with rainbows of gas and oil into the East River. A strong odor of fish wafted through the air.

Most of the steel grates were down over shop windows, but the bakery's generator hummed through the propped open side door. A tantalizing smell of fresh cookies drew Taina in through the front.

She tucked the dog under her arm but needn't have bothered. The counter girls fussed over the animal like he was a newborn infant.

"Give me a half pound of those cookies, a buttered roll, and tea with milk and two sugars."

One girl filled the box, tied it with thin blue and white string pulled from a metallic vessel hung from the ceiling. The other buttered the roll and prepared the tea. Did she wash her hands after Zeus had licked her like a Popsicle? He was her dog, anyway. Still.

"Seven dollars." The old-fashioned cash register tinged.

Taina gave her ten, then put the change in the till. She ate the roll, balancing the box of cookies on top of the cup, letting Zeus trail his lead on the way to the *botánica*.

One of the regulars held Josefa's door open for Taina. *"Muy buenas, nena.* She has a flood in the basement."

A bucket rattled from somewhere behind the curtain.

"¡Buenos días!" She called downstairs.

"¿Quien es?"

"Taina. Do you need help?"

Feet shuffled. Metal clanked. Zeus trapped Canela under a display cabinet. The cat hissed and swiped a few times, but the dog wouldn't retreat.

"Play nice." Taina turned the lock on the front door and went down.

"You're out early today." Josefa, wearing rubber rain boots and a housedress, hobbled around with a mop.

Taina's sneakers skidded on the floor, covered with about an inch of water. "Give me that, Josefa. If you fall you'll break something."

The *santera* didn't argue and emptied a full bucket into the slop sink. Taina opened two grimy, cobwebbed windows to let in fresh air. She swabbed. Josefa dumped. It took a few passes, but finally the floor was drying—and cleaner than it had been in a long time.

They washed their hands, and then Taina helped her up the stairs.

"Ay, nena, don't get old. The dampness seeps into my bones and won't let go." Josefa eased onto her stool behind the counter. "Make me some tea, please. And brew some using six drops of this for yourself. You need it." She handed over tea leaves as big as fingers and a brown bottle.

She lit the gas burner with a match and filled the kettle. "What is in this?"

Josefa smirked. "The headaches are troubling you again, *verdad?* Have you noticed they worsen when you are bleeding?"

The woman could divine without even trying. "This potion brings down the worst periods I've ever had in my life." Taina poured boiling water into two cups.

"It's true that cohosh increases the flow, but the red raspberry leaves tone the muscle and ease the cramps. Don't cheat. Full droppers."

"Can't you leave out the cohosh?" She sipped gingerly, determined to make Josefa think she was drinking when she really wasn't.

The *santera* pursed her lips. "It helps the headaches the rest of the time, *sí?*"

"They're magickally induced." Taina opened the cookies and pushed the box across the counter.

"It's all related. *Pues*, how can I help you today?" She chose two cookies with raspberry jelly and rainbow sprinkles.

"Someone set a fire in my apartment. Two gangs are after me because of work-related conflicts. There's been an earthquake and a hurricane on the anniversary of my family's death."

Josefa didn't affirm or refute the sentiments. "What is the question?"

"My job is negotiating a truce with people who do terrible things to each other. How can I do that without giving up my humanity?" Concealing the full truth from an advisor wasn't a good idea, but Josefa was sharp enough to divine it anyway.

"Ask Arnaldo. He knows how things work around here."

"He has some sort of pact with two other men. One set a fire— to warn me. He knows who killed my family and wants me to back off. The other man is trying to seduce me. Both are threatening Arnaldo because he's 'looking after me.'"

Josefa blew out and shook her head. "Arnaldo is always involved in things like this. I found out his birthdate."

"How?" Why seemed a more likely question, but according to him, Josefa had the reputation of being a matchmaker.

She rummaged through some papers. "I did some readings for his grandmother when he got into the drug trouble and got arrested."

"Well?" Would she be as merciless in interpreting his chart?

"He has lots of empty houses."

"Meaning?"

"Your combined charts are more interesting. In his Eleventh, the sector of friendship, hopes, and dreams, he's got Pluto and Uranus, and all of the rest reflect a focus on mastery, security, comfort, and sex-u-ality." The sparkle in Josefa's eyes augmented her emphasis on the carnal aspects.

"I recall my Eighth house was empty. You know the sex one. How about his?"

"Mars and Mercury in the Eighth, Taurus, very close to Venus and the Sun, again reflecting desire for pleasure and mastery."

"So he's a horny, alpha witch, and I'm not."

She burst into laughter. "You struggle between work and pleasure, personal comfort, and your higher calling."

"Noble, but frigid." Despite the banter Taina wasn't feeling as jolly as the *santera*.

Josefa's smile faded, but a trace remained. "Don't be so hard on yourself, *nena*. You thought of me this morning and helped clean up the mess downstairs." She handed Taina a tri-colored, chocolate frosted confection.

She bit into the sweet treat, but bitter tears stung her eyes.

The truth hurt, even if she lived it every day.

Josefa patted her arm. "Your Moon is either counterbalanced in squares, trines, or opposition with other planets. That's why you are in constant conflict. You've had a hard life and have earned some respite."

"And this means what in relation to Arnaldo?" Did she really want to hear that the horny, alpha, savior male was destined to dominate the wimpy, dependent, conflicted, opposed, bottled-up, squared, and turned into a hopeless stalemate female?

Josefa put on her glasses. "Earth and water make mud, a symbol of fertility. Your fire signature gives you drive, ambition, and courage. You'll run a circle around him before he even notices you've moved."

"Josefa, I'm not looking for a relationship."

She stared Taina down. "You need to douse that fire and the memories of it. Arnaldo can bring you back to life."

The woman had tapped the essence of her soul, but the last thing she wanted to hear was how to make mud with Arnaldo.

Josefa hunched over the papers. "Both of your Ninth houses are empty. No contracts." Her glasses came off for emphasis. "Your Eleventh, for friends and lovers is empty."

The word empty had begun to take on another dimension of misery.

Josefa's eyebrows rose. "The spirits of the *orishas* work in many ways. Petition *Yemayá*. She will quench the flames. All your physical ailments are related. Blood is red. Fire is red. Passion is red."

She hesitated, then knitted her hands together and concentrated hard on the murky water in a fountain. "I hear *Elegguá*...no, *Yemayá* calling to you. Whatever happens between you and Arnaldo will bend to her will."

Josefa went behind the curtain and returned with two bottles of that foul brown and pink liquid. "Another banishing and cleansing bath will negate the influence of those evil men. Ah, cleaning and divining exhausts me. Next week I will read your cards and advise you further."

"Of course." Maybe astrology wasn't the answer or was it just that they were answers she didn't want to hear.

Josefa pushed papers across the counter. "Here are the charts. Study them for any insights. Pay me what you think they're worth. You did, after all, mop my floors."

Taina gave her two twenties. "Blessed be." She clipped on Zeus's leash.

Blood flowed out of her like water, though the cramps had eased. Her Moon was on the cusp of void. Would it be safer to walk or take a cab? A crapshoot, like everything else in her life.

As she got to the door, once again stuck shut, Josefa called out. "Men do nothing for women but make their lives difficult, Taina. Arnaldo isn't perfect, but I know him since he was a boy. When I thought of any other men, then of you, *Elegguá* intruded. He has strange alliances. Even without seeing their charts, that omen is not good."

Taina almost asked more about *Elegguá,* but she could study more about what that *orisha* represented. She gave one huge tug, and the door opened. She closed it with an equal amount of effort and studied the picture of the Seven African Powers in the window.

Elegguá didn't seem any more threatening or dangerous than the others, but something in Josefa's voice had indicated otherwise.

Raul looked like something out of a GQ photo-shoot, while Arnaldo, when he wasn't cleaned up and on best behavior, was only a shade less dark in appearance than Lupo. No, appearance wasn't a good judgment parameter. *Elegguá's* influence notwithstanding, werewolves and dhampirs represented the undead and worshiped only themselves.

Chapter Thirty
The Melting Pot

Traffic lights were flashing by the time Taina got home, and so were her messages.

Arnaldo: "The landlady told me you went out in the eye of the storm, even though the mayor said everyone should stay inside. Turned out to be nothing. Call me."

Simone: "Buses and subways are expected back on or close to schedule tomorrow so we'll be open for business. Hope you had a romantic weekend. Don't ya just love storms?"

"Taina. Now that Arnaldo's diversionary tactic has blown by, I'll be waiting for you to call."

Her blood chilled. Of course Raul knew where she lived. And he wasn't giving up.

The cramping in her abdomen returned with a vengeance. She trimmed the candlewicks and rekindled the flames, then doused herself with the foul-smelling solutions and soaked in clear, cool water. The only thing that changed was the addition of nausea to the mix.

She'd barely finished toweling off and getting into a nightgown when Zeus, who'd been standing guard at his window yapped. His front paws rested on the windowpane, and his tail stood at attention. The dog ran to the door before the bell rang.

"I'm not answering, Zeus."

Footsteps clopped on the stairs. Arnaldo had the key! She put on a light bathrobe. She ignored the first tap, the second harder rap. By the third try, the banging resounded in her ears like a gong.

"Taina, you there?" The fear in his voice tickled her already queasy stomach.

"It's okay, Arnaldo. I'm sick and need to rest."

"Can I come in?"

Now she was just being mean. "Sure, but just for a minute." She opened the door a crack.

Arnaldo stood, hands on hips, as stern as any judge sitting on a bench. "Got company you don't want me to know about?"

"Ay, señor. No." She moved back and gestured for him to enter.

He bent to pat Zeus, then stared into her eyes. "You look terrible."

"It's been a rough week, Arnaldo. All this funky shit with the earthquake and the hurricane, and…"

How did she wind up in his arms, sobbing on his shoulder?

He smoothed the wet hair. *"Ya, mamita.* And what?"

She pushed away and composed herself. "This is the anniversary of the fire. This was the first time I've been in The Bronx since it happened."

He looked down. "I know."

A dagger of pain penetrated her head. She swayed. Her vision clouded over. "I need to lay down." Taina put her hands over her eyes to block out the light.

Arnaldo helped her into the bed and tucked the sheet over her. Her head sank into the pillow like a lead weight.

"Did you eat?" He brushed the hair away from her face and slipped his hands under hers to massage the temples.

"I'm not hungry."

"No wonder you have a headache."

"Josefa gave me something, but it makes my cramps so much worse." Taina reached for the medicine bottle on her nightstand.

He watched her put six drops of potion on her tongue. It usually eased the throbbing within a few minutes. But then the bleeding would increase.

Arnaldo crossed his arms over his chest, still perched on the side of the bed.

She had to get him out of here. "Can you get me some tea and yogurt?"

"Sure." He disappeared into the kitchen.

All she had to do was say she was better. Guzzle the tea. Eat a few spoons of yogurt. Lock the door behind him. Suffer in silence.

"Is it like this for you every month?" Arnaldo came back with the cup and container.

Taina could already look at him without her eyes hurting. "Just since I've been in The Bronx."

His brow furrowed. "What did Josefa say?"

"All female stuff that you don't want to know."

"Maybe you need to see a real doctor—not a witch doctor. Get it?" He elbowed her arm and cackled.

This wasn't the time for clever word play. Taina took two spoonsful of yogurt. "I can't call in sick again tomorrow." She swung her legs out of bed and struggled not to sway or hold onto anything as she walked.

"I can tell you want me to leave you alone. Call if you need anything." The door slammed behind him.

Zeus's tail wagged, and he whined as he watched Arnaldo go.

"I can't get involved with him, puppy dog."

He whimpered and stretched out on the window seat, looking away from his mistress in disagreement.

Taina included the dog in her rant. "You and the fairies are asking for miracles I don't have in me. Just because Arnaldo is the only game in town doesn't mean I have to play."

The dhamp and the werewolf had given up their humanity. Arnaldo had crossed over and came back, leaving a critical piece or two of himself behind but he was, at least, fully human.

All three wanted her because she was a witch with powers they coveted, and because she was a woman. Which, right now, she was very sorry about.

Taina ran for the bathroom.

~ * ~

"So, this *Boricua* Women's Shelter might have potential for selected clients, but taking a tour wasn't convenient." Simone flipped through the report.

"Well, to be fair it was the afternoon of the earthquake, then the hurricane hit. I'll have to make an appointment with Mr. Rivera and go back to take a look at the facilities." Taina had become very good at this game.

Plea bargains with obviously guilty criminals also made her uncomfortable. But undercover cops and defense attorneys colluded with enemy stooges all the time to get their man—or get their man off.

Time to learn how to swing from the tangled vines in the urban jungle.

And try to forget by doing mundane things: riding the subway, grocery shopping, walking Zeus past the Coca Cola deliverymen every morning for a snack—and going nowhere near Ritual Rock.

Magick-free, she had no headaches, no uncertainties.

But after a long, lonely Labor Day weekend, the heat and anxiety had risen to the ceiling. "When does it start to cool off around here? I thought September was the end of summer."

Sandy changed into sneakers. "More toward the middle of the month. It's still summer until September 21, right?"

"Actually, September 23 at 9:27 PM." She'd once looked forward to equinox, but not now.

"Not too anxious for cooler weather, are you? I thought you were from the tropics." Simone filed some papers.

"There's no relief from the heat around here. See you tomorrow."

Taina allowed herself to be swept along with the tide of humanity headed to the subway who'd been packed into the train like canned fish. As her stop approached, she elbowed through but didn't make out the door before it closed.

"Shit." She pounded the door, then kicked it. Of all times to miss the transfer point.

None of the other occupants of the car raised an eyelash at her childish commuter tantrum. Nor should they have done so. The pressure was getting to her, and it was always better to stay clear of bottled-up spirits about to pop a cork.

It built in her chest, and her heart pounded as the train stopped and started, stopped and started. Nothing unusual for rush hour, but if she didn't get out of this pressure cooker soon she would explode.

They pulled into the next station, and she was the first one off. Sucking the sour, stifling air below ground did nothing to alleviate the knot in her chest.

Competition for a cab was fierce, so she crossed the street and insinuated herself into one that had just discharged a passenger. "Prospect and 149th Street. How much?"

"Fifteen at this time, miss. Bad traffic." The cabbie didn't wait for her assent.

She settled into her seat. Time to move out of this neighborhood, away from the melting pot of species who'd never be able to learn to co-exist.

~ * ~

Taina walked Zeus in the empty lot instead of the park, pausing him to mark every hydrant and lamppost.

The familiar whirr and whoosh of pigeon wings drew her attention to an exceptionally large bird with deep green iridescent stripes on its wings perched on a trash bin. "Hello, Bridge Rat. I haven't seen you for a while."

He bobbed his head. "Hawk Claw and I have deployed our best sentries to this sector. They normally patrol upper Manhattan so they're familiar with the mundane and magickal culture of urban wastelands. The Bronx is particularly unsettled right now."

"So it seems. Was my mother aware of the danger?"

"Of course. She did her best to protect you, but the burning times were very terrible. Since birth, your power shone like a beacon. It attracted a lot of attention." His beady eyes blinked, and his neck toggled like cogs on a wheel.

"It still does. Most of it the wrong kind."

Bridge Rat hopped onto the ground in front of her and pecked at some crumbs. "Indeed, the cauldron is bubbling. And it will boil over before long. Lady Taina, none of them have ever obeyed any law, mundane or magickal. That's why you are here—to impose reason, tolerance, and balance."

"Bridge Rat, that makes no sense. You've told me to align myself with Arnaldo." She stamped her foot and the pigeon, putting on a good show for the mundanes, flapped away.

He alighted on top of a battered plastic newspaper container. "Things must be skewed before they can be put right. Reports from the field indicate that your comportment and your strategies are quite effective.

"Strong males of any species will rebel against a stronger female. You must not be afraid to use your power against them, my lady. Soldier on. The fae have your back. And we are preparing for the final phase."

Hearing it couched in military terms made it more ominous. "Is the battle near?"

"I feel an odd energy surge, but I'm not clairvoyant, Lady Taina. Seek guidance from your advisor, your own scrying, your own instinct." He brushed one wing against the back of the bench and flew into the trees.

"*Coño*. Let's go home, Zeus. I have to go to work tomorrow." She picked up the dog and hurried to beat the advancing twilight.

A legion of pigeon sentries lined the wide expanse of 149th Street, roosting on windowsills, awnings, streetlights—wherever they could find a claw hold.

By the time she arrived home, the battalion commander himself was ensconced in the dormer eave of her apartment. Rat sentries poked their heads out from behind the garbage pails. Their whiskers twitched in acknowledgement.

Magick simmered underground, kissing her feet like bubbles in a pot of boiling water. Late-summer lethargy notwithstanding, ignoring that would be a like not doing repairs and waiting for a transformer to blow or a water main about to burst, burning up or flooding everything in its path.

Not only the season was about to change.

Chapter Thirty-One
Esbat

A whiff of fall blew down the street. The crisp, acrid essence replaced the warm, soggy must. For the first time in as long as Taina could remember, the tropical girl wasn't in the tropics.

Fire hydrants weren't spraying, and the kids chased each other through grass littered with dry, brown leaves that had given up early. What would next summer bring? If she lived that long.

She squinted against the glare of a setting sun. Zeus's ears pricked. Although the dog was on alert, and no doubt the fairies were in the trees, it seemed more than foolish to close her eyes.

She gazed at the courtyard gate, beyond which lurked all those terrible memories. Raul's building was out of the range of vision, but for the first time she appreciated her family's apartment had formed one point of a triangle linking Ritual Rock to the damp/were alliance.

What had Mama known? How had she concealed her worry from two daughters and mundane husband? Had her father known who—and what—he was taking on when he fought against noise and littering and loitering in and around their building? No matter how hard she tried, even immersed among the mundane, doing mundane things, Tania's magickal legacy intruded.

The sun disappeared behind the buildings. Kids ran back to their mothers. Dusk began to paint the sky with purple. Though she didn't have candles and her mindset wasn't right, this was as close as she would get to a solitary esbat for tonight's full moon.

A new disturbance flowed through the energy field around Ritual Rock, though there was no other sign of werewolves. Zeus applied nose to ground led her past the peculiar part of the rock formation facing the street, which today appeared more like a portal appended to the granite slab than it ever had before. A faint yellow glow marbled the granite, barely distinguishable from the white veins snaking top to bottom.

Dirt bubbled, bathing her sandal-clad feet. To mundane eyes it was just dust being kicked up by wind, but hot werewolf breath churned in that underground lair as they did whatever lycanthropes did until the cover of darkness.

Zeus stopped, one foreleg raised like a pointer's, gaze intent on the portal.

"You found them buddy, but we're not hanging around." She picked him up and almost bumped into the African woman holding a tea light inside a votive jar, guarding it from the wind with one hand.

"Blessed be." Taina bowed and stepped out of her way.

"And blessed be to you as well." The woman's voice conjured the image of a foreign land, her tribal dress the thought of drums, dancing, and song. "Will you join me for a circle in tribute to *Yemayá* on this night?"

"She is my *orisha*, well at least the once who I've been advised to honor at this time." Synchronicity was the goddesses's way of showing their pleasure.

"Yemayá means much to my people, and now that I am separated from my family and friends, knowing she looks after them gives me much comfort." The woman's smile did nothing to hide the sadness in her ebony eyes.

"My name is Taina. Might I know yours?"

"I am known as Yoruba."

"Yes, but just once around. It isn't safe after dark." Taina fought hard to walk slowly as the woman inched deosil, chanting under her breath in a language reminiscent of French.

Tania tried to open herself to the moon goddess but was distracted watching for anyone or anything to emerge from the shadows. Her breath caught as, on the final round, Raul's silhouette appeared on his customary seat upon Ritual Rock.

The woman, deep in prayer and meditation, ignored or did not take notice, but the dhampir smiled and nodded before gesturing like a magnanimous priest to continue. True to his word, he did not disturb their worship. In fact, he might be the only reason Lupo hadn't done so already.

They continued around, out of his line of sight. Energy flowed like an ocean current, predictable, calm, deliberate.

A few deep breaths later, something moved Taina to chant. "This is the time of the bearing of fruits, of change realized. To she who awakens yearning in the heart and who is the end of desire, we look on her shining face and ware filled with love. Merry meet."

The goddess, or the *orisha*, filled Taina with a bottomless sense of peace, of hope. Warmth spread out from her core. Moonlight oozed from her fingertips. The first sincere smile she had in a long time parted her lips. When awareness returned, Yoruba had already turned the corner.

Taina forced herself to stay in the moment until she rounded Ritual Rock. The closer she drew to the werewolf portal, the faster the magick flowed from her. She clenched her fists to try and preserve as much as she could.

Her companion likely sensed it as well and halted.

"It's not safe to proceed. We're being watched." Taina pointed to where Raul sat.

Yoruba's chin did not drop, and her eyes did not narrow. "I believe that the *orishas* will protect me. But if you are fearful, then take your leave."

Taina's cheeks burned with embarrassment. She was behaving like a coward—just what Raul and Lupo counted on. "No, I will unbind the circle before departing."

"You lead this time, Miss Taina." Yoruba handed over the candle and gestured.

She put Zeus down to stand guard and struggled to be mindful of the purpose of this devotion—though the moon was merely a pale white disc in the still orange and purple sky. The goddess departed, along with the sense of gratitude, of welcome, of peace.

Her flesh crawled as if covered by flies. Her scalp tingled and burned. The energy turned funky, evil, conflicted.

They reached the starting point. Taina handed Yoruba the candle.

She took it, blew it out and sliced a passage in the air like taking an ax to a log. "Blessed be. Take care for sure, but remember to always be strong, believe in the protection of our *orishas*. Far too many have been frightened and turned off their path."

Taina did not want her to leave. "I am fortunate to have met you tonight. So mote it be."

Their spirits once again touched, emitting a spark of light.

Yoruba walked across the park in the opposite direction.

Zeus, who'd followed behind Taina as if attached to her heel, strained to leave.

She didn't need any more encouragement to hurry after him, glancing over her shoulder, all the while scanning the street for any sign of dhamps and weres.

The night of a full moon was no time to be out after dark in The Bronx.

~ * ~

The smell of gasoline, of smoke, burning flesh, screams, her mother's arms, the relief of fresh air as mama kicked out the window, her mother's incantation, her last kiss, flying, drifting slowly, thudding into the man's arms.

He caught her as if she'd been tossed like Daddy used to play with her, not for her life.

"Shit, what do I do with it?" He smelled like sweat, reefer, tobacco. His green eyes darted.

"Give it to a fireman. We've got to get the hell out of here."

Screams, sirens, he held her against his chest, elbows poked, water sprayed, droplets like rain, steam, metal clanked. "She threw her little girl from that window. Someone get this kid into an ambulance. We're going into the apartment—for recovery."

Another pair of arms, a stiff, hard coat, heat, soot-stained face, funny hat. Clanking. "You're okay."

Every time the script played in her mind, more details crystalized. Taina sat, threw off the covers, got ready to run.

Zeus regarded her from this window post as if to say, "What's up with you?"

Her heartbeat gradually slowed. No matter that she had the fae on guard, no matter where she moved, the nightmare would never go away. Who had been speaking to Jesús?

She and Zeus beat the deliverymen to their breakfast, and she headed to the courthouse early to rebuild some good will lost by the multitude of absences.

By the time Simone and Sandy arrived, Taina had more than enough time to clear her inbox, tidy up her files, and even make coffee.

"Plans this weekend, Taina?" Simone started the traditional Friday morning pep rally.

"To rest—a lot."

"Not gonna see your fella?"

"Things aren't going well between us. Too much personal stuff."

"Aw, too bad." Sandy sipped and booted her computer.

Taina wandered into her office. Her charts showed that she was too intense on the job, which was true, and that her relationship with a partner was gaining positive momentum—which wasn't.

The last long, solitary month had shown that removing herself from the magickal vortex wasn't running away. She'd still be working close by—and close to the law enforcement officials who could protect her while she tried to nail the killers.

This had to be the last full moon in her apartment.

Chapter Thirty-Two
Zombie Encroachment

Summer refused to quit. Whatever relief the sundress offered was offset by dodging delivery trucks and leering auto mechanics distracted from their other body and fender work. By the third catcall, Taina's nerves were as frayed as an overstretched rubber band.

She enabled auras to scan the area for colored glare. The grease monkeys bled mundane gray into the haze.

A locus of energy pulsed in her gut like a radar blip. A man with a yellow aura disappeared into a *bodega*. She hurried past. She visualized a spiral of white light around her, infusing through the top of her head, through her body, all the way down to her toes. Energized, centered, protected, she entered the danger zone.

One of the mundanes dashed across the street and got in her face. "*Ay, chica.* You lookin' for a good man?"

The back of her arm met his face and slammed him into the brick face of a windowless factory. He stood back up, dazed. If he'd had a red or yellow aura, she'd have drop kicked him into oncoming traffic.

A glare and one forceful exhale later, the other backed away. The mundane gangstas, too street-wise to fuck with this bold Bronx bitch, retreated. The pigeon sentries atop a ramshackle awning hadn't had time to act.

Jesús rounded the corner just across from Miguel's shop and headed for the beer cans scattered around an overflowing, wire-mesh trash bin. This was her chance to ask him if he remembered anything about that night and who he was with. To find out if his zombie brain could recall anything.

Taina was within sprinting distance of the main drag, a few blocks from her house. Just a simple question, he wouldn't know the answer, and her curiosity would be assuaged. She could find a new neighborhood, never think about him again, read about *Las Tombas* and *Los Sangueros* in the newspaper.

She didn't dare walk past abandoned warehouses that served as fronts for *Las Tombas's* zombie tombs. Taina ducked into the dubious safety of Miguel's garage.

As always, he stopped whatever he was doing and rushed over. *"¿Nena, que pasó?"*

"I'm going to look for a new place today and want to take the car. If it's not too much trouble."

He grinned. "Good thing I didn't sell it. Finally taking my advice?"

She'd spare him the details. "I'm tired of being a prisoner in my apartment."

"It only gets worse in winter when it's cold and dark. I'll be back in Culebra before the snow flies. Got a deal going to buy me out." A dreamy look came over Miguel's face, as if he'd seen a vision.

His excitement and anticipation energized her. *"Que bueno.* I might decide to keep my car. Let me pay you something for keeping it for me."

He found the keys and led her to the back lot. "My pleasure. Just be sure to come back to say goodbye." He opened the door, and his eyes teared up.

"Of course I will." She kissed him on the cheek, then regretted it when she caught sight of the mechanics gawking.

Well-practiced in the ritual, she waited for him to open the steel security gate, then pulled out into the back street, prepared to run over anyone who got in her way.

But there were only a few mundanes hosing off produce trucks just back from their early morning deliveries. Spray from the power-washing hoses splattered like bullets against the windshield. Taina turned the corner and headed north on the Bruckner like she'd succeeded at a prison break.

The northern end of The Bronx, lined with strip malls and row houses interspersed with big apartment buildings—some still with soot stains from the burning years—seemed like paradise.

No magickal vibes, gray auras, and a few gangstas, but nothing like the South Bronx that teemed like an uncovered nest of roaches. While immersed in the misery, she'd never appreciated how difficult the last two months had been.

Distance would let her do her job with minimal interference, especially if Raul honored his end of the bargain and kept Lupo under control. And without Arnaldo pressed into being her de facto bodyguard, the burner would be turned down before the pot overflowed to give the unholy triumvirate time to rebalance.

The apartment on the second floor of a four-family building would allow her to bring Zeus and was near Bronx Park and the Number Five subway line. It was no bigger, no better than the one she had, and needed a lot of cleaning and painting.

But it was available on October first, and the landlord agreed to call her landlady for a reference. Taina left a $100.00 deposit and headed home.

Dusk had just kissed the sky. Where would she park, and how would she get home safely? She took Southern Boulevard and drove past *Sonrisa,* hoping to see Arnaldo and let him volunteer to help. Like he always did.

A flock of birds flew so low they almost grazed her windshield. Several pigeons followed.

Her shoulders rose on either side of her neck, and she gripped the wheel. Fairy soldiers never chased real birds, and she'd never seen them shift into sparrows. Maybe they weren't fae, and there was a real hawk around.

A car pulled out of a spot almost directly in front of *Sonrisa.* Parallel parking was a skill New Yorkers had raised to an art form— and she was far from practiced at it.

A dull thud came from behind, and she slammed on the brakes. A yellow-tinged zombie pounded the car as he worked his way around to the front. Each blow rattled the fillings in Taina's teeth as the swings with a metal baseball bat got progressively more forceful.

Spittle dripped from his mouth. Rotted teeth hung from his gums and threatened to fall out as his lips curled up in an evil clown's smile. His clothes, merely rags, stank like piss even through the closed windows.

Taina advanced slowly, but the skeletal figure hanging onto passenger side mirror picked up his feet and took the ride.

Sweat, the nervous men's-locker-room kind, soaked her armpits. Taina braked hard to try and dislodge him. Instead, he used the opportunity to clamber onto the hood. When she blew the horn, his grin turned to a whatever-teeth-he-had-left snarl.

The zombie jumped down, leaving a few clumps of stringy hair on the car, then raised the bat behind his shoulders like a home-run-derby competitor.

She didn't wait for the glass to shatter, for him to grab her, bite her, or goddess-only-knew what. She floored the accelerator and two clomps later, both he and the baseball bat were under her car. Crying, shaking, ready to puke, she pounded on the steering wheel. "Please don't die. Please…"

The birds circled again.

Arnaldo ran down the street after them. "Goddamn fairy bastards buzzing my house like locusts. What the hell…" Whatever he saw had to be awful given the fact his eyes looked like two full moons with a reflection of a third where his mouth should have been. *"Ay, coño, mami.* No recycling that motherfucker."

Taina opened the door, stepped out and took a few steps toward the front of the car. The street was empty of people, though she did see flashes of yellow in the deepening shadows. "I had no choice. He would have killed me." She couldn't bear to look.

"Of course he would have. When Lupo is holed up with the weres, zombies run amok. The mundanes don't know why, but the energy is so wacked out they just pull down the blinds and hide. But not Taina Aponte. No, she just walks right into it."

Taina cried like a kid whose father had slapped her up the side of her head. "Fuck you! I was coming here to ask you to walk me home."

The stink was so putrid she retched. While doubled over, spitting a mouthful of vomit onto the street, Taina caught sight of the zombie's head squashed like a tomato under the front wheel. His brains looked like overcooked curly pasta smeared into the tire treads. The rest of his body lay chest down, arms snapped off at the shoulder, one hand still holding the mangled bat. No blood, only mounds of green, snot colored flesh and powdered bones littered the ground.

The falafel sandwich that had tasted so good going down blended in with the rest of the splatter on the ground.

"You'll get used to it. He would have bashed your pretty little head in and made a meal of *your* brains. Remember that." Arnaldo patted her back.

She dug through her purse for a tissue. Stomach acid gurgled, and her throat screamed for a drink of water. "Call the police!"

"You're crazy! Get in trouble for killing a dead guy? I'll get a pail and shovel and take what's left of him to the zombie graveyard. Without a head there ain't nothing they can reconstitute."

She put her head in her hands and started to cry again. "I've never killed anyone."

"Knock it off. They're just shells of a human form. Useless. Zombies know nothing except what their master has drilled them to do. Go down to *Sonrisa* and wait inside. I'll take care of everything. In fact, there are a few more of them hanging around that might drag him away once I get him in the can." Arnaldo kicked the body parts into a pile of what looked like a garbage bag that had been run over a few times.

Her knees wobbled like jelly. He helped her down the street and grabbed a green pail marked for paper recycling and a spade. She couldn't take her gaze off the scene as he scooped up the remains like she did with Zeus's poop and dumped it in.

Arnaldo whistled through his teeth. "Come and get it, you miserable zombie motherfuckers. When you gonna learn not to mess with witches?"

Three of them shambled out of alleyways—all toting bags full of cans and bottles.

"Clean up the mess good. Lupo will be pissed if he finds out you went hunting while the weres had their orgy." Arnaldo got in the car and backed into the spot like a true Nuyorican. He jumped out and ran after them. "Don't forget to give my shovel back. And that pail better be back in my yard, or I'll tell Lupo on you."

What was she doing there, among these miserable creatures and a witch who'd compromised all of his morals and always descended to the level of the least common denominator?

How could she forget she'd killed someone with her car and fled the scene? In two months, Taina had become more like Arnaldo because it was just too much damn trouble to follow the rules. The damps and weres and zombies hadn't changed her. She'd done it all by herself, with a help from her witchy friend.

He disappeared with the remaining zombies. Taina paced, contemplated calling the cops to report she'd hit someone who'd only been slightly injured and walked away. They wouldn't be able to piece together anything meaningful from the gore splattered on the grill and undercarriage of the car.

But not until she was sure Arnaldo was back from cleaning up her mess and safe inside, so he couldn't be implicated in disposing of the body.

The thud as a zombie threw the empty garbage pail over the fence brought back the moment a wheel ran over the guy's head. Fighting back the nausea, heart beating like it was coming out of her throat, Taina went outside.

He drove the car from the parking place and gestured to open the gate. Only magick could have allowed it to fit through the narrow opening. "What are you doing?"

The passageway constricted behind it.

"Gotta hose it down along with the pail. Don't want Lupo snooping around. Doubt he'll even miss one of his grunts but…"

"No! I'm going to call the police and tell them—"

"Hell you are." He took her by the shoulders. "Fughetaboudit. It was just another piece of road kill."

"It was once human!" The memory of running over a duck along a dirt road in PR came back, as it did from time to time.

Along with the recollection of the poor thing looking straight into her eyes as Taina had slammed on the brakes and tried to stop. And of herding the orphaned ducklings into her car as tears dripped onto their downy backs. And of driving to a pond to release them, hoping another mother duck would care for them though she knew it was hopeless.

And of returning to feed them bread and birdseed every day until they disappeared—either adopted or eaten, though she really didn't want to know. And they were a hell of a lot sweeter than a zombie, except the guy was a vestige of a man…

The spatter of water on metal jarred her out of the trance.

She tried to grab the hose, but Arnaldo wouldn't let go. Their shoes were soaked and the car washed clean of any evidence except the dents and dings left behind by the baseball bat.

He restrained her arms as she pummeled his chest. "*Ya.* Enough. Forget about it."

A bubbling puddle gurgled into the street and down the sewer.

Taina dissolved into his arms like salt into water. "It was self-defense. The police would have understood. But now that you destroyed the evidence, I can't prove anything."

He held her tight and kissed the top of her head. "*Una Tomba* running wild is dangerous. I know, because I almost got to that point. Except I got arrested and put away long enough for me to realize what was happening. That fucker would have killed you or dragged you away beaten senseless for Lupo to work his own brand of magick on."

Taina pushed away. "The law…"

He shook her again. "*Las Tombas* have none—other than blind allegiance to their leader. Stop trying to bring Lupo, and Raul for that matter, into compliance with mundane rules or you're gonna get killed—or worse."

Sobs swallowed her breath. "I'm moving. Found a place today. Up north. I can't take it around here anymore."

The crow's feet on his face deepened. "You were warned, but you can't get away now. Even if you go all the way back to PR, they won't give up. You're in as deep as all of us.

Arnaldo relaxed his grip. She turned her back. The water spigot whined, and the spurting ceased. Rubber thwacked as he rewound the hose.

She stared at the dark stain in the street where the zombie ceased to exist. It could have been oil dripped from a truck, or the gooey residue of garbage crushed beneath the wheels of a car.

Like the memory of a mother duck, and her orphaned babies set free to live or die according to the whims of nature, it penetrated her soul. It conjured a memory of the shrouded remains of her family wheeled by as she gulped air from a plastic mask.

Arnaldo's arms wrapped around her from behind. "Leave the car here until tomorrow. I'll walk you home to get Zeus. You can come back and stay here, if you'd like."

"I'll decide later."

The lost duckling had returned to the scene of the crime, and an ex-con was advising her.

A horn blared. Arnaldo pulled her out of the way of a truck barreling down 149th Street. "C'mon, Taina. Shake it off." He nearly dragged her back to the apartment.

The exhilaration of realizing there was a parallel world just a few miles north where Taina hoped to re-enter the mundane life had vanished. The zombies, if they were sentient enough, would be able to identify her and Arnaldo to Lupo—or the police. Not even Zeus's excitement and sweet kisses could re-kindle hope.

Señora Duarte peeped through the window as they entered, then ducked back behind the curtains.

The message that popped up on Taina's phone explained why. "Your landlady tells me someone set a fire set outside your apartment a couple of weeks ago in retaliation for something that happened at the courthouse. I'm sorry but come and pick up the deposit. I can't take any chances."

She raised an arm to hurl the phone against the wall.

Arnaldo stopped her. "It doesn't matter. You still have to finish what you started."

"And I don't need you to keep grabbing and holding me back. I'll do what I damn well please. Goodbye."

"Why don't you come back with me?" Now that she'd entered the lawbreaker's league, Arnaldo swaggered more than usual.

"No. I have to go to work tomorrow. I'll pick up the car tomorrow night."

"Taina, I'm only trying to help."

"Please, Arnaldo."

He shook his arms in the air as if summoning the gods to his assistance. "So you can stay here and ruminate? Are you going to run to Raul again, to see if he can make it all better?"

So, the dhampir had told him of their meeting in the park. "I am not going to tell anyone, and I hope you won't, either. Since you ruined the evidence, you're just as complicit as I."

"Stop talking like a lawyer and start thinking—and acting—like a witch." The apartment door slammed behind him, followed by thunderous footfalls on the linoleum, the final thud of the heavy building door, the exterior gate latch clicking.

Normally, the noise would have raised worries about disturbing the landlady, who'd just screwed herself into more time with a troublesome tenant.

Chapter Thirty-Three
The Werewolf Advance

Tension crackled in the air. With no clear source, and no outlet, it swirled around Taina, whipping up a tornado of anxiety. Every footfall, *clank, clunk, thud, creak*, siren, crying baby, telephone—everything kicked her in the back of her head.

Nothing helped—potions, meditation, *Agua de Azahar*, chamomile, aconite.

She flattened herself against the subway walls and walked in the middle of the street. The full moon had come and gone, and Lupo hadn't retaliated. She needed to relax.

She'd pored over the newspapers, even searched police reports to see if anyone had reported a missing person or found a badly decomposed body anywhere in The Bronx. But even after five days, fear found its foothold in every moment.

If her work performance slipped any further, she'd be fired. But every time the phone rang, she fancied it was a detective wanting to ask her a few questions about something someone saw happen on Southern Boulevard last Sunday night.

The car was still parked mere feet from the crime scene, begging to be noticed. Tonight, she'd have to go and bring it back to Miguel.

And face Arnaldo, and the fact he was right: She had to be prepared to kill before being killed.

Zeus leaped around her feet as she came in the door. She kicked off her shoes and slipped into sandals. "Come puppy." She carried him down the stairs, and his kisses soothed her like aloe on a burn.

The sun was going down, and she dared not go near Raul and Lupo.

The dog strained, and Taina let him lead her toward the few patches of grass on the opposite side of the street, next to the abandoned gas station where the fairies had gifted him to her.

Growls, almost imperceptible, rippled through the air. Zeus raised his head, snarled, his head swiveling side-to-side. But there was no one. Nothing. Not even a shadow, the flicker of an aura. Only a prickle of fear that raked down her back like sharp fingernails.

"Let's get out of here, Zeus." They started across the street, but a caravan of trucks had the light and pushed them back.

She tapped her foot, waiting for green. Zeus yelped.

Something seized the back of her shirt and tore it off one shoulder. Her cry got lost in the thick, furry palm clamped over her mouth. The smell of stale tobacco, of body odor so stale it had putrefied, and of rotting teeth wrapped around her like a moldy blanket. Still more wolf than man, Lupo guffawed with excitement.

Taina bit down, stomped, twisted—but the thick body dragged her through a hole in the chain link fence, kicked through the decaying plank covering what used to be the restroom entrance, and shoved her inside.

He grunted and struggled to hold onto her with an arm around her neck and a hand over her mouth. The other meaty paw moved up her skirt and ripped off her panties.

All the strength she could muster didn't loosen his grip. She couldn't let him rape her, then bite her, then change her, but no magickal spell came to mind.

Every time he pushed her down and his pulsing cock brushed closer, Taina bucked like a wild horse. Which one of them would tire first?

Lupo slapped her, then smashed her head against the cinder block wall.

Taina's neck cracked. Her arm went numb, but she refused to surrender. The window covered with worm-eaten wood swam in her sight, then everything blurred. Her tongue tangled on the only spell that came to mind, and she couldn't organize the diffuse, conflicted energies around her.

Her knees wobbled and buckled. Lupo knelt behind her and groveled with delight, then shrieked like someone had cut off his arm. His grip loosened.

Taina crawled out from under him and toward the door. "Zeus, where are you?"

She turned toward his growl and saw Lupo, on all fours. The dog hung by his teeth off the werewolf's balls, all four paws flailing, claws scratching whatever parts of him they could reach. Lupo gyrated trying to dislodge the pooch, but Zeus wasn't letting go.

"Come, Zeus. Now." She hauled herself up by holding onto the splintered doorframe but couldn't get her legs to hold her weight.

Another figure squeezed through the broken plank and nearly knocked her back down.

Unmistakable licorice scent, velvet voice, even in this situation. "Stay in here, Taina. There are more weres outside."

With no choice but to trust Raul, Taina sank to the floor.

He held Lupo by the nape of the neck and magickally muzzled him with a twist of his palm. The willowy dhampir held him fast but couldn't subdue the werewolf's flailing forelegs.

Arnaldo broke through whatever was left of the ramshackle door like a superhero, tore off his shirt, and pinned Lupo's forelegs in a makeshift straitjacket. He did his deep breathing, intoned something under his breath until the werewolf hung limp in Raul's hands.

Zeus let go and scurried to Taina's side.

The werewolf quivered like a bug that just got a shot of insecticide.

She unleashed her fury on him. "I thought we had a deal. You stay out of my way, and I'll stay out of yours. You reneged. That's a big word. Do you know what it means or are you just stupid?"

Lupo's hairy fists clenched so tight they looked like paws.

Arnaldo twisted the fabric to get a better hold as the angry werewolf regained consciousness. "Knock it off, Lupo. We're not letting go until you settle down."

"You're not letting him go, period!" Taina's vision began to clear. The sight of the trio struggling like a bunch of kids after a playground scuffle flipped her pissed off circuit breaker. They'd laid bare what Arnaldo had described as a magickal triangle to maintain 'balance,' which was nothing more than a show of male dominance.

"I've got ten fingernails worth of the wolf man's DNA material, plus whatever hair and slobber all three you left on my skin and clothes. There is bound to be some there to prove who assaulted me.

"Then, Raul, I'll share that you intimidated me in the courtroom, and that Lupo spread scat all over my fence, which I also saved for analysis. I'm not playing your games."

While Arnaldo and Raul caught their breath, evil, dark magickal energy bombarded Taina, but with Zeus in her arms she finally found her center. She breathed white light in through the top of her head and it spiraled down into her core, expelling all their dirty filthy thoughts, wishes, and intentions. She blew a silvery cloud around them. Even the hairy, brutish werewolf twitched.

Raul and Arnaldo hauled Lupo to the door his yellowed teeth protruding over his lips, dripping saliva.

Raul, panting with the effort, called to whomever, whatever was waiting in the now-darkened lot. "Take him back to your lair until he sleeps off his fur. If I as much as see any of you on the streets before that, you'll be dog food."

Two *Las Tombas* soldiers, humanoid but still covered with dark fur, lifted Lupo under the shoulders and half-carried, half-dragged him out, leaving a trail of dark blood behind.

"Why did you let him go? You said you could control him. Seems like that isn't true, Raul."

"He can't be seen in this state." Raul huffed.

"And why is that your problem?" She knew the answer but wanted to see how he covered up the conspiracy.

"I can't be everywhere, Taina. I told you Lupo was crass, unsophisticated, and wouldn't honor you the way you deserved. You need to be under my protection." The dhampir made a good show of damage control.

"I've offered you protection, but you insist on staying alone." Arnaldo was not going to be upstaged.

"I'm not a toy, a treat, a tidbit, or a bargaining chip. I want nothing to do with either of you."

"Taina, please reconsider. Your fae friends didn't get Arnaldo here on time. What if you'd been bitten?" Raul's voice could melt butter.

"And raped." They seemed to have forgotten that, even though she was half naked on the floor of a filthy, abandoned restroom.

Arnaldo put himself between Taina and the dhampir. "You got your facts wrong, Raul. The pooch made short work of gelding the wolf man. We just did bouncer duty."

Both extended their hands, inviting Taina to choose her savior. She retrieved her shoes, her purse. Smoothed her hair. Pulled down her skirt. Covered her boobs the best she could. Took out her phone. Dialed 911.

"I've just been assaulted in the abandoned gas station near the corner of Prospect Avenue and 149th Street. This guy tried to rape me, but two passersby scared him off. Please hurry, or he'll get away." Taina closed the phone.

"Now get out of here, unless you want to be called into court to testify against your 'friend.'" She waved at both of them, using all ten fingers worth of evidence.

Raul's voice turned sharp as glass, cold as ice. "Don't tell the police you know who it is. Or else."

"I'll tell them whatever I goddamn please." The exertion set her wobbling, and she sank back to the floor.

He turned to Arnaldo. "I think you can convince her why that isn't a good idea." Without waiting for either to respond, he slithered into the night.

Arnaldo, shirtless, reeking of sweat and werewolf musk, walked over and extended a hand to help her up. "Lupo could counter any claim that he assaulted you with an accusation that you killed one of his friends."

"Because you wouldn't let me call the police, and my car is parked in your yard with who-knows-what evidence clinging to the hood."

"I brought the car back to Miguel on Monday. After two car washes."

She still wasn't taking his hand. "Lupo and I have been going at it for more than a month. And there is a record of him threatening me in the courthouse."

He exhaled. "All alleged, with no evidence. And each case is considered separately. Believe me, been there, done that—from the other side."

Red lights flickered as the police pulled into the lot.

"I'm telling them his name, everything."

Arnaldo knelt next to her. "I got here as fast as I could and have been, and always will, protect you the best I can. I don't make demands, only suggestions. Let the cops analyze the DNA and come to their own conclusions. Please."

The flashing strobe and cop's flashlights illuminated his face, etched with sadness. She took his hand and let him haul her up.

Zeus padded to her side and stood, head high and proud, at her service. Taina swayed and almost threw up—a combination of the dizziness, the fear, the stench, and the implications.

Arnaldo held her against him. "Over here, officers. My friend ran after the creep. She's trying to be brave but is hurt real bad. Please call an ambulance."

~ * ~

Simone waited with Taina outside Lincoln Hospital while Arnaldo hailed a cab.

"I told the on-call advocate not to bother you." Taina hugged her.

"Nonsense. I wish I'd met this gentleman under more pleasant circumstances, but I'm so happy you have such a source of support." Simone patted his shoulder.

"I try and look out for her. You take the first one." He opened the taxi door.

She backed away. "Taina needs to get home as quickly as possible."

"But you have to go to work. Another one will be along." Taina pushed her forward.

"Okay, but don't even think of coming back until next week." Simone slid in and waved goodbye.

Five AM. Taina couldn't keep to one train of thought, which they assured her was a result of a concussion. In the mundane world, sure. But not in hers.

How about that really neat team magick trick Raul and "gentleman" Arnaldo had used to gain control of the raging werewolf? Evidence enough that they'd worked together before and were now trying to keep their triangle of deceit in balance.

Raul's arrival had been too well-timed, too convenient, and he performed as if on the set of the hottest new teenage vampire flick. But Arnaldo had taken Zeus to *Sonrisa* before coming to the hospital. Then he'd stayed for the entire ER marathon while every orifice was probed and swabbed for evidence against the "unknown assailant" whom she'd 'seen around the area' and believed was stalking her.

Crisp fall air smacked her in the face. The sun still hadn't cracked the darkness, and the moon still looked full, bathing the street in an eerie glow. Arnaldo flagged down another car.

"Where to?" The driver studied the two of them carefully. Couldn't take any chances in this neighborhood.

Arnaldo opened the car door. "The nurse said someone should keep an eye on your for the next twenty-four hours. And remember that my man Zeus is waiting at *Sonrisa* for us. Okay?"

She had no fight left in her. Did it matter where she slept off this nightmare? "Sure."

He answered the cabbie's annoyed glare as they got into the back seat and he slid next to her. "2344 Southern Boulevard. Once I get you settled I'll get breakfast for all of us."

"Just fantastic. I'm going to lose my job, my apartment, and soon enough, my life."

Arnaldo moved closer. His voice dropped to a whisper. "It's a good thing that Zeus has got your back. And those fairy birds are really annoying, but they didn't quit until they caught my attention and told me you were in trouble. But the offer of a job and place to stay still stands."

"I don't trust any of you." The nausea was getting worse.

He turned away. "You're putting me in league with Raul and Lupo? Sure, I've done things I'm not proud of, but I stopped—all of it. I'm an honest man and ethical witch, and proud of it."

The cabbie was dancing in his seat to some weird Bollywood music that stabbed Taina between the eyes with every pluck of a sitar. The floodlight in front of *Sonrisa* went on as they pulled up to the front gate, making it hurt even worse.

Arnaldo paid, helped her out, and inside the perimeter gate. But not before her gaze found the dark spot, the indelible mark in the street that had smudged her soul.

Zeus was waiting by the door, his tail wagging like a metronome.

Taina bent to pick him up and swayed, trying to keep her balance.

"C'mon, Zeus." Arnaldo took Zeus from her then carried him inside.

They headed through the deserted canteen and upstairs.

Taina patted the dog before Arnaldo placed him on a bed he'd fashioned from an old pillow. A metal pot served as a water bowl. "You rest there, puppy. I need a bath."

Arnaldo still had plenty to say. "My fondest memories of Serena, and why I wish she was still around, was how she taught me that if you believe the goddesses will listen, the magick will work, no matter if it's time to conjure or banish."

Taina could not escape the ill-timed magick lesson. "Arnaldo for me, a void full moon is nearly impossible to deal with."

He took her hand. "You can't survive here by waiting for the right planet to be in the right house, or your moon phase to be correct. Void of course? Deal with it. If you hole up and pray to the *orishas,* hoping one of them will shine their divine light on you, you ain't ever gonna get out.

"That's why Abuela became a recluse and hid out with all the other little old ladies. And why Serena took the witness protection offer. They wouldn't let go of their Tarot, astrology, their crystals, their herbs, their potions. You gotta be a stinking *sato* mongrel. No purebred frou-frou types gonna make it here.

"No offense to Zeus. He's a gangsta. *Ay señor*, him hangin' off Lupo's stuff, I mean those teeth could do some serious damage..." His voice faded into a chuckle.

"Are you saying I should just cast off what I've been taught, my beliefs, my ethics?"

"Worship whatever gives you the advantage." He held up his crucifix, pointed to a statue of San Lázaro on the shelf surrounded by dusty seven-day candles. "Money from Catholic Charities keeps *Sonrisa* open. If an *orisha* speaks to me, I'm there."

He gestured to a collection of beads and rosaries hung on a rack. "But I can conjure weather magick whenever I want, without any help, or at least any I'm aware of. Sure, I pay to play—everyday."

Arnaldo rummaged for a bar of soap and found clean towels, a T-shirt big enough to fit her like a dress, and a comb. "I'll be right outside. Leave the door unlocked in case you get dizzy." He turned on the taps to fill the tub, then left.

Warm water soothed her aches but floating on her back to rinse her hair offered only temporary respite from the throbbing in her head. By the time she got dried and dressed, he had made up the sofa bed and Zeus was nestled at the foot waiting for her.

Arnaldo's booming voice delivered a sledgehammer to her head. "I know what Josefa said about me and don't give a shit about my empty houses, my part of fortune, my moon, sun, my Neptune, Uranus, Pluto, and my North and South nodes in fucking retrograde. That's why I'm stuck here and why I've been dealt the cards I have. It's my choice how to play them.

"The only thing in astrology that makes sense to me are those trines, the squares, the inconjuncts. Balance. It's all a game of moving stones from one plate to the other. Maintain balance, anyway, anytime, you can."

"What are they holding over you, Arnaldo?"

"A lifetime of screw-ups."

He took her hands. His voice deepened, and his face moved closer to hers as he said, "We could form a Grand Cross. You and I on the horizontal, and Lupo and Raul the far points on the vertical line. "Maybe it's age. Maybe it's desperation. Maybe it's my final opportunity. Makes no sense. We're so different. You're so much younger. But I want to be with you, not against you."

Taina almost raised her lips to his, but reason intruded. Lupo and Raul had tried, each in his own way, to snag her. Now it was Arnaldo's turn to pile on the bullshit.

The dog whimpered.

She pulled away. "Arnaldo, I need to do this myself, for myself. Trouble is I'm too weak and too inexperienced."

He nodded. "We all have weaknesses. Lupo's is stupidity.

Raul's is ambivalence. Your's is an inability to trust your judgment and use your powers."

"So, what's yours?" she asked.

"Mine," Arnaldo stared, blank-eyed, over her shoulder at the brick wall outside the window, "well, mine is running from my past. Someday, it is going to catch up with me. Just like it catches up with each and every one of us. How about some breakfast?"

"That's the best idea I've heard in a long time." Taina hauled her aching, exhausted body over to the kitchenette.

He wrapped his arms around her. "I really wanted you to go back to PR, get the hell out of harm's way. But you wouldn't. Now stop worrying about karma, kickbacks, ethics, your moon, your sun, your stars, your planets. Get ready to kick some magickal ass."

Why, all of a sudden did his arms exude such tenderness, his voice such calm, his strength such confidence?

Zeus, still on the foot of the bed, rested his head on his front paws.

Arnaldo looked down on her. "Once I realized you weren't going to give up, shit happened. I fell for you."

Chapter Thirty-Four
A New Alliance

Somewhere between Arnaldo tucking her under the sheets and now, a buttered bagel and a takeout coffee cup had appeared on a snack table by the bed. An air conditioner whirred—its white noise as soothing as the soft cotton blanket wrapped around Taina. Zeus snoozed atop her feet—his warmth and weight a connection to reality.

She stretched, wiggled her toes, lifted her head. Nothing hurt. "Time to go home." The second the words were out, a familiar dread and pain settled in her gut like a virus lurking until the right moment to overwhelm its host. "What time is it?"

No one answered. Zeus looked up, then put his head back down, eyes wide, ears pricked, indicating both interest and surprise.

She swung her legs over the side of the bed and strained to see the clock on the microwave. Five o'clock, and it had to be PM since pale sunlight diffused through the windows. Now her head, neck, and right arm ached. She'd slept twelve hours and could still sleep more.

A shiver ran through her, and she draped a blanket over her bare arms. Zeus, hauled along for the ride, gave up and hopped down to follow as she went to turn off the air conditioner.

Arnaldo's heavy footfalls rattled the metal saddles on the linoleum. "Hey, sleepyhead. How ya doin'?"

Nope, it hadn't all been a dream. "Good."

"You were asleep when I got back from the store and haven't eaten anything since yesterday. Let me get you something fresh. Whatdaya feel like?"

She took the bagel. "It's so cold in here, this is well preserved. Just warm up the tea, and I'll be fine."

He obliged. "I was hoping you'd stay for the weekend. At least until things settle down and we see if there's going to be fallout."

The offer cut her down the middle, with one half relieved and comforted and the other suspicious and unsettled. "I have no clothes, no toothbrush, no makeup."

The microwave beeped.

Arnaldo brought her the tea. "No problem. I found a pair of your shorts and a T-shirt when I picked up Zeus. Didn't want to go burrowing through your underwear drawer, though."

Taina sipped. Perfect. Just the way she liked it. How did he figure that out? "Arnaldo…"

He looked away. "I know. You want your privacy. You can handle everything. You have to go to work on Monday. But, Taina, I might not make it in time when something happens—and you know it will."

All of a sudden he was concerned with her privacy? After the stunt he pulled, ogling her after the fire? After seeing her about to be raped by a werewolf and the aftermath?

"Arnaldo, if I make it look like I'm dependent on you for protection, Raul and Lupo will continue to play monkey in the middle with us. I didn't give his name, because I don't want them retaliating against you. But if the DNA shows..."

"It won't. Zombie and were DNA is too jumbled. I know from experience. Dhamps are more human than animal, which is why Raul watches his fangs—and his dipstick." He spoke with an ex-con's worldly experience and classy vocabulary.

"How about you take me home, and we'll see how the energy flows." She took a bite of the bagel. Her jaw ached where Lupo had whacked it.

Arnaldo smiled like he hadn't expected even that. "Eat, get dressed, and I'll go straighten up after those rowdy seniors downstairs. I got someone to supervise the teens tonight."

She nodded and kept chewing.

He rolled onward. "Taina, I'd feel better if we made contact when you're coming home from work. And next week is equinox."

The memory of their harvest celebration surfaced, along with the benevolence it had left behind. "Another block party?"

"Nah. But we could do something."

"Why not?"

Taina visualized him doing a happy dance on the way down the stairs. Had he really fallen for her or was this an act? Had the fairies put some sort of charm on him? Was this more of Josefa's magickal matchmaking? And why was Taina not minding, even though she wasn't buying it?

The vibes normalized and being out in the daylight routed memories of the attack. Until they walked past the gas station, now surrounded by yellow crime tape. The adrenaline rush, the fight reflex, the bravado dissipated.

Sweat poured off her, she trembled. She needed to find a new place to live. If she started that discussion now, Arnaldo would never leave.

He walked the perimeter of her apartment, palms down. "Seems like this protective shield is intact. And you got your feathered bodyguards on duty."

"I'll be fine, Arnaldo. The phone is working. Zeus is here. I've got food."

"Hot as hell in here, though. And you gotta keep the windows locked."

"The fans do a good job," she lied.

"*Bueno.* See you tomorrow?"

"Yes, I'll call you when I'm leaving, and we'll meet in the middle." She herded him to the door. "I appreciate everything you've done for me. You're a good friend, but…"

"I know. Wrong flavor." Disappointment dulled the sparkle in his eyes.

As soon as he was down and out, she opened the window.

The fairy's wings whistled as he fluttered inside. "We got Master Arnaldo there just in time."

"Thank you, Bridge Rat."

"At your service, as always. But he does not meet with your favour?" He cocked that silly pigeon head at her.

"I don't like men, Bridge Rat." Why was she lying to the fairy? She was more attracted to Arnaldo than she'd been to any man or woman.

"Choosing one sex over the other for conjugal relationships has never been something fae worry about." He chuckled.

"Yeah, well…"

"But of course, humans require a male and a female to reproduce. Why would anyone not want to couple to make a baby if they only have to share once or twice?" His pigeon eyes blinked rapidly as his head swiveled.

She flopped onto the sofa. She was coming out to a fucking pigeon. Discussing human reproduction with a goddamn bird. "Bridge Rat, I don't want to bring children into this miserable world with anyone, anytime. I want to see justice done, then live in peace until I join my family again. Perhaps my next life will be better."

Bridge Rat flew after her and perched on the back of the sofa. "Pity, since it is the will of the gods and goddess that you and Arnaldo unite, in body, mind, and in spirit to go forth and eliminate the terrible blight on this portion of the Earth. To be sure, it will be a task accomplished by your offspring, the perfect melding of the light and the dark. But we immortals are, by necessity, patient."

She leaped to her feet. "Are you saying I'll be back here in my next life if I don't finish this time? That it's my karma?"

More blinking, but Bridge Rat stopped bobbling his head. He raised his beak as if his disguised fairy chin was elevated in contempt. "Karma is a word witches use, not fae. I suggest you consult your sources for the answers to that, my lady."

"I don't know who or what to believe. I've heard your side of the story, Josefa's advice, Arnaldo's warning, and Raul's and Lupo's manifestos. I know what side I'm on but feel everyone is against me." She picked up Zeus.

Bridge Rat hopped onto her shoulder. His claws pinched her neck and, like acupuncture needles, relieved the crick. "There, the energy was quite bunged up. Should flow better now. Really, Lady Taina, how you could question fae allegiance is beyond my understanding. But you'll do what you must, of that I am sure."

His wings rustled as he disappeared through the open window into the night, headed west, probably to deliver the news to Hawk Claw. Their savior, the White Witch, would not lend her womb out to save The Bronx. She'd take her chances that the next time would find her a toy poodle living on Fifth Avenue.

Were the fairies prophets, or minions of the gods? Was Josefa a gifted astrologer or a common matchmaker? Was Taina's bisexuality an excuse to not get close to anyone?

"Fuck them all. Fuck it all. I'll do what's right for me." She hugged her loyal pooch, closed the window, and turned on the fans.

~ * ~

One week since the werewolf attack, and all remained quiet. Taina walked a straight line at work, not saying much to Sandy and Simone, and nothing to anyone else. The DNA evidence wouldn't be ready for a while and, if Arnaldo was correct, it would never be.

Maybe she could fulfill the fae prophecy by showing Lupo and Raul she wouldn't be intimidated and keeping Arnaldo out of the crossfire. But she wasn't a Libra, and when she lost her balance, someone would get hurt. Well, around there the chances of getting hurt were pretty high anyway. Taina rubbed her temple.

Checking in with Arnaldo every night, having dinner while he played basketball, then walking home with him might be less about protection and more about her own needs. She'd ignored all the warnings about coming here, and then leaving. Perhaps when the weather changed, the confusion would lift, a door would open, and she'd be able to move on. Well, it had, only not in the way she imagined.

"Plans this weekend, Taina? It's supposed to rain." Simone packed her bag.

"Just dinner."

Simone elbowed Sandy and winked. "A romantic one, I hope."

Taina smiled. "Maybe."

She almost told them she was bi. But she just dug out her Metrocard and headed for the subway to pick up Zeus, her implements, and some snacks.

Chapter Thirty-Five
Autumnal Equinox

Freshly bathed, wearing as little as she could without being arrested or propositioned, Taina collected candles, her athame, and her abalone shell. She tucked a bottle of salt water into the bag, some matches, and sage for an outdoor sabbat.

Dark clouds raced through the sky. The sun, trapped above, had given up for the day, and the moon, now barely a sliver, wasn't likely to have any more success penetrating the gloom. If the rain would just hold off, they could light their candles, perform a New York City-style ritual—quick and dirty—and have a drink and something to eat.

Zeus stood by the door, leash in his mouth.

"No way am I going anywhere near the park without you, puppy dog. But it's too early." The longer she waited, the less time they'd be together, and the less chance of complications.

Something called Taina's attention to her Tarot deck. Not something she did often enough, or trusted to interpret for herself, but… She opened the wooden box, shuffled, and tapped the pile with the flat of her hand. "What's going to happen with Arnaldo and me?"

She spread three cards, facedown, on the lace altar cloth. Her heart pounded, and she walked away. "I don't want to know."

Taina closed and locked the window. The downdraft blew those cards, plus a fourth and fifth, onto to the floor. Two stared up at her, demanding to be heard.

The gray-haired Hermit, heavily cloaked, leaned on a red staff for support, his face impassive, eyes straight ahead, walking a golden path holding a lantern aloft.

Followed by Temperance, in the same colors of bright blue, green, and gold with blood-red highlights, wings unfurled, eyes cast seductively over her right shoulder. She poured water from a higher vessel to a lower, standing upon a sea of blue with two tiny fish behind her, eyes snickering.

"Am I tempting or seducing Arnaldo, or Raul and Lupo?"

Taina upturned the third and dropped it like a hot pot. The Star, golden hair flowing loose, naked, knelt upon the yellow path, her robe discarded behind her.

Female breasts drooped, but her arms exhibited masculine musculature, and hairy legs, and abdomen. A whirl rose upward from a concealed pubis.

Overhead, a red, blue, and gold central star, with three smaller ones were arranged symmetrically, yellow, blue, yellow on either side. Two trees with yellow reed branches, stood in the background leaves folded, with two indistinguishable red figures atop, watching her. The larger in the foreground, leaves opened, hosted a bright blue bird watching her pour the same two red and gold pitchers of water into a flowing, sky-blue stream.

"Oh, Goddess." The cards never lied to spare feelings or coddle those in denial.

Zeus peered over a shoulder like he knew what he was looking at.

The two other cards wouldn't likely add any clarification. "Am I supposed to throw off the cloak and embrace my desires, follow Arnaldo on this path? Please, help, *Yemayá*?" Taina petitioned the *orisha* before realizing the words had come from her lips.

She exhaled fear, inhaled strength, resolve.

First, the Two of Swords, upside down. A brunette in a blue gown held two sabers crossed in front of her chest, a silken blindfold pulled almost completely over her eyes.

Upended cards always meant either a stalemate or moving in the wrong direction. "I don't want to fight or to see the truth."

Taina looked closer. The woman squatted on a white hassock before a body of water roughened by waves, the outlet guarded by two huge boulders. A pregnant belly rested on her thighs. "Okay, okay so the fairies said Arnaldo and I were destined to have offspring—and I don't want to. That's all it means. No one will ever force me to reproduce."

Her hand trembled as she overturned the fifth. The Ace of Swords, also upside down. She turned it right side up and studied the blade, held aloft by an androgynous arm, dangling a gold crown and an olive or palm branch.

"Yes, I want peace and justice, but how do I find it?" She left the cards on the altar.

"Let's go, Zeus." Taina picked up her bags and hurried to the meeting place, between her apartment and *Sonrisa* and the eastern junction of *Las Tombas* and *Los Sangueros* territories.

~ * ~

Humidity hung around them like a damp shower curtain. The odor of moldy earth emanated from piles of sodden leaves heaped around the sewers. The stagnant air, the steamy heat— Taina closed her eyes, visualized walking through the tropical jungles. But when she opened them, she was still in The Bronx. "This is what it feels like in PR."

Arnaldo looked at her from the corner of his eye, still scanning the street. "Do you wish you were there now?"

She struggled to keep her mind clear of fears, open to possibilities, the only way to walk the path of destiny. "I wish for peace and tranquility. I want to show you the island. Introduce you to your heritage. It's so lush, so green, the water is so clear, so blue." Something drew her closer, and she took his hands.

He swallowed. "Maybe someday."

Magickal rituals always liberated her deepest feelings and desires. Was it the disconnect between her conscious and unconscious that made acting on them such a disaster? How could she avoid it? Should she?

She let go, and they entered the deserted park. Raindrops condensed out of the mist, soft at first, like gentle teardrops, then harder, pelting them like stones. The trees offered some protection, but water sluiced off Ritual Rock and pooled around it before cascading downhill into the gurgling sewers.

"We can forget about candles tonight." The bag in her hand was drenched, the matches and incense ruined. Zeus looked like his legs and belly had been dipped in milk chocolate.

"No fall equinox under the moon and stars." Arnaldo stripped off his sleeveless tee shirt, raised his face and palms aloft, allowing the water to run down the front of his body.

His lips moved in a silent confession as he walked deosil to banish transgressions or regrets, tracing the fingers of his left hand over Ritual Rock.

"They're still there, even if you can't see them." Despite the abominable heat and humidity, she shivered.

Visualizing the sun turning the corner toward winter, slowly moving away from the Earth, only intensified the chill. Her life was changing as rapidly as the weather. She was turning toward the dark period of her life, perhaps the end of it. But tonight was not the time to think of that. A piece of everyone died in fall and winter, only to be reborn in the spring. Perhaps next spring, she would be back in Puerto Rico, and Arnaldo would come visit.

"Let this pain I harbor pass. Let peace replace vengeance. Let clarity of purpose replace confusion, despair." Water rose to her ankles, jolting Taina out of meditation.

Rain fell over the empty streets like a sheer wall of water. A few cars, a bus plowed through the flood, wipers flapping wildly. She traveled backward to keep the deluge out of her face, maintain her focus, seal the circle, then bumped into Arnaldo.

They laughed, and he pulled her back against him under an outcropping to deflect the worst of the downpour. His body was solid as stone, and she allowed herself to lean against him. His beard and wiry chest hair prickled against her skin in a not-unpleasant way. There was no mistaking he was a male and she a female.

Zeus pressed himself against the rock but remained vigilant as his mistress let her guard drop.

Arnaldo flattened against her midriff, and he leaned down and whispered in Taina's ear. "Blessed be the Mother of all life. Blessed be the life that comes from Her and returns to Her."

They should have shared a cup of wine and burnt offerings, but instead both pressed their right hands on the granite and marble formation and walked deosil, Arnaldo still behind her, left hand on her shoulder.

Energy pulsed within the stone, a simmering volcano, dark, fraught with fear, confusion, despair. No, not tonight, this was a joyous occasion. Taina took her hand off Ritual Rock, turned and placed it on Arnaldo's shoulder then directed her gaze downward to the circle.

A soothing green aura glinted off the muddy path they'd trod. He always spoke of hope, and her spirits rose. Together they could do good works. The rain again drove them to shelter under the rock ledge, hidden from view of the dhampir's perch.

He divined her thoughts. "Hope is all we have, Taina." He placed both his hands on her cheeks, leaned in to brush his lips down her neck. His hand slid behind and down her back and drew her close. "You're trembling."

Was it cold, fear, arousal? "Yes, all we have is hope. I think we've done all we can outside tonight."

But she didn't move. The smell of his damp hair, the power in his arms as they surrounded her exuded contentment, even as they stood in monsoon-like rains that had transformed St. Mary's into some kind of magickal water park.

Las Tombas and *Los Sangueros* couldn't be far away, but tonight the witches had claimed this space for the witches.

"I'm lovin'this!" He released her, raised his face, opened his mouth to drink in the rain, and spun like an actor on a Broadway set. "I smell pineapples and coconuts."

Taina picked up the torn bag. "Piña colada, virgin of course. She unscrewed the cap, took a sip, handed it to him.

Arnaldo drank nearly half the bottle in one gulp. "That is delicious."

"Finish it."

"No, share the rest with me."

She guided him to their starting point, then cut through with her athame. Taking turns drinking from the bottle, they waded upriver down the middle of 149th Street, bathed in the fuzzy glow of streetlights, giggling and laughing like drunks. Zeus followed at their heels, closer than if he was leashed, head wagging along with his tail.

Taina opened the perimeter gate, and they hurried under the awning. The dog shook muddy water all over their legs while she fumbled with the lock.

"Let me do it." Arnaldo used a magickal kick to get it to turn. "Is it okay if I come up?" His eyes asked the next question she answered.

"Yes." Her voice was, gruff with desire and anticipation.

She led him upstairs.

Chapter Thirty-Six
Night Magick

Drunk on magickal energy, they stumbled over their own feet and skidded on the wet linoleum staircase. Tank tees and shorts with no underclothes clung to their bodies, leaving no mystery.

Arnaldo dried Zeus with a towel. The dog sank onto his fluffy pillow with a contented groan.

Taina shoved the Tarot cards aside and lit candles before setting them on the table at the four points around the room. "How about a snack?"

Arnaldo came up behind her, held her like he'd done in the park. "I'm not hungry for food. You look so beautiful and relaxed, like the rain washed all your worries away."

She turned and rested her cheek against his chest. "What will happen if this goes any further?"

"Who knows? Who cares?" The raspy whisper faded as his lips found hers, his hands moved up the back of her shirt, the around to the front, stopping over her breasts.

Their hair loosened and draped down their backs, and sodden clothes dripped a puddle of water around their muddy feet. They fell against the wall.

Taina eased the shirt over his head, ran her hands over his chest, her palms over his nipples. He lifted the tank top over her head, pausing to kiss her before it slipped onto the floor, and then he took the time to stare in appreciation. They stood naked to the waist, inches apart.

All Serena's reasons not to be there, and a few of Tania's own, ceased to matter.

Pressed against him, she squirmed with desire. "Let's go into the bedroom."

"Nothing personal, Zeus, but we need some privacy." Arnaldo closed the door behind them.

He watched as she found a towel, dried off her hair, her legs, and lay on the bed. He knelt over her, slid off her shorts, and then she did the same for him.

Sheets, soft, smooth, soothed her tingling skin. His hands calloused, rough, hot, traced every inch of her until she caught fire. His tongue probed her mouth, his breath sweet as a tropical night. Drops fell from his curls, releasing their body heat into a steaming fluorescent aura. He smelled like damp earth, like summer sweat, fruity, fertile. Then he touched her *there*.

"Oh yes." She opened herself to him, wild, wanting, welcoming. He was hard, throbbing, she, soft, yielding, gentled by his caresses.

"Wait." He grappled through the pockets of his discarded shorts and pulled out condoms.

"Forget about it." She'd take the morning-after pill tomorrow.

"I was clean last time I checked but never take chances. You put it on, nice and slow." He propped himself up on his elbows to watch.

Taina's brain loved him for that. But the rest of her body tensed like a rubber band stretched too tight as she rolled on the bright yellow rubber with a cantaloupe scent.

They thrust, slithered, kissed, stroked, gasped, moaned.

He ruffled her hair, pulled her on top of him, touched her with every muscle, every limb, every goddamn part of his body. "Look into my eyes."

She saw bright pinpoints of light. More than fucking, more than making love, some cosmic phenomenon.

So different than her fiancé, who'd been too timid, too inexperienced to take her where she wanted to go. And from Serena, a woman who knew what a woman wanted and needed, yet left some part of her untouched, unsatisfied, unfulfilled. Arnaldo was magick, performed magick, made magick.

"Yeah, mama." He locked her in a grizzly's embrace.

"I am not your mama." Taina bit his neck.

"Go, baby." He nibbled her ear.

"And I'm nobody's baby." She gyrated like an exotic dancer.

"That's right, Taina. Work it." He reached up to caress her breasts and pressed deeper into her.

The awkwardness of being naked, the fear of making noise, of anyone knowing they were pleasuring each other, the good girl, the submissive witch vanished. She kissed him like he'd kissed her.

He rolled over, straddled her.

"Don't go." She clutched his arms.

"Don't worry." His hands moved from her nipples down her belly to her mound.

"Don't stop." She growled like Zeus.

"You like that?" he whispered.

"Yes." She fought the urge to scream, which would surely have *Señora* Duarte summoning the cops, if the bed creaking and moving over the floor like a clunky magick carpet hadn't alerted her already.

Seated between Taina's legs, he flicked fingers over her sweet spot like a tongue, the length of him penetrating to her core. She met him, but he teased, withdrawing almost out of reach. He allowed her moment with him deep inside before pulling away, grinning at her desperation.

"Stay there, stay there." She grabbed his ass to hold him still.

"Not yet. Look at me." He kept her on the edge of the pleasure-pain divide.

Every muscle tightened, she arched her back, strained toward him, a tingling mass of nerve endings on the verge of firing at the same time.

Arnaldo groaned with the effort of restraint. His hands massaged every inch of her body.

Taut, near the breaking point, she trembled. *"Ay, por favor, damelo."*

He thrust deep, withdrew, thrust deep, withdrew, watching himself, watching her, lips apart, tongue dangling.

"Oh. Oh. Oh." The rubber band snapped, and she convulsed.

Pleasure, pain, pleasure, pain, pleasure, pain. Whose? Impossible to tell until she, still shuddering, twisted away.

"Not yet." Guttural whispers kept time with his slow, deliberate movements.

Another wave, deeper, more peaceful spread through her.

"Good, baby, good. Feel your power, the pleasure, oh shit." He screamed into his own ecstasy, eyes wide, still gripping her tight.

Then they lay still, their heaving chests and hearts beating, drenched in sweat.

"Te amo," he whispered.

"Sí, como no." The idiom seemed particularly apt for. Yes, but no, implied "of course" but in plain English she'd heard to never believe a guy who professed true love right after he came.

Would he disappear now that he'd had her? Would he expect

her to tag along like a pretty little familiar? Or wear her like another gold icon to a god he didn't really believe in, to rub Raul's and Lupo's faces in the fact they hadn't succeeded in conquering her, but he had?

His nuzzle, his gruff response to her unspoken thoughts brought her back to the tangle of arms and legs. He pulled away, attended to the condom. "Fucking things ruin everything."

A moment later he was back. She didn't fight the peace surrounding her like this hulking man's embrace.

~ * ~

Taina stirred each time a car drove by too fast or voices outside pierced the night. Zeus whimpered in one of his puppy dreams. Arnaldo sprawled across the entire bed like he owned it, draped a heavy arm over her, intertwined a hairy leg with hers, brushed her feet with his calloused toes. He murmured, from time to time and tightened his grip, as if afraid she'd run away.

She slipped out from under his arm, disentangled her legs from his, flattened her body on top of him. He smiled, stretched like a cat in a sunny window, clasped his arms around her and purred. "Am I dreaming or this really happening?"

"Yes, it is." His beard scraped her cheek, on the border of pleasure and pain. He nipped her earlobe.

Arnaldo stroked down her back, cupped her ass, and pulled her against the length of his now rock hard shaft. He knew just how to tease, half in, half out, but this time she was in control.

"Not yet." Taina pushed herself up, straddled him, leaned forward enough that her lips brushed his chest. Her hair tumbled over his shoulders.

His hands moved up her thighs, across her belly, as if he was tracing the outline of her womb, then up her belly to her breasts to cup them in her hands. He thrust his pelvis toward hers, his mouth fell open, and he groaned as she gyrated out of his reach.

"You're gonna kill this old witch, mama." Arnaldo's eyes glazed over with lust. He clenched his teeth.

Taina had him where she wanted him right now, under her spell, at least for this moment.

She licked her lips, rolled on the condom he snatched from under his pillow, and settled herself down on him. "Is that what you want?"

His spell-kissed hands traced her body like feathers, eliciting shocks of energy wherever they went.

Sunbeams diffused through the windows, dust motes sparkled in the haze, bathing the room in an ethereal light. Sweat pooled between them as their bodies danced, joined. Their eyes locked, and the intensity of the gaze drew them even closer, if that was possible.

She collapsed onto him and shuddered as high voltage ran through her. He lingered until it hurt so good. "Stop, enough, *ya*."

"No baby, no, *más, más*. Ahhh!" He pressed inside her, as if wanting to be swallowed.

Taina, sated, held him tight, murmuring into his ear. "*Ya, hijo. Ya, ya.*"

He went limp, and she melted on top of him; the two of them breathless, empty and yet full at the same time. The prickling of his beard too much for her jangled nerve endings, Taina nestled her cheek against his shoulder.

His hands traced her shoulders, her back, her ass, her thighs. She raised her head to look at him, read the adoration in his eyes even before he spoke.

"I'll do anything to protect you." Anything." Tears pooled, then leaked down his cheeks.

She wiped them away, rested her head in the crook of his neck. Fire and earth, paralegal and ex-con. Both witches, mutated by the tribal magick of their ancestors melding with the sun and moon, god and goddess.

Would the differences complete the other? Would her Water bathe his Earth, and in turn mute the Fire, the anger burning inside her?

Streetlights pricked the nighttime haze. A warm breeze rustled the curtains; a whisper of pigeon's wings penetrated the silence. The fae would be pleased. Zeus pushed through the door, hopped onto the bed, and settled at their feet.

Arnaldo's breath turned to a soft snore, like a kitten with a cold. Her foot rested on his like the rung of a ladder raising her up to the sun, stars, planets, the moon. But why did she not trust the charts, the cards, the goddess, the *orishas*? Why did she not trust him?

Chapter Thirty-Seven
Special Magick

Early-morning light diffused through the windows. They were so different: Her skin and hair warm honey, his caramel and chocolate, snapped together like a jigsaw puzzle

Arnaldo's physical strength weighed on her like a sleep-deadened limb.

His voice was uncharacteristically soft, his cuddle hormones surging, and he wrapped her in a bear hug. "Everything is changed now."

He appeared younger, despite the scruffy beard and bed head. An impenetrable shroud of remorse hid his true feelings from her supercharged, empath's brain.

"What's wrong?" Was he thinking of Serena, wishing he was younger and could do it all over again? Was Taina a proxy, a do-over?

"Nothing." He reached down to pet Zeus, who was holding the leash in his mouth, whimpering. "I'll take him for a walk while you get dressed." He put on his shorts and shirt, stretching the connection almost, but not quite, to the breaking point.

"Thanks." She went to brush her teeth. Was the mascara smeared under her eyes, tangled hair, and cellulite too much of a reality?

She stepped into the shower and stood there far too long, letting the water wash away the remnants of their lovemaking. Would the feelings go down the drain with it, tangled in a moment they could never recapture?

The smell of dark roast coffee greeted her as she stepped out of the bathroom wrapped in a towel. A faint afterglow still lingered; he kissed the top of her head and plunked down a cup of the brew, toast, and eggs. This would never last.

"Yeah, everything is changed. With the two of us committed to each other, part of each other, we can't lose."

"I think you're rushing this, Arnaldo."

His lips puckered, then flattened. "Guess I'm further under your spell than the other way around. I need to go back to *Sonrisa* and make sure everything is okay. No way can I stay away two nights in a row. Don't take that wrong, all right?"

"I understand." The idea of being alone again clogged her throat.

"I'm sure you'll say no, but how about coming over to spend the night? I'm closed tomorrow, so we'll have all morning to, to do whatever we want. And all day together. I'll come back here with you Sunday night."

"Sure." What was she agreeing to?

Arnaldo's chin retracted. His eyes widened in shock. "Really?" A smile softened his face again.

There hadn't been a warm human body since she and Serena broke up, and a male presence in Taina's life and her bed, for years. Here, in this moment, it seemed the cards had set her on the correct path.

But would one misstep plunge her over the edge of an abyss into the dark places she'd vowed to never visit?

~ * ~

Perpetual rain failed to douse the fire. The air conditioner alone was enough reason to stay at *Sonrisa*. That and Arnaldo getting up to take Zeus for a walk, make her breakfast, and stare gooey-eyed at her lounging in bed.

But now they were back in her hazy, hot, and humid apartment, her territory, not his, and tomorrow was a workday. There would be a quiet dinner, another shower to cool down, one more night before the charm disappeared like smoke.

She dried the last of the dishes. "Did Josefa perform some matchmaking spell, or did you mix up some *brujería?*"

Arnaldo lounged on the sofa, hands behind his head, feet up on the coffee table. Very much at home. "You made the piña coladas."

"What if Raul and Lupo retaliate?" She plopped down next to him.

"They will. Let me worry about it." He fidgeted despite the bravado. "But there is something that can give both of us more power to stand against them."

She'd been waiting for this. "Dark magick?"

"Sex magick."

Was he joking? "Anything like that weather shit you conjure with no effort?"

He laughed. "No. This is really hard. And intense. We have to focus on what we want to accomplish while making love. I mean really focus. When we're both there, out goes the spell."

Yeah, he had to be kidding. "Sounds like something in a romance novel."

"It links us in body, soul, mind, and magick. Nothing to do with performance, but we don't seem to have any problems with that anyway." Arnaldo helped her to her feet and slid the robe off her shoulders. "Wanna give it a try?"

"Why not?" She leaned against his bare chest, savoring the smell of Ivory soap, the coolness of his skin against hers.

"First we agree on something we want to accomplish together."

"Like uniting against Lupo and Raul?"

"Pretty complicated for a first try, but sure." Arnaldo's boxers were no match for his enthusiasm.

The now-familiar ritual of tumbling into bed and grappling each other like rock climbers about to fall into a crevasse needed no rehearsal.

Already connected by whatever spell had overcome them, fine-tuned during the weekend marathon, their bodies conformed to one another's. He enveloped her from behind like a starfish trying to open a clam—arms around her upper body, his legs around the lower, his hands moving up and down from her groin to her breasts, and everywhere else she wanted him to touch.

A condom wrapper tore between his gritted teeth. "Turn around. Look into my eyes."

Taina sat on his lap and aligned her mind as well as her body with his.

"Ready to make some magick?"

The question brought her back from the edge, wide open, receptive. Fuzzy green energy swirled around them.

"Yes." Taina focused on a vision of the two of them, walking down 149th Street, sending *Las Tombas* and *Los Sangueros* scattering, shielding their eyes from the blinding light.

"C'mon, spells tumble out of your mouth like liquid sugar when you're not trying so hard. The mundanes lap up the dregs." Green light twinkled in his eyes.

Her eyes swam in water as blue as the tropical sea. Drops fell like rain onto their shoulders.

"Goddess of light,

Bless us with your sight.
Offer us your might,
As we begin this fight."

"That's more like it." Arnaldo entered her, and she gasped, struggling to keep the image in front of her as her eyes clamped shut.

"Keep your eyes open. On me. Don't move." The command, at a time when she was so vulnerable, shocked like electricity.

"Goddess of light,
Bless us with your sight.
Offer us your might,
As we begin this fight."

She remained immobile while he did his magickal tickle but couldn't hold back. "Oh, oh!"

"We can do this, Taina. We can." He took up the chant as her voice failed.

"Goddess of light,
Bless us with your sight.
Offer us your might,
as we begin this fight."

Every muscle in her body quivered with shocks that surely could knock the dhampir and werewolf off whatever thrones they were sitting on.

"Ya, mami, ya." Arnaldo stroked, trying to calm her, before he went limp from the effort.

Her mind empty, unable to move, Taina let her eyes close. She danced, clad in a white feathery cloak, amidst puffy clouds.

~ * ~

Arnaldo disentangled himself.

She snapped back into a room spot lit by reality, by bright sunshine. His departure, though it was only in inches, stung like scraped knuckles or a paper cut. "Am I allowed to move?"

He pushed himself up on one elbow, tousled her hair, then stroked her cheek. "It was so perfect—you right there, right then, right where I wanted you."

Despite the power in his arms and a hand as big as her face, his touch was as gentle as one of Zeus's kisses.

"The most intense sex I've ever had." She pushed herself up and sat cross-legged. "But the way you ordered me around..." It had to be said. "Did you make magick like that with Serena? Were you thinking of her?"

He ruffled her hair, kissed her hands. "Where did you get that idea?"

"You're so damn moody. And I know the two of you must be talking about me."

He got fidgety again. "Serena and I are ancient history."

"I'm not sure I believe you." There was still some glitch in the connection, like a loose screw or blinking light bulb.

"Have you thought about her or any other lovers when we're together?" Arnaldo rested on his elbow. "I certainly haven't."

"No. But is there some deep dark secret the two of you are harboring? She won't answer my calls or emails."

"When a relationship dies, people hurt. I know she's scared—for me, for you, maybe for herself." If Arnaldo was bluffing, he was doing a great job.

Until he knitted his hands, which gave her the real answer. "Taina, I want to get you the hell out of harm's way. Sometimes that creeps in, no matter how hard I try." A bear hug attempted to distract the conversation.

She studied his eyes but only saw that post-coital, awestruck stupor. "You don't always act like it."

He drew her closer. "Someone, something somewhere is pulling strings, and we just have to be puppets, no matter how tangled up it gets. As long as we link our purpose, our minds and bodies will follow."

"I'm not ready for any commitments, Arnaldo. Especially when everyone wants to control me."

He shook his head like a dog just out of an unwanted bath. "I'm lonely. You're lonely. We both have issues, and we can help each other solve at least some of them." Arnaldo leaned forward to kiss her, the sheet across his crotch askew enough to betray his intentions.

The clock radio clicked on. An announcer's voice jarred Taina out of Arnaldo's grasp, and out of bed. He leaped to his feet and followed.

"Are you all right?" He smoothed her mussed hair, stroked her cheek.

"Look at the time! I have to go to work." Now for the honeymoon hangover, the tenderness between her legs, the abrasions on her soul, another upending of her life.

He nearly fell over, laughing. "So much for magick, *mamita*. What those judges and lawyers got that I don't?"

"Money." She turned the taps on the shower and waited for the water to get hot.

As she washed her hair, soaped her body, rinsed, Taina watched his silhouette, shadowed through the curtain, pacing.

She poked her head out, covering herself with the clammy plastic. "Hand me that towel and give me some privacy—please."

He did as ordered, then paused near the bathroom door. By the time she had run a brush over her teeth and through her hair, he was dressed, arranging pillows on top of the neatly tucked sheets. "Next time, breakfast in bed."

"Can you walk Zeus? I'm already late." Taina pinned her still drippy hair up and gathered her things.

"I'll take him with me. You can come by and get him after work."

An obvious ploy for him to ensure she'd see him tonight. Though she belonged with one of her own kind, she'd never belong to him.

"Sure, be there about six." Taina ran down the stairs, back into the reality of heat, haze, humidity.

Arnaldo had held off Lupo and Raul for years. Did he really need her to get involved? Her hand went up.

A gypsy cab crossed from the left lane to the curb, nearly crashing into another car. "Where to, miss?"

"The courthouse." Taina got in and didn't ask how much the fare would be.

She'd already spent more than she'd budgeted, so what was a little more?

~ * ~

Maybe it was coincidence. Maybe it was the morning-after pill she bought on her lunch hour, just in case any of those condoms had a hole in it. Maybe it was some curse. The bleeding started like someone opened a faucet.

Taina tipped the brown bottle nearly upside down and sucked out the last drop of Josefa's potion. The one that made her hemorrhage but got it over with and killed the worst of the headache. She rummaged in the toiletry cabinet they kept stocked in the office for clients.

"What do you need, Taina?" Sandy looked up from her computer.

"Anything super maxi. And serious drugs." She grabbed a tampon, a pad, and a bottle of ibuprofen.

Sandy laughed and came over. "Take four of those. I mean it. Prescription dose and it slows the bleeding, too."

"You sure? I just took some herbal remedy."

"Do it all the time. Just eat or your stomach will turn inside out."

"It already did that." Taina plunked into a chair and spilled out four white pills.

Sandy brought her some water. "Here you go."

She downed them in one gulp. Nothing worked right in The Bronx, not even her body. "Where can I get birth-control pills? Or an IUD? Quick."

"He must be really special." Sandy's shoulder massage soothed the ache.

This all seemed so normal, so mundane. The kind of girl talk she used to have—before she'd acknowledged being bi, and when she had second thoughts about compatibility with her ex-fiancé.

"He's so into me. I don't know if I can reciprocate." That they could understand. Even she couldn't get her brain to process the undercurrent of magickal intrigue.

"You deserve to have someone pay that kind of attention to you. Here's the name of my gyn. Tell her I said to call. She'll get you fixed up before next weekend." Simone handed her a card.

Chapter Thirty-Eight
Yesterday, Today, Tomorrow

Taina didn't know who would understand the situation, but she knew she could trust the *santera* to tell her the truth. "So much has happened, Josefa. Lupo Lopez attacked me last week, in retaliation for me getting involved with cases of his that didn't turn out in his favor. Raul Rivera and Arnaldo both stopped him, and they're trying to convince me to quit my job at the courthouse and come run their centers."

Josefa frowned. "*Sonrisa* I know of, but what does that stinking drug dealer pimp claim he's running?"

"*Boricua* Women's Shelter." Taina had already said more than she wanted to but just you should never conceal things from your doctor, your lawyer, or your *santera*.

If steam could have come out of Josefa's ears it would have raised the temperature another ten degrees in the stuffy *botánica*. She pounded on the counter. "If it weren't for him, Arnaldo wouldn't have gotten... Well, he was always a follower. But I'd like to go break Raul's door down and twist his *cohones.*"

Why had she said anything? "Josefa, *por favor,*. I don't want you anywhere near him."

"I have my ways of exerting influence." A sly smile crept over Josefa's face. "*No ten miedo, hija.*" Her lips mouthed a silent prayer—or curse.

"Arnaldo is trying to protect me, and..."

"You've become lovers. I can see the bright light in your eyes. The glow on your face." Josefa grinned. "*Que bueno.* Let me do a quick reading."

"I did one for myself last week. That's why I allowed things to...happen."

Josefa gestured toward her reading room. "Are you happy?"

Taina settled into the now familiar chair. "Yes, but it's going to make things very complicated when Raul finds out."

The *santera* adjusted a cushion behind her back. "Why, are you in love with Raul?"

"No! But I don't think I'm in love with Arnaldo, either."

"Ah, in lust. Nothing wrong with that." Josefa smoothed her tablecloth. A wicked grin spread over her face, as if she was watching them perform sex magick through a supernatural window, seeing the powerful energy still pulsing around them.

"I'm afraid the two of them will start fighting over me." Taina squirmed, to quell the unease as well as the cramps and backache.

"They've been fighting for years." Josefa shuffled the deck, cut it, and closed her eyes. "Taina Aponte. Yesterday, today, tomorrow." She laid out three cards, turned them over, opened her eyes, frowned. "Hmm."

Taina tempted to grab them herself, leaned forward. "What?"

"Yesterday. The Four of Swords. A personal battle has just ended. You've let your guard down and found momentary peace. But it is time to prepare for the next round. And there will be many more." She turned the card so Taina could see the androgynous knight laying on its back, sword lying by the side of the bier.

Three blades pointed downward at the abdomen, chest, and head. A window, its view obscured by stained glass, overlooked the knight's legs and feet.

"Today. Justice. Every action you take will have an effect. But the vindication you desire is at your fingertips."

The queen, in red robes and gold-and-jeweled crown, held a sword upright in her right hand, a balanced scale in the left. The luminescent gemstone securing the cloak around her neck, as well as her delicate hand, drew Taina's interest.

"Tomorrow. The Wheel of Fortune. Your luck is turning and a new phase of life is beginning, but destiny allows you little choice."

The wheel, adorned with black runes, rested upon the back of a red, half-goat/half-human being followed by a yellow snake. A bird with a book in its talons, wings unfurled, and a winged lion and goat or lamb rested upon the clouds in the northeast, southeast, and southwest corners. And in the northwest, a golden-haired angel read her own volume. The image of an Egyptian-masked half-man/half-lion sat atop the wheel.

Josefa's chin bobbed against her chest, as if she was asleep. Taina pushed the cards back toward the *santera,* not daring to disturb the trance. She watched the lacy hands on a gold clock adorned with fake flowers and butterflies, move minute-by-minute, taking far too long to tick off five lines.

She inhaled a breath so deep, Taina rose from the chair to be sure she was all right.

When she snapped back to awareness, a look like a doctor giving a terminal diagnosis shrouded her face. "Monday, beware on Mondays. *Elegguá's* day. Put his *macuto* on your altar. And stones from the park, from near that big rock your kind like so much. Sprinkle some rum over it and burn avocado leaves."

Just the name conjured visions of fire, of evil. Fear licked Taina's insides. "He's the devil, isn't he?"

"*Elegguá* walks among the dead, controls the crossroads, metes out justice."

"I know I must fight, Josefa. But can't I propitiate a gentler *orisha?*"

"No, be vigilant on Mondays, the day *Elegguá* rules." Josefa rocked gently side-to-side.

"Why not *Oya?* She is a warrior with power over spirits and the dead." Even as she begged like a spoiled child, Taina knew the answer was no. One did not chose *los santos, los santos* chose them. She was being directed to worship the saint whose colors were that of fire, her ultimate fear, the very thing that had stolen her family.

Could Josefa hear her? Was she ignoring the entreaties?

After what seemed like many minutes, Josefa spoke. "Serena and Arnaldo both declined my advice and tried spell-casting to drive evil away. Your mother too." She opened her eyes, came back to the room. Her glare chilled the air.

Taina shivered. "My mother?"

Josefa's eyes narrowed, as her chin rose. "I put my faith in the saints. My magick is prayer, sacrifice—and I'm still here."

"How does one propitiate the devil?"

"*Elegguá* walks with *Yemayá*. She still calls for you and has great influence over him." Josefa took off her glasses, her demeanor softened. "Are *las migrañas* better?" The woman was an expert at distraction.

"Yes, they are."

"So my potion has given you clarity of thought, the ability to see through the interference of others who mean you harm. Wait outside while I prepare more for the days to come." Josefa hobbled to the velvet curtain, looked at Taina, and shook her head before disappearing.

While Josefa worked, Taina paced. Whatever Josefa was brewing must be quite intricate. The shop bell tinkled, then the sticky door scraped over the floor.

Yoruba entered, the sparkling bronze-colored fabric of her skirt so tight over ample hips it was a wonder she could walk. Bead necklaces adorned her neck, draping gracefully over the brown blouse interwoven with gold thread that made her sparkle like a jewel. She held her head, wrapped in a matching turban like a princess.

Taina's heart lightened. "Blessed be, Yoruba."

"Blessings to you, Miss Taina. Where is Miss Josefa?"

Taina's gaze was drawn to the beads around the woman's neck adorned with carvings of skulls and other ghoulish icons. "Making me a potion. For female troubles and migraines."

"Ah, yes, performing magick will cause that." Yoruba spoke with no malice, no judgment in her voice. "But the spells I cast *leave* people with headaches and female troubles." She chuckled.

No, this wasn't a like mind.

"You favor this?" She picked up *Eleugga's* head—having sensed Taina's gaze on the half-black/half-red face with seashell eyes resting on a shelf.

"No, he frightens me."

"There is demon and angel in all of us." The exotic dialect conveyed a special eloquence to Yoruba's words.

Josefa shuffled in and nodded to both of them. She held a brown bottle and a seven-day candle with the same arrow-headed black-and-red icon stenciled on the front. "How can I help you, *señora?*"

"I need these, please, *madame.*" Yoruba handed her a list.

Josefa read it. Raised her eyebrows. "*Un momento.* Let me pack up Taina's things." She cackled. "Don't want to mix any of these in by mistake."

There was no coincidence the three of them had come together there, today.

Synchronicity was a sign from the goddess to proceed. "I met Yoruba near Ritual Rock a few weeks ago."

"That park is a magnet for those craving filth and depraved orgies." Josefa said. "It's best to stay away lest you get caught up like your mother did, thinking she could magick her way to a deal with the dhampirs and werewolves."

The revelation stabbed Taina in the gut. "So that 's what you've been holding back from me about my mother and her involvement. Are you saying that Mama trying to intervene with Lupo and Raul was responsible for the arson? Did my father know anything about this?"

Josefa sighed. "I surmise your papa viewed your mother's magickal dabbling as harmless at best, useless at worst. Both were fearless, though. And honest, which was their downfall."

"I should not speak ill of them however, given the lack of my success helping Arnaldo's *abuela* deal with him. No different than any mother or grandmother in the South Bronx, desperately trying to keep her children and grandchildren safe and away from the temptations of dark magick. Perhaps if your mother, his *abuela*, and I had been willing to use dark arts, things may have been different."

Taina's unease gave way to hope. More pieces of the puzzle were snapping into place, but only the edges were complete. The center was covered in a mishmash of magickal practices, but maybe the three of them together could fill in the blank spaces.

"There is great power at Ritual Rock, if one knows how to control it." Yoruba's teeth gleamed. But first, one must embrace the dark in order break through it." She seemed to have divined Taina's thoughts.

Josefa always ignored what she didn't want to hear. She dropped a ball encrusted with black-and-red beads into Taina's left hand, then fixed an *azabache* bracelet dangling a red fist onto her right wrist. "This will quell the jealousy, the *mal de ojo* circulating around those men."

The minute Josefa's hands left her's a stabbing pain took the left side of Taina's neck. She dropped *Elegguá's macuto*.

Josefa picked it up, and packed it with the candle, the potion, and the beaded ball in a brown bag. "Thirty dollars for the reading and supplies."

Taina's fingers still tingled, and she had trouble grasping the bills in her wallet. "Thank you."

She grappled with the door. It didn't open. She tugged again with her entire weight, but it refused to budge, trapping her in a hive of dark magick. Panic ricocheted between her shoulders like ping pong balls.

While Josefa was stowing the cash in her drawer, Yoruba pulled the door open with no effort and whispered in Taina's ear, "I saw you in the park with your man, making love and magick in the rain. Don't be afraid to dance with demons, Miss Taina. But when you don't like the music, stop dancing."

Taina forced herself to not run.

Chapter Thirty-Nine
Dark Moon Rising

Bad moon day. Full—and Arnaldo's was void. He'd scoffed when Taina had mentioned it, but lately he'd been acting like he had a bad rash, constantly fidgeting, ornery, complaining about everything.

Señora Duarte stepped out to drop trash in the can. Without a backward glance, she was inside the foyer and could have pushed the buzzer to release the gate latch from the inside. Instead, she slammed the front door shut, forcing Taina to burrow in her purse for the keys.

If looks were bullets, her back and Arnaldo's ass would be full of holes even though he was always polite to her landlady and even took the pails to the curb on garbage and recycling nights. Taina couldn't blame the woman for hating her.

The dog danced around her feet, dragging his leash. At least someone was happy with the current routine. They'd meet and make dinner. Arnaldo would walk her home, kiss her goodnight like he meant it, but then plead the need to sleep at *Sonrisa* to keep watch and to protect each other during the full moon.

But she needed to maintain her own space, even though her sheets were far too cold and shadows far too much like dark swords stabbing the night. But the uneasy alliance between her, Josefa, Yoruba had ensconced Arnaldo in the dark magick realm, a place she was not yet prepared to walk deeper into than she already had.

"We need to find a new place to live, Zeus." Taina changed out of work clothes and packed an overnight bag—just in case they didn't make it back there tonight.

Darkness fell earlier and earlier these days. Despite unseasonal warmth for the last two weeks, the waxing moon cast an ever-burgeoning chill over The Bronx—and their relationship. Instead of growing closer by seeing each other every night, the rip current of magickal energies swept them out of the lifeboat and left them struggling to keep from going under.

Taina's gaze fell on her altar. The wilted leaves around *Elegguá's* candle and *macuto* should be changed. And the water in the *Yemayá's* abalone shell was murky with white flecks of mold. That was no way to treat an *orisha*.

She rinsed the shell and added fresh salted water, the crumbled the avocado leaves into a cauldron and dropped in a match. They flared and smoked, leaving behind a heap of ash and the acrid smell of singed grass to assuage *Elegguá*. No time for prayers or the proper propitiation. Not good.

"Come, Zeus."

He scampered down the stairs and seemed to know he couldn't sniff every stinking thing along the way. Dusk had already touched the horizon. Arnaldo was waiting in the usual meeting place—in front of a variety store—passing time perusing boxes of irresistible trinkets like potholders, cheap perfume, and wooden spoons. A pair of bright pink leggings labeled '*Especial, dos por $10.00*' hanging from the awning wrapped around his head when the wind blew.

In another time and place it would have been hysterical. But she was not in the laughing mood.

"You're late." He crossed his arms over his chest.

An accusation, but likely motivated by concern. That she knew, but the tone didn't propel her to give him a hug and kiss. "Trains were running slow, and I needed to…"

"I see you brought a bag. Staying with me tonight?" The self-assured smirk was enough to make Taina want to slap him. Even Zeus, who usually greeted his new best buddy by nearly climbing up his leg, studied him for the best place to sink his teeth.

"Maybe." She fought back tears. She'd never expected this to last long, but it was dying faster than a spring flower in the heat of summer. "It's the full moon."

"I know. So let's move it." He took the bag from her. "We need to get inside."

They hadn't gone more than a block when the skeleton-adorned yellow truck rumbled by way too fast for the crowded streets. A bunch of teenagers wearing doo rags and chains, but as gray as mundanes could get, rushed after it.

One straggler, a skinny black kid whose feet were too big for his gangly body, with so little facial hair he probably was about thirteen, tried valiantly to keep up. He cut across the street and down an alleyway.

"Hakeem!" Shock and terror, flashed across Arnaldo's face. "Where ya goin' man?"

The boy didn't hear or pretended not to.

Arnaldo shoved the bag back at her. "I gotta stop him."

She'd never seem him move so fast. Taina grabbed Zeus and ran after them.

Barely a block away, like a video game on slow motion, the *Las Tombas* death truck slowed to a crawl, right in front of *Sonrisa,* daring the kids to clamber over the hood in the same initiation trick that had caused Taina's accident.

With the blackout windows she couldn't see who was driving, but it had to be *Una Tomba* doing Lupo's bidding. Like the zombie who attacked her while his boss was holed up in the bunker.

"Are you crazy? Knock it off!" Arnaldo screamed, but the kids weren't hearing it.

Hakeem went last, jumping over the hood of the yellow truck and off the other side just as a car turned the corner. A horn blared, tires screeched, someone screamed. *Thud. Thunk.*

The death truck kept going, nice and slow, like it had nothing to do with what had happened to some crazy kid.

Time paused. Taina covered her mouth to hold back the vomit, remembering the zombie. The crowd gathered. A woman ran out of a building and shrieked. A keening rose into the air, so shrill and anguished it drove daggers into Taina's heart.

Hakeem lay under the tires of an innocent man's car. But unlike her, this driver didn't run.

He sobbed and pounded his fist on the hood of the battered sedan. "I didn't see him. I tried to stop."

Hakeem's mother sat cross-legged in the middle of Southern Boulevard, cradling the limp bloody body, rocking, howling. "My baaabyy. Sweet Jeeesus, My baaabyy."

Arnaldo knelt next to her, tears dripping down his cheeks, shaking his head. "I'm so sorry, Mrs. White." He looked up at Taina, eyes swimming with sadness.

"I'm sorry." She mouthed the words, then lowered her gaze, desperate to flee, but she couldn't leave Arnaldo alone.

Sirens prickled along her spine. Taina knew the individual sirens well. An ambulance whined and whelped when going through red lights. The fire engines screamed, and its horn blared for drivers to move. The police car's *woo-woo, woo-woo, woo-woo* grew closer.

She was trapped there, in this moment, on this boulevard of bad spells and broken dreams, in this neighborhood, in The Bronx, where everyone knew exactly what type of siren each branch of emergency service used.

No matter where she went those sounds never let her forget she'd snubbed the evildoers' advances, taken them to task for their crimes, and now she had doomed herself to live watching innocents suffer and die. It had started with that pregnant woman in the subway. Only fate had been kind that day.

Cops herded the crowd back while the emergency medical technicians pried the mother away from her son's body by promising to see if there was anything they could do to help him. The woman was bereft enough to accept at least a glimmer of hope. Taina appreciated them for that kindness.

Arnaldo moved to the curb. She placed her hand on his shoulder. Zeus sat motionless at their feet, tail still, ears drooping.

As if pulled by a magnet, the mother, drenched in her son's blood, bypassed Arnaldo and threw herself into Taina's arms. "Me baaaby. Why? Oh dear Jeessus. Me baaaby."

She rocked the mother like a fussy infant and swayed with her in a women's dance of grief, lending her whatever strength she could, gifting her the last thimbleful of comfort dredged from a soul already leaking like a kitchen strainer.

The mutual stroke of hands on hair, pats on the back, and tear-moistened cheeks brushing against one another sufficed where words meant nothing. *Nada.*

"Ma'am, you should come with us."

Only the promise of seeing her son once more pulled Mrs. White from Taina's arms.

The cops led the woman to a police cruiser. The boy lay on the ground next to the car like a discarded rag doll. They etched his broken form in yellow chalk.

The driver sat in another cruiser, staring silently ahead. A gray-haired, blue-clad white man, ME emblazoned on the back of his T-shirt, walked about snapping pictures. He directed the EMTs with a nonverbal hand code, to cover the body with a black cloth.

Life oozed out of the ragged tear in Taina's soul, reopened by the innocent boy's death. She had been too young to fully understand her family had died, but flashes of that night, and ghostly noise danced between flashes of red light cast by the strobes.

She turned to offer some solace to Arnaldo on the loss of one of his kids, but nothing came out of her mouth.

"Let's go." He pulled her into *Sonrisa*, through the deserted senior citizen center, up the stairs.

"This is my fault." Taina mopped her eyes, walked back and forth across the creaking wooden floor, then tore beads off his rack, threw them on the floor, stomped on them. "How could the gods, the *orishas*, the saints, whoever the hell they are, let this go on?" She'd angered them by inattention, her offhanded treatment, bastardized magick.

"No, don't say that." Arnaldo pinned her arms. Stopped the pacing. Held her as tight as he could and pressed his lips so hard against hers it seemed he was going to swallow her. "Let's get cleaned up."

"They're watching us. Watching me." She broke free, rubbed her arms like that would get them off, keep them off. "Our sex magick made things worse."

"Taina, they're testing our bond, our resolve. We have to push back just as hard."

Even in the face of this, it came down to power, to possession, to domination. "They call me the White Witch, but I'm no savior. I'm responsible for two murders now."

"Taina, the mundanes don't know why, but hope oozes out of you. They latch onto you like frightened children. *Las Tombas and Los Sangueros* are afraid of that power and will shake you, break you, try and change you. The dark is fighting with all its might, but if we stay focused and centered we'll defeat them."

She paced. "I can't stand your ability to stare death in the face and turn your back and walk away. Hakeem wasn't a zombie like the one you dumped in the trash."

Arnaldo wasn't relenting. "This neighborhood is more famous for death than life. They even have advertisements for memorial T-shirts posted on the fences along the Bruckner service road. I do the best I can to give my kids hope. I tell them what it was like to be a junkie and almost dead. But they're seduced by the promises of cool stuff and money."

"No. I don't want any more of this!" Not even the full moon would keep her there tonight.

Something between pain and battle-scarred resolve registered on his face. "Raul and Lupo are trying to turn you against me. And isolate us."

Taina sank to the floor and sobbed. Zeus climbed into her lap. Arnaldo held her from behind, his face buried in her hair, his own tears running down her neck.

She fell back against him, but he didn't waver. This little witch was too afraid to go out there alone in the dark with the werewolves running, she, the lover of a man whose full moon was void of course, who could accept collateral damage.

Arnaldo spoke, his voice husky, his touch devoid of any passion, while the magick between them dissipated into bloody droplets. "Just remember one thing. No matter what happens. Protecting you and the kids. That's all that matters to me."

~ * ~

The fallout cooled faster than the weather. Arnaldo no longer spoke about sex magick. Was that the only thing eating him from the inside out? She took cabs, checking for gray auras before closing the door, back and forth from work and tried to stay away from paranormal creatures. She didn't want to risk another murder.

Nearly a week after Hakeem had died, after the traffic safety rally and funeral, half the moon had disappeared, sucking with it even more precious light. Even though the sun had not yet set, only a few mundane miscreants trawled St. Mary's Park, waiting for cover of night.

She was there, her mundane voice insisted, to walk Zeus. But the inner witch had made her come to this powerful sacred place to perform a banishing spell. To try and rid this neighborhood of at least one sliver of evil.

Taina cast a circle, walking deosil until energy surged through the soft earth into her bare feet. She lit her candles as dusk fell. No business being there. No reason except a summons from an unrecognizable voice.

Zeus growled and took his place at the north point. Fairy shifters on guard duty rustled in the branches above, and crimson and yellow leaves rained down around her like petals of flowers tossed at her feet by adoring subjects. "Are you trying to tell me something, Mama, Papa?"

Not even the wind answered.

Unable to focus, to center, to connect with anything, anyone, Taina tried her best.

"Waning light,
bring with you the fight,
cleanse the night.
Waning light,
bring with you the fight,
cleanse the night.
Waning light,
bring with you the fight,
cleanse the night."

No tingle of energy alighted on her scalp, no sense of peace or purpose lifted the specter of doom pressing on her chest. She extinguished the candles and waited while the wax hardened. As she placed the last one in her bag, her shoes scraped on stone, followed by the telltale smell of licorice. Had her homage to *Elegguá* summoned this demon?

Zeus's eyes were fixed on the dhampir. Furrows marred Raul's face, showing his true age. The smirk turned downward in a snark. Gleaming fangs protruded onto blood-red lips.

She sensed his unease, which had allowed the glamour to slip and his true nature to emerge.

"Your bodyguard let you out of his sight?"

His voice, deep, hard, prickled the back of her neck, but she wouldn't show fear. "I don't consult with Arnaldo, nor ask his permission to go anywhere. I answered a summons, did what I needed to do, and am leaving."

"If your parents could, they'd tell you to run. To leave. To go far from this place."

How dare he intrude on her private ritual? "I have as much right as you to be here."

"You are a fool, Taina Aponte. Arrogant, willful, stupid, ungrateful. I've offered you more than any other initiate. And kept my end of the bargain by protecting you from the wolf men. You defied me by reporting Lupo's attack to the police, stirring up dirt that should have been left to settle. You refused me, then dared give yourself to that mongrel. And flaunted it by cavorting in the rain.

"The time has come, White Witch, for you to face the consequences of ruining my credibility, disrupting my business, causing dissention and rebellion in my clan." Raul groped for her, but vestigial circles closed around his feet.

Someone, something there protected her. Taina stepped into the tangled spirals of energy pulsing around her. "I never promised to join you."

Saliva foamed at both corners of his mouth. "You will be conquered, brought under control."

An anguished sigh tickled the boughs overhead.

"And what about the vow to honor your mother?"

Raul struggled to break free of the pulsing, green shackles. "I will do what I must to protect my legacy. With or without your consent."

A gust of wind spiraled black dust around his feet. Pain shadowed his face. Raul clutched his temples, body trembling. "I ccccan not allow her to ddddestroy what I've built."

Taina picked up Zeus, who'd not moved a whisker, and picked her way through the circles to the sidewalk. She watched Raul wallow in the misery as his mother's spirit spiraled around him like a dusty swarm.

He tugged at his fetters and shrieked in fury. "You will grovel at my feet, *bruja sucia*. You'll beg for mercy, eternally sorry that you fucked that filthy half-breed witch." He raised his right fist and shot a beam of red light into the tree.

One of the shifters, trapped and vulnerable in its mortal form, fell to the earth with a thud. The glamour ebbed. The twisted, burned fairy glimmered and began to disintegrate. Raul stomped it into the ground.

Taina's heart seared with grief at the sacrifice the fairy had made. But she dared not return to offer it a proper thanks and burial.

Clutching Zeus to her chest, she ran down the double yellow line in the middle of the street. Mundane car horns blared a warning, while demon-haloed soldiers heeded their master's summons and emerged from doorways and alleys. Lupine howls drowned out the sound of her labored breaths.

She was afraid to go home and endanger *Señora* Duarte, so against her better judgment, she returned to *Sonrisa*.

Chapter Forty
Dark Void Moon

The sky, a weird, whitewashed blue, peeked out from behind clumps of gray clouds. Taina blinked to clear the haze. Another migraine on the way.

Cutting ties and loose threads was all that remained to do before leaving New York forever. She'd failed in her quest to avenge the dead, but success carried too high a price for the living.

After work, she walked directly from the subway to Timpson Street. Miguel had called three times for her to come sign the title so he could finally unload the car, but she feared another werewolf encounter. Now she had no choice. It was being picked up tonight.

Her void moon had passed, but the shop was deep into *Las Tombas* territory. She hurried past the strip of auto body shops, then saw Jesús rummaging through a trash can.

This would be the final opportunity before she left to see if he remembered anything about catching her, and if he had any inkling of a clue about what happened that night. He was so close to the corner, and so close to Miguel's, she could see her car parked on the sidewalk in front of the garage bay.

Jesús would either remember or not. It would take her a minute to sign the papers and get home well before sunset.

A yellow glow reflected down the entire length of Austin Place. Jesús aura was too pale, too weak to generate that kind of energy.

Why hadn't she brought Zeus?

But as long as she stayed near this busy intersection, whatever *Las Tombas* were around couldn't muster enough power over her in the ready state she was in until the sun went down.

"Jesús!"

The zombie, stooping to pick up a can, rose empty-handed and swiveled his head. *"Quien es?"* His eyes focused on Taina long enough to stop rolling in his head, but he stared straight past her.

"It's Taina. Let me help you." She bent as gracefully as possible in a skirt, collected two sticky cans, and paused to dump some stale beer—and a drunken bee—out of one before depositing it into his plastic bag.

"Gracias." He grinned, and his green eyes showed some spark of recognition.

Now that she had his attention, she reached out to touch him. He trembled as her energy infused into him. His hands shook so violently he dropped the armload with a sickening clatter. Beer splattered all over her legs and feet, but she didn't let go.

The positive melding with the negative inside the shell of what used to be Arnaldo's best friend caused the man to quake, his knees to buckle.

The niggle in her gut told Taina her spirit had connected with his. "Don't be afraid, Jesús. I'll help you pick up the cans, but I want to ask you something first."

He stopped shaking and looked at her, eyes wide in shock. The memory of those surprised green eyes looking down on the sooty, choking child he'd just caught washed over Taina.

She fought to keep her center and locked her knees so they didn't collapse together in a heap. With her free hand, she flicked the on her phone's recorder.

Her slow deep breaths brought the zombie to her steady state. Jesús stood tall and smiled.

"Do you remember catching me? They tell me you were the man who saved my life." Tears leaked from her eyes, unbidden.

The zombie's eyes gleamed with moisture, as she lent him enough memory to bypass the gaps in his damaged brain. "I looked up and saw the lady screaming, and the next thing I knew, you were in my arms."

"Thank you, Jesús. How did the fire start?" The magnitude of this moment was so great she couldn't hold her center. She trembled and fought to stay in control.

Jesús's gaze clouded over. She regained the connection. This was too important to fuck up.

He shook his head. "Huh?"

More deep breaths, and his chest rose and fell in tandem with hers.

"How did the fire start?"

His sick grin faded, as tears ran from his eyes. "We needed a fix. Lupo paid us to throw gasoline and a match. Poof! Then Raul delivered us his best shit."

No surprise there. "Who helped you, Jesús?"

"Arnaldo. We always worked together."

It took a moment to process, to be sure she'd heard correctly, to comprehend.

Taina pulled her arm away like she'd been burned. "Arnaldo? Arnaldo set that fire?" Flames lit up her brain, and it became clear what he'd been hiding. Why he acted so odd. Why he'd tried to get her to give up, to go home when they'd first met.

Drained of her healing energy, Jesús raised his eyes, and a frown came over his face. Any glimmer of sentience vanished.

A flock of pigeons streamed down the alleyway and swarmed around Taina, the frantic beat of their wings in time with her fibrillating heart. The birds came so close, so thick, she covered her head, afraid they were about to peck her eyes out.

Gunshots pinged against metal cans and ricocheted off the sidewalk. The flock drove her behind a garbage can then disappeared, but not before a few pockmarked fairy bodies littered the street then evaporated into the supercharged air.

She cowered, trembled, tried to think. The smell of gasoline infiltrated her nostrils. She retched and vomited. A rainbow of fluid cascaded down the street bathing her shoes in a stinking mixture of gasoline and motor oil.

You have to get out of here. She coughed, crawled toward the corner. More shots pinged off the asphalt. Yellow fog surrounded her. Taina could just make out the outlines of hairy brutes pummeling Jesús with their fists, beating him over the head with bats. He fell to the ground, rolled side to side, trying to get out of their way, moaning, then went still. His body only moved when they kicked it.

Another set up. Another act of senseless violence. *¡Bastante, ya!* They'd taken enough life and there would be no more.

Taina scrambled to her feet and ran toward the mob. "Stop!" Bolts of white light from her outstretched hands pierced the yellow haze. *Las Tombas* paused and looked toward her, standing in the middle of a river of gasoline. And blood? She patted herself. Had she been hit?

One picked up Jesús's limp body and heaved him over a shoulder. The gang ran past her, deep into their territory. She clutched at their garments as they passed, but her hands stayed empty, stinging from contact with their dark magick.

Sirens wailed far in the distance. She started to follow the gang, then stopped as Lupo's form appeared out of the shadows.

She held up both hands. "Don't come near me or I'll kill you."

He swaggered closer. "You'll never pin anything on me, witch. On the contrary, they'll wonder what the righteous advocate was doing here amongst the common whores. And why you make up stories about people that can't be substantiated by any facts or evidence. But they'll find bumper damage on that car to match my police report of a hit-and-run. With you at the wheel. And a sworn statement that Arnaldo disposed of the body."

Fury overrode any other emotion. She visualized him exploding into bits and hurled a bolt of white light energy at him.

Lupo staggered backward.

A wall of pressure built behind her. Taina turned her body enough that she could keep one eye and one outstretched palm on him and one on whatever the hell was coming from the other direction.

Raul, in black leather, coalesced from the mist. A red cape fluttered in a hot breeze like flames, taunting her with memories of the night her parents died. "Taina." His voice was liquid poison, dark, smooth.

They would not silence her before she delivered that audio file to Michael Kelly. "Back away, or I'll kill you both." *Goddess, Elegguá, Yemayá, someone help me defeat these monsters.*

They roared with laughter. Their weight against the protective field she'd conjured pressed against her from both sides, but she pushed back.

The dhampir chortled. "No mercy for you, witch. You smiled in my face then defiled yourself by consorting with that filthy, mercenary murderer. Now face the consequences of your choice."

The all-too-familiar cacophony of sirens drew closer, closer screaming to blast their way through rush hour traffic.

Lupo howled, and he and Raul vanished. Jesús's overturned cart lay on the corner, surrounded by a mountain of cans and bottles.

A crumpled heap lay in the street in front of Miguel's shop. Her pockmarked car dripped a steady stream of rainbow-colored fluids.

"No. No. No!" Even before she got to his side all of her hope was gone.

"Miguel." She cradled him in her arms. His eyes stared into hers as blood seeped out of his chest and neck, drenching through her clothes to her skin.

She put pressure on the wounds to try and stem the flow. "Help is on the way, Miguel. Hold on."

He coughed up blood clots. "I had too much honor to run. Go back to Puerto Rico, *nena.*" His eyes rolled back.

"Please, don't die. Not here, not like this." She laid him on his back, put her mouth over his, and breathed her life into him.

She put her hands on his chest and pressed, but more of his essence oozed out with each compression. His spirit departed. Any sense of his presence vanished.

She dragged him back onto her lap as her backside sank into the fetid puddle that surrounded them.

Police cars drove down the sidewalks from both directions. Cops leaped out, guns drawn, and prowled from car to car, scanning for any remaining threats .

One yelled into a two-way radio. "All units, Timpson and 149th. Two down. Gasoline everywhere. Possible sniper. I repeat, we need all available units to Timpson and 149th, EMS, HazMat, the ME, the DA."

The air exploded into a soundtrack for a movie in which she was a star, but unfortunately more than an actress.

A helicopter whirred overhead. Taina dissolved like sea salt into a cauldron of hot water. The camera rolled, and she watched from somewhere above and beyond.

The stench of gasoline, the metallic odor of blood, the filth and gore covering her, buttons torn off her blouse, skirt hitched over her behind, nothing concerned her, a specimen, a victim exposed, physically and emotionally for everyone to see.

An ambulance plowed through Jesús's detritus, smashing it into bits of metal and glass.

The cops turned circles, guns pointed in every direction, including at Taina and Miguel.

"Cover me." One cop emerged from behind an open car door and tiptoed toward them. "Put your hands up." He pointed his firearm at Taina.

He'd do her a favor by shooting, but she obliged. "I don't have a gun. Please, help my friend."

He pointed the pistol toward the ground but didn't holster it. "Miss, have you been hit?"

A child's hazy image of her family's body bags swirled in a sea of teardrops: The firefighter taking her from Jesús, giving her oxygen, staring into her eyes, stroking her hair, soothing her.

It evaporated, and the adult Taina crystallized in the bottom of a cauldron of bloody, chemical soup. "They shot Miguel. They shot Miguel." She rocked his limp body like a baby.

The director might have yelled, "Cut, it's a wrap" at that very moment.

In her zeal to uncover the truth, she'd released and recharged the demons. Then descended to their level.

Arnaldo had killed her family.

By trying to avenge her family's murders, she'd killed Miguel.

The cop yelled into the assemblage. "All clear. One DOA, but let the paramedics in here for the woman. Nobody light a match or even answer a fuckin' phone or we'll be blown to Brooklyn. Let HazMat get to work on the spill."

Still holding Miguel's corpse, Taina dragged herself one step further toward a reluctant reality.

Two medics, wearing gauzy orange HAZMAT suits with FDNY on the shoulder patches, ran toward her opening a collapsible chair, ripping equipment off their belts.

A female, a badge visible through the gown read Bradshaw, covered Taina with a blanket.

The female's face was partially concealed by the mask and goggles, but dreadlocks flicked like Medusa's snakes as gloved hands pried Taina's arms off Miguel's body. "We gotta get ya outta here."

She crouched behind and hooked her arms under Taina's.

Her partner, a dour-looking Latino, grabbed her under the knees. "One, two, three."

As they lifted her from the street to the transport chair, Miguel's body plopped into the puddle, splattering the mess over all of them.

"Shit, we're all gonna need to be decontaminated," Bradshaw muttered.

They wheeled Taina over the curb, out of the gutter. Bradshaw changed her gloves, peered under the blanket and unbuttoned Taina's blouse.

She unhooked Taina's bra and examined her chest. "Just lookin' for any bullet wounds."

She focused on the woman's competent, kind eyes, her motherly voice. The guy was working on her legs, but stopped at mid-thigh, no doubt leaving the choice bits to his partner.

Bradshaw cut into the waistband of Taina's skirt, peered beneath her blood soaked panties, at her ass, until satisfied. "Doesn't look like she's been hit."

The man, Gutierrez, changed his gloves and took her blood pressure. He held her wrist for a moment, averting his eyes, pausing to scribble on a clipboard.

The two paramedics stepped back as a cop in plain clothes pushed his way through the wall of blue uniforms. "This your purse, miss?" He held up her bag.

The phone! All this could not have been for naught. "Is my phone over by that cart?"

Another cop came over. "Right here. It couldn't have been a robbery because your wallet, keys, money, credit cards, they're all here. Can you tell us what happened?"

Taina clutched the phone to her for safekeeping. Her gaze drifted to Miguel's body, still lying in the street. Yellow police tape surrounded him. Firefighters, in full gear despite the blazing heat, tossed some sort of grit on the area outside the cordoned-off portion. Another cop snapped pictures of Miguel, of her.

She envisioned the jurors as images of the half-naked woman and the dead body flashed before their eyes. Here, so close to Hunts Point, they'd speculate she was a hooker, that she'd caused a jealous rage, a war between a pimp and a john. "Please get him out of that mess."

"Miss, I'm Detective Morillo, special gang task force." He did the perfunctory shield flash. "We have to wait for the medical examiner before he's moved or that area is entered. And the homicide detective and the assistant district attorney are on the way as well. In the meantime, please, tell us what happened."

She looked at up at him. "I need to be sure he's sent back to Puerto Rico. To his family. To Culebra. It was me they were after."

He raised his eyebrows, nodded like a shrink, and persisted. "What happened?"

"They took Jesús too. The guy collecting cans. Beat him to death. Carried him off." She clamped her hands over her face to block out the images, the smell of shit. She tasted blood, gasoline, grit, and she spit like a bum into the street.

Blood still crusted in her knuckles, under her nails. Her seared skin seared and peeled off as she rubbed.

"Go on, tell me what happened next."

What could she tell him that he'd believe? To get him to pick up Lupo, Raul, and Arnaldo and put them behind bars, without bail? Nothing. Nothing. He'd not believe a thing, write in his notebook that she was a hysteric making up stories about dark magick to cover up the fact she was a hit and run hooker.

"The only person I'm going to talk to is Detective Michael Kelly. He knows me, and my situation." There was no way to explain this to him either, but at least she'd have time to think about it.

"Kelly?"

"He told me I could call him, anytime."

Morillo's patience wore out. "Listen, miss. This scene has all the markers of *Las Tombas*—beatings, gasoline. This whole block could have gone up in a fireball. They'll be back for you, believe me. You'll need protection, you'll need relocation..."

Clueless cops on her tail would prevent her from doing what she needed to do. "I work for the court. You can't force a crime victim to accept anything. I want to go home. I want to get cleaned up. I want Miguel sent back to Culebra. And I want to speak to Detective Kelly."

"What did you mean by your fault that they were after you?" The tone of his voice was too sweet, too suave, too leading.

Now she needed a lawyer to add to the bitter brew. He hadn't read her any rights, and she wasn't saying another word. "I have the right..."

He screamed into the crowd, "Jesus fucking Christ. Can somebody please find Michael Kelly? And get her name, address, and get her the hell out of here." Morillo stormed off.

Bradshaw, now without mask and goggles, came back to Taina. "Let us take you to the hospital to get checked out. You're covered with blood and have to get preventative meds for HIV and hepatitis. You need a post sexual assault exam. The detective will meet you there."

"No, I'm going home. Please take Miguel. I can't stand seeing him lying there like that."

"The medical examiner is here now. Once he's done, they'll take him. Let the cops watch you, or you'll wind up just like that."

"You've been very nice, Ms. Bradshaw. Bright blessings to you. But I just need to go home." Taina struggled to her feet, clutching the blanket around her. Her legs wobbled like overstretched rubber bands.

"Officers, we're done. Medical assistance refused." Bradshaw stopped smiling. "These people don't play nice, girl."

Where were Bridge Rat and Hawk Claw now, to see Lady Taina, the White Witch, half naked, covered in blood, gore, and gasoline? Their capes would get seriously messed up.

"I'll take you home, miss." A cop stepped forward. "But you have to give us your name."

"Aponte. Taina Aponte. Victim's Advocate, Bronx County Courthouse."

He looked up from writing. "Let's go, Ms. Aponte." He led her by the arm.

Morillo stood fuming in front of a cop car. He opened the door and gestured her into the back seat. Like a criminal.

He snarled at her like she'd fired the shots. "Every stitch of your clothing goes into a plastic bag. You'll be asked to provide some specimens for forensics."

She slid into the back and slithered down so as not to see the carnage as they drove past. She'd never come down this block again.

Chapter Forty-One
No Turning Back

The cop opened the passenger door. "Miss? I'll take you upstairs."

Taina took his latex-gloved hand. Neighbors, summoned by the symphony of sirens and a hovering helicopter, gawked. The regulars at the bar came out to watch. Clutching the thin blanket around her, she lowered her head, hid her face.

He escorted her inside the fence. "You could have avoided all this by going to the hospital."

She resisted the temptation to tell him to go fuck himself. "I could have avoided all this if the police kept the gangs off the streets."

"Let's get inside your apartment. The ME and detectives will be here as soon as they can."

"Taina!" Arnaldo pushed through the crowd. His mouth fell open. His gaze tracked from her head to her bare feet. "*Ay Díos.*"

If she hadn't had been as drained and disconnected as an amputated limb, she would have attacked and beat the shit out of him.

The cop rescued the motherfucker. "You have to wait out here until they collect evidence, sir." He hustled her up the front steps.

"Evidence? What…" The door closing behind them cut off his words.

Señora Duarte rushed out of her apartment, horror painted on her face. "Taina! Are you hurt?"

"No, *gracias a Díos, señora.*"

"I've got to get her inside." The cop almost dragged Taina up the stairs.

She fumbled in her purse for the keys. He took it and fished through like a pickpocket looking for buried treasure. Once inside, she stood just outside her circle, surveying the neat and tidy room she'd left this morning for a routine day of work. Zeus scampered toward her, then stopped, whimpered, and retreated to his bed and stared, his eyes sad, limpid, more aware than any mere animal could be of the intense anguish washing over her.

Now Miguel was dead. Jesús too. Arnaldo had killed her family. Arnaldo had killed her family.

Too much to absorb at one time, or to make sense of. She tore at her hair.

"Arnaldo's your boyfriend? I know him from *Sonrisa*." The cop left the apartment door ajar.

"What the fuck does that have to do with anything?"

He put his hand up in surrender. "I don't want to give him a hard time."

"Go easy on him? I'm one of the victims!"

Saved by the doorbell. The cop looked down the stairs. "Up here."

Footsteps rapped on the linoleum. A woman in ME blue came in, carrying a case. "Ms. Aponte?"

Taina looked around. "I don't see any other bloodied, gore-encrusted victims in this apartment."

"I'm sorry, ma'am. I know how difficult this must be. Any evidence we can collect might give us a clue as to who killed Mr. Santana. The sooner we get this over with, the sooner you can get cleaned up. And that very anxious, eh…gentleman waiting downstairs can come up to see for himself that you're okay."

Taina's bravado melted like candle wax. The desired information had been obtained. But Miguel was dead. Her family was dead. Everyone she knew was in danger. And the person who was supposed to be helping and protecting her was the murderer.

"Ms. Aponte, did you hear me? Why don't we go into the bathroom?"

Taina shook her head to clear the cobwebs. "Yeah, okay."

They'd sent a female, assuming Taina would prefer that. Truthfully, the woman's saccharine demeanor creeped her out.

Ms. ME closed the door but didn't lock it. "I need you to undress and put all the clothes into this bag. Then I have to collect some specimens. Unless you want to take the easy way out and go to the ER."

"My friend was just murdered. There is no easy way out." Taina stripped off whatever was left of her blood and gasoline soaked bra, shredded skirt, and sodden panties, and dropped the mess into the bag.

Ms. ME averted her eyes. "Now the nails." Her latex-gloved hand made it seem more impersonal, yet more intrusive. Practiced fingers dug the gunk out from under each with a toothpick, then clipped them all.

"Finally, I'd like your permission to collect vaginal fluid, urine, and saliva samples and two tubes of blood. They'll be analyzed for a variety of things—drugs, bacteria, and viruses, including HIV. These are the things that would have been obtained in the hospital."

"You can take whatever you want." They'd find nothing amiss. Taina signed the form, leaning on the toilet tank, taking care not to smear blood all over the paper.

She took Taina's upper lip and ran a spatula around the gum line, top and bottom, and stuffed it in a foil pouch. "Put this swab into your vagina and then into the tube. It will be tested for semen, as well as for infections."

Taina complied.

"Thanks. Here is a urine cup. I have to watch, I'm sorry. This is to maintain the chain of evidence."

"I thought I wasn't a suspect." Squatting in front of a stranger, stark naked, to pee in a cup was further than she would go. "I think that's all I'd like to donate tonight then."

"Well, I guess I can wait outside, and you could pass it to me. There's no one else in the apartment."

Taina's advocate hat couldn't quite fit over her bloated head right now. If she didn't do it, it would appear like she was hiding drug use or prostitution. And that was what Lupo had set this up to look like. "All right."

Ms. ME obliged and stepped out, but it took Taina a while to pee on demand.

"You okay, Ms. Aponte?" She opened the door a crack.

"This enough?" Taina screwed the cap on.

"Plenty. Let me take the blood samples, then you're free to shower and get dressed. And your boyfriend can come up."

Her advocate's head slipped past the obstruction. "Let's get this straight. I was free to shower and get dressed from the beginning. I'm doing this because I have nothing to hide and don't want my name or reputation dragged into the sewer by some fucking ADA trying to pin a charge on me and get a promotion. And that is not my boyfriend."

"Right or left arm, Ms. Aponte?" Ms. ME stretched the tourniquet between two hands.

Taina held both arms out. Everyone proclaimed innocence. But she'd killed Miguel by selfishness, not something admissible, discoverable, and provable. But real, nonetheless. "How about one tube from each?"

She rested Taina's right arm on the sink, tied the blue rubber around it, poked, swabbed. "One stick is sufficient."

A pinch, pressure, the snap of rubber. How much pain had Miguel felt when the bullets invaded his body? What unspeakable agony had her family endured as flames engulfed them?

"All done. Press and hold. Again, Ms. Aponte, I'm sorry. I do appreciate your willingness to cooperate with the investigation." She taped a bandage over the stinking pin stick.

Taina ripped it off as soon as she left. She heard Arnaldo fussing and peeked out.

"Hey, listen, officer, why don't you wait outside while I help her get cleaned up?" He patted the cop on the back, and they whispered like she wasn't in control, wasn't able to speak for herself.

She was too scattered to even rebuke them. The cop went out of the apartment.

Then he saw her. "Taina." Arnaldo squeezed through the partially closed door. "What happened?"

"They killed Miguel and Jesús." Saying it hurt as if the bullets were puncturing her body, the bats bashing her head in. "They set us up."

He swallowed hard. "Lupo and his thugs?"

"Both Lupo and Raul were there, but *Las Tombas* soldiers beat Jesús and fired the shots. It was like something out of a war movie."

"Those two never leave their stinking imprints on anything." The arrogant bastard was sure he'd never get caught but had another think coming at him.

He pushed his way into the bathroom expecting a submissive kitten to crawl into his lap. "Let's get you into the shower."

Taina pummeled his chest with her fists. "I don't need any help from a murderer. You killed my parents and my sister. You'll die in jail right next to those two. I have *Jesús's* confession taped, and Detective Kelly is on his way over here right now to hear it."

He backed away. "Jesús doesn't even remember his own name."

"I healed him. Now I know why you tried to scare me away." Taina's anguish meter surged. She'd waited most of her life to be able to look her family's murderer in the eye and, though meaningless, the moment had finally arrived. How come it had to be like this?

Arnaldo staggered back even further. "People were dying everywhere around me. Of overdoses. Of AIDS. Of gunshots. Of stab wounds. Lupo paid for the gasoline. I dumped it around the foundation of the building. Jesús couldn't get the match to light, so I did it for him and tossed it like a cigarette butt. Sparks flew and ignited the curtains. Raul gave us drugs as payment." He put his head in his hands.

She punched him in the chest. "Three lives ended with the flick of a wrist."

Tears streamed down his face. "I was running from everyone at that point in my life: the dealers, other addicts, the gangs, the police. All the while high on heroin with a speedball toke or crack booster. What was one more crime at that point? I didn't know what I was doing."

The cold, callous way he stated it hurt as much as hearing it. "You killed a man and a woman and a child. And nearly killed me— and didn't even have the balls to tell me the truth." *How could she have been so stupid?*

"Taina, I knew the minute you found out you'd never look at me again."

"Oh, and going back to prison had nothing to do with it?"

"I did my time and make up for the wrongs every day of my life. You now have the same weapon as I to control Raul and Lupo and could leverage that to do good for many innocent people." He tried to put his arms around her.

"Get the fuck away from me, murderer!" Taina pushed him so hard he banged into the wall.

He wiped a snotty nose on his shirttail. "I'll do anything to prove I'm sorry, including going back to jail. "But please, give me a few days to find someone to run *Sonrisa*. I can't let those old folks rot in their apartments like Abuela did. And those kids, Taina, they need someone, a road map to get them out of here alive, undead."

He groveled like an idiot, kneeling, hands clasped as if in prayer. "That place is my life's work and if it fails everything I've done will have been for nothing."

"Get up. Now." She stared out the bathroom window at the traffic going up and down like the world was not caving in around her, like nothing was wrong, that things were just fine, like it was just another day.

He put his hands on her shoulders. "Tell them not to send a tactical squad, and to come after I close up so the kids don't see me in handcuffs. I'll go willingly and confess to what I did. Nothing will bring your family back, but I'll spend the rest of my life in prison to prove to you that freedom is not my motivation. When they lock me up, please don't let all my work go down with me. Please."

She wanted to spit in his face. "Miguel is lying in bloody,

gasoline-soaked clothes in a morgue. What did he do to deserve that? And what about Jesús? He was your friend too."

"This is a war, Taina. They fought despite the risks. Just like you."

"I don't want to hear about collateral damage."

Arnaldo backed away. "You can cover your eyes and your ears, but nothing will change unless you fight back as dirty as they do. I would still love to be by your side doing it."

She needed no more reminders of her own complicity. "Get out of here."

Arnaldo ran for the stairs.

Zeus scratched at the door, whimpered, then ran to the window and leapt onto the radiator. His head cocked as his gaze followed Arnaldo down the street.

Taina, still naked, and sticky and bloody and smelly, picked him up and watched her lover, her protector, disappear around the corner.

"It's just you and me, Zeus."

Her gaze went to the altar. "Goddess, *Elegguá, Yemayá,* someone, help me."

Chapter Forty-Two
Along the Boulevard of Bad Spells and Broken Dreams

Even after the water gurgling down the drain no longer ran pink, and the smell of oil was swallowed by scented soap, the images, the odors, the shame, the grief remained.

The cop outside paced the sidewalk, no doubt anxious to get back to his own life. She locked her door, grabbed the phone, and dialed.

No spell needed this time. Serena answered on the second ring. "Taina, I woke thinking of you today."

"I bet you did." She struggled to keep the emotion, the judgment out of her voice. "Lupo Lopez and Raul Rivera tried to kill me today. With real bullets. But my friend, an innocent man, was in the way and he died. Serena, it's a mess. They're going to say I was a hooker, or a thief or both, trying to cover up another crime I was set up for."

"And Arnaldo?" Her voice quavered.

"He confessed that he set the fire that killed my family."

"Arnaldo did a lot of bad things when he was using." There was no surprise in her voice.

Fury bubbled inside. "You knew? All this time? And you sent me directly to him? Why didn't you tell me?"

Serena's sigh sucked what was left of the air out of the room. "There is a path that must be walked, a destiny to be fulfilled. If you knew Arnaldo set the fire, you would have called the police before you knew him and saw all the amends he's made."

"It's a good thing you're lecturing from over a thousand miles away. You pretended to love me, then conspired with him on a plot to cover both your tracks."

"Hija, I told you not to go. Leave everything you can't carry. Get on the next plane back to Puerto Rico."

"I'm not a fucking coward like you. And there is nothing for me to come home to."

"Taina, *tu abuela* wouldn't allow you near me. After she died, I sought you out, tried to teach you what you needed to know. It is not my place to question the goddess on her intent. Her will be done, she who is all knowing."

"*Bastante ya* with the will of the goddess, my path, my destiny, with all this bullshit. You and Arnaldo are like two snakes hatched from the same egg. I hate you, Serena. Live with those as the last words you'll ever hear from my mouth." Taina slammed the phone down.

She moved like a robot through the apartment, dusk's claim of the street the sole marker of time. Zeus stationed himself on the radiator cover in front of the kitchen window, eyes scanning the scene, taking an occasional break to lick salty tears off Taina's face as she sat in front of her altar.

Smoky sage filled the room, but smudge could never banish the stain on her soul, the shock of Arnaldo's betrayal, the pain of what she'd done to Miguel. She stared at her parents, trying to connect with them, wherever they were, for some guidance. But the room was devoid of spirit, and of spirits, a hot, lonely box, sealed up tight against the outside world, a police car parked in front to ensure no one got in.

She doused the sage with *Agua Florida.* Fragrant steam banished the weedy aroma.

Engrossed with watching dark spirals disperse, the bell startled her. The knock on the door grew more insistent, the voice louder. "Taina, Detective Michael Kelly, NYPD. Are you okay?"

She opened the window to let more air in. "Let me get some clothes on." She fanned with throw pillows, blew out the candles, and covered the altar with a white cloth.

If she waited any longer, he'd kick the door in. Taina took a deep breath and unlocked it.

Kelly showed his badge. "I'm glad you had them call me, Taina. Can I come in?"

She gestured to the sofa. "Please sit down."

He took a seat. She settled on the opposite side. All very proper police procedure. No matter what they said, she was a person of interest.

"I got a look at the scene. It's a miracle you're alive. Can you tell me what happened?"

Like lawyers advised their clients, she'd just stick to the facts.

"I went to Miguel's to sign the title for a car he sold for me. There was a bum on the corner, collecting bottles and cans. I was talking to him, and this bunch of thugs came and started to beat him up. When I screamed, Miguel must have come out. It all happened so fast. There were gunshots, then lots of smoke." She didn't start to cry for dramatic effect, but Kelly probably thought so.

"Go on."

"That's all, besides the sirens, blood, the smell of gasoline. That still makes me sick, after…" Taina clasped her hands to stop them from shaking and took deep breaths.

"Okay, Taina. I know that's a trigger for you. Did you recognize anyone?"

This was the moment she'd been waiting for all her life. She had the evidence. "A gang beat up the bum and kicked him and smashed his head like a pumpkin. I saw Lupo Lopez and Raul Rivera, but they weren't carrying any weapons. I have no idea who shot Miguel."

Kelly scratched his chin. "Rivera and Lopez together? That's unusual. Can you tell who the gangs were flagging?"

Arnaldo was right. The cops were clueless to the fluid conspiracy between the dhampirs and werewolves. "Some were tagged with yellow, some with red."

"Taina, this was a typical *Las Tombas* scene, deep in their territory, with gasoline all over the place. We found a bill of sale for the car on Miguel's desk. Lupo Lopez was the buyer. That's his alibi for being there. Are you sure you saw Raul?"

"Yes."

"What were you talking to the bum about?" The furrowed brow negated his benevolent smile. Had he already heard allegations of the hit-and-run?

"I asked him if he was hungry and was going to give him money to buy food." Why was she lying? Why not just tell him Jesús was the man who had caught her and that she wanted to thank him?

Kelly wasn't stupid. He'd remember the name. Surmise that Raul and Lupo were threatened because Jesús had just given Taina the information she had been searching for.

Serena's admonition replayed in her mind. *"If you knew Arnaldo set the fire, you would have called the police before you knew him and saw all the amends he's made."*

Kelly's nose scrunched. He sniffed like her words smelled as suspicious as the lingering incense. "Taina, why wouldn't you tell Detective Morillo all this?"

"I was too upset, and he was too aggressive, telling me they were going to put a guard on me and take me to the hospital."

"I'm going to be honest with you. Miguel was shot with a semi-automatic weapon. If one of *Las Tombas* tossed a match with all that gasoline, the entire block would have blown up, including you and all the first responders.

"The fact that you were there, that you survived, and yet wouldn't tell him anything, raised some suspicions about your role in the incident. Others have suggested you'd been visiting Miguel Santana frequently, having dinner with him, that there might have been some sort of romantic…"

She jumped to her feet and got in his cool, calm, collected cop face. "That is not true! He knew my father, and we were good friends. Are you saying I was a party in this attack? Or that I'm withholding information?"

"You're a criminal witness. You will be asked to answer questions, over and over. And we'll ask you not to leave New York City until the investigation is complete."

"My friend died in my arms. I saw another man beaten to death. All I was doing was selling my fucking car. Don't I have the right to walk down the street? Have dinner with a friend every now and then?" If she played Jesús's statement now, any question that she was complicit would be erased. Lupo and Raul would be picked up. Arnaldo too. She could go back to Puerto Rico.

Play the victim, or play the tape?

"Taina, I explained to Morillo what happened when you were a kid. He understands the scene, the gasoline, and the sirens could have affected your emotional state."

She couldn't sit still. "No more until I have an attorney."

Kelly followed her to the window. "I know this is a terrible thing, but you did refuse medical, and by association, psychiatric care, and social services. And, as I understand it, you don't want police protection."

"I don't want to be tailed." She walked to the door, hoping he'd take the hint. She needed space, time, to figure this out.

Kelly was too experienced to not know she was lying. "Taina, is someone putting the squeeze on you?"

"No more than anyone else who lives in this neighborhood." That was number three. There were chickens in a neighbor's alleyway. She half-expected a rooster to crow.

"You're in danger."

"No shit."

He turned the detective's thumbscrews a bit more. "I think you were getting too close to finding out who set the fire that killed your parents and sister. Rivera and Lopez are teaming up to silence you and anyone around you. If you don't think you need a guard against two gangs, you're crazy.

"When you first came to me desperate for answers I explained how frustrating it was for us to never be able to get witnesses to tell us anything. Now you're doing the same thing."

"Thank you for your concern, Detective Kelly." She opened the door. Her insides squirmed like worms.

He paused on the way out. "The perpetrators are getting up there in age. And they're training replacements. When you're ready to tell me what you know, call my phone number." He handed her a card. "Anytime. I'll be sure you get a new identity and passage to wherever you want to go. In the meantime, can I let the police at least stay outside overnight when the gangs are most active?"

How could she do what she needed to do with the police up her ass? "I decline any extra police protection."

He shook his head. "Detective Morillo will be in touch. I'm sure he'll have more questions. Losing your life isn't going to bring your family back. If you're hiding anything, you're enabling them to continue this." Kelly closed the door gently behind him.

Miguel had once said *"It's everyone's fault, and no one's fault."*

Sending Lupo, Raul, and Arnaldo to prison wouldn't end it. There were legions of loyal gang members trained and ready to step in and take their places until the immortals served their time and got out. While Arnaldo rotted in jail.

In anarchy, when no one is in control, the battle is for control. The real reason for the fight is buried, forgotten. She'd gotten lost, just like Arnaldo, and was no longer part of the solution. She was part of the problem.

~ * ~

Taina paced like a caged animal. An eerie quiet descended with the night. If she stayed there, *Señora* Duarte would be next. The protective spell around the apartment would only hold up for so long against the combined forces of *Las Tombas* and *Los Sangueros.*

She could call Kelly, tell him she was afraid, accept his offer of relocation—just like Serena did so many years ago. Go to Puerto Rico, or the Dominican Republic, anywhere. Lose herself in the masses, be a paralegal with a terrible secret.

But now Taina needed air, and Zeus needed a walk. "Fuck *Los Tombas* and *Las Sangueros.* We're going out."

She picked up the dog's leash.

He hurried to the door, anxious for a stroll. Could the animal comprehend the danger they were in? She envisioned white light around her, drew its protective force inside, and went out into the night.

A slice of waxing moon slashed the velvet sky. The brightest stars twinkled through the streetlight and pollution haze. "Miguel, if you're looking down, please, forgive me."

Only cars rumbled over the elevated Bruckner.

Graffiti-adorned security doors covered most shop windows, save for the fried-chicken place and the Chinese takeout spilling crowds of raucous mundanes onto the sidewalk, eating out of paper cartons and wiping greasy fingers on their clothes like nothing had happened just around the corner.

Taina walked past her childhood home, the scene of the crime that had brought her back, given her this legacy to honor, this burden to carry. She paused, then hurried toward Paloma.

The counter man looked up as the bell tinkled but didn't smile or acknowledge her. Anger tinged with sadness swirled through the air. He was Miguel's friend, and no one could have missed the army of police cars and fire trucks blasting to the scene. And a fucking helicopter hovering above the scene, even if it was about a mile away.

"Dos ordenes pollo guisado to go." She wasn't hungry, just desperate to recapture a time when Miguel was alive, to turn back the clock, to make it unhappen.

The man eyed her like a chicken to hack into pieces for the stew. "You're the *puta* who was with Miguel when they shot him."

News traveled fast. "He sold my car, and I went to sign the title. That's all."

The cook ladled out the rice and dumped the chicken on top. Practiced hands sealed the plastic cover to the foil plate, topped it off with napkins and cello bags of utensils—all while throwing knives with his eyes. When the pictures got out, there would be no way in hell to prove her innocence.

"Tell that to his wife and his daughter. Tell it to God when your turn comes up, *pu-ta.*" He shoved the plastic bag, reeking of garlic and abject disgust, toward her. "You're going to hell. *Buen provecho.*"

Taina blinked back tears. Miguel knew the truth, and he was the only one who needed to forgive her. She dropped a twenty on the counter.

"I don't want your dirty money." The man crossed his arms over his chest.

"Give it to the church." She snatched the bag then ran.

Zeus wriggled in her arms, and she put him down. To stay away from the park, she cut through the side streets past the homestead houses and found herself on Southern Boulevard. *Sonrisa* bustled with kids in droopy pants, wife-beater tees, and basketball shoes—as usual for that time of day.

Arnaldo, in a doo rag, shorts, armpits dark with sweat, just like the first day they'd met, did a layup and scored. "I might be old, but I'm good."

The kids playing with him under the lights on this unseasonably warm October night took the ball and ran cross-court. Arnaldo saw her, stopped, opened his arms and shrugged, then waved for her to come in.

She shook her head.

"Please," he mouthed.

She walked to the gate, called past him to the kids. "Anybody hungry?"

They rushed over. "Yeah, miss. Whatcha got?"

Taina handed the bag through. *"Lo mejor pollo guisado en El Bronx.* You behave yourselves now."

They tore into it like starving dogs. "Arnaldo, get us some soda."

"We need plates."

"Go inside and get them, you freaks. I'm not a waiter."

"Thanks, miss." They crowded through the door, leaving the two of them facing each other, the chain link fence and Arnaldo's strong protective spell between them.

He reached through and patted Zeus on the head. The dog licked his hand.

Arnaldo stared at her, tears glistening in his eyes. "I'm sorry about what I did, and that I was not honest with you. I've spent all my life trying to make amends for my past."

"Spare me, Arnaldo." She turned to leave but caught sight of Jesús, sprawled in a plastic lawn chaise, eyes wide and unblinking, unseeing, unknowing.

Some of the hatred drained out of her fractured heart. "You found him?"

Arnaldo opened the gate and gestured for her to enter. Taina knelt beside Jesús. She stroked his battered face. There was no response.

"I searched the dumpsters." Arnaldo's voice creaked like a rusty hinge. "Almost left him there. He was bad off enough before, but now he can't move or speak. Maybe I should have walked away, but he's my best friend. I can't forget what he was like before he was changed."

Tears ran down his face, and he made no attempt to stop them or mop them up. "We aren't bad people, Taina. We had no one to show us the right way and got sucked into the trap Lupo set and addicted to the drugs and sex Raul provided. We didn't set out to hurt anyone." He put his head in his hands.

Even such raw emotion seemed self-serving.

"You're both still on Earth while my family is just bones and dust in a graveyard. Demonic scat, that's all the two of you are, with one difference. Jesús saved my life while you ran like a fucking coward to save your own hairy ass."

She took Jesús chin in her fingers and gazed into his eyes, willing white light to swirl through him from the top of his head to his toes. With each breath, it tornadoed through his body, infusing life, banishing death.

He blinked. His eyeballs, bloodshot with snakes of torturous clotted veins, swirled toward her, pupils pinpoint as his eyelids fluttered against the brightness.

She sensed his awareness returning. "Jesús, I will do my best to heal you."

His gaze fixed at a spot on the wall, which could have been the electric socket or a spider web stretched between the moldings.

Arnaldo put his hands on her shoulders, his eyes round as saucers. "When did you realize you had such powers?"

She shook his arms away, stood, and brushed the dirt off her hands. "Right about the same time I realized you were a filthy, lying murderer. You mean nothing but pain and death to me. Clean him up, please. I'll come back another day to see if I can do more."

She'd let him wonder if he'd been turned him in, let the knife of uncertainty twist in his gut as long as she could.

Arnaldo picked up the zombie like a ghoulish groom carrying a bride over the threshold. He whistled and two kids came running.

"Whatcha' doin' with him, Arnaldo?" one young man asked.

"Carry that chair upstairs for me. Help me fix him up."

The two boys hefted the chaise and disappeared.

Arnaldo paused. "I hoped that being around the kids would help. But you're right. I'll set him up away from all the confusion and everyone gawking at him."

She walked out and watched the boys in the backyard playing basketball instead of playing chicken with cars, or shooting up, or snorting, or lighting fires.

In her mind's eye, she saw Jesús immobile on a plastic chaise lounge in the corner of a staircase landing like some corny Halloween decoration.

Chapter Forty-Three
Goddesses, Saints, Sinners

Lights twinkled in apartment windows like dispossessed fae spirits. The housing projects that had replaced their forests rose around Ritual Rock. Now shadows tinged with red-and-black demon halos slithered through the trees. A smattering of distant stars tried valiantly to brighten the dark sky, but the new moon hid its face in shame.

Zeus led, tail and ears pricked. A white aura lit the ground, and Taina stepped into the circle for protection. Bridge Rat flew out of a tree and landed at her feet.

He transformed and greeted her with the customary bow. "So the gauntlet has been thrown, my lady. Have you accepted the challenge to duel Lupo and Raul?"

The eternal fae enthusiasm was particularly disturbing tonight. "I have not. Maybe you're used to battlefield slaughter, but I'm not anxious to be a part of any more of it."

"She who has been chosen is often reluctant to take on the task, but it is the will of the goddess."

Enough theatrics. "Whose goddess, Bridge Rat? A lot of names are bandied about, depending on one's persuasion. The One True One has an awful lot of competition, and her voice is lost among all the squabbling for my attention."

"Ah, so you refer to the deities described as *orishas*, who bear many names, many faces."

"*Exacto. Los santos* who are asking for some rather weird shit from me."

He rose and hovered at her eye level. "Gods and goddesses and their manifestations are as personal to the faithful as invocations and sacrifices. Surely you understand the concept of duality, of the male with the female, the black with the white, the good with the bad."

"The *orishas* Josefa talks about have an endless permutation of forms." Did she really need to school fairies?

"Devised by human's need to hide their beliefs, to worship according to the norms of your societies or risk death. But, Lady Taina, you have never been one to lose yourself amongst the baffles and babble.

"Follow the voice that speaks loudest to you, which touches the place in your soul longing for solace and respite. Compromise is a necessity of the human condition that even we fae have made by taking on the forms of mundane creatures."

Ay, por favor. "Bridge Rat, why didn't you and Hawk Claw just tell me all this when we first met? It could have avoided a lot of complications."

He put a long, green finger to his cheek, cocked his head, and smirked. "As I recall you were far from receptive and your ears, your mind deaf to the message."

Stinking fae tricksters.

Her turn to wag a royal finger in his face. "You knew I was looking for information about my family. But you pushed me closer to Arnaldo, all the while knowing he was involved with Raul and Lupo in their murder. "You wanted to entrap me so I could advance the fairy agenda and fulfill the prophecy of a god or goddess you worship. But innocent people have died. A young boy and a dear friend. Now I'm going to die too. Not that I care, mind you, but I would have liked to have the opportunity to see Raul and Lupo get their due before they annihilate my soul."

Bridge Rat swept his cape over a shoulder. "Our agenda is to repair the destruction of the environment and the quality of existence for all. Neither witch, nor dhampir, nor lycanthrope will relinquish control. The fae could have fled with the rest of our kind and left humans to implode under the weight of their own stupidity."

His atypical vehemence poked a hole in Taina's pumped-up bold, bitchy, Bronx balloon. "Where does that leave me now?"

His characteristic big-lipped grin returned. "No offence intended, Lady Taina. You are a fine specimen of humanity, which is why you were chosen for this task. If only there were more like you." His voice drifted off like a wistful, jilted lover hoping for a beloved's return.

The light in his eyes fed directly into Taina's and emptied into her soul.

"Use of your gift will honour your family. Death has never frightened you—as it doesn't those who have been fortunate to escape from its grasp. Remember, the thing you desired most is what you have discovered. What you do with that newfound closure is your choice. But choose wisely. As you have seen, the god and goddess do not take disregard of their will kindly when meting out their own form of justice."

She crawled out from under the crush of his words. "I'm a victim too!"

"Perhaps the legal system humankind has devised provides some reward to those who have suffered at the hands of others, but immortal justice does not. It is now time for you to decide your fate." Bridge Rat raised his right hand, fist clenched, toward the sky.

His wings beat furiously, the whine rising above the *duh-duh, duh-duh, duh-duh* of trucks lumbering over metal plates on the elevated Bruckner, jumbo jets roaring along their takeoff and landing routes, sirens wailing, and horns blaring.

Hawk Claw swooped out of the sky, a white bundle in his talons. He landed atop Ritual Rock, flapped his wings and transformed, a neatly folded, feathered garment in his hands.

A ray of sun pierced the cloud cover and surrounded Ritual Rock with pulsing white light. "Lady Taina, this battle must be led by a female witch who straddles the borderline between the mundane and magickal world, the embodiment of the goddess, a giver of life. The donning of this cloak will signal your willingness to fulfill her will."

The whole scene was like a really bad movie. "There are thousands of female witches in New York City. Go find someone else."

Hawk Claw smiled. "Dark magick left a stain on Arnaldo's soul, one which he was not responsible for, but had to overcome, nonetheless. Only the blameless victim of his transgressions can liberate him from the curse inflicted on him before he was even born. When you and he share your bodies, your spirits and your minds, those energies meld into a source of power strong enough to counteract those who do evil with no remorse and defile the Earth and all her children by their malevolent actions."

He gestured to his vassal. Bridge Rat bowed to his lord, took, and shook out a finely woven cloak with snowy white feathers along the hemlines. The fairy alighted in front of Taina, proffering the garment. "I offer you the sacred cloak of the White Witch. Long have we awaited the moment when the chosen one would lead us into battle."

The power, the energy emanating from the jeweled clasp raised goose bumps on her arms. She reached out, enthralled, then terrified, pulled back. "I came to New York City to find out who killed my family. I now know and will see them put in jail. If I survive, I will go away."

Bridge Rat bowed his head, his wings and ears drooped as much as his normally smiling lips. Zeus whimpered, looked up at her with a curious mix of sadness and surprise.

Hawk Claw fluttered to her, got on one knee, and took her hand in his. "There are still twenty-four hours until Samhain—and the Dark Moon. A most beneficial time for dispersing and banishing. Take the enchanted cloak and moonstone. Not until you fasten it about you will you be bound."

Leading a battle charge singlehandedly against *Las Tombas* and *Los Sangueros* was the worst kind of suicide—committing to a living death.

And without Arnaldo, the person she hated most in the world right now, there was no chance.

But it wasn't death that scared her. "What if I am changed?"

Hawk Claw did not hesitate, did not loosen his grip. "You have already been changed, my lady. Irrevocably altered."

Bridge Rat approached. "The sacred stone will illuminate the path if you have the courage to take the first step."

War waged in Taina's head. She needed to meditate, to rest. "Then you will come to me tomorrow to retrieve the cloak should I decide not to accept?"

"I shall not entertain such thoughts." Hawk Claw stepped back and dropped her hand.

"But of course, my lady. I shall call for you tomorrow as the sun begins to set." Bridge Rat fluttered around her and folded the cloak over her outstretched arms.

The feathers tickled her hands. The stone pulsed, emitting energy that surged through her like an orgasm, causing her knees to buckle. Surely this was a talisman with great power.

Bridge Rat, Hawk Claw, and Zeus stood tall, staring up at her like she was the goddess herself. Flocks of birds fluttered overhead, alighting in the trees, silent. Rats and squirrels scurried out of the shadows and paused before dipping their heads.

The giddy laugh came from somewhere deep inside her, then deteriorated into heaving sobs. She was a bumbling, misfit witch just over five feet tall, expected to lead a fairy king and his vassal, a flock of birds, rodents, and a tiny dog into battle against two violent gangs bent on subjugation of humankind.

And the prick that had killed her family, seduced her, and lied to her about it was now her knight in tarnished armor.

"Until tomorrow eve, my lady." Hawk Claw spun and transformed before he flew off.

"Lady Taina." Bridge Rat did the same.

Birds lining the power lines tucked heads under their wings and slept. Rats scampered back into the subway grates and sewers. The squirrels ran up tree trunks and disappeared.

Taina sat alone, with her tiny familiar, in St. Mary's Park, in the South Bronx, on the eve of a Dark Moon, holding a magic cloak and a powerful crystal.

Would she survive until she got home?

She ran, as fast as she could without having a full-blown asthma attack, and Zeus as fast as his legs could carry him. As she passed the abandoned gas station, three humanoid forms walking on all fours approached. Their sickly yellow auras glowed like bug lights luring disoriented insects to their incineration.

Zeus stood in front. She tucked the cloak under her jacket to keep it safe and out of sight. The three lycanthropes circled, moving closer, closer, closer.

She summoned white light. Her left index finger spun a ring around her and Zeus. She reached for her athame, clutched the grip in her hand, and prayed to no one in particular for forgiveness, for strength. The leather warmed, and when she pulled the knife out, the blade seemed longer and glowed like a white-hot flame tinted with a rainbow of color at the heart.

The weres stopped, lowered their heads, prepared to attack. Zeus stood his ground at the apex of the circle. Taina eased into fighting stance and extended her weapon.

One leaped for her throat, but the protective circle deflected his trajectory. He landed well outside, stunned. The other two would not make the same mistake. They moved to opposite poles, west and east.

As she'd done that night, Taina allowed evil thoughts to take hold, centered and herself. As they pounced, she slashed their bellies, relished the feel of blade ripping into hairy flesh. Roaring with pain, they tried to crawl out of her circle, but she jumped forward, stabbing the back of one's neck. Before he stopped quivering, she'd done the same to the second and finished off the third lying dazed on the ground at the north pole.

"One for Miguel, one for Jesús, one for my family." She wiped the blood off her blade on their fur and stepped over the bodies, then picked up Zeus and moved on.

Shadowy figures dragged the fallen weres back to the lair for funerary rites. They'd be shredded or new zombies would emerge from the remains, too stupid and vapid to be of any threat if their master was not right there with them.

Without pause, Taina tossed her fouled jacket and shoes into the junkyard dumpsters with the rest of *Las Tombas* detritus. If she was to battle monsters to the death, there could be no remorse, no disgust, only the pleasure of victory, the thrill of the kill.

Raul and Lupo appeared, staring defiantly like they did through the smoke as she'd cradled Miguel's body.

Neither she nor Zeus broke stride, with her athame leading. "Killing the two of you is all that remains. Then I'll command the scavengers to chop you up and drop you in the landfill where you belong."

"Tough talk, but Arnaldo isn't here to help you, *chica*. Little girl, that's what he calls you, isn't it? His little *puta*. Whose little dog won't survive if he bites me again." Lupo growled. His yellowed lips dripped putrid saliva.

Raul grinned. Fangs dug into his lips, drawing blood. He blew her a kiss. "Soon. Soon I will have my way with you, *bruja sucia*."

Taina extended her hands, held her breath, concentrated her energy, then blew out forcefully.

"Stay away, away you'll stay.

Harming none, harming never."

One time sufficed. The were and damp staggered back.

"Get out of my way." The jewel and white cloak, still pristine, was already exerting influence, her mind so clear, she could sense their surprise, their unease.

Lupo gestured to his lackeys, who lumbered after him down an alley.

Raul hid his confusion better than the werewolf—or so he imagined.

"I'll save the final conquest until Samhain. There will be many to witness the subjugation of the White Witch and feast on her blood— among other things." Ever graceful, he twirled like a dancer and slipped into the shadows.

She'd won this round, but could she do it again when her adversaries were better prepared? All she had to do was go home, call Detective Kelly, play the audio, accept his offer of safe passage, and she'd be free to leave. Raul, Lupo, and Arnaldo would be behind bars.

Without leaders, the gangs would disintegrate into squabbling mobs and annihilate each other. No collateral damage to bloody her hands further.

Mission accomplished.

A police car and fire truck sat in front of Taina's building, strobe lights flashing. Uniformed men scrambled around the building. The unmistakable whiff of gasoline met her sensitized nostrils. Zeus whimpered.

Señora Duarte waited by the front door, trembling, twisting her fingers around each other. Tears dribbled down her cheeks. "They left a can filled with gasoline and nails inside the gate. If I didn't go out to chase away a flock of pigeons and see it..." She started to sob. "You have to leave."

"I'll be gone tomorrow." Tonight, she'd taken the next step on the slippery slope by using her magick to harm, not heal, and to endanger innocents.

The cop who'd taken her home from the murder scene was back on duty. "I think you can see why we're putting a guard on you, whether you like it or not. These guys aren't going to stop until they kill you. I suggest you stay inside. We've got a car in front and around the back as well."

He turned to *Señora* Duarte. "Don't worry, ma'am. It's all cleaned up, and we'll keep watch until those men are caught."

The moonstone heated Taina's skin until it tightened and seared like a bad sunburn. They would never catch "those men." Never. They weren't men, and the police had no inkling.

"Lo siento, nena." Señora ducked into her apartment.

Zeus scampered up behind Taina as she unlocked the door. A hot breeze blew in through the open window along with a whiff of gasoline mixed with garbage and diesel fuel.

She placed the cloak on her altar, opened the kitchen window, and she turned off all the lights, save for a black candle behind a clear bowl of water. The flickering created an exact image of a flame, a demon's halo, in the center. No surprise that was in her future. But did the portent mean the flame would be her downfall, that the moon was complicit?

She lit *Eleggua's* and *Yemaya's* candles and burned sage and rosemary incense in the abalone shell. Next, she took a piece of parchment paper and tore it into three pieces: one for each of her enemies.

"Lupo Lopez.
Banish him into the fire.
Banish him now as I desire.
Raul Rivera.
Banish him into the fire.
Banish him now as I desire.

Arnaldo Arroyo.

Banish him into the fire.

Banish them now as I desire."

They ignited as soon as she dropped them, one by one, into *Elegguá's* candle jar.

If she chickened out, ran away, hid, caved, gave in, or gave up, the *orisha* of justice might see to it that the trio received the punishment they desired. But if she stayed to exact revenge, maybe he would grant her a quick, merciful death as well.

When she peered out the window, the police car still sat, backed in, on the sidewalk, allowing the cops free vision of anyone approaching. As her eyes adjusted to the dark, the outline of three rat sentries appeared near the garbage pails.

Taina stuck her head out the window. Bridge Rat perched in the eave, looking every bit like a pigeon roosting for the night. He bowed his head to acknowledge her and resumed watch.

She lowered the window, leaving it open enough for some air to enter, jamming the still bloody athame between the upper and lower sashes.

"Blood of your brothers avenges that of my mother.

Enter with risk.

Its bite will not miss.

Blood of your brothers avenges that of my father.

Enter with risk.

Its bite will not miss.

Blood of your brothers avenges that of my sister.

Enter with risk.

Its bite will not miss."

Taina meditated in front of the flickering candles and inhaled cleansing sage to banish the tarnish on her soul. She kissed her mother, her father, and her sister. Zeus padded into the circle, walked widdershins, then crawled into her lap and rested his head on Taina's arm.

The answer came to her, as obvious, as certain as the fae prophecy. Avenging the death of her family by watching more innocent people killed was not what her mother or father would have wanted.

The White Witch would go to the park tomorrow night. She would not flee. She would not waver.

She would not let them take her alive.

Chapter Forty-Four
El Día de Los Muertos

The night before Samhain, her birthday—and death day—candlelight flickered on the ceiling as if Taina was inside a church—or a mausoleum. The only comfort for the vigil was Zeus's pittering heartbeat, his whispering breath, his total devotion.

The plan unwound like a ball of yarn rolled across the floor by a playful kitten. *Señora* Duarte wouldn't miss the troublesome tenant, as long as Taina left the apartment habitable. And furnished.

The police investigating her death, or disappearance, would find instructions on the computer where to locate the cellphone with the evidence against Raul, Lupo, and Arnaldo.

Enough to implicate the three of them in the fire as well as vindicate her, who, though claiming she was innocent, was facing prostitution, manslaughter, and conspiracy charges trumped up by the very men—or so they called themselves—who'd masterminded the plan.

She packed her few treasures into a postage-paid box, ready to send to Serena with a key and instructions on how to contact Detective Michael Kelly to go empty her safe-deposit vault.

The rambling diatribe on tear-stained paper, well suited for a suicide note, apologized for the last tirade, admitted Serena was right, and that Taina Aponte should have stayed in Puerto Rico.

Her sacred implements, cauldrons, stones, and candles would be with her on Samhain. Part of the crime scene. Serena might want them. Good idea. Taina left a note in the apartment to forward all mail and personal effects to her in PR. In a big FedEx box. Prepaid.

Everyone would learn she was a witch after she died. There would be some buzz, but it would vanish like the bees and butterflies as soon as the weather turned cold.

Arranging her own death was easier than expected. Very few possessions, no attachments, enough money to be comfortable, but no more. She'd been preparing to die all her life.

Simple instructions: "I desire cremation, then interment with my family in Section 5, Row 44 in the old section of St. Raymond's Cemetery, along with the remains of my loyal dog. The money to pay for all final expenses is in the safe deposit box. I bequeath all my furnishings to *Señora* Atilia Duarte. All funds remaining in my bank account should be used to fund programs for women, children, and seniors at the *Sonrisa* Community Center on Southern Boulevard." The neat script wavered as she wrote the last sentence. Who would be left to administer to it—and to Jesús? She couldn't die with that on her conscience.

Taina crinkled up the paper and re-wrote it from the beginning, this time stipulating that all remaining funds shall be placed in a trust for the sole use of programs for women, children, and seniors, as well as the custodial care needs of Jesús Rivera, an invalid living within. She wrote a check and mailed it to the funeral home to cover the expenses of sending Miguel's body back to Culebra, along with a note for his family offering her deepest regrets for asking him to sell her car.

She took Zeus for his final treats from the Coca Cola deliverymen and the bakery girls. He ate until his belly drooped and tail wagged like he'd already died and gone to heaven.

Tears rolled down her face.

"What's wrong, miss?" The counter girl gave her a tissue.

"Allergies," she lied.

Taina withdrew cash from the machine and hid the dog inside a shopping bag while she went into the vault. The crucifix her grandmother had given her glimmered. Taina fastened it around her neck, and it settled into the hollow of her throat.

That would mean a lot to Papa, and to Abuela, when Taina died out of the state of Catholic grace later that evening. Would the pantheon of gods and goddesses assure a reunion with her family, or allow her soul to be interred in some hellish afterlife or the body of an earthworm?

Why not get her nails done while Zeus was groomed? The shop was empty, and the Asian girls spoke almost no English. Taina didn't want to talk anyway. Black polish with a red flower design would concentrate the energy flow from the tips of her fingers to the tips of her toes, as well as augment the luminescence of the moonstone.

Her final purchase: rat poison and capsules of peppermint-flavored fish oil large enough for her to stuff the pellets into, yet thick-walled and enough to sit in the corner of her mouth until she bit down. She'd die before any change took place, the final middle finger to Raul and Lupo.

Simone and Sandy deserved more than a note. Her only communication with them had been a message the night of Miguel's murder that she needed a leave of absence to recover and deal with the aftermath.

Taina worked up the courage to call, just before five, when the two of them were in a hurry to leave, to get back to their lives. As much as they cared for her, that distraction would not make the call seem rushed. Sandy answered.

"It's Taina." Her voice sounded distant, tinny, like she was already on her way to some other place.

"You okay?" Simone's voice echoed on the speaker.

"We'll wait for you to come back, honey." Sandy's voice could soothe even the rawest soul.

"I'm not sure when I'll be ready. This is getting very complicated." If she said anything morose they'd call the cops. "I miss you both." That was the truth.

"Take all the time you need. Call us if you need anything. Anything at all. And Taina..." Simone was probably wagging a finger at the phone.

"Yes, Simone?" She couldn't help but smile.

"We believe you. We believe in you. I told the DA and that detective you'd been set up. I'm glad I contacted them about those previous incidents. It's all on record, and I'll fry their asses in court for not doing more to protect you."

Taina could have argued that she'd declined the protection, and was, in fact, under protection now. But there was no need to defend her honor. Dying would do that. Prove that. Let the mundanes think what they wanted.

It was the magickal world she'd truly lived in—and would die in. "I love you both. Let's have lunch when things settle down. My treat."

"Great idea." Sandy chimed in. "How about City Island? It's near the water, and you'll love it."

"Sure. Later, okay?" Taina disconnected before she lost it, then allowed herself a long stint of crying, the kind that made your nose snotty and your eyes look like you'd been sucker punched. That made your chest hurt, your throat sore, your head throb.

She left the window open, with a warm breeze blowing through, and allowed sleep to claim her for a while, savoring the soft cotton sheets, the sumptuous pillow-top mattress, the odd floral and salty conglomeration of candles burning on the altar.

~ * ~

Taina bathed but dared not languish in the tub lest it wash away her resolve. She sprinkled herself with *Agua de Azahar* and dressed in a flowing white dress she'd bought on a whim, but never had the occasion—or courage—to wear. That had likely been some portent as it complemented the fairy cape. The hemline at her ankles allowed freedom of movement. Black ankle boots were the only shoes that would suffice for a fight.

Like the typical Amazonian super heroine, her breasts bulged out of the crisscross top. She combed out her hair and fluffed it over her shoulders for modesty.

"Fuck it." She pulled it back and into a tight braid. "If there was ever a time to be bold, bitchy, and Bronx it's now."

White had never been her color, but purple and gray eye shadow with black liner and mascara lent a demonic touch. Taina lined her mouth with the same dark pencil she used on her eyes, and an old lipstick called 'Love Bites.'

The effect was overdone even before she used a brush to scatter sparkling, pink powder over her cheeks, her neck, between her breasts. For the ultimate act of sacrilege, she left the gold crucifix around her neck, *el azabache* on her wrist, *los macutos* in a reticule.

Perfect for Samhain, and for Halloween, only this wasn't a masquerade. It was a coronation—and an assassination. And her birthday, but there hadn't been cards or presents for many years.

Dusk cast shadows over the room. Taina swung the cloak over her shoulders and fastened the gold clasp to hold it secure. The moonstone, mottled with a dense gray, pressed against her chest. A burning sensation spread throughout her body. The silken gown rustled as she walked, and the feathered trim on the hemline of the cape tickled her shins.

She glanced in the mirror at a ghoulish bride, black nails, blood red lips, heavily lined eyes in sharp contrast to the purity of the gown and cloak. Zeus, snow white and smelling sweet as bougainvillea, sat by the front door, waiting.

The cops were still out front. She gathered the gown to make a pouch for the dog then added her lipstick-athame wand, candles, matches, and rat-bait pellets to the reticule and looped it over one shoulder.

With the police on guard, the dormer window above the alleyway offered the only escape. She squeezed through feet first, then slid down the pitched roof until she could reach a rung of the fire escape.

Heavy steel window guards obscured the bizarre sight of a crazy woman, dressed for a costume party, lowering the fire escape ladder and climbing down. The gown flapped around her legs, but Zeus stayed put in the folds of the enchanted cloak.

The Earth thrummed as the dead prepared for Samhain, and their yearly moment to return, even if it was only a symbolic romp. Howls, whimpers, screams emanated from alleyways. Sinister laughter, bottles breaking, and metal cans clunking joined the click of her heels on the pavement.

She started down the middle of 149th Street and released Zeus from his snugli. He walked as if attached to her right heel.

A flock of pigeons chased by a hawk flew high in the sky, its deep blue twilight razor sharp. To the mundanes, it would appear the birds was pursued by a predator, perhaps one that had snatched a fledgling from its nest. But she knew better.

Wings left silver streaks of magick in their wake. Hawk Claw led them through maneuvers. They swept in circles, plunged, dove, then ascended rapidly.

The yellow-and-red skeleton trucks drove past, delighting trick-or-treaters out with their clueless mothers and fathers. Soon the kiddies would be safe inside and the battle would begin. Only she could see the shadow of the moon and its power sent a chill down her back, though the temperature and the humidity rivaled any midsummer night.

Bridge Rat appeared next to her. "You have taken the first step in the long march, my lady."

Taina held out her palm, and he alighted in it. "I'm scared, Bridge Rat."

"You're mortal, so of course you're frightened. Be assured you will have legions behind you, Lady Taina. I will inform Hawk Claw that you have donned the cloak of the White Witch, accepted the challenge to lead us into battle to take back this land, restore it, and allow all to live in harmony once again."

Big talk for such a creature. How much help would they be?

"I will meet you at Ritual Rock, after you claim your territory and invite those who present themselves and pledge loyalty to enter your realm."

"Don't go, Bridge Rat."

"No one can do it all, but all united can do anything." Then the fairy left her.

Chapter Forty-Five
Drawing Down The Moon

Dread hung in the air. The scant light of the waxing crescent, obliterated by an early moonset, guaranteed almost twelve hours of darkness for demons to frolic with the dead. The predicted rain would extend the ghoulish celebration.

Taina passed Raul's apartment building at the juncture of *Las Tombas* and *Los Sangueros* territory. Female silhouettes stood at every window on the first floor, directly over Romeo's Lounge.

Were his women sending her a message of support or waiting for the males to return with the conquered White Witch—the one they'd be burning or burying if the plan worked out the way she anticipated?

Rosa Nuñez waited on the corner. As Taina passed, she raised her hand, lowered her head, then looked away. Such extreme courage to defy Raul and offer even a token acknowledgement to her master's enemy.

So, Taina's defiance had given his women some measure of hope—at least one glimmer that this folly had not been a complete waste.

Darkness closed in as she entered the park. Ritual Rock blocked the window glow from surrounding buildings. Falling leaves covered the ground like a scarlet and gold carpet, cushioning her footfalls, pricking her toes. Those that remained on the trees dropped like confetti with each whisper of wind.

She had little chance of success in drawing down the moon, normally performed by a high priestess surrounded by a coven. Why would a goddess accept the invitation of a miscreant to descend and join a solitary circle?

Rats scampered out of sewer grates. Birds glided across 149th

Street and alighted on the utility wires, awnings, benches, and trash cans.

Her racing heart slowed, and resolve returned. Centered, Taina unpacked her supplies, set up a cauldron of salty water, walked her circle to place and light her candles. She tousled Zeus's freshly washed coat, tickled the perfectly trimmed fringe on his belly. He licked her face, his breath warm, tinged with the lingering aroma of the raw beef she'd given him as a last meal. His protective force mingled with hers, and their powers coalesced. She brushed her lips and cheek across the dog's head and stood. Four paws hit the floor with a gentle thud.

Ready, he signaled.

"Ready." Taina clasped the athame in her right hand, a wand in her left.

Lupo glided in from the left, Raul from the right. Hands on hips, feet about a foot off the ground, they moved closer still. Couched in the protection of night, powers at their height, their countenances reflected surety, purpose, and their true nature.

Lupo's beard and hair morphed into one mass of mane. His hands, covered with fur, burst through fingerless gloves. He growled a welcome to Raul, who chuckled in response.

Six pit bulls leaped out of the skeleton trucks. Three wore yellow collars, three red, and they looked at Zeus and licked their lips.

Demon-haloed soldiers, half flagged yellow and half flagged red, stood at attention behind their leaders. Chains, the ones they'd use to imprison, claim, and mutilate the White Witch, clanked.

The candles sputtered as evil drifted toward the circle, but they did not go out. The werewolf and vampire touched down.

Taina held up her hands, wand and athame at the ready. Zeus ran the circle for reinforcement as fast as his four tiny paws could move, yet not one iota of his concentration on the creatures waned, not one drop of energy was wasted on a tail wag, ear prick, or warning snarl.

Raul, fangs fully extended, stained crimson, pale and nude from the waist up, clad in black leather pants, dangled the red flag of *Los Sangueros* from a pocket.

Lupo, bare-chested and as furry as a real wolf, wore loose trousers and a belt trimmed with the yellow of *Las Tombas.* They outstretched their arms and glided closer, cloaks limp in the void around them.

Strength, augmented by energy rising through the ground, flowed through Taina's fingertips. The werewolf and dhampir stopped as they met resistance. Lupo's grin was hard to appreciate in the fur-covered face, but Raul's toothy sneer broadened.

The pair planted their feet wide apart, signaling no intent to back off. Taina's palms remained outstretched. She would not yield, her concentration would not waver, she would fight their advance.

Arnaldo strode out from behind Ritual Rock. A black silk cape hung off his shoulders. Shirtless was gentleman's choice for the night's festivities, and the leather loincloth he wore exaggerated the musculature of his thighs. A glistening, fresh tattoo of *Changó* adorned his left breast and war paint beams of light glimmered over his six-pack.

His appearance was no surprise. Long co-conspirators, the trio had ample reason to silence her. This moment was bigger than the sum of bodies, more significant than personal tragedies or foibles. The forces of good and evil were channeling through all of them. The goddesses, gods, *orishas,* the demons, and the dead had drawn them here, merely subjects for their own capricious wonts.

Arnaldo walked to the edge of her circle. "I'll stand or fall with you as fate dictates. May I enter?"

Something, someone took control of her tongue.

"Yes." She raised the athame and sliced down like a remote-controlled automaton.

He bowed and stood behind her.

Despite her fury, hatred of the man ebbed as his power entered the circle even before his physical body. No longer a murderer, a spurned lover, a betrayer of her trust, his quest to right the wrongs conjoined with her's, even if they were no longer united in their mortal bodies, in their mortal lives.

Empowered her familiar and the fae, Taina turned her back to the East.

"Goddess of light,
Come forth this night.
Bless us with your sight.
Offer us your might,
As we begin this fight."

She paused, momentarily stunned by the familiar rhyme that had rolled off her tongue.

"Goddess of light,
Come forth this night.
Bless us with your sight.
Offer us your might,
As we begin this fight."

Arnaldo put his right hand on her right shoulder. The third time they recited it together, and other voices augmented the chant.

"Goddess of light,
Come forth this night.
Bless us with your sight.
Offer us your might,
As we begin this fight."

Josefa's and Yoruba's voices joined them, strong, chins high in defiance, arms linked, as they walked toward the circle.

"They're bringing in the old ladies." Raul's cackle echoed through the ranks.

Lupo howled his amusement, and his soldiers joined their throaty calls with their master.

The women looked at Taina. Unwilling to break her concentration for even a second, she cut the circle with a rapid downward slash. "Enter, but stay behind us."

They stepped out of Taina's field of vision, but a pulse surged through Arnaldo's fingertips into her. Another jolt passed through the chain of power and positive energy as Josefa and Yoruba added two more links.

The moonstone against Taina's throat glowed, illuminating the familiar path around Ritual Rock. "Follow my footsteps, remain linked until we complete the circle."

She began, one step, feet together. Another step, feet together. Another step, feet together. Rhythm channeled through her until she skated across the ground, leading them around from candle to candle.

Yoruba's floral perfume, Josefa's musty herbs, Arnaldo's musk, and Taina's own nervous sweat tinged with an odd citrus essence scented the air. The earth trembled. A cool breeze brought a shower of leaves down upon them.

Raul and Lupo tried to move forward, but Arnaldo pressed his palm tightly against her back. The jolt ran through her, toward the dhampir and the werewolf, and they had no choice but to stand and wait.

Las Tombas and *Los Sangueros* stood at ease behind their masters.

The chain reached the starting point.

Her wand and athame pointed, Taina paused. "Now backward, just the same."

One step, feet together. Another step, feet together. Another step, feet together, linked right arm to right shoulder. The goddess must have been pleased and allowed a tiny crescent of moon to re-emerge in the western sky.

Tears of joy ran down Taina's face. This rag-tag coven had pleased the goddess, and their righteous cause had been affirmed.

Raul lost his patience. "This fight is between you, White Witch, and us. No one else. Unless you'd like it to be."

"You've not hesitated in killing innocents to taunt me." There would be no more loss of life. How Taina would yield this power, and the consequences, was her responsibility. "Josefa, Yoruba, Arnaldo, when we reach the starting place leave the park. Burn offerings for me this night."

The power dipped when *las brujas* complied, but his hand remained heavy on her. "This is my fight as well."

Josefa's invocation of the *orishas* faded into the background. Yoruba hissed like a snake. Beads clacked as she flicked her wrists so rapidly the bones tapped together. Before her presence departed, Yoruba's tongue clicked like rocks tumbling in rough surf.

Raul and Lupo's heads bobbled to the rhythm of Yoruba's clicking. They took a few steps back and covered their eyes as a giant glowing golden serpent unfurled, fangs extended, and slithered toward the pack then exploded into a shower of sparks.

Taina's breathing slowed to conserve energy. To concentrate it, she waved her wand and held the athame aloft with her left to block *Las Tombas's* and *Los Sangueros's* new advance.

Raul shook his hand, and a bolt of light bounced off Taina's palm to outline her entire body in a quivering pulse of electricity. Pain ripped through her.

Raul hit her again, and she stumbled forward.

Lupo charged on all fours, knocking Taina's feet out from underneath. Her face and chest smashed against Ritual Rock. She held her breath to avoid discharging the energy she'd need to fight them off, but the pressure rose in her gut to an intolerable level.

She struggled to push herself up, but her arms remained weakened, her legs unable to move, her athame and wand scattered outside the sundered circle.

The dhampir and werewolf stood inches from her, towering above her. Green energy bubbled out of the ground, and Raul and Lupo fell backward into the dirt. It splashed around them like water, dousing them in a magical pool.

Zeus padded in front and licked her face.

Wings rustled. Hawk Claw's mighty talons clicked on Ritual Rock. Rats and squirrels scampered along the ground.

Arnaldo rebounded from wherever he'd been tossed. His right hand once again touched her shoulder. "Get up, now! *¡Subite, ahora!"*

She got her arms to work, and on the exhale, a burst of his energy pulled her to her feet.

The sex magick had enabled their bodies to respond to each other, even if they were not looking at each other. Taina's face burned. Blood dripped from her nose and soaked the bodice of her gown but sluiced off the cloak like crimson raindrops.

She slipped a poison capsule between each cheek and lower gum and grinned at the dhampir and werewolf. She had twenty minutes to repel them before it would kill her.

Lupo charged again.

She braced, but it was Zeus who yelped in pain and crumpled into a heap.

"No!" She lunged to pick up and cradle the animal in his last moments, gasping as pain ripped through her core. Zeus's life force ebbed. She trembled and tried to maintain the field in front of her.

Raul shrieked with laughter. "Soon your blood will run in the of the street, and I'll wipe it up with that filthy mop, witch."

The werewolf grunted his own form of mirth, yellow fangs bared. "They're coming to arrest *you*."

The dhampir raised each hem of his cloak and spun, sucking the free flowing energy off the ground into a vortex around him. He halted and flung it at Taina and Arnaldo.

Dry grass and leaves ignited. Flames spread toward them. Evil crackled in the air as the spirits, liberated from bondage in some hell or purgatory, clamored at the junction of the veil between the living and the dead.

Those unhappy, tortured, or doomed to eternal damnation strained to pass, to escape, to return to earthly existence behind the champions of the undead.

Raul and Lupo advanced, pushing her repellent spell aside like a lace curtain.

Arnaldo kept one hand on her shoulder. "Focus. Remember, united in body, mind, and purpose, no one and nothing can stop us. *La esperanza es todo que tenemos.*"

Zeus was dead. Her parents were dead. Her sister was dead. Miguel was dead. And these foul creatures were responsible. Killing them was all that mattered.

The pit bulls circled closer, closer, closer licking their lips as they neared Zeus's body. Taina spit the rat-baited pellets out of her mouth. "Arnaldo, use your free hand to spill my purse."

He fumbled with the reticule that hung askew over her shoulder, and the remaining poison capsules rolled across the ground.

The dogs lapped them up.

Taina cracked a ribbon of light like a whip and drove them away with a shot of pure white energy. They yelped, licked their wounds, and ran off. Filled with enough poison to kill a human, it wouldn't be long before they'd succumb.

Yemayá's beads scattered, *el azabache* and her implements sank into the sacred earth.

A flicker of heat rose to a flame in her belly, diffused through her limbs, oozed from her fingers, her toes, escaped through her nose, her mouth with each breath. A fog drifted toward the advancing dhampir and werewolf.

White light blinded Taina as the barrier between her and her family imploded. The clock re-wound, time reversed, holding her in a moment she did not want to revisit. But she accepted her fate—surely going to meet them across the veil meant they would escort her along with them to their exalted place, whatever or wherever it was. Her poison gone, this was the only hope for relief.

The smell of gasoline, of soot, swirled around her head. Ash tickled her nose.

"¡Papa, aydudame!" Ana screamed.

Papa picked up her sister and dropped to his knees. Her mother crawled on all fours toward Taina's bed as flames licked the rug. She nestled against her mother's chest. Their hearts pounded, they rasped for breath as one. Thick smoke clogged their throats.

Mama kicked out the window. "Bright blessings, mi amor. Never forget we will always be with you.

White light, shine bright.
Banish the night.
Bring back the light.
White light, shine bright.
Banish the night.
Bring back the light.
White light, shine bright.
Banish the night.
Bring back the light."

Shards of windowpane grazed Taina's cheek, her lip. She tasted blood, gulped fresh air. Her stomach lurched as she tumbled, headfirst, arms flailing. "Mama!"

There was no answer. People ran around like an uncovered nest of roaches. Jesús, younger, alive, smelling like bad reefer and stale beer, walked under the window as if led by a leash, opened his arms and caught her. "Holy shit!"

Taina stared into the man's surprised eyes. She bobbled in his arms.

Green eyes darted side to side. He shoved her toward the monstrous figure in a stiff coat, red hat, with a face unrecognizable as human, streaked with soot.

"Mama?" Taina looked up as torchieres of flame shot from the windows. Sooty raindrops fell; her hair matted to her head under the spray.

Jesús ran. "Shit, that woman threw the baby to me."

"We've got to get the hell out of here." Arnaldo, younger, thinner, bushier hair, eyes bloodshot.

Details popped out like blisters on her burned skin.

Another pair of arms grabbed her, a stiff, hard coat, heat, soot stained face, funny hat. Clanking. "You're okay, one."

More screams, sirens, the fireman held her against his chest, elbows poked, water sprayed, steam billowed. "Someone get this kid into an ambulance. We're going into the apartment."

Sirens wailed. Metal ladders clunked. Hoses scraped along the ground. The men grunted with effort.

"Watcha got? Detective Kelly, shag haircut, jeans, Keds sneakers, peered into the cab of the truck.

A fireman wearing no gear, with a fancy uniform led Kelly aside. "With this much gasoline it's amazing the whole building didn't blow up. The girl's mother threw her out the window. She's DOA, along with the father and another kid."

Kelly pounded the fire truck door with his fist. "Fucking bastards. When will this stop?"

Police radios chattered.

Taina's chest ached to breathe. The monstrous man holding her ran. Other men surrounded her. One pressed a plastic cap over her nose and mouth. She wriggled. They held her still. "Breathe, baby, breathe. Ya, nena. No ten miedo. Respira."

"Mama, Papa!" Her words were swallowed by the mask over her face, her cries drowned out by yelling, more sirens.

The fireman covered Taina's face with his hand, but she could see through the gaps between his fingers. Three shrouded bodies passed, and she could tell by the sizes which was Mama, Papa, and Ana.

She bit his fingers, ripped the mask off.

Patient, gentle, the man soothed her in Spanish as he put the oxygen back on. "Vámanos, mami. Ay Dios mío. I hope this kid is too young to remember anything."

"Mama!" Taina screamed. "Help me!"

Fury surged through Taina like molten lava. The mist cleared. The light dimmed.

Arnaldo blew out, and torrential rain extinguished the flames. He inhaled until steam swirled around their feet, then exhaled a chill wind. Snow blanketed the singed grass, snuffed out burning embers, and glowing skeletons of fallen leaves. Frost tipped the wrought iron fence spikes.

"Mama, Papa, Ana!"

"We are here with you, *hija.*" Mama finally answered.

They sang. Each voice, her mother's, her father's, and her sister's were distinct. "Happy birthday to you. Happy birthday to you. Happy birthday dear Taina, Happy birthday to you. *Cumpleaños feliz. Cumpleaños feliz. Cumpleaños, querida Taina, Cumpleaños feliz.*"

"The time has come." Hawk Claw, in full fairy regalia, fluttered onto Ritual Rock. He raised a golden sword, the hilt encrusted with rubies, emeralds, sapphires, and diamonds. When it fell, birds of all sizes and shapes swooped. Rats charged.

They transformed into fairies, brandishing blades that spread gleaming light as they swung furiously at *Las Tombas* and *Los Sangueros,* smoting them by sheer surprise and magick seen only as streaks of green and purple light in the night.

Yellow and red orbs shone over the snow-kissed grass as restless spirits were banished to their graves. Shrill squeals of ghosts, the undead, the banshees, and all ilk of those who lay just beyond the veil echoed in a cacophony of mournful keening.

Spectral energy coalesced behind Raul and Lupo, fortifying them with supernatural strength, emboldening them to finish the fight and eliminate the obstacles to the rebirth and domination of all things evil.

Taina sucked as much air as she could into her lungs. The energy field around her quivered as she drew it in. It built to a crescendo, whirling like a tornado inside. Her mouth opened, and she spewed forth her venom.

"White light, shine bright.
Banish the night.
Bring back the light.
White light, shine bright.
Banish the night.
Bring back the light.
White light, shine bright.
Banish the night.

Bring back the light."

Pure quicksilver flew from her fingertips and knocked the werewolf and the dhampir onto their asses. She raised her hands and hurled another salvo. They writhed, screaming, on the ground as light crackled around them like exploding firecrackers.

The werewolf lay amidst the pit bull pack, which was gasping their final breaths. His clenched fist shot a bolt of green energy directly at Taina. She crossed her arms at the wrists. It seared her skin, but bounced back, hitting Lupo between his yellow eyes. He fell backward and twitched until going still.

Raul struggled to sit, and his pallor blurred into the snow-covered ground. Specters, ghouls, disembodied streaks, and flecks of spirits darted about in confusion as those who had welcomed them back to the living hemorrhaged power.

Taina hit Raul again.

"White light, shine bright.

Banish the night.

Bring back the light.

White light, shine bright.

Banish the night.

Bring back the light.

White light, shine bright.

Banish the night.

Bring back the light."

Orange sunlight kissed the horizon, its glow magnified by the snow. Lupo's soldiers whimpered like starving pups and dragged their master toward his cave at the base of Ritual Rock. The portal slammed behind them like a prison gate.

The waxing crescent moon, still visible through dark clouds, remained defiant, low in the brightening sky. Raul got to his feet, trembling and staggering toward the legions of dhamps, weres, and zombies and dismissed them with a wave of his hand.

Rays of sun poked holes in the clouds. Golden light flared, then burned white hot—releasing a swirling fog that smelled like honey and cinnamon and gingersnaps. It trapped the remaining spectral images and sucked them into the earth as if they'd been flushed down a toilet. The dhampir's pallor faded as the moon surrendered and the sun took charge of the sky. His skin returned to its human state.

Raul backed away, clawing at his eyes. He swept his cape around him and vanished. Frosty grass steamed under the heat of the rising sun. Cold mist swirled around Arnaldo and Taina's feet. She shuddered and fell to her knees, fighting to stay conscious. She searched through the haze for Zeus's body.

When she found a solid mass and tried to lift it, up popped Bridge Rat, in his fairy form, holding the lifeless dog in his hands.

"Fear not, my lady." He pressed his lips to the animal's and squeezed his chest, but Zeus dangled limp in his arms.

Hawk Claw's regal cloak swooshed over the snow. The jeweled scepter touched the crown of her head. "All hail the victorious White Witch. The battle will be long, but the fairy kingdom stands with you against those who ravage the Earth and its good folk." He bowed.

Las Tombas and *Los Sangueros* soldiers, clothes torn, bloodied by fae sword strokes, dragged their dead and dying to the dumpsters.

Several fairy bodies, twisted and broken-winged, littered the grass around Ritual Rock. Hawk Claw waved his sword, and they dissipated into wisps of smoke.

How many more innocent lives would she be called to account for? The goddess's fury and her mother's spirit waned. Breathing hurt. Taina's head threatened to explode.

Her vision blurred. "So many of your kind have sacrificed themselves tonight."

Hawk Claw helped Taina to her feet. "We are all united, all equals, all prepared to pass from this world if called by the goddesses and gods in service of righteousness. Rise and lead us, unmasked, on a victory march."

She took two steps and staggered.

Arnaldo caught her, took her into his arms. He wrapped the enchanted cape around her quaking body. "Please, forgive me, *Bruja Blanca*."

She couldn't find words to say that she would not join him, that she would not forgive him. That she hated what he'd done and how he'd deceived her. But the will to reject the comfort of his arms failed her.

"Your familiar, my lady." Bridge Rat carried Zeus to her.

She clutched the dog to her chest. His tiny heart fluttered against her fingers. His ragged breaths blew puffs of warmth against her breasts.

"Thank you, Bridge Rat." Tears of joy bathed her, Arnaldo, and Zeus in whatever magick the goddesses had instilled in her this night.

The fairies extinguished the smoldering fires with a snow squall, covering the ashes of their dead with a white coverlet.

No mundanes would know that a battle had transpired here—that a fight too long in coming had been waged—and won. Their ability to see the assemblage, the magick, the triumph was impeded by apathy and disbelief.

Arnaldo carried her along the double yellow line down 149th Street toward Southern Boulevard.

Hawk Claw and Bridge Rat flanked Arnaldo's right.

The fae army padded behind.

"Put me down please." She'd walk this boulevard of bad spells and broken dreams on her own.

Arnaldo lowered her feet until they scraped the asphalt and found a toehold. Taina pulled the snow-encrusted cloak around her and moved on. She gathered a breath from deep within and circled her arms, hurling silver light down both sides of the street.

Los Sangueros and *Las Tombas* stragglers snarled, spat, and retreated into the shadows, back alleys, and darkened hallways as the White Witch passed.

A police car turned the corner. The fairies vanished, leaving Taina and Arnaldo alone in the middle of the street.

Regiments of pigeons, hawks, sparrows, and seagulls now sat in formation upon power lines, streetlights, and roofs, bowing heads as she passed. Rats poked their noses, whiskers twitching, out of the sewers, manhole covers, subway grates, garbage pails, cardboard boxes, and cans in rubble strewn lots.

The patrol car stopped. A cop rolled down his window. "Trick-or-treat is over now. Go home before we haul you in for lewdness and public intoxication." He and his partner shook their heads and guffawed as they drove off.

"You should only know what is yet to come." Taina stayed on course, her head held high.

"We'll fight them together, won't we my lady?" Arnaldo smiled. "That's what the fae call you, isn't it?"

She did not care to respond.

He walked, two steps behind her, down Southern Boulevard to *Sonrisa.*

Chapter Forty-Six
A Prophecy Fulfilled

Taina put one foot in front of the other. Her bare feet burned from contact with frost-coated asphalt. The cloak warmed her, but the jewel had punched a raw, red brand on her chest.

Arnaldo held one arm and encircled her waist with his other hand. There was no trace of carnal passion in his touch, merely the reassurance of a fellow soldier.

Her knees wobbled like a newborn foal. The mammoth effort expended more than her body could stand.

He swept his hand down like an axe to allow them through the defensive shield around *Sonrisa*. He picked her up and carried her through the gates, up into his apartment.

The cloak brushed over Jesús, lying inert on the plastic chase, staring into space, a red seven-day candle next to him burning in between statues of St. Lazarus and St. Jude.

Touched by the magick dripping off her, he shuddered. His head moved like a rusty cog toward Taina, and he smiled.

Clad only in the skimpy chemise and frost covered cloak, all traces of the fire vanquished, a chill settled into her bones, ice crystals circulated in her veins, froze every muscle into spasm. She quaked like a feverish child.

Arnaldo laid Taina down on the bed and wrapped the cloak around her and rested the injured dog on her chest. He started to undo the clasp, then pulled his hands away from the pulsing jewel as it burned his flesh.

She tugged until the clasp opened and dropped the moonstone on the floor beside her. The very act attenuated the magick and the pain. The still pristine cloak fell away, revealing the blood-spattered gown, dampened by snow, clinging to her curves. Her breasts peeked through the thin silk, nipples firm, erect from the cold.

Arnaldo covered her with an itchy, wool blanket.

"There is no hope of ever beating them. I don't want to live with the specter of this swirling around me every day." She kicked the annoying coverlet off.

"I might control the weather, but you can control the sun and the moon, the dark and the light." His countenance softened by exhaustion, he humbled himself.

"Just leave me be." The fae spell woven into the cloak had penetrated her body like a long, sharp sword.

Energy bled out, draining her life away. A perfect ending to her quest.

Let Arnaldo explain why his girlfriend's lifeless body was in his bed.

Unable to move, each breath spreading pain throughout her body, Taina surrendered to death and waited patiently for her family to come to welcome her.

"That kind of exertion would have killed a lesser witch." He tucked the cloak around her, trapping even more magick inside the folds, unwittingly finishing the job.

Samhain dreams delivered her to the place she wanted to be, but a transparent partition prevented passage.

Mama, Papa, and Ana romped upon a cloud, surrounded by blue sky, laughing, hugging each other. They regarded Taina, stone-faced, unwelcoming, then turned away.

She banged on the glass. "Let me in. Let me come with you."

Only Mama heard. She shook her head, raised her outstretched palms. A brilliant flash swallowed them and drove Taina back.

Abuelita coalesced out of fine mist, kneeling by her bed, her room just as Taina remembered, rosaries clicking, candles flickering. "Hail Mary, Full of Grace, the Lord is with thee. Blessed art thou amongst women and blessed is the fruit of thy womb...." Her voice cut off before she could finish the prayer.

Abuelita tucked the gold crucifix in a clenched fist, bowed her head and, she too, vanished.

Miguel walked through a door, his body once again whole, bathed in a golden light. A benevolent smile projected forgiveness, patience, and as much fatherly love than the man she'd called Papa. His eyes widened in shock, he clutched his chest, fell into the clouds and disappeared, snatched from her once again.

Grief sickened her stomach, weighed heavy on her heart. She retched, fought to breathe. A frantic newborn baby's cry emanated from swirling grey fog. Taina struggled to see past the whirls of light, but a blindfold of darkness covered her eyes. Though she was prepared to enter heaven or some Otherworld, it was not ready to receive her.

"...Santa Barbara, San Lázaro, San Cristobal, San Francisco, Santa Teresa, Santa Lucia..."

Whispered words penetrated her muddled brain. Silk brushed prickly skin, soothing the frosty burn. Fragrant raindrops fell on her face, her chest, her arms, her legs, her feet.

Taina opened her eyes to a crimson cloth, embroidered with orange and gold symbols and figures that danced as it snapped around her.

Josefa, eyes open and fixed, did not interrupt the *sacurate*, but Arnaldo, seated just outside a ring of flickering candles, rose and moved toward Taina.

He didn't pass the *santera* at work but made eye contact and smiled. Josefa splashed *Agua Florida* from a bottle and brushed damp hands through Taina's hair, across her throat, down her arms. She refreshed her palms and continued along Taina's abdomen, thighs, and lower legs, ending with the bottom of her feet.

Only then did she pause, blink, or address either Taina or Arnaldo. "I have done all I can."

Josefa placed a basket next to the bed containing Taina's implements, *los macutos, el azabache bracelet, Yemayá's* beads and the shell, still stained by green-tinged witches' earth. "Visit me when you have healed so these can be properly discharged."

She turned to Arnaldo. "Banish and cleanse this place, then bathe and feed her."

"Just let me go." Taina could barely get the words past the clot in her throat.

Josefa smoothed Taina's hair and stroked her face. "You must stay with us a bit longer. It is not yet your time. The *orishas* are pleased by your courage."

Arnaldo approached the bed. "She'd probably like it better if you give her a bath while I clean the house."

"No." The *santera's* eyes shot bullets into him. "You made this mess. Only you can clean it up."

Josefa gathered her things. "Keep those candles burning, day and night. Pray to San Miguel for protection. And San Lázaro for healing, for all here need both."

She poured *Agua Florida* over Jesús, and her footsteps hobbled down the steep stairs. Each clunk of the *santera's* descent reverberated up Taina's spine.

Warmth replaced the chill in her core. She rose to a sitting position.

Arnaldo brushed tangled hair off her face. "Let me get you something to eat. Then I have to get busy." He lit candles on his corner altar.

Water ran. The faint odor of hot wax mixed with sulfur from the matches. Arnaldo peered out the window and, seemingly satisfied that all was secure, tucked the cloak around her again.

He rummaged in the kitchen and carried a cup of tea and a plate of crackers and cheese to her. "I thought you were dying so I called Josefa."

"I was." She gulped like a drunkard, then nibbled the snack. Her head, so heavy she could barely keep it up, bobbed against her chest.

Arnaldo walked to the landing where Jesús lay, motionless, silent, one of the living dead. "You keep watch, *amigo*. Taina and I need some sleep." His footsteps echoed on the uncarpeted stairs.

The doors rattled, and she heard him chanting but couldn't make out the words as he reinforced the perimeter against the inevitable retribution.

Taina awoke again when the plate hit the floor and crackers scattered. Arnaldo came running. She started to get up, and to clean up.,.

"Déjalo, mami." He picked the food up and tossed it into the trash. "You want more?"

She shook her head. "I'm worried about *Señora* Duarte, Josefa, Yoruba…"

"The cops are still keeping an eye on things at your apartment. After some rest, I'll take my kids and rent a truck to move your things over here. I'll cast a protective spell over *Señora* Duarte and the property. Josefa and Yoruba can take care of themselves, at least for now."

He sat on the edge of the bed. "You know you'll have to stay here for a while." He paused, waiting for a reaction.

Let him make his plans. She'd fight with him later.

"I'll build a wall so you can have your own room. But now, I have Josefa's orders to follow. Let me get you cleaned up." He poured a packet of bath salts labeled *El Baño de Elegguá* into a cauldron and immersed a cloth.

He dabbed her face, rubbing gently to clean off the dried blood. He slipped the cloak and soiled peignoir off one shoulder and sponged her neck, chest, before repeating it on the other side. Taking care to keep her covered with the magickal cloak, he cleansed then massaged the painful stiffness out of her neck muscles and lower back.

Lingering between sleep and wake, the real and surreal, Taina allowed herself to be manipulated like a mannequin

The cloying, floral scent waned as Arnaldo finished and dumped the liquid in the cauldron down the sink but lingered in her damp hair spread over the pillow. Her eyes kept closing despite the effort to stay awake. Her skin itched and burned.

"Take this away, please." She barely got the words out.

He folded the cloak neatly and covered her with a soft, mundane cotton blanket.

"Sleep, Taina. I'll be here watching." Arnaldo perched on the edge of the bed.

She expected him to lean down to kiss her, but he simply sat quietly. It was only then she appreciated the exhaustion etched on his face, bloodshot, droopy eyes, the slight tremor in his hands.

Arnaldo staggered to the bathroom. The magick had left him as drained as she.

A pungent odor of turpentine tempered with cloves wafted through the apartment as he mopped the floor. He ran water in the sink and commenced with the syrup-sweet purifying solution.

Arnaldo came back into the room, one hand holding onto the wall, then the kitchen counter, then a sofa arm, the other carrying a dish of burning incense. He might not believe in Josefa's magick but obviously wasn't taking any chances.

Taina's lungs held their breath against the assault. The asthma inhaler was back in her apartment, so she'd just have to do without.

He parted the curtains. Two steel gray pigeons sat on the sill, and their heads swiveled toward him, bobbed. He raised his hand to acknowledge the fae guard, and their attention turned back to the scene below them.

The rumble of snowplows, angry car horns, the whir of tires skidding, the clank of a loose manhole cover, signaled the return of daylight, of normalcy, of some semblance of human control over the supernatural.

He hobbled to the bed, settled himself on the other side, and lay down with a sigh of relief, smelling like a cross between a cigar lounge, a funeral home, and a fruit store whose goods were a few days. What their relationship would become in the aftermath of the last twenty-four hours, once the exhaustion of such powerful magick waned, remained elusive. But for now she was safe.

The metronome of his breathing, slow, deep soothed her.

Though winning was far from assured, but without each other, neither had a chance.

This man who, a moment of youthful foolishness, had killed her family. Now he'd saved her life.

Taina had vowed to be alone. But the goddesses, *the orishas,* the saints, whomever was in charge, had other plans. She stared out the tiny, grimy window at the fairies in disguise drawn from other sectors serving as sentries for the White Witch locked away in her castle, awaiting the siege.

She had to give up her dreams, her goals, her independence, and her privacy so no one else would have to lose their families like she did.

So no more kids would wind up like Hakeem, and no other upstanding businessmen would be cut down like Miguel. But how could she live in *Sonrisa* without any room to call her own, with Jésus a living sculpture on the landing?

Taina answered her own questions. *You could have married Jaime. You could have made a life with Serena. You were advised not to come back, told to leave, cautioned to stay away from sleuthing. You did this to yourself.*

Jesús lay catatonic on the plastic chaise, his body twisted like a pretzel under the blanket.

Candles in a rainbow of colors flickered at his feet, in the corners, on the altar. Josefa had called out all the *orishas* on this occasion. Taina would help to heal what was left of the man that had saved her life. Tomorrow, or the next day, or the day after that. It would all have to wait until some other day.

Zeus looked up at her from a cushy floor pillow, adoration in his eyes, his matted coat still bloodied. He tried to move but whimpered with pain and lay still.

Taina stared into the flames of *Elegguá's* candle, inhaled the pungent scent of his bath salts on her skin. The trickster, the guardian of the crossroads, intermediary between the dead: her *santo.*

Arnaldo's breathing thickened with sleep. He remained separate and apart, respectful of her boundaries, awaiting permission to move closer, which she could not, would not grant.

Taina slipped out of bed and went to pee. In the bathroom mirror, she regarded her scratched, bruised face, stringy, sweat-matted hair, smeared lipstick, and mascara-blackened eyes. The image of a crucifix was branded in the hollow of her throat, the golden one snatched away by the ghosts—or the goddesses, to be reclaimed upon her death.

Two soda bottles awaited, one with the foul, brown banishing bath, the other with an electric-pink purifying one. She stood in the tub and poured one, then the other over her, shivering as the cold liquid dripped around her, retching at the unsavory stench. Defying the *orishas* once again, she turned on the taps to rinse it away.

Steam rose around her like cloud. Evil spirits, the detritus of battle, swirled down the drain, leaving her cleansed.

She toweled off, teased the knots out of her hair with Arnaldo's comb, wishing for her brush and her flannel nightgown to warm her. But all she needed to fulfill the mandate of the goddess and gods, to avenge her family's death, Miguel's murder, and the subjugation of innocent women and children was in this tiny bachelor's apartment.

Zeus limped to her side, weak and broken by Lupo's attack, but like his mistress, very much alive. He raised his eyes, which smiled at her in canine adoration.

She pulled a discarded newspaper from the trash and spread it on the floor. "No walk this morning, Zeus. When we're both feeling better, we'll visit the deliverymen and the bakery. But we need to live here now."

The dog did his business, circled, and plunked back down. She bundled the urine soaked paper into a plastic bag and left it outside the door.

Outside the window, the two birds swiveled their heads, directing beady eyes on her, before turning back to their watch. A rat scampered, back and forth, around the perimeter of the chain link fence surrounding *Sonrisa*.

Los borinqueños, die hard New Yorkers, *Nuyoricans* and people from lands that had never seen snow, walked around the magickal protection which couched the entrance and obscured the view of anything but the tiny storefront where senior citizens would soon arrive for bagels *con* cream cheese, coffee and *salsa*.

All would tell stories of this year of intense heat, of earthquakes and hurricanes, and the Halloween when snow fell from the sky. Few would recognize it was magick being re-balanced, about to upend everything that everyone had come to know, to expect.

While under suspicion for a criminal complaint, she'd have to fight to keep her job as well as defend herself against all manner of unsavory claims. And face the detectives investigating the murder case, backpedal, and tell half-truths. Claim duress. Get her own victim's advocate.

Taina breathed deeply and opened herself to embrace the will of the *orishas*.

Acknowledgements

Many thanks to Andrew Richardson who has been with me on a writer's journey for almost twenty years. And to April Grey and Rayne Hall, whose writing and editing advice have been invaluable in seeing this manuscript through to completion.

I am grateful to Deborah Blake for her ongoing tutelage and encouragement of writers of the paranormal and all things witchy. This Bronx girl remains indebted to all who have not only survived and thrived but have made heroic contributions to halting the spread of urban blight and enabling rebirth and rebuilding of our neighborhoods.

Lastly, *muchas gracias* to *Las Boricuas*, who have welcomed this *gringa* into their lives and their culture both in Puerto Rico and on the Mainland.

About the Author

Carole Ann Moleti lives and works as a nurse-midwife in New York City, thus explaining her fascination with all things paranormal, urban fantasy, and space opera. Her nonfiction focuses on health care, politics, and women's issues. But her first love is writing science fiction and fantasy because walking through walls is less painful than running into them.

Boulevard of Bad Spells and Broken Dreams was inspired by her life, and her life's work, as she roamed the streets of The Bronx as it has morphed from an emblem of urban blight to a vibrant and ethnically diverse borough in New York City.

Her short stories have been featured in the *Ten Tales* Series: *Haunted, Seers,* and *Beltane,* and *Bites, as well as in Hell's Kitties, Hell's Mall,* and *Hell's Heart.*

Excerpts of her memoirs, ranging from sweet and sentimental to edgy and irreverent, have been published in a variety of literary venues. Carole was awarded the *Oasis Journal* award for best nonfiction in 2009. She has also contributed to the award winning feminist anthologies *Shifts and Impact.*

Carole loves to hear from her readers. You can find and connect with her at the links below.

Website/Blog: http://caroleannmoleti.com
Newsletter: http://eepurl.com/bfNver
Facebook: https://www.facebook.com/CaroleAnnMoletiAuthor/
Goodreads: https://www.goodreads.com/goodreadscomCmoleti
Pinterest: http://www.pinterest.com/caroleannmoleti/
Twitter: http://Twitter.com/Cmoleti

~~~

If you enjoyed *Void of Course,* we think you'll love *Hidden,* by Amy McKinley, book 1 of the *Five Fates.*

CURSED SINCE BIRTH.
HUNTED BY GODS.
A LOVE THAT DEFIES DESTINY.

TURN THE PAGE
FOR A PEEK!

Excerpt

Jade froze, her paintbrush hanging mid-air above her palette. The light streaming in diagonally through the bay window cast an eerie, surreal frame over the room.

Whispers seduced and coerced.

She scanned the painting. Buildings cast long, ominous shadows, stalking the pedestrians as they made their way to and fro, huddled against the misery of the evening. A man lay sprawled, his lifeblood staining the sidewalk crimson. Half in a deserted alley, he was yet to be discovered. This was the detail Jade concentrated on. She blended a burnt red and used careful brush strokes to complete the scene as the portrait fell prey to the darkness that burned inside her.

Without meaning to, her gaze was once again drawn to the slain man. She reached up and touched the blood seeping from his body, her fingers coming away wet. Bringing her hand to her nose she closed her eyes and inhaled.

Instead of the cloying scent of her oils, she inhaled the coppery twang of blood.

Stunned, her mouth parted on a silent scream. *No!* Darkness bubbled to the surface, invading her senses with a roar. Unable to fight the invasion, her heart beat an increasing crescendo. Part of her didn't want to struggle, not with the temptation of death on her hand.

Deep inside, a macabre shadow stretched. Hungry for more, its long arms clawed for purchase with each breath. Changing her, as part of her argued for the better. The other part—the one that gloried in her fire-kissed hair and shimmering eyes—cried against this crime and screamed for redemption.

She crouched to welcome the demonic strength as the parasitic monster grew inside her. Evolving into a fierce predator, she was able to taste, weigh, and measure the souls who sifted through her fingers.

Still, she fought for space in her own body. For control.

But with the scent of blood, of death, of prey teasing the monster—she was losing fast. *It's happening.* Unshed tears burned her eyes. Finally. The curse of the three Fates had begun. With her.

Slowly Jade stood, bit down on her lip and welcomed the pain. The distraction would help fight the transformation. Dipping the brush into the Caribbean blue, she swirled then began to paint a shimmering cove. The vision soothed the beast that lurked just beneath, but it was temporary, and Jade knew its evil would soon mutiny. The Fates' curse would change her over time, unleashing an unstoppable power within her to annihilate the gods who created her and anyone who got in her path.

Including her family.

Succumbing to a surge of menace, Jade dropped the blue-tipped brush as her back snapped straight and her mouth opened on a silent scream as she lost control. Every cell stretched to accommodate the new presence. Shivering from the effects of her altered state, she briefly shut her eyes, adjusting. When she opened them, her painting was before her, and she viewed the scene anew. Cocking her head, she closely observed a woman who tightly clutched her rain slicker about her body.

This one will not make it home tonight.

~ * ~

Jade's parents' castle was heavily warded so no one but family could trace directly inside. All others were re-routed to the perimeter walls. Safety was imperative to Xavior, King of the Trynd demons.

Controlling the slight tremor in her hands, Jade strode forward in search of her mother.

Moving a long strand of hair over her shoulder, she caught sight of its fiery color. What the hell is this? She tugged it closer into view and studied it. She'd always been able to maintain her glamour, something that was crucial to her disguise in the human realm and also as a further deterrent against those who hunted her. A small fang snuck out to nibble on her lower lip as unease settled deep in the pit of her stomach. She was sure gold shown in her eyes and her lips no longer were blush pink but a brilliant red with shimmering undertones of gold, having shed their camouflage as well. The loss of control was one more sign of the battle she faced.

She strode through halls, lowering her eyelids to half-mast as she attempted to shield the worry she was sure was reflected in her eyes and nodded to the many residents she passed. Light filtered through the slitted windows placed high above, fashioned after arrow holes—the height of a seven-foot demon and a palm-width wide. Evenly spaced, ancient wall sconces set securely into red sandstone with black accent stones, glowed when darkness fell. She took in the familiar sights, the comforting smells, the laughter, and the banter of those who traveled the corridor.

Nothing of her surroundings soothed her.

The subtle squeak of her shoes increased and her vision wavered as anger and despair hit her like a brick wall. Smells assailed her senses and the walls of the corridor seemed to close in, making her want to accost anyone within arms' reach. Her focus shifted to that of a predator. The door to her room drew closer as she dragged her claws along the stone wall. The grainy scrape music to her ears.

Wait! No. She attempted to wrestle control from the beast that resided inside her. Jade rolled her shoulders and shuddered. The darkness expanded and slithered into dominance.

Bending her head, she snarled as she neared her quarry, her instincts flaring. The other residents regarded her warily as they gave her a wide berth. With satisfaction, she felt the claws on her left hand sharpen to razor points. Rounding the corner, she spied her step-demon, Xavior, and several of his guard. And with them—her prey.

"Jade?" Xavior greeted her. At over six feet tall, he had eyes that were pools of black and lacked their crimson shards as he was not in battle mode. Onyx horns with deep red tips curved out of his short, midnight hair.

As the group neared, Jade growled low in the back of her throat, baring her fangs. One of the guard's jaw dropped while another paused. They'd lost precious seconds with their mouths gaping before reaction set in.

Using the advantage, she lunged to the side and attacked. Her left claws swiped at the jugular of the unadorned demon walking alongside her father's guard. Blood spurted as the demon was unprepared for the attack. Still, countering her, he went for her head with fangs exposed and horns straight up—a clear sign of aggression.

The closest guard reacted and grabbed the bleeding demon. It took two others to restrain Jade.

"Lock him up and see to his wounds until we can straighten this out. Bring Jade with me." Xavior's commanding voice sliced through the hall. Several paces down the hall, Jade and Xavior entered her room. After he shut the door, he turned cool, onyx eyes to regard her likely enraged ones.

"Release her." Keeping his gaze on Jade, who paced like a caged animal, Xavior addressed his guard. "Leave us."

The door slammed shut with a thud, and Xavior's deep voice wrapped around her. "Are you okay?"

She whirled, working hard to regain full command over her body which vibrated with pent-up hostility. "No. I smell death on him, I see what he plans. He needs to be eradicated from this realm. Let Hades deal with his eternal rotting soul." She sneered.

"He's from another clan and is requesting to join our ranks, but if you're that opposed, we won't let him in," Xavior said calmly.

Jade slowed her pacing and sat on the bed. Tossing her head back, she breathed in and out through her nose several times. She half turned to see Xavior observing her every move. Her stomach sank. "I'm in big trouble, aren't I?" She fought the urge to bury her face in her hands.

"It's clear what's going on." His warm voice settled around her. "Have you told your mother?"

In a slow side-to-side, she shook her head. "I was on my way to find her. I thought we could put our heads together with the prophecy and figure out what will create this blasted balance and fix this...situation."

Smiling sadly, he clasped her hand. "We'll face your fate together, Jade. This one will be surmountable. You have the ability to overcome anything you set your mind to."

"Thanks for the vote of confidence, but I'm not so sure. It's pretty powerful stuff."

"Have faith in yourself." Xavior ruffled her hair before he headed out the door. "Your mother's having breakfast; go to her and get started."

Flopping back on her bed, Jade pressed her palms into her closed eyelids and pushed out a breath, trying to stay the emotions swamping her before she found her mom. She would scour the heavens and every realm imaginable to find her balance, to stop the prophecy. She'd forced the darkness back in its shadowy box. It hadn't been easy, but she managed. A chill crawled over her skin despite the heat.

It was so much simpler when she and her sisters were young. At least then they were all together within the castle. As sisters, they'd vowed to do whatever necessary to avoid bringing death upon those they loved.

For Jade, it had already begun.

Chapter Two

Jade's temples throbbed. She headed toward the east turret where she knew her mom favored her morning meals. As she burst into the room, Aiesa gasped. A fork clattered right before Jade's brother, accompanied by shrieks of joy, jumped up from his chair and ran to her.

She pasted a wide grin on her face as she bent to pick up her half-brother. His arms wrapped around her neck was the sweetest thing ever. As she sunk into his embrace, she inhaled deeply, closing her eyes. He had the best little demon smell. She clutched him to her until he squirmed.

Releasing him, she realized that for the first time in a while, her shoulders were relaxed. Opening her eyes, she met her mom's gaze over her brother's shoulders.

Her mother's dark hair hung down in a fall of midnight. A storm of worry shone in her eyes. Aiesa half rose, her mouth forming a circle. *Damn.* Tension rocketed back up again. Nahl pushed at her, forcing her gaze back to him.

"Hey, little demon, you're looking very handsome this morning." Jade tweaked his nose.

He favored both their mother and step-demon with hair black as night and ebony eyes. And lucky for him, he inherited Xavior's olive-toned skin, but not their mother's deep red lips. On Mom, they looked stunning. On a boy, well…not so much.

"I'm fierce, not handsome." Nahl frowned at Jade, grasping her long tresses and tugging.

"Fierce and handsome." She chuckled. "What mayhem have you got planned today?"

He beamed as she sat him down, then scampered back to his food. "I get to go to Kristo's to work on magic. We're going to turn beetles into snakes."

"That sounds like fun." She snuck a peek at her mother, who hadn't taken her gaze off Jade since she entered the room.

Nahl's laugh turned wicked as he gazed at his sister with glee sparkling in his eyes. "Then the snakes into spiders."

Jade winced. "Wonderful." She couldn't stand spiders as her mischievous brother knew very well.

Aiesa rested a hand on his shoulder. "Why don't you head over early, Nahl? Cade can escort you there. He's in the war room with your father. Go find him."

"Okay, Mom." He hopped off his chair then gave a quick hug and kiss to their mom and Jade before he raced from the room.

"I can't believe how much he's grown since the last time I saw him."

"Hmm, why don't you have a seat, Jade?" Aiesa melodic voice cracked through the room ensuring Jade's compliance.

"Sure." After sitting, Jade glanced nervously around the bright room. The sunlight streamed in, illuminating the blue and green mosaic tiles. The room emanated coastal waters, salt-kissed breeze, and tropical scents. All it lacked was a bit of sand.

With a little illusion, Aiesa used to take her daughters to breakfast on the beach in this very room. It had been heaven. *Perhaps that's why I'm drawn to California in the human realm.* Unable to avoid it any longer, Jade met her mother's gaze.

Grasping her hand, Aiesa asked, "The fiery orange circle around your eyes is new. How long has the Fates' curse been active?"

Icy fingers crawled up Jade's spine, and her stomach churned with worry with her fears confirmed by her mother's words. "Not too long. Some days are worse than others." She grimaced. "Like today."

Her mom's arms came around her in a warm embrace, exactly what she needed.

"I hate this. I hate what the Fates forced on my babies." Aiesa's voice shook with frustrated rage. "Damn Zeus for pushing them too far and setting all this in motion." She pushed out a breath.

"Mom, it's not your fault."

Jade and her sisters were raised with the prophecy handed down from the Fates, a wretched curse for mere amusement, using them to aggravate the mighty gods. But the sisters just wanted peace, and Jade wanted love. They never wanted this.

Everything began because Zeus demanded deaths before their time, one in particular. Power crackled, and the king of gods vied for supremacy against beings immune to his tyranny. They saw things he did not and time was needed for the soul in question. Provoked by his interference, the Fates wanted Zeus out of their hair and brewed up a cursed plan altering fates to keep the mighty god distracted and effectively away from them.

A balance of sanctuary existed. But if left undiscovered, if the sisters didn't find their key, the family would pay the full price. The curse felt like a ticking time bomb. The key was balance and each sister had to find her own.

The prophecy foretold that the sisters would target the gods. Jade shuddered. If that happened, the gods would sacrifice her family. She and her sisters grew up knowing they were the harbingers of death and destruction. None of them wanted the fallout to touch their family.

Aiesa held Jade's shoulders, her voice a whisper. "What's it like?"

Jade hesitated as she searched for the right words. Stillness settled over her as she withdrew into herself, brushing gently against the evil that resided deep within.

She merged, becoming more than herself, and the words that fell from her mouth were a mix of her own and that of what resided within. "Like my very soul is being compromised at times, and then at others, the most natural thing in the world, and that's what terrifies me the most. It's like being seduced by something inside me that's pure evil."

She heard this hiss of air as her mother sucked in a breath then growled on her exhale. "Those bitches."

Jade's gaze cleared as she shook off the sense of skimming her dark counterpart. *Gods, Mom, I know I'm nearing the end.* Cautiously, she glanced at her mother, afraid of the condemnation she would read on her face. Yet there was none. Eyes of obsidian swam with unshed tears and unconditional love. Her long, midnight hair framed a face that had seen battles, death, and would survive no matter the odds.

"You've begun killing?" Aiesa froze, here gaze anxious.

Jade splayed her hands across the table, her voice, devoid of emotion, echoed within the room. "Souls born of evil. Humans. For now. How long until I take an innocent's life? How long until I target a god and am set down *that* path?" A silent tear tickled its way down the curve of her cheek.

Aiesa reached up and smoothed it away. Pulling her in for another hug, she gently rubbed her back in soothing circles, offering what little comfort she could. "How are you doing it?"

Ashamed, Jade knew she needed her mother's help. It was better to lay it all on the line rather than hide it from her. Sighing, she leaned back, creating space to explain. "Through my painting."

Tilting her head, Aiesa shoved a dark lock of hair over her shoulder.

"It consumes me, either in anger or passion. Either way it sets me off, and I can't seem to stop it from taking over." She rubbed her hands over her face, raking them through her hair, tugging gently. "I can see what's going to happen in the scene, then I reach in and alter it. In the very beginning, when I saw the news, I'd see crime scenes that were exact images from my paintings. They didn't show the event, but they reported it, and parts of the pictures were right there on the screen. I stopped watching after two came true."

"This isn't going to help, but I didn't expect you to be the first tormented with this transformation."

A laugh bubbled up, breaking the tension inside Jade. "Really? Who did you think it would be?"

"Oh, Ria, I suppose. On the outside, she's so controlled, but on the inside, she's constantly bombarded with others' emotions. Having to deal with so much all the time, I've always worried it would make her an easier target."

I'm glad it wasn't Ria, or any of my sisters. "I thought you'd say Layla. She's such a hothead." Jade rolled her eyes, thinking how easy it was to rile her.

"I guess it's impossible to tell. Why don't you spend the night here? I'll get the prophecy, and we can take a crack at it, see if we can't come up with some sort of a solution."

"I was hoping you'd say that." Jade squeezed her mom's hand.

"What, you thought I'd turn my back on you?" Aiesa appeared shocked.

"No, of course not." She clasped her mom's hands quickly before her mom rose to retrieve the written words of her curse.

Jade sat back down, suddenly exhausted. Through a veil of tears, understanding dawned. She was running out of time.

~ * ~

With a sheet of parchment that had the words of the prophecy written out in full carefully spread between them, Jade huddled close to her mother.

She and her sisters had been required to commit the horrid thing to memory, but…she needed this.

Confused for a moment, she studied the sheet. "Mom, this isn't your handwriting."

"No, it's your father's. Helios wrote it down ages ago. He wanted to make sure we had the correct wording, that we were prepared, and if we needed to, we could go to him."

Jade shifted, resting on her elbow, eyeing her mom. "Did you ever?"

"No." A sweet smile bloomed across her face. "I have Xavior. He's my heart and soul. I'll always have fond memories of Helios, but Xavior is my true mate. He is my counsel, and I'm his. I leave the choice in your hands. But there are risks in seeking Helios's aid. Even with the knowledge of who ordered the Oneiroi to hunt you, there may be other gods who seek your death. That's why we thought it was best to keep you hidden."

When Jade and her sisters came of age and were ready to set out on their own, their mother had known the optimum place to hide them was among the humans. "I know, Mom. It's okay. I get it."

Her heart ached at the love she saw in her mom's eyes. *I hope I have what you do someday.* She shifted her attention to the paper she held between her fingertips and the words flowed from her lips. After she read the first few, her mom's rich voice joined hers.

"When darkness meets dawn, the time of the five nears.

Beware in the dreaming for they come.

Bequeathed from the father, one common thread they'll share.

In three lunar phases, all is revealed.

Fear what isn't seen.

Death and destruction unto the gods will rain,

Unless a balance is struck, fulfilling what is longed for most."

Her mom tapped her lip. "Helios and I went over and over this as you already know. We only pieced together a few of the lines and, even then, we weren't sure we had them correct. But if we go through them again maybe we'll see something different."

Her finger slid down the page, stopping at the beginning of each line as she read. "The opening clearly has to do with him and me and the birth of all of you. The second line must be a result of the gods who are displeased with your birth and who fear the powers you possess that may expose their secrets or even kill them."

"That's when some of the gods decided to sick the Oneiroi on us?" Jade's sarcasm bled through at the thought of the dreaded dream gods.

"So it seems. When I told Helios about you, he remembered the prophecy and realized it was about our daughters. Because having quintuplets wasn't exactly a common occurrence. My news definitely struck a cord. From conversations he'd overheard, the Oneiroi would be called to begin the hunt.

"You know they come for their prey in the dreaming, their playground. The Eye, the magical amber your father gifted all of you, was meant to keep you safe while you slept." A slight frown wrinkled her mom's forehead. "You are using it, aren't you?"

Jade nodded as she thought of the five-point grid of amber, strategically aligned, that she slept with to keep her safe. Hidden. All the sisters did. "It's so wrong." She blinked away tears of frustration, her body rigid.

"The Fates like to meddle. I wish I knew what their goal was. Do they want you to defeat the prophecy, or do they want it to unfold with the demise of the gods?" She shook her head. "It plagued Helios and me that you were the ones targeted. Why not go after one of Zeus's children? Did they think he would repeat his father's history?"

Aiesa tucked an errant strand of hair behind Jade's ear, running her hand down to her shoulder for a gentle squeeze. "No matter what, we'll figure it out. The line about your father, 'Bequeathed from the father one common thread is shared'. Now, I'm still not sure what that means. You must have something from him. It could be the amber, but I don't know. Maybe some power inherited that we haven't discovered yet."

"True. It has to be something we all share. I could use a new power about now." Jade rubbed her forehead. "We all have similar coloring. Although, I'm not sure how that would help us. Let's look at the rest. Three lunar phases, yeah…I have limited time. Three weeks. That sucks. I think that's the line I've dreaded the most. And now… Isn't the last line about the Oneiroi? To fear what I can't see? Did we ever determine that?"

Aiesa's nose wrinkled. "No, we didn't, but I never thought it was. Well, that could be you, but it may reference one of your sisters or someone else entirely."

"Okay, maybe we won't worry about that one right now." Jade massaged her temples, the tension getting to her.

"I know this is…trying. Prophecies from the Fates are never easy." Aiesa's lips pinched together. "And when you're the one affected, it's horrid."

Jade groaned. "Right, okay. Let's just keep going."

"The last line tells of being consumed, raining death upon the gods, and retaliation by those who remain unless balance is found. Finding your balance could end this."

"I always thought the answer was my painting. It brought me such peace, at least until lately." Jade hunched her shoulders in memory of her recent canvases.

"That's your power."

And my curse…

Jade stared at her mother; she was at a loss. "I thought I had it all figured out. My painting gave me such satisfaction and so much power—a sense of completion."

"And you were doing the right thing as it was your power driving you. Although, its progression may very well have been the catalyst that activated the curse."

Realizing her mother was probably right, Jade stifled a grown. No wonder her mom discouraged them from further developing their talents.

"However, that's not what will balance you. There is something else deep inside you, and you need to find it. What is it you're desperate for? Something you want or something you do that you can't live without? Think about it—it'll come to you."

Jade nibbled on her lower lip and stared past her mom into the shadows of the room. Her stomach knotted. Images rolled through her mind. *I know what I want.* Absently, she spun a strand of hair around her finger. *Love. But could it really be that simple?*

Her mom stirred, and Jade shifted her gaze back to her. A soft smile graced her face. "It seems like you may already know."

"Yes, but so far it hasn't been easily attainable. I want a love like you and Xavior share." Shrugging, Jade puffed out a breath. "I've dated, and…it seems to elude my grasp. I've really never experienced anything besides a passing attraction. And then being half demon there's the complication of *mates*. Do all mates find each other and fall in love?" *Do I have a mate?*

"You've always longed for companionship, for a male to love and cherish you. It will happen when it's supposed to. And when you find him, all those feelings you've hoped for will be there."

Aiesa wrapped her arms around Jade in a hug as she'd done when Jade was young. But this time, her mom couldn't fix the problem, and they both knew it.

"There are only a few cases I've heard about where mates did not find each other and then fall in love. Mates are usually fated to be together, in all ways," her mom said.

"Okay, this gives me quite a bit to think about. I'm going to head back to my apartment. I'm supposed to go into work tomorrow. Next time I'll stay overnight."

Hugging Jade close, Aiesa gave her a quick kiss on the forehead before releasing her. "I understand. Make sure to come to Xavior or me. We're here to help, Jade. Anytime."

"I know. Thanks." Standing, Jade traced back to her studio apartment.

She arrived bathed in the soft glow of moonlight and shivered. It wasn't the moonlight that had her on edge. The slide of the silvery caress was comforting, like her mother's embrace. She turned wary eyes upward to her skylight, seeking the Fates. Something was coming; she could feel it with every sense of her being. How soon until her world turned completely upside down?

The real question though...*what* was coming?

Out Now!

What's next on
your reading list?

Champagne Book Group promises to bring to readers fiction at its finest.

Discover your next
fine read!
http://www.champagnebooks.com/

We are delighted to invite you to receive exclusive rewards. Join our Facebook group for VIP savings, bonus content, early access to new ideas we've cooked up, learn about special events for our readers, and sneak peeks at our fabulous titles.

Join now.
https://www.facebook.com/groups/ChampagneBookClub/

www.ingramcontent.com/pod-product-compliance
Lightning Source LLC
Chambersburg PA
CBHW070846260626
47170CB00007B/2520